The Night We Became Strangers

Other Books by Lorena Hughes

The Queen of the Valley

The Spanish Daughter

The Sisters of Alameda Street

The **Night We Became Strangers**

LORENA HUGHES

KENSINGTON
PUBLISHING CORP.

kensingtonbooks.com

Content warnings: Parental death, terminal illness, murder

ISBN: 978-1-4967-5246-8 (ebook)

ISBN: 978-1-4967-5245-1

First Kensington Trade Paperback Printing: October 2025

10 9 8 7 6 5 4 3 2 1

Printed in the United States of America

The authorized representative in the EU for product safety and compliance is eucomply OU, Parnu mnt 139b-14, Apt 123
Tallinn, Berlin 11317, hello@eucompliancepartner.com

*To Ximena, my first friend, and to my mom
and Tía Norma, for the inspiration*

PROLOGUE

She was certain that her husband was having an affair with another woman. And not just *any* woman.

She held the final proof in her hands: a powder blue silk scarf with three painted doves that his mistress had left behind. Of course, she knew all about this scarf. It went way back. It had once belonged to her. But she was in no mood to reminisce. All she could think about was one thing.

Revenge.

Yes, they were both going to pay.

And she had the perfect ally for this mission.

Shoving the silk scarf in her purse, she donned her gabardine trench coat, her white beret and gloves, and left the house. The radio drama was starting in less than an hour. She had just enough time to make it to the station and talk to her unsuspecting ally.

Just enough time to design and execute her plan.

She rushed down the cobblestone street, expertly dodging the familiar cracks with her heels. After a few blocks, she saw the building. Without hesitation, she pulled the door open, her mind racing, the tremor in her hands barely manageable. She'd never felt more hatred than she did at this very moment.

And there was only one way to appease it.

"We interrupt tonight's musical programming to
deliver an emergency news cable.
According to a report from our correspondents, a huge ball
of smoke and fire has descended on the city of Latacunga.
Baffled citizens watched with amazement as the clouds
dissipated, revealing large discs with bright lights. Their
attitude is hostile. A powerful ray emitting from these
strange crafts is destroying the city."

PART I

The Theater of the Mind

CHAPTER I

Matías

Quito, Ecuador, February 12, 1949

The chaos in the street woke me up. The bedside clock indicated that it was five minutes after 9:00 p.m. I'd grown tired of waiting for my mother to come home and had fallen asleep on top of the covers with my clothes still on. It was unusual for her to be gone so late at night—she never left home after seven. My father, well, that was a different story. He was gone several nights a week to play cards with his friends. Tonight was one of those nights.

I couldn't pinpoint with precision what noise had awoken me. A loud screech? The clash of metal? There was some sort of collision outside my window and people were screaming. I moved the curtain aside, pulled my window open, and leaned over the white metal sill to peek at the street three stories down.

Don Jacinto's 1946 Buick Roadmaster had just hit another car. I could imagine the scene I was about to witness. Don Jacinto was fastidious about his automobile. If either I or my friends so much as touched its smooth chassis as we walked by, he would curse at us, call us *vagabundos*, and immediately wipe our fingerprints with a red flannel specially designated for that purpose.

Don Jacinto owned the barbershop across the street, but he

constantly kept an eye on his beloved vehicle. I had to admit that sometimes we messed with his car just to get a reaction from him, me being the primary instigator. At my thirteen years of age, the barber's outbursts were hilarious and broke the monotony of those sleepy weekday afternoons in my dull neighborhood, if only minimally.

My predictions were all wrong. Instead of the brawl I envisioned, Don Jacinto got out of his car and extended his fat arms, conciliatory, toward González, the pharmacist, who got out of his Chevy and reciprocated the hug.

"I'm sorry, *vecino*, it was my fault," González said. "I shouldn't have stopped so abruptly."

"No," Don Jacinto said. "It was completely my fault."

"How about that news, huh?"

"Terrifying, Señor González. Absolutely terrifying."

All around them, people were running up and down the street, frantically. Nobody was stopping to look at the car damage or offer an opinion. Curious bystanders, who normally surrounded an accident scene to voice their assessments of guilt—unconcerned with the preservation of evidence or the status of the victims— were nowhere to be seen tonight. People were minding their own business as though they were late for an important appointment.

I rubbed my eyes. Was I still dreaming?

My parents and I lived in a three-story house in the heart of downtown Quito—a house entirely too big for the three of us and our maid, Delia, but it was only a few blocks away from my family's newspaper, *Crónicas*. It was convenient and comfortable, and my father's family had owned this property for generations.

"Niño Mati!" Delia said, bursting into my room.

Her sudden presence and the use of "niño" followed by the diminutive of my name annoyed me. Didn't she realize I was no longer a child? I was taller than my mother and just a bit shorter than my dad, for God's sake! Even at school they called me "Señor Montero."

"Something horrible has happened!"

"Yes, I saw. Don Jacinto's Buick hit the pharmacist's Chevy."

"Martians have landed!"

If I weren't so irritated with her, I would've laughed. She must be demented, or sleepwalking.

"Let's go to the kitchen, and I'll prepare you a *té de tilo*," I said as a peace offering.

"No! There's no time for tea! That's not what I'm doing the last minutes of my life."

"What on earth are you talking about, woman?"

"They just announced on the radio that Martians have attacked Latacunga, and there have also been UFO sightings over the Galapagos Islands!" Her voice trembled a little. "Come!"

Questioning her sanity, I followed her to the living room on the second story, where my dad kept his Telefunken radio covered with a piece of white cloth to prevent it from getting dusty.

"Where's my mom?" I asked.

"I don't know. She's not back yet. *¡Virgen Santísima!* Maybe the Martians got her!"

It was hard not to laugh at the stupidities coming out of her mouth. I expected her to burst out laughing any second, but Delia didn't have a sense of humor. She was always businesslike and busy. No time for chitchat or distractions. Then how could she have fabricated this outrageous lie? I'd never known her to possess any acting skills, either, and her performance, I hated to admit it, was credible.

Wearing her pink nightrobe and curlers on her head, she approached the radio and turned the volume up. Stranger than her senseless ramblings was not seeing her in her customary light blue uniform.

"This is unbelievable," the radio announcer was saying. "People are running through the streets. They can't escape! Listeners, the city of Latacunga has been destroyed by a swarm of aliens, and they're headed for Quito! I repeat: they're headed for Quito!"

His voice sounded broken.

"Dear listeners, our civilization is wounded," the man continued, dramatically. "Our species is facing its own extinction. Ladies and gentlemen, let's accept the inevitable. The incredible news we're delivering is coming to us from legitimate international agencies and, of course, sources at our own capital's daily newspaper, *Crónicas*, which operates in this very same building. This news bulletin is brought to you exclusively by Naranjada, the unbeatable orange soda. Now in pineapple flavor, too."

What was this nonsense? As a heartfelt *pasillo* resumed, Delia got on her knees, her long, bony fingers coming together in a praying gesture, her slender frame being swallowed by the oversized cotton robe. At the top of her lungs, she recited the Padre Nuestro.

"Kneel down, Niño Matías!" she ordered. "Let's pray for our salvation."

I hesitated. I needed to know if what Delia and the radio announcer were saying was true. And I wouldn't find that out on my knees.

Without speaking another word, I darted toward the stairs and out into the street.

CHAPTER 2

Valeria

Ecuador, July 1957

I lost my parents to twenty minutes of radio drama. I never knew exactly how it happened, and nobody wanted to tell me the details, but my life was never the same after the incidents of February 12, 1949—incidents I was determined to uncover now that I was finally an adult and free from the hasty exile my Tío Bolívar had forced me into.

One thing I knew: There was a name that couldn't be spoken aloud, one related to the events of that evening that had become taboo in my family.

My mother's name.

The shiny red train from Riobamba to Quito was packed this morning. Navigating between legs and arms, valises and boxes, I made my way to an empty seat by the window in one of the back rows. Bodies boiled around me and something putrid permeated the air. Somehow, it didn't bother me. Neither did the thought of being crammed into this closed space for the next six hours. Today, the future looked bright. I was finally going back to Quito after eight long years locked in a boarding school. I set my two valises, which held all my belongings, in the compartment over my head and squeezed in front of a woman with a black hat and blue poncho.

"*Permiso*," I said, reaching the window seat, but she didn't answer. She clung onto a cage with a green parrot inside. "What's its name?" I asked.

"Tico," she said.

For the next six hours, that was all she said. The parrot, however, kept repeating his cheerful "*hola*" in a high-pitched voice, way after we'd made each other's initial acquaintance.

I kept my gaze outside the window, where green pastures extended. My thoughts were lulled by the train's prolonged whistle and the discordant rattle of the engine, sporadically interrupted by the wind sneaking through the window's gap. I entertained myself counting Holstein cows and horses and *campesinos* wrapped in ponchos. A boy and a girl cheerfully ran beside the railroad tracks and waved at us. I waved back.

What would become of me when I arrived in Quito? I certainly had a lot of plans. And dreams. My life has been shaped by nothing but dreams.

I was the family pariah—there was no doubt about it, though I didn't understand why. Of course, Tío Bolívar would tell a different story. He'd say he'd sent his only niece to a prestigious private institution so she could receive the kind of education most women of her time could only dream of. He'd boast about how I grew up surrounded by girls my age, cared for by loving nuns in a quaint little town, rather than alone in a cold, empty house. He'd brag about how I sang in the school choir and how impeccable my needlework was. I had left Riobamba, ready to become the perfect wife.

But if you asked me, I would say I never understood why I couldn't move in with my uncle's family. I would've loved to grow up next to his daughters—two older cousins I'd idolized during my childhood—and his four sons, in spite of how rambunctious they'd been. It was apparent that I wasn't welcome in Tío Bolívar's home. If at least I had a sibling of my own to commiserate with, things would've been more bearable, but no, I was an only child, so my parents' tragic fate was mine to carry alone.

My family's rejection had always stung, but I tried not to dwell on resentment. Tío Bolívar showed his affection in other ways. He visited me once a month, bringing along expensive dolls, dresses, and stylish saddle oxfords, and taking me out for *helados de paila*. I looked forward to those Sundays with embarrassing anticipation. No other girl in my school had an uncle who showered her with as much affection as he did. Nobody else sported the latest fashions, even if it was only on weekends when I could finally remove the plaid school uniform I was forced into from Mondays to Fridays.

When I was fifteen, however, he gave me the most precious gift of all—one that I was sure to cherish all my life and would establish the path to my dreams.

A Kodak Brownie 127.

Behind the lens, the world looked more interesting. I could frame a moment just right and keep it forever. Being that my late mother's best friend and her husband owned *Crónicas*, one of the largest newspapers in Ecuador, I was certain I could get a job as a photojournalist. All I had to do was ask my Tío Bolívar to talk to them on my behalf.

I felt the shape of my precious camera inside my camel leather bag and turned toward my travel companion, beaming with anticipation. There was yet another reason for my excitement, perhaps the strongest one.

I was finally going to see Matías again.

"Isn't it a beautiful day?" I said.

The woman frowned, while the parrot repeated *"hola."*

Tío Bolívar was waiting for me at the train station in Quito. The rain had stopped, and he stood alone by a puddle of water reflecting his dark suit, thin black tie, and the cigarette that always dangled from his mouth. He must have been approaching fifty, but he didn't look it, not with that open forehead—free of wrinkles—his dark mane peppered with erratic gray highlights, and his pudgy cheeks. Tío Bolívar was my father's younger brother, an accountant who'd been consumed with work responsibilities and a large family, and who, from one day to the next, had been solely in charge of a disgraced radio station and an orphaned niece—me.

I'd hoped that at least my youngest cousin would've come to the station with him. Last I heard, his two older boys were married and so was his older girl. The only girl who remained at home was Graciela, whose biological clock was desperately ticking at twenty-one, and two younger brothers, ages sixteen and eight. I hadn't seen any of them in years because I spent every holiday and summer breaks at my dad's cousin's house in Ambato.

My dad's cousin, Amparo, was a middle-aged, crooked woman with jet black hair that she religiously dyed every three weeks. Her dark pixie cut created an interesting contrast with her pasty white skin and her many wrinkles, not to mention the overwhelming rouge on her cheeks to match her bright, carmine lips. Everyone called her Doña Amparito, and she had always been kind to me. She was a distant cousin and very busy with her *fonda*, a humble restaurant where I helped during my breaks. She had never married, but her parents had left her the business and a one-bedroom apartment. By the end of my visits, my back was in shambles from having slept on her sofa for weeks.

It always baffled me that I couldn't go back to my hometown during the summer break. I knew Tío Bolívar had his hands full with six children and a radio station, but I'd always had the feeling that this forced separation was deliberate.

"Look at you, Valerita," Tío Bolívar said, whistling. "All grown up."

I hated the nickname *Valerita*. Why did people in Quito always add diminutives to names?

"*Hola, tío,*" I said, running my gloved fingers by my mint swing skirt, attempting to flatten the many wrinkles that the long train ride had left behind.

He picked up my two valises, and I followed him outside the

station. As we passed by a window, I glanced at my own reflection. Flying hairs expanded like sun rays all over my high ponytail. I did my best to comb them with the palm of my hand. I'd wanted to make a good first impression on Tío Bolívar's family, but that was not going to happen.

We got into a teal-and-white 1955 Ford Fairlane. The scorching leather seat burned the palms of my hands as I settled on the passenger seat. Tío Bolívar unrolled the driver's window and started the vehicle.

"How was the trip?"

I'd forgotten all about his nervous energy, which seemed to come and go with his moods, but today, it was fully activated. He kept nodding his head with quick small movements, even though I wasn't saying anything.

"Long and tedious," I said. "But I took some pictures."

"You still have the camera I gave you?"

"Of course!" I perked up. "In fact, Tío, I was hoping you could introduce me to the Monteros. I would love to work for *Crónicas* as a photographer."

In spite of being good friends with my parents, I wasn't sure the Monteros remembered me after so many years. I had many memories of Mrs. Montero, my godmother, and her first husband coming for dinner at my house, and bringing their son, Matías, to play with me.

We stopped at a red light. He tapped his thigh repeatedly.

"I don't know, Valerita. Things have changed."

Valeria.

"Oh, yes, they're no longer in the same building as the radio station, right? I heard about that."

He lit a cigarette, eyes squinting. He didn't say anything, so I filled the silence.

"For nine months, they printed the paper at *El Día* until they fixed their printing press and got their new building." I wanted to impress him with my knowledge. A photojournalist, after all, must be well informed.

As the light switched back to green, he accelerated, his gaze back on the road. "Well, we'll see about that."

I didn't like the dismissive tone of his voice, but I was prepared for this. I had been planning my response for the last three years. "I know it's not customary for women to work, especially at a newspaper, but I think I can do it. I've been practicing so much, and my friends say I'm really good." I tapped the bulge in my bag. "I brought some photos to show you. Besides, I don't want to be a burden to you. I can make my own money."

"Oh, you don't need to worry about that," he said.

He gave me a sideways smile, but didn't say another word as he drove toward downtown Quito.

The city had grown vertically in the last eight years, and imported vehicles crammed the streets. As we drove past Cine Pichincha, a big sign advertised Silvia Pinal and Pedro Infante's latest movie, *El inocente*. I was finally in the capital and could watch a variety of Mexican and American films whenever I wanted, not the same old film over and over again.

I lowered the window to breathe in the city air. There was noise all around: vendors announcing to the world that they had plenty of oranges and tangerines at cheap prices, cars honking, the brakes of an old bus behind us, construction workers whistling at an attractive woman sauntering down the street, a crowd laughing.

Quito was alive. And I felt invigorated by it.

Tío Bolívar lived in an old two-story house a few blocks away from the infamous radio station that, according to hearsay, was slowly regaining the credibility of its listeners. As we entered the dim vestibule, my heels clacked against the mosaic tile. A warm, yeasty aroma permeating the air left no doubt that something tasty was in the oven. It also made me realize how hungry I was. But it was way past lunch time.

"Marga!" Tío Bolívar said, calling his wife.

I had a vague recollection of Tía Marga. She'd been pregnant when I left, that much I remembered, because I'd been fascinated by how enormous a human belly could grow. She'd had little to say back then, at least to me, but had been a pleasant woman with big brown eyes. Last I heard, she'd had a son, Joselito.

It was a shock to see Tía Marga now.

She'd lost all the pregnancy weight and then some. A life of hardship reflected on her face with bulging cheekbones and brownish blemishes across her skin. Her eyes, which in her youth had been the focal point of her face, now looked muted and somber. Her mane, held in a tight bun, was more gray than black. How could that be when Tío Bolívar looked so youthful?

"Look who's here," he said in a cheerful tone that came out forced. He set my luggage by the staircase as his wife came toward us.

"*Hola, Valeria,*" she said, extending a weak hand for me to shake. "Forgive my appearance, but I was in the kitchen." She was wearing an apron splattered with flour. "Goodness, I didn't remember you having so many freckles!"

I did my best not to touch my nose, which in summer months became covered in freckles due to my long hikes, mostly to get the perfect shot. I owed my fair skin and toasted caramel hair to my mom, but I was not about to ruin the mood by mentioning her.

"Did you tell Valeria about tonight?" Tía Marga asked her husband.

"Not yet."

"What about tonight?" I asked.

Discretion was not my forte.

"Oh, we're having some friends over for dinner," he said. "To welcome you back."

"The Monteros?" I asked, barely able to hold my excitement. These city people took advantage of every moment to celebrate.

He avoided my eager gaze. "No, not them. Other friends I want you to meet." He picked up my suitcases. "Is Graciela upstairs?"

"Yes, she's getting the room ready," my aunt said.

As we started our climb up the stairs, a boy came running down and nearly bumped against Tío Bolívar and me.

"Hey, watch it!" Tío Bolívar scolded. "Why don't you behave like a gentleman for once and say hi to your cousin?"

"Hi, cousin," he said with a quick, dismissive bow. His long bangs nearly covered his eyes.

"Her name is Valeria," Tío Bolívar said, maneuvering my two valises as his young son attempted to rush past him down the stairs and reached the bottom with a leap. "And this is Joselito," he said, with a resigned sigh.

"Hi," I said.

But Joselito was already running to the front door. All I'd been able to assess was his short tan pants and suspenders. Tío Bolívar and I renewed our climb.

"You will stay in Graciela's room," he said. "We only have four bedrooms, and the boys use the other two."

I had a few memories of Graciela. She'd been taller than me, and her hair had been so straight that the pin curls her mamá worked so hard on creating every morning would wane by the middle of the day. I looked up to her since she was the cousin closest in age to me. When I first moved to the boarding school, I'd sent her letters filled with drawings. She'd answered a couple of them but slowly, and sadly, our correspondence had died.

She was nearly unrecognizable now. For one, she was shorter than me, and the once self-assured child who'd encouraged me to climb rooftops and dared me to eat dirt in order to borrow her bicycle would barely look me in the eye.

Her hair came down to the nape of her neck, held on one side with a rhinestone barrette, and she was still attempting to curl the bottom—with mixed results. A tailored blouse and a pencil skirt highlighted her small frame. Her fingers were long, her wrists tiny. So much so that when we shook hands, I was afraid I might break one of her bones.

"Graciela, help her get settled, will you? I have to go back to the radio station for a couple of hours," my uncle said, bringing my luggage inside the first room to the right.

My cousin nodded. I'd yet to hear her voice.

"Thank you, Tío," I said as he headed to the stairs, and I followed Graciela into the bedroom.

This had been the girls' room before—I remembered as much. It had once been a pink paradise with flower-print curtains and a rosy doll crib that matched my cousins' furniture. Well, the room had drastically changed. The wallpaper was more subdued now, with tiny olive leaves spread throughout. Gone were the two canopy beds from their childhood in lieu of two twin beds with matching sage bedspreads. A night table with a walnut RCA Victor radio stood between them.

"Oh, you have a radio," I said, applauding. Back in the boarding school, we'd only been allowed to listen to an hour of radio a day, after dinner, while we did our needlework. I always picked the station, and invariably, I chose a *radionovela*, as I was enthralled with the stories of unrequited love and betrayal. But if there was still time, we'd listen to a Colombian radio station that featured live bands playing *boleros* and *guarachas*.

"Do you like *radionovelas*?" I asked her.

She started to smile, but as she did, she immediately covered her mouth with her hand. She nodded.

"Which is your favorite?" I said, and the two of us said in unison. "*¡El derecho de nacer!*"

As she opened her mouth to speak, I realized the source of her shame. Her front teeth were terribly crooked, to the point that one seemed to be climbing on top of the other. As soon as she was done speaking, she covered her mouth again.

Caray, this was a big leap from the poised child she'd once been.

"Come meet my brothers," she said, heading for the door.

Joselito was not in his room, but his colorful marbles were. So was his train set—pieces scattered all over the floor. This bedroom had once belonged to the oldest son, as I recalled, but he was a married man now and had moved to a house of his own.

We didn't linger and Graciela opened the next room. A teenage boy raised his head from a book filled with numbers and formulas. On his desk was a strange contraption built with metals and wires in some sort of mysterious circuit.

"Germán, say hi to our cousin Valeria."

"Hi," he said, barely moving his chin up and making no attempt to get up to greet me.

While my aunt and her maid killed, plucked, and baked a couple of chickens, Graciela helped me unpack my valise. She was thrilled to have new reading material and peeked through several of my textbooks.

"You can have them," I said, as I'd already read them.

I showed her my camera and told her about my plans to work at the newspaper. She listened in pensive silence, but didn't utter an opinion. The one thing that fired her enthusiasm was to help me pick a dress for tonight's dinner with my uncle's mysterious friends.

I wanted to look my best, so I chose a black crepe top with a creamy taffeta skirt that Amparito had sewn for me. She had a talent for duplicating any magazine design with cheaper fabrics.

My cousin wore a sky-blue sleeveless dress with a matching flare skirt. She pinned my head up in a twisted bun and I borrowed her blush and lipstick since the nuns didn't let me buy my own makeup. But that was about to change!

Together we headed down the stairs, where I could hear my uncle's voice and some laughter. Nothing this exciting had ever happened to me since the days my parents were alive and hosted dinner parties themselves.

The stiff petticoat under my skirt slightly scratched my legs as I descended the stairs. "Your brothers are not joining us?" I asked Graciela.

"No. And trust me, it's better that way."

She still covered her mouth when she spoke, but in the afternoon, there had been times when she'd forgotten her problematic teeth.

Tía Marga had changed into a navy dress with lace sleeves. She sported a pair of glasses that were somewhat incongruous with her fine gown, but she looked much better than she had in the afternoon. What a little grooming could do to a woman!

"Here they are!" Tío Bolívar said, opening his arms to welcome Graciela and me as we entered the parlor.

In the muted living room were an older couple and a young man—a redhead. Out of habit, I pinched Graciela's arm. I couldn't help it. My friends and I pinched each other whenever we spotted a ginger—that was how rare they were in Riobamba.

She screeched. Then covered her mouth with her gloved hand.

"Sorry," I said.

The older woman, wrapped in some kind of fur, blatantly stared at me.

Tío Bolívar cleared his throat. "Well, here she is, my niece, Valeria. She just arrived from Riobamba this afternoon."

The two elders assessed me as if I were bacteria under a microscope. They were older than my aunt and uncle. The man's hair was mostly white, and his fair skin signaled that his son might have inherited his coloring.

"These are Mr. and Mrs. Recalde," my uncle said. "And their son, Félix."

Félix was very slim and somewhat clumsy. He nearly tripped as he extended a hand to greet me. His face was covered with freckles (and to think that my aunt had criticized mine!) but he had nice soft features—a harmonious face with chestnut eyes and reddish eyebrows.

"Nice to meet you," he said in a barely audible voice.

The portly maid I had met in the afternoon entered the parlor, carrying a tray filled with wine glasses.

"Please, have a drink," Tío Bolívar said. "Let's toast for this evening."

In what could be considered an overexcited move, I reached out for my wineglass first. I'd never tasted alcohol and was eager to try. I took a quick sip as Graciela elbowed me, shaking her head.

"Wait for the toast," she whispered.

I nodded. What would Señora Flores, my etiquette teacher, say if she'd seen my abrupt indiscretion? Everybody else picked up a glass with the grace that had failed me and waited for Tío Bolívar to speak.

"I'd like to make a toast for our guests of honor"—he raised his glass—"and of course, for my niece, who's finally back with us. It's such a joy to have you here."

He winked at me.

Tía Marga was the first to utter a "*¡Salud!*" followed by everyone else's.

I loved the drink's sweet bubbly taste that, based on the empty bottle sitting on the cupboard, was champagne—not white wine, as I'd originally thought. I was shocked at my family's splendor and extravagance! They must have really missed me.

As we sat around the dining room table to enjoy the two chickens, skillfully paired with parsley potatoes and rice stuffed with green peas, I had the opportunity to quietly observe my uncle's interactions with his guests.

There was something odd about this encounter. I had been led to believe that these were close friends who were coming to welcome me, but my uncle treated them with the same deference one treats an authority. His nervous energy was at its height until two glasses of beer set him at ease, and he started telling jokes and laughing even before delivering the punchline.

The hefty meal was followed by the creamy apple cake my aunt had been baking earlier—she apologized for preparing such a "simple" dessert. The guests were gracious but left promptly after dinner, which was even stranger because in Quito, invitations were a long affair. I still remembered the endless nights of drinking and dancing at my parents' home that I'd peeked at from the upstairs banister when I was a young girl.

It would take a week for me to find out the real reason for the gathering at my uncle's home.

HAPTER 3

Matías

February 12, 1949

Pandemonium reigned on the streets of Quito. Not only did I witness Don Jacinto handing out the keys to his Buick to a random passerby, who immediately declined the gift—somewhat offended ("What am I supposed to do with this *now?*"), but I also had to dodge a mattress that nearly fell on my head from a four-story building.

People around me ran aimlessly, some still in their pajamas and night robes. A few were getting into their cars, others on bicycles. Some carried suitcases, baskets, blankets, knocked on neighbors' doors relentlessly and shouted that the Martians were coming. It was like a dream where nothing made sense. If only I could find my mother, we could navigate this odd trance together. But she'd been acting so strangely in the last few days. Tonight's disappearance was a clear example.

Where on earth was she?

My grandfather's house was an option, but it would be too long a walk, especially against this torrent of humans around me. Maybe she'd gone to see my father at the club where he played cards?

My friend Benjamin's older brother, Carlos Cortés, was standing outside Casa Manuela, arms folded across his chest, his back leaning against the white stone wall of the colonial building that housed one of the most popular restaurants in the area. Next to him was a table and on top of it, a radio conveniently placed outside the restaurant for all to hear the news.

"What's going on?" I asked him. "Do you believe this shit?"

He brought a finger to his lips, signaling me to be quiet. People stopped their hasty walks and circled the radio to listen.

"We ask our citizens to be alert and attentive to a new official bulletin. At this moment, we are communicating with important government officials and the military. This just in: We have a report from the Mariscal Sucre airbase. The aliens are now in Cotocollao. An armed group from Vencedores Battalion has come to the enemy's encounter but unfortunately, the Martian attack is so overwhelming they have destroyed everything in their path. There are many dead—dead and wounded." A more agitated, urgent voice came through. "The airbase in Mariscal Sucre has been taken by the enemy and destroyed! They're exterminating *everything*!"

Around me, people spoke in unison, some more panicked than others.

"Quiet!" Carlos said. "Let us hear!"

Someone on the radio was announcing that the chief of communications from *Crónicas* was about to speak. After clearing his throat and stumbling with his first words, the man mentioned the specific locations where the Martians had allegedly landed already. Familiar names of nearby parishes were listed in scary succession.

"If the data we are receiving is truthful and accurate, we must understand that the mortal enemy has us surrounded. A few more stops and they'll be in Quito," he continued in a solemn voice. "We are not aware of what's happening in other countries as international news agencies have suspended their broadcasts. We are also ignorant of the fate of our reporters stationed in Cotocollao and whether or not our army has come into contact with the enemy. This is all the information we have at the moment. Thank you for your attention.''

A woman's scream broke the listeners' unnerved silence. Bringing her hand to her chest, she seemed to be having some sort of fit.

"A doctor! Please! I need a doctor."

An older gentleman grabbed her by the arm. "Someone call an ambulance!"

Another man guided them toward his car, which was parked by the curb. The rest of the listeners dispersed in all directions.

A man running towards us stopped short. "What's happening?" he said, eyes wide. "I've been running but I don't even know why."

"I—I'm not sure," I said, feeling dumb at the thought of repeating what I had just heard. "Apparently, the aliens are coming?" There *had* to be a logical explanation for this that didn't involve extraterrestrial creatures.

Before I could say anything else, the man darted toward the plaza.

"Where's Benjamin?" I asked Carlos, as he started walking away.

"I don't know, but I'm going home to die with my family."

I couldn't tell if he was joking or being serious. Benjamin and I had always looked up to his brother, Carlos, who was almost seventeen. This kind of statement was *not* what I expected from one of my personal heroes.

A part of me thought this a joke, but another—more visceral—part was starting to worry. Why would the radio station *and* the newspaper make up such a lie?

I was only a few blocks away from the building that housed my family's newspaper and Radio La Voz. Maybe I could get some answers there. The porter knew me and would certainly let me in.

One of the bartenders from Casa Manuela stepped outside, carrying a tray with small glasses. He had removed his jacket, and under his armpits, two puddles of sweat stained his white buttoned-up shirt. He started calling people in, offering them free drinks. In his other hand was a full bottle of a transparent liquor.

"*Tomémos, cholitos,*" he was saying, inviting his compatriots to drink with him as he generously poured what looked like *puro* into the shot glasses.

Several passersby obediently took a glass, or two, and gulped the liquor, which I had only tried once—much to my regret. I was certainly not going to try it again tonight.

As I walked past La Iglesia del Sagrario, a strange vision came into view. A priest—standing in front of the church's gigantic double doors, arms lifted toward the sky—was surrounded by a small crowd who knelt in front of him. He was speaking in Latin, in that solemn tone priests always used during mass. But instead of listening in silence, the parishioners were responding indistinctively, all at the same time. I approached them so I could make out their words.

"Bless me Father for I have sinned," a man said, in tears. "It's been two years since my last confession."

Wait, were they all *confessing?* In a group? *Out loud?*

Another man was ahead in his confession.

". . . with the neighbor's wife. I had too much to drink, Heavenly Father, but it only happened once. Please forgive me, *Diosito lindo.*"

Words like *stealing, lying, cheating, blasphemy,* and a whole list of sins and regrets—many involving carnal transgressions—were uttered at the same time while the priest made the sign of the cross in a gesture of mass absolution.

I resisted the temptation of confessing my own bad thoughts and continued toward Plaza Grande. A couple, holding hands, nearly bumped into me. I recognized Guillermo Salas and his fiancée, Rosa-something. He had been at my school but graduated last year.

"We're getting married, Mati," he said.

"But I thought your wedding was planned for July."

"No time, my friend, no time."

The two of them rushed toward El Sagrario without more than a goodbye wave.

When I reached the large independence square, I was shocked to see so many people gathered there this late at night. Quito was normally a quiet, peaceful town, and most people went home after dark. This plaza was perhaps the most important site in the entire country as four significant buildings surrounded it. First and foremost, the presidential residence, El Palacio de Carondelet, with its long row of Tuscan columns in the front. I looked up at one of the second-story windows wondering, for a second, if the president was aware of the chaos taking over our capital. Was he watching? Come to think of it, my father had mentioned in the morning that President Galo Plaza was out of town for some important event.

South of the presidential palace was one of the most important churches in Quito and a true landmark, La Iglesia de la Catedral with its infamous *gallito* on top of one of its domes. The *gallito* was an iconic iron rooster who happened to be the protagonist of a famous legend that all children learned about in school.

Currently, a crowd rushed toward the dozen stone steps that led to the front entrance. I could already see that many were desperately knocking on its carved double doors to be let inside. As most believers, they probably thought they wouldn't be safer anywhere else.

Two more buildings surrounded the tall monument in the center of the plaza built in honor of the country's independence. One was known as the Palacio Arzobispal—the archdiocese's headquarters—and the other one was the Palacio Municipal, which harbored the mayor's offices.

Where were these illustrious citizens now? Hiding underneath a table? Begging God to forgive their sins? Or laughing at all of us from behind one of those dark windows?

Perhaps one of the oddest things about the desperate *quiteños* around me was that once they reached the plaza, they didn't just settle there. Instead, they grabbed their luggage or mattress once again and took off running—destination unknown.

Diagonal to the government palace was Hotel Majestic, where another group stood in a line that went all the way inside the

Renaissance building. This was the first house built during the founding of the city in the sixteenth century. My guess was that these individuals might be waiting to use the telephone—as it was one of the few places in the area that had one. It wouldn't be too far-fetched to assume they wanted to call their loved ones to say goodbye, or maybe to warn them about our imminent apocalypse?

The doorman had taken it upon himself to remove a large mahogany radio so everyone could keep updated on the Martians' progress.

"It is now nine thirteen, courtesy of our favorite orange refreshment, Naranjada. Ladies and gentlemen, your attention please, all of us here at the station would like to extend our gratitude for your undivided attention as we follow these unprecedented and tragic events. Friendly listeners, we ask you not to leave our side. Radio La Voz will continue to provide the latest news about the Martian invasion. We pledge to continue until the moment that—God forbid—we might fall, unequivocally, in the hands of the military supremacy of our raiders from outer space."

After that dramatic outburst, the announcer introduced a government official, Minister Díaz Granados. "Citizens, as minister of defense, I ask the citizens of Quito to remain calm. We're organizing the defense and evacuation of the city."

Evacuation?

I didn't even know where my parents were. How was I expected to leave the city? Something fell from one of the top floors of the hotel and shattered at my feet. It was a ceramic piggy bank containing someone's life savings. I stared at the broken object, trying to make sense of this upside-down world.

CHAPTER 4

Valeria

1957

I would always think of the first week at my uncle's house as a different time, a period of wondrous youth, of innocence. I still believed I could achieve all my professional dreams while having the family I'd always longed for.

How mistaken I was.

The day after the dinner party with the Recaldes, I'd showed Tío Bolívar my photographs and I asked him to introduce me to the owners of *Crónicas.*

"I don't know," he'd said, noncommittally. "Since they moved locations, we haven't been in touch."

That made sense. The newspaper had once shared the same building with my family's radio station, La Voz, but after the tragedy, the station had closed for two years and *Crónicas* relocated. From Amparito, I had heard that my godmother, the widow of the newspaper's owner, had remarried her husband's first cousin, so the newspaper remained in the Montero family. What wasn't clear to me was who exactly was running the company now.

Maybe Matías?

The thought of seeing him again, after so many years, was exhilarating. I waited a few days for Tío Bolívar to say something about the job at the newspaper. Had he talked to them? All I wanted was a job interview. I knew I could charm my way into a photographer position. But he never said a word. Because I had, if anything, an impatient nature—my teachers had even called me reckless, which to me had been a compliment—I decided to take matters into my own hands.

The previous day, Graciela had taken me around town. She'd shown me several churches in Quito, an amazing assortment of impressive and distinct architecture—all in close proximity to one another. She had also pointed at the new building of *Crónicas* newspaper. To my delight, it wasn't that far from my uncle's house. She hadn't said anything else, and I knew better than to ask. I was already used to those awkward silences from Doña Amparito and Tío Bolívar whenever I mentioned that institution or anything related to my parents. But I had taken note of the street and the landmarks around the building.

Today I was going there.

I'd carefully prepared my outfit: a flower-print taffeta dress with a tucked bodice and a full pleated skirt. A matching headband was the final touch. Doña Amparito had sewn this dress for my birthday, and I'd been waiting for the perfect opportunity to use it.

Today was the day.

I didn't want to give any explanations to my family, so I waited for my aunt to rush to seven o'clock mass, for my uncle to go to work, the boys to school, and Graciela down to the bakery to get the daily bread.

I donned my gloves and camera bag, which also held my precious photographs, and sneaked outside. After a fifteen-minute walk, I was standing in front of the *Crónicas* building, a solid brick structure that looked nothing like the ornamental building that had originally housed them. I wondered if it had been on purpose. I greeted the guard at the entrance and asked to speak to Señor or Señora Montero. He was hesitant to let me in without an appointment, but I insisted. I said I was a family friend and wanted to surprise them. For good measure, I even added that I was a close friend of Matías's, though that might be a stretch.

The guard squinted a bit, assessing me shyly from head to toe, his chubby cheeks sweaty.

"Señora Montero is going to be thrilled when she sees me," I reassured him. "She's my godmother."

"I'm really not supposed to."

I tightened the hold of my bag against my side and produced a smile as a last resource.

"But I guess I'll make an exception for you."

I knew the dress would work.

He pointed at an elevator behind me and told me to go to the fourth floor and ask the receptionist for Mrs. Montero.

My first time inside an elevator! The day was going to be momentous in more ways than one. The ride upstairs took a minute, at most. I barely had time to retouch my lipstick, but everything had to be just right. As I pushed the door open, I could barely conceal the tremor in my hands.

The fourth floor was hectic. People coming in and out of offices, phones ringing, laughter coming from a hall. I kept my eye out for Matías, clammy hands inside my gloves. Would I recognize him? Would he know who I was?

I approached the receptionist and said I had an appointment with Mrs. Montero. The girl was so busy answering phone calls and taking notes, she simply pointed at an office in the back.

I took a deep breath and headed there before anybody could stop me. There was a label on the door that read EXECUTIVE EDITOR. I was about to knock when I heard a man's raised voice. It would be imprudent for me to interrupt, so I stood there for a moment, smiling shyly at a couple of men who walked past me but seemed too busy to care about who I was or what I was doing there.

I couldn't wait to start working here. Now I could hear a woman speaking. *That must be her!*

Her voice was measured and somewhat conciliatory. She was

just how I imagined her to be: a magnanimous leader who would, no doubt, give a fellow woman an opportunity. I was in awe of women who worked, especially in this kind of environment, where I'd only seen men and only one female, the receptionist.

As the male voice sounded closer, I took a long, deep breath, perfecting in my mind what I was going to say. The door opened abruptly, and a young man—about a head taller than me—stood in front of me, his thin black tie swaying as his chest heaved up and down. I slowly glanced up.

Holy Mother, it was *him*.

He looked at me as though I was an apparition of the Virgin.

I took in the rich, earthy fragrance of his cologne. I couldn't formulate a single word, much less a coherent sentence. The shine in his eyes was the same. The Roman nose that somehow fitted his face harmoniously was different. So was the sharpness of his jawline and the greenish stubble. But his hair still had that sandy brown shade I'd loved.

He was more virile than I'd pictured in all my imaginings. After an endless silence, I finally spoke—barely. "Matías?"

He frowned, trying to place me perhaps.

"It's Valeria. Remember me?"

He seemed taken aback, as if he hadn't thought of me in a hundred years. Or maybe he didn't remember me at all. How embarrassing.

Not knowing what else to do, I extended my hand, and he took it—briefly.

"Excuse me," he said, and walked past me. He didn't remember me, whereas I'd been thinking about him *constantly* for the last eight years. Mortified, I recalled all the times I'd signed "Valeria de Montero" on random pieces of paper and how incessantly I'd talked about him to my girlfriends at the boarding school since the day I arrived.

"Who's there?" the woman behind the cherry desk said.

I stood up straight and entered the office. Mrs. Montero had hardly aged. If anything she seemed more sophisticated, more beautiful. But she must be near forty already. I made my way inside the spacious room. If I hadn't been so nervous, I would've surely appreciated the lovely sitting area preceding the desk, with its leather chairs and orchid arrangements, the paintings of horses plastering the walls, the view of the city behind her.

"*¿Madrina?*"

She was wearing a chocolate two-piece suit, pearls around her neck, and medium-length curls over her shoulders. As I got near her, recognition seemed to sink in. I had pictured hugs and a lot of catching up, not the grave expression that set on her face.

"I'm Valeria Anzures."

"I know who you are," she said, her tone definitely hostile. "What are you doing here?"

Where had my masterful speech gone?

"Well, I . . . I just got back. I graduated from high school, and I thought . . ."

She was standing up, showing off her chic pencil skirt, her shapely legs as she approached me. A jasmine scent accompanied her. "Who let you in here?"

"I'm sorry, I thought . . ." It was now or never. "I just wanted to show you my photographs. I—I want to be a photojournalist, and since you and my mom were such great friends, I thought—"

Her laughter was anything but joyful. It was bitter, filled with a hatred I never thought possible. "Do me a favor, *niñita*, get out of here and don't you ever come back." She opened the door, without touching me, though for a second I thought she was going to slap me. Her amber eyes, so lovely, looked murderous.

I stepped outside as fast as I could, only to hear the door slam behind me.

CHAPTER 5

Matías

February 12, 1949

"We have in our studio the mayor of Quito," the announcer said.

"People of Quito," a different voice said. "Allow us to defend our city. Our women and children should go to the high surrounding areas in order to leave the men free for action and combat."

It was undeniably our mayor. I recognized his hoarse voice and his meticulous cadence over the radio waves. How ironic that only a few minutes ago, I had resented Delia for treating me like a child, but now I didn't know if I wanted to be considered a man "ready for action and combat."

It was impossible for me to unglue my feet from the ground—panicked as I was. I was still standing by the console radio outside the hotel, just like the statue of independence in the center of the plaza. The Archbishop of Quito had spoken, too, and this insanity was starting to seem more real by the second. If at least my parents were here, I would know what to do. Could they be at the *Crónicas* building? My dad, who had taken over the newspaper after my grandfather passed away, worked days, but if there had been some sort of emergency at work—and this certainly qualified as one—he would be there. It was, truly, the only place I could think of going other than the club where he played cards, which was past the newspaper building, anyway.

The voice on the radio blasted again. "It is now nine sixteen p.m. in the capital of Ecuador, courtesy of Naranjada, the unbeatable orange soda. Now in pineapple, too. Just a few moments ago, the minister of government entered our studio. Listeners of Radio La Voz, we have here with us the distinguished Eduardo Salazar Gómez."

"Unfortunately, compatriots," he said, "I suspect our weapons do not have the mechanical capacities to counter those of the colossal enemy."

I didn't hear the rest of what he had to say. Something had finally snapped inside of me. I had to get out of here. I crossed the street, heading resolutely to the *Crónicas* building. It was the only way to get answers. As I crossed the street, a woman's voice called out.

"Someone help me! Please!"

She was sitting on the curb, in obvious distress. A few people trotted ahead of me, clinging on to their scarce belongings. An older woman marched beside me with short, quick steps, her head low, her hands holding her cardigan together, her hair in a knotted bun.

"Hey!" I called out, but she kept walking, repeating a prayer to herself.

"*¡Ayúdeme, por favor!*" the woman on the curb continued to plead for help, and she was looking directly at me.

But I was just a kid. It looked as if she'd fallen. Surely, I could help her get up. I strode down the street toward her. Only as I got close to her did I realize she was pregnant.

"I think the baby is coming," she said, looking up.

"Right now?"

"Yes." She was rubbing her lower back. "The baby was supposed to come in a couple of weeks, but I think I precipitated the delivery when I started to run. Please don't leave me."

"Where's your husband?"

"I don't know. I was all alone at home. When I heard the news on the radio, I went outside to find him."

I empathized with her as we were in a similar situation—trying to find our loved ones in the midst of this near-apocalypse—but at least I didn't have a gigantic belly nor was I about to deliver in the middle of a stinky street.

"Where's your house?" I asked. "Let's take you there."

"A few blocks that way," she said, pointing back, where it was much darker and not at all where I needed to go, "but I don't want to go home. It feels like this baby is coming out *right now* and it's even worse when I walk. You have to take me to a hospital!"

A hospital? Did it look like I had the means to take her to a hospital? I didn't even have a bicycle, nor did I know where the nearest medical center was! Maybe I looked older than my thirteen years of age. I was, after all, the tallest in my class.

"All right," I said, "let's go back to the plaza to see if someone can drive us there. Hold my arm."

I leaned over and she grabbed my arm, but the minute she stood up, a copious amount of water gushed between her legs.

CHAPTER 6

Valeria

1957

Ever since my parents died, I'd get into these moods that the nuns referred to as "the devil brewing inside of me." It would start like temperate water over a flame, with tiny bubbles slowly forming along the edge. The bubbles would grow and fill the surface, and before you knew it, the scalding water would transform into magma ready to explode and destroy everything on its path. With time, I learned to control my *rotten temper*, as they called it, and being that this was Graciela's room and my uncle's house, I knew I couldn't toss all the books on the floor or destroy the ornamental chair, much less crash the oval mirror in the vanity table, as satisfying as the clashing noise might be. So, I settled for nervously pacing back and forth in the small space between the two beds.

I had never considered the possibility that Mrs. Montero, my mother's so-called best friend, would deny me the opportunity to work at the newspaper. And in such a spiteful way, at that. *Who* did she think she was? On top of all, Matías had avoided me as if had leprosy. I'd never imagined he would become so arrogant with age.

The door clicked open, and I stopped my pacing.

Graciela entered the room in a coral dress. "Where were you?"

I thought nobody in the kitchen had noticed me sneaking back into the room. "I went to *Crónicas* to talk to Mrs. Montero."

Graciela sat on the bed, bewildered. "Why would you do that?"

"I told you. I want to work there."

She sighed.

"She was so rude, *prima*. I don't even know why. She told me to never set foot there again."

Graciela scratched her forehead, folded one leg on top of the other. "I should've warned you."

I sat in front of her. "Of what?"

"I knew this would happen."

"Tell me!"

"After *that night*, there was a big fight between my dad and the Monteros. I think it had to do with the broadcast of that awful novel. They blamed our family for the tragedy. The newspaper's owner died and so did a few employees who had nothing to do with the broadcast. They also lost their printing press and had to print their newspaper at *El Día* until their machine was repaired."

"But whatever happened is not my fault," I said.

"Yes, but ever since, our families haven't spoken or had any relation whatsoever. In fact, *Crónicas* doesn't advertise our shows, not that my dad tries anymore."

I crossed my arms. "I don't understand why my father did something so stupid."

Graciela shrugged.

"Who knows? My dad doesn't like to talk about that night, so I recommend you don't ask him, either."

CHAPTER 7

Matías

February 12, 1949

The *Crónicas* building was only a block and a half from the plaza, and yet, it had never seemed so far.

I helped the pregnant woman take short steps toward Hotel Majestic. Someone in there ought to know what to do with a woman in labor—certainly better than me. I knew nothing about such bloody affairs, having neither siblings nor smaller cousins, as I was the youngest in the Montero line.

My only concern was that no one would care enough to help us. In the massive panic we were all immersed in, people were only looking out for themselves. It was strange what I had seen already. Either people were fleeing—in no particular direction and with no specific plan—or they had resigned themselves to their imminent death. And the way they were dealing with their ominous fate was either by drinking their sorrows away (because, let's face it, there was no better way to confront the end) or confessing their sins and getting a last-minute absolution from God through His representative on earth, the priest. However, if a priest was not readily available, then the affected party had to grant the needed pardon. Why, just a few minutes ago outside the hotel, I had witnessed a husband admitting to his wife an affair with a co-worker.

"I can't take it anymore!" my companion said, taking tiny steps and holding on to the bottom of her belly. Now that the light from the hotel illuminated her face, I could see that she was not much older than me, probably still under twenty. She was pretty, too, even with that grimace on her face.

Outside the hotel's entrance, the radio was still on, announcing its doomsday news. Each report more dramatic and terrifying than the last. I had been gone for about three minutes. What had I missed?

"Other stations are covering the news," a man stepping out of the hotel lobby was telling another.

Were the Martians in town already?

I glanced at the sky. Maybe I could identify some UFOs, but the only view in sight was that of the full moon above our heads.

"Look!" someone else said, pointing at bluish clouds amassing in front of the moon's face.

"I don't see anything!" a woman answered.

"There! It's the Martians!"

"Is there a doctor around here?" I said, desperately. "This woman is about to have a baby!"

"I am a doctor," another man with spectacles and a wavy comb over said. "Let's bring her into the lobby."

The announcer on the radio made us pause. "Attention, please: It is now nine twenty in our nation's capital. The informative bulletins you're hearing, ladies and gentlemen, are brought to you by our exclusive sponsor Naranjada, the orange beverage that can't be beat. We have now established a connection with our reporters in Cotocollao. Go on, fellows, we're listening."

"Thank you, Reinaldo. Indeed, we're reporting from the north side of the old plaza in Cotocollao, nearby the church's front entrance. Attention, main studio, are we on the air?"

This voice was extremely familiar.

"On the air, fellows, on the air!"

"This is Leopoldo Anzures reporting."

Valeria's dad.

"I'm going to try my best to describe the incredible scene I'm witnessing. The night is clear, except for dots of stars in the sky. At scarcely one hundred meters from where I stand lies a cylindrical vessel, half buried in a vast pit where just a few minutes ago was a park. It has a diameter of—I don't know—fifty meters, and the vegetation around it is scorched. Unfortunately, it's hard for me to make out what's happening there as curious spectators have gathered around the cylinder."

"Stand back, stand back!" an authoritarian voice demanded.

"From what I can see," Don Leopoldo continued excitedly, "the metal on the sheath looks smooth, with a dazzling sheen, like nothing I've ever seen before. Now, ladies and gentlemen, there's something else I haven't mentioned, but it's hard to ignore. Please, listen!"

"Get back! Move! Someone keep those idiots back!" the other voice said.

"Do you hear it?" Valeria's dad continued his detailed account. "A humming sound is coming from inside the cylinder and, *Virgen Santa*, the hatch is opening! The *Thing* is unscrewing! And now something's wriggling out like a gray snake."

Shrieks and screams muffled Anzures's voice.

"*¡Dios mío!* The things I'm witnessing. It's hard to describe what I'm seeing, but it's quite a spectacle. A huge, elongated creature is coming out of the cylinder. It unfolds an arm—not an arm—a tentacle! Several of them! It is, without a doubt, a Martian! The face—I can barely look at it—it's indescribable. Black, gleaming eyes. A mouth in a V shape, dripping saliva. Olive skin glistening like wet leather. It's now emerged heavily from the cylinder, as if fighting gravity, and there's another creature behind it—as big as a bear."

Another shout of terror came from the crowd.

"These creatures—these Martians—they can barely hold their own weight. They seem to have fallen back inside the pit. Meanwhile, the contour of the cylinder is glowing, expelling a luminous, greenish smoke."

Someone near him was shouting, "*Run, run!*"

"It's truly something out of a modern *Arabian Nights*, dear listeners! A humped shape is now emerging from the pit, and oh, my Lord in Heaven, there's some sort of a mirror or a disc spanning from it and shooting a scorching yellow beam. Oh, no, it's hit some kind of dwelling and as far as I can tell, the house is now gone!"

There was a loud detonation, gun shots, and howls.

"An Army's tank has been destroyed!" Leopoldo said. "And my legs! My legs have become paralyzed! I can't move, but maybe it's just my own panic. The metallic arm has turned toward me and it's about to shoot at me. Ahhhh! What's happening to me?"

There was silence. And then, the announcer again.

"Leopoldo, Leopoldo, can you hear me?"

The listeners around me were just as quiet as the radio signal. Even the pregnant lady and the doctor had remained still.

"Can anyone hear me?" the announcer, Reinaldo, was saying. "My God, what's happened? Kind listeners, did you hear that? It was a cry of agony! Leonardo Anzures, our beloved colleague, appears to have perished."

I couldn't fathom what was happening. I knew Leonardo Anzures well. He was the owner of the radio station, the artistic director, and a reporter in his own right. But above all, he was a good friend of my father's, and Valeria's dad. For the first time in the evening, I thought about little Valeria and what she might be going through. Both of her parents worked at the radio station, and I had just heard her father disintegrate under some sort of lethal yellow beam. God only knew where her mother was.

How would she ever recover from this?

That is, if there's life after tonight.

A heart-wrenching scream came from the top of the hotel and echoed all around the plaza. The shout was followed by a human body and then a thump on the curb.

I shut my eyes.

Had someone just *jumped* off the building?

This last action seemed to throw people over the edge. The yelling, the running, the negotiations with God returned.

"*¡Dios Santo, ayúdanos!*" someone beside me shouted.

"Hey, boy, help me bring her inside," the doctor, snapping from his shock, told me.

The pregnant woman rested one arm on my shoulder and the other one on the doctor's. Slowly, we guided her toward the glass double doors.

"Dear listeners," the voice on the radio returned, more subdued than earlier, "we have been informed of serious disturbances in the streets of Quito due to this radio broadcast. We would like to announce to our citizens that there is no Martian invasion. What you're hearing is a completely fictional radio drama by Radio La Voz. Remain calm. This is *only* a radio drama."

CHAPTER 8

Valeria

1957

"*Venga, mijita,*" Tío Bolívar said, as I entered the living room, where he sat with his newspaper and his cigarettes. "I've been meaning to talk to you."

This was the first time we had been alone since he'd picked me up from the train station a week ago. Their house was always hectic, with my older cousins coming in and out with their spouses and children, Joselito stepping on rugs and hardwood floors with muddy shoes, my aunt relentlessly cleaning or preparing something to eat for her unannounced guests. It seemed like she, Graciela, and the maid were always doing dishes. I myself had helped them in the kitchen a few times.

I sat on a settee speckled with embroidered rosebuds and stared at him. Maybe Graciela had already mentioned my unpleasant encounter with Matías's mother.

"Do you remember the Recalde family?" he said.

How could I forget? It had only been a week.

"Yes." I rested my chin on my knuckles.

"What did you think of Félix?"

The redhead? I hadn't given him a second thought. "Nothing."

He sighed, leaning forward, and set his cigarette on an ashtray strategically placed on an end table by his sofa chair. A scent of ashes emanated from his suit.

"The Recaldes are important people," he said. "They own two of the biggest radio stations in the country." He had already started with his nervous shakes, but it was too early for a drink. "Listen, *mijita*, La Voz never fully recovered from"—he cleared his throat—"the tragedy."

They kept calling it "the tragedy" and talked about it as if it had been an accident of nature, not a deliberate act.

"We lost advertisers and, more importantly, the trust of the people. The Recaldes have an upstanding reputation in the community. If we, hmm—if we associate with them, it could be very beneficial to our station. We could buy modern equipment, hire actors to renew *radionovela* transmissions, acquire better scripts, bring in big bands for our evening shows."

"And how would we *associate* with them?"

He pulled out another cigarette from a box he always carried in his shirt's front pocket. He didn't answer until he'd taken the first drag of smoke.

"Félix is a good boy, but so shy. The Recaldes have been trying to find him a wife for some time. I think he'd make a great husband for you."

"For me?" I said, incredulously. What was this, the Middle Ages?

He nodded.

I stood up, afraid that anything I said would come out in the form of a scream. With time and punishment, I had learned to control the anger that lived inside of me.

He stood after me. "Wait, Valerita, think about it."

Valeria.

"Where are you going to find a better husband? These people are decent, well-respected, and they have a luxurious home in La Mariscal, a new residential neighborhood north of us. You will love it."

"Tío, I told you last week I want to work, I don't want to get married. Not yet. Certainly not to a man I met for two hours and don't even know what his voice sounds like."

He set his hand on my forearm in an appeasing gesture, circles of smoke between us.

"Look, you don't have to answer right now. Take some time to think about it. Talk it over with Graciela, and then we can speak again. There's no hurry."

I wanted to ask him why he didn't tell his own daughter to marry Félix, but I decided not to say anything else. Getting into a fight with my uncle wasn't a good idea. I was staying at *his* house, after all, and had no other place to live. As far as I knew, he'd sold my parents' old house, and the money had been used to restore the radio station and to pay for my education and upkeep.

Fighting tears of frustration, I turned around and headed for the stairs.

When I opened the bedroom door, Graciela immediately shut down a thick folder, as if I'd caught her reading—what? Something forbidden? She tried to hide it among other books in the bookshelf's bottom row, but I'd already seen it, and I intended to check its contents as soon as I got a chance.

"You won't believe what your dad just told me."

She dodged my gaze, flipping imaginary dirt from her skirt.

"Oh, no," I said.

"What?"

"You already knew, didn't you?"

She opened her dresser's top drawer and removed a leather-bound album. "Come here, I want to show you something."

I sat next to her. She opened the first page. It was a photo album filled with black-and-white postcards inserted in tiny corner frames, all from different cities: Valparaíso, Mar del Plata, Río de Janeiro, Maracaibo, Veracruz.

"Where did you get these?"

Graciela pressed her lips together, as if trying to fight a smile.

"My fiancé works for a fishing fleet in Manta and travels all over the world transporting tuna. He sends me postcards from every location." She was openly smiling now.

"I didn't know you had a fiancé. When are you getting married?"

"I don't know. Oscar is trying to save enough money to buy us a house."

"Are you going to move to the coast?"

"Probably. Although he has family here, too. That's how we met."

"How long have you been engaged?"

She kept turning pages. "Since I was eighteen."

Based on my calculations, that was three years ago. "When did you see him last?"

She shut the album. "I think you should accept Félix. He's a good man. I've known him since he was a young boy. He's not arrogant like his parents *at all*. You should take advantage of this opportunity, Vale. They don't come often for girls like us."

"*Girls like us?*"

"Girls followed by tragedy."

CHAPTER 9

Matías

February 12, 1949

In mere seconds, general panic turned into rage.

While the doctor and I helped the pregnant woman into the hotel lobby and set her on an ivory couch, an angry mob had gathered in the plaza and, among screams and curses, they marched in the direction of the radio station.

"These sons of bitches! We'll show them!"

"*¡Desgraciados, van a ver!*"

A mass of people gathered outside the vestibule's window, shouting threats and irate words, then advanced toward Chile Street. I looked at the doctor, and he nodded. Slipping on the green-and-white checkered marble floor, I rushed out of the hotel and followed them for the next block. The crowd consisted of mostly men carrying large sticks and rocks, but a few women were partaking in the mutiny as well.

"*¡Matías!*"

Someone yelled ahead of me. I recognized the voice and face of my friend and neighbor Benjamin among several others.

"Benja!" I said.

Squeezing through the multitude, I finally reached him.

"My dad's inside the building!" he said, pointing at the five-story *Crónicas* building coming into view.

Benjamin's father, Raúl Cortés, was the newspaper's editor-in-chief. He and my dad had also been friends for years. It was not unusual that Raúl would be there tonight, as sometimes editors stayed late to solve problems that may arise with the next day's edition, or to read the front page, or to write their own opinion pieces. On occasion, my dad would stay late as well, particularly if some political drama had developed in the evening and he had to oversee the new story and front page.

"Do you know if my dad is there, too?" I asked.

"I don't know!" He had to scream to be heard as the horde around us was getting rowdy.

As the mob reached the building, they tried to open the metal door, but it was locked. They banged on it relentlessly. Others threw rocks at the windows or hit them with their sticks, cracking some of them. Someone got hold of a brick and threw it at one of the windows, shattering it.

Among the crowd, I spotted one of my destitute cousins—those we never mentioned. They were older than me by two or three years—twins—a man and a woman. One of my aunts had made a "questionable marriage," according to what my mom had related to me, and had basically been disowned by my grandfather, so they apparently lived in one of the poorest neighborhoods of Quito. But I had seen photos of them that my mother had showed me in utmost secrecy a couple of years ago.

He stared at me, which told me he knew exactly who I was. I waved at him as a sign that I knew who he was and didn't hate him, but he turned away and kept walking toward the building, a torch in his hand and a rolled newspaper under his arm.

I lost sight of him as people began gathering outside the building like ants on a piece of watermelon.

"We have to go in," I told Benjamin, "and warn the people inside what's going on."

"How? The door is locked!" Benjamin said, testing the doorknob again. He barely had enough room to move as the mob was squeezing him against the door.

I pushed bodies aside and made my way toward the glass window, where the linotype machine could be seen. I wiped the glass with the corner of my shirt and tried to look inside, hands and face pressed against the cool glass.

The linotypist stood by the machine in his navy smock, staring at us with a puzzled expression. I bet some technicians and operators were not even aware of the unfortunate broadcast yet. There was some movement behind him, but I couldn't tell who the people were. The crash of another window startled me as a bulky rock broke through the glass. People proceeded to throw burning newspapers inside the building. The very same pages of *Crónicas* were feeding the burgeoning fire.

"Stop!" I yelled. "What are you doing? There are innocent people inside!"

But the crowd was blinded by rage. A man, slightly taller than me, was about to hurl a large torch inside the building. I tackled him to the ground, but as soon as I got up, someone punched me on the side of the face. I fell on a couple of women who were directly behind me.

They shrieked.

"Sorry," I said, attempting to stand.

"Here!" Benjamin said, offering me his hand. Somehow he'd managed to escape the mass of people pressing him against the entrance.

The brakes of a truck caught my attention as its driver was parking the vehicle across the building and forcing people to move out of his way without regard for human life. The back of the truck was filled with rocks that the mob proceeded to grab and throw against the building.

How did they know to bring rocks?

The smell of gasoline became overwhelming.

"What are you doing?" I asked everyone and no one in particular.

This was my father's building, my grandfather's legacy, the pride of the Montero family. A newspaper my father worked very hard to print every day at the sacrifice of his own family time. A paper that had cost him his own blood, sweat, and tears. Now these bandits wanted to destroy it because of a stupid *radionovela*? It didn't seem fair.

"Someone, please, call the police! Call the firefighters!" a voice shouted behind me, but I couldn't discern whom it belonged to.

I attempted to push away the vandals who kept throwing rocks and burning newspapers, but a few of them restrained both my arms.

People had truly lost their minds. A cluster of men managed to bust the door open. Men in navy smocks fled out. Some were welcomed into the street with a shove or a punch—even though they clearly had nothing to do with the disastrous broadcast.

"Where the hell is Leopoldo Anzures?" a voice in the furious crowd shouted. "This is all his fault!"

"Come out, you *malparido*!"

"Now comes the second part of the invasion, *cabrones*!"

"Please, someone call the firefighters!" One of the *Crónicas* workers said, between coughs.

As the flames grew, we could hear the screams of people inside. More and more employees found their way out, but as the fire spread, a group of people attempted a human chain to descend from one of the higher windows—with disastrous results. All five or six of them fell to the ground.

I shut my eyes, but I feared that the scene I'd just witnessed would stick with me for the rest of my life. I brought my hands to my throat where a big lump grew painfully. After minutes that seemed like hours, a fire truck finally came to the rescue, its siren a welcome, heaven-sent sound in the midst of the uproar.

"What took you so long?" a concerned woman demanded from a firefighter attempting to unfasten the hose from the truck.

"Most firemen and policemen are in Cotocollao, fighting the so-called Martians," the firefighter said, annoyed. "The rest of us thought the calls about the fire were part of the radio drama."

As a second firefighter descended and helped the other one unravel the hose, two angry citizens threatened them with a thick stick.

"One more move and we'll kill you!"

Others got hold of the first firefighter. A man in a military uniform ran inside *Crónicas* before anyone could stop him.

I managed to escape the grasp of the faceless mob. Something told me that my father, at the very least, might be inside. I had to do something. Covering my head with my sheepskin jacket, I entered the burning building.

CHAPTER 10

Valeria

1957

Tío Bolívar first came onto my radar the day after my father's radio station recklessly transmitted the infamous adaptation of *The War of the Worlds*. Until that catastrophic day, he'd been a distant uncle that I would bump into at the station hallways or see in passing at family dinners during Christmas or New Year's Eve while I was busily playing *las escondidas* with my cousins—hide-and-go-seek had always been my favorite game. So, I was understandably baffled when he came to my house in the middle of the afternoon and took me out for ice cream without preamble.

I suspected this outing had something to do with my parents' absence. Neither one had spent the night at home, and I'd been worried sick about them. Fortunately, there had been Ada, always Ada, my beloved nanny, to look after me.

Tío Bolívar bought me a two-scoop mango ice cream flanked with banana slices inside a crystal tulip glass. Two scoops! My parents only ever bought me one.

"Valerita," he said. "I'm afraid I have some upsetting news."

I set my spoon aside after a small taste.

"There was an accident last night," he said, his fingers trembling slightly over the checkered tablecloth. "A fire at the radio station."

A *fire*? There was still mango residue on my lower lip.

"Unfortunately, your parents didn't make it."

What was he saying?

"It happened so quickly." He tapped his unlit cigarette on the table's surface. "I—I don't even understand what happened myself."

There must be a mistake. "No. You're wrong."

"I wish I was wrong."

"I want to see them!" I said, standing.

"No, wait, sit down. Nobody can go in there. The firefighters and the police are the only ones allowed. They're trying to recover the bodies. I—I'm sorry, *mijita*." He grabbed my hand. "I wish I could give you better news."

"But how do they know they were there?"

"We heard their voices on the radio just a few minutes before the fire. They were performing in the radio drama. Others saw them there, too. They were on the third floor, so the chances of them escaping are slim. We have no way of knowing, at this point, how many people made it out, but the fact that nobody saw them leave the building and it is now"—he glanced at his wristwatch—"four o'clock is pretty telling, considering the fire started at ten last night."

I couldn't believe it. I *didn't* believe it. "How do you know they're not hospitalized?"

"I was standing outside the building. I saw all the people who were taken to the hospital. Besides, I called all the hospitals this morning."

"Take me there."

"To the hospital?"

"To the radio station."

For a long time, he didn't say anything but simply scratched his chin. He hadn't shaved and his growing beard was starting to join his mustache and sideburns. His eyebrows also had given up and decided to form a bridge over his brow and form one long eyebrow.

I stared at my ice cream as it slowly melted.

I'd always heard employees say bad things about my uncle: that he was mean, that he was greedy, that he drank too much, but I appreciated that he spoke the truth to me. He didn't treat me like a little girl, but a person with a functioning brain. He could've lied to me to soften the blow of my parents' death, like so many adults in my life would do subsequently, to spare my feelings, but he agreed to take me to the radio station to see with my own eyes that what he was saying was true.

I didn't know if Tío Bolívar was good or bad, or if what he had just told me was the truth. All I knew was that from that day on, I would never eat mango again.

The harmonious strings of a guitar woke me up after midnight. I turned to my cousin in the bed next to mine, but she was asleep. The music seemed to be coming from the street. I thought of my cousin Germán, who'd been talking incessantly about saving money for a *requinto* guitar during dinner, but the truth was that whoever was outside was an experienced musician, or a group of them. The chords appeared to be from more than one guitar.

I sat up, rubbing my eyes. The tall light post from the street partially illuminated Graciela's dim room, and I could see my cousin's silhouette as she sat up.

"*¡Sereno!*" we yelled in unison, dumping our covers to the floor and leaping toward the window.

"Wait!" Graciela said, as I attempted to open the lacy curtain. "You can't show too much eagerness. You have to play hard to get."

"You realize the serenade may not be for us, right?"

Besides, I didn't want to play hard to get with Matías, if, in fact, it was him who had brought me a serenade after realizing it was me—his childhood girlfriend—at the newspaper the other day. Well, the term *girlfriend* might be a bit of wishful thinking on my part.

"Open it slowly," Graciela instructed with the expertise her years granted her.

Maybe it was her sailor finally coming back. How disappointing *that* would be.

"All right," I said, gently moving the curtain aside.

A duet delivered the first lyrics of "Perfidia," one of the most popular *boleros* of the last fifteen years. The harmonious baritones—so rich and melancholic—brought about unexpected emotions. If this went on much longer, I might start tearing up.

"Who is it?" Graciela asked, still hiding behind the wall.

I squinted. "I can't really see. There's three of them."

"Are they standing under our window?"

"Yes."

She brought a hand to her chest and for once forgot to cover her mouth as she smiled. What could only be described as a toad was bouncing in my stomach as I tried to distinguish who the third man was. I'd already discounted the first two singers as strangers, but I still held the hope that the third one might be Matías. Back at the newspaper, I'd been impressed with how favorably he'd aged. He'd certainly been cute for a thirteen-year-old, but those were some awkward years for everyone, and he hadn't reached his full potential yet. Not until now.

Under the streetlight, the third man's hair was starting to look copper to me. He finally raised his head.

Oh, no.

Félix Recalde.

I dropped the curtain and took a step back.

"Let me see," Graciela said, removing her front curlers and peeking outside eagerly. "Ohhh . . ." She sounded equally disappointed. "Félix."

I crossed my arms.

"It's still a nice gesture," she added.

I sighed. "Well, what are we supposed to do now?"

"Wave, I guess."

One voice rose above the others. It was an impressive tenor, with a projection that filled my arms with goosebumps. When I looked down again, I was shocked. The voice belonged to none other than Félix. But how could that be when he'd barely been able to speak last week?

Graciela and I stared at each other, our mouths agape. She turned on the lamp on her night table and subsequently, waved at the men.

"Do you know the other two?" I said, waving more reluctantly than my cousin.

"No. But one of them is really cute." She covered her smile. "The tall one in the back. You see him?"

At that moment, a man in stripped pajamas—Tío Bolívar—stepped onto the street and effusively patted Félix in the back. Then, he waved at me from downstairs, displaying his widest smile.

I realized then it wouldn't be so easy to ignore his plans.

CHAPTER II

Matías

As I burst inside the *Crónicas* building, I realized some of the malcontents were already in there. They were carrying typewriters, rolls of paper, and other valuables outside. The man in the military uniform, who apparently was helping a woman get out of the building, was hit over the head with a typewriter. What was wrong with these people? If I hadn't been so consumed with panic and so desperate to find my father, I would've run behind the assailant and hit *him* with the typewriter, but the man quickly disappeared from my view.

From what I could see through the clouds of smoke, one of the linotypists was already helping the military man get up. I needed to hurry if I was going to make it alive. I'd been in this building several times, so I knew where my dad's office was, assuming he was still there. With a burning chest and watery eyes, I made my way through the smoke toward the staircase. Two men were coming down. I'd seen them before—they were reporters.

"Hey, kid, don't go up there! It's dangerous!"

"Is Agustín Montero in here?" I managed to ask.

"I haven't seen him," one of them said.

"Get out of the building!" said the other.

The two of them rushed toward the front. I climbed the concrete stairs, coughing the entire way up. Halfway through the stairs—on the landing—I saw a female form in a two-piece suit, her legs partially exposed. She was lying down and apparently unconscious.

I leaned over her. I needed to see her face, so I moved her arm out of the way.

"¡Mamá!" I yelled.

Her eyes were shut, her body awkwardly contorted. I needed to get her out of here. I tried to lift her, but I wasn't strong enough, so I hoisted her up from the underarms and dragged her down the stairs. She was heavier than I'd anticipated, and the heat on my face was overwhelming, but I managed to get her to the first floor. Once downstairs, I ran into one of the technicians in blue smocks.

"Help me, please!"

The man lifted her by the ankles, and we crossed the foyer toward the front door. She started fussing and coughing as we moved her. What a relief! I'd been terrified that she might be dead.

In the street, the mob was now letting the firefighters do their job, as if they'd finally come to their senses and realized what they had done. We carried my mom away from the crowd and found a clear spot on the ground. I placed my jacket underneath her head for support and knelt beside her.

"Your father," she said, between coughs, "he's still inside."

I turned toward the burning building. It seemed enormous, insurmountable. The flames had spread to other areas since we came out. The two firefighters who were trying to fight them were not being too successful. How could I—barely a teenager—go back in there?

CHAPTER 12

Valeria

1957

I hadn't expected to see Matías again so soon. But how could I not? This was an unprecedented event that required all media sources to come together. Somehow, I thought that as proprietor, editor, or whatever function he had at the newspaper, he wouldn't be here.

And yet, he was. Standing just a few steps ahead of me.

We had all gathered in the Quito airport, where two Mexican stars were arriving to film a movie with our one and only Ernesto Albán.

The minute Tío Bolívar had mentioned—in passing—that the two celebrities, Juliana Isabel and Alejandro Toledo, were coming today and he was going to do his best to get them to come to the station and sing at our evening show, Graciela and I had begged him to let us come along. He'd grudgingly agreed, but it seemed like all the other radio stations in the city had the same idea, not to mention that all the newspapers were eager to report the extraordinary visit.

Obviously, I'd brought my camera along. I was determined to get spectacular photos of the teen idols, but was frankly, a bit in-

timidated when I saw the slick cameras the professional photographers were carrying. What I needed was an exclusive, a photo like
no other, and I wasn't going to get something unique standing in
the same spot as all of these photographers.

At least that was the plan when I squeezed through men carrying cameras and microphones all the way to the front, where
I spotted Matías by the railing, looking at the runway through a
floor-to-ceiling window.

Correction, Matías with his hand on the small of some woman's
back. She turned to him, giggling, and he whispered something
into her ear. Something that got her laughing even more.

I forgot my strategy. I no longer cared about the picture.

I could only stare at his profile with a mixture of eagerness for
him to see me and fear that he might. I hadn't even looked at myself in the mirror before rushing behind my uncle after lunch, and
who knew what my hair was doing by this point of the afternoon?
But I hadn't wanted my uncle to leave without me. I'd barely had
a chance to grab my purse, my camera, and Graciela's hand.

How people changed! I could already see it. Mati had been
a melancholic, introverted kid, but the way he was flirting with
this . . . woman! And laughing. He would never have done that
when I'd known him. He had been quietly observant, with a wisdom, if you will, that I loved. He had been so kind to me even
though I was three years younger and some people claimed I was
annoying. I liked to think of myself as spirited, instead.

There was a brawl of some sort behind me. "Hey, what's wrong
with you?" a man with a camera said.

"I was here first," said another. "You took *my* spot."

He shoved the other. The one with the camera lost his balance and landed on top of a few fellow reporters, who complained
loudly. As I faced the front again, my eyes met Matías's for just
a second, but then he looked away and focused on the brawl behind us.

What had I ever done to him to deserve such indifference? I'd
written him a letter after I arrived at the boarding school telling

him how sorry I was about his father's passing—he'd also been at the building during the fire—but Matías had never answered or given me any condolences over my parents' deaths.

He hadn't been the only one who'd lost someone! I had lost both parents, not just *one*. I hadn't even been able to attend their funeral, as my uncle had said it would be "traumatic" at my age. I knew one day I had to gather the courage to visit their graves. I just wasn't ready yet.

Since everyone was so immersed in the fight between photographers, nobody seemed to notice when the Aerovías Panamá plane landed on Ecuadorian soil. It must be some kind of sign that only I would have this exclusive. I took a shot at the plane and then noticed a door to the side being opened and an airport employee stepping out.

I pushed through the bodies, briefly spotting my uncle and cousin absorbed in the enfolding drama and headed to the ajar door. Before I stepped outside, I glanced back at the crowd of reporters. Matías was staring at me. I held his gaze for an instant, then darted outside.

I welcomed the cool breeze on my face as it had been so stuffy inside the terminal. My relief, however, was short lived as a few raindrops hit my nose. I had failed to bring my umbrella, and I could also feel my bun, or what was left of it, coming undone.

As the plane taxied closer to the building and stopped in front of the picture window, the loud cries and cheers of women above me became deafening. I looked up and noticed for the first time a rooftop balcony on the second floor filled with girls. It was jampacked, and the eager fans were screaming at the top of their lungs. The shrieks became louder—if such thing were possible—as the boarding stairs were set in place and the plane's door was lifted. Following the flight attendant, Alejandro Toledo and his characteristic strawberry blond hair appeared on top of the escalator.

As he waved at the girls, I feared a hysterical teenager might jump from the rooftop. Alejandro Toledo was one of the biggest stars in Latin America at the moment. He had achieved fame sing-

ing rock 'n' roll in Spanish and had recently started an acting career as well. Some of the girls at the boarding school had plastered
walls and armoires with newspaper clippings of him.

Not I—I wasn't easily starstruck.

Hiding behind a baggage cart, I approached the escalator. From
the side, I took a photo of him. It may not have been the best one,
but it was an exclusive photo. Following Alejandro Toledo were
two large men in suits. As the singer descended the escalator, the
crowd chanted "Alejandro! Alejandro!" while others kept screaming. I resisted the urge to cover my ears.

Close behind them, the beautiful Juliana Isabel emerged from
the plane in a bouquet-print dress with a wide skirt that enhanced
her minimal waist. She looked so glamorous with her hair wrapped
in a lavender satin scarf, with gloves and sunglasses on. Someone
behind her had already opened a striped umbrella and was preparing to protect the young actress from the rain.

I moved a little and squatted until I could capture her full body
through my lens. I snapped another photo.

"Excuse me, *señorita*."

Before I got a chance to turn toward the male voice behind me,
someone snatched the camera from my hands.

"Wait! What are you doing?"

It was one of Alejandro's guards, who'd already reached the bottom of the stairs.

"Give me that! It's mine!" I said.

"I'm sorry, *señorita*, but you're not allowed in here, and Mr. Toledo doesn't want to be photographed before the press conference,
especially from that angle."

I struggled to recover my property, but the man was so tall, and
he held the camera so high, I couldn't reach it. I snatched his other
arm, but he pulled away from me with ease and walked behind his
boss, who hadn't even bothered looking at me.

Juliana Isabel descended the staircase with her assistant holding the umbrella close behind me. I was too shocked to utter another word. Even worse, I was mortified by the possibility that

someone—more specifically, Matías—might have witnessed the embarrassing scene from the window. I didn't even want to think about how ridiculous I must look with my hair and clothes drenched. At least the rain freshened my blushing cheeks—one small mercy.

As the celebrities and their entourage entered the terminal, I stomped back to the door where I'd come from. Who the hell did that man think he was to *steal* my camera? If I didn't know the entire world—more or less—was watching, I would've chased him down until he returned what was rightfully mine.

On top of all that, I didn't have a single photo to show. Stupidly, I'd thought the Monteros would be so impressed with the photo of Alejandro Toledo, they would offer me a job on the spot. How could I be so dumb to let that gorilla take my camera?

I tried to pull the door open, but it was locked! The rain had gotten so hard I could barely see where to go or what to do. There was movement on the taxiway as luggage was transported from one place to another and technicians would come and go, not to mention airplanes, like giant birds, in close proximity. I was livid, but more at my own stupidity.

As I briefly contemplated my possibilities, covering my head with my purse, the door opened abruptly. Thank you, *Diosito*. Matías pulled me inside before I could get a word out.

The crowd of reporters and photographers had spread somewhat and in their place were passengers headed in different directions.

"Thanks," I said, too embarrassed to look him in the eye. Had he seen my entire, humiliating ordeal?

"Your uncle is looking for you," he said, curtly.

So, he knew who I was!

"What about the press conference?" I said.

"They moved it to the hotel." He wouldn't even look at me. As if I were some disgusting rodent. Instead, he searched for someone among the faces around us. His little girlfriend?

"Valeria!" Graciela called out, surprisingly pushing passengers out of her way as she approached me. My uncle followed behind.

"Well, I'll see you later," Matías said and left before I had a chance to say goodbye.

I couldn't believe how *arrogant* he'd become!

"Where were you?" my cousin said. "We've been looking for you all over."

Tío Bolívar was furious. Apparently, they had wasted time looking for me instead of rushing to the hotel where Alejandro Toledo and Juliana Isabel were staying to speak to them first. I didn't even bother giving them any explanation, and when my cousin asked where my camera was, I simply said an evil man stole it from me.

CHAPTER 13

Matías

February 13, 1949

When my mom woke up at the hospital, I'd been sitting by her side for over eight hours. There was still no word from my father.

I should have gone back into the Crónicas building.

The nurses and doctors had been busy all night tending to women in premature labor, people who had suffered various accidents—in cars or on bicycles—while trying to escape "the invasion," and victims of heart attacks who'd panicked after they'd heard Valeria's dad apparently being disintegrated by an unidentified hyper-advanced weapon.

I still didn't know if Leopoldo Anzures or his wife had made it. At the moment, my biggest concern was my father.

"Mati," my mom said, her voice hoarse. "What happened?"

She was asking *me*? That was what I wanted to know. *I* was the one full of questions.

"They burned the building," I said.

"Who?"

"I don't know. People who were mad."

"Mad?"

Had she lost her memory?

"Wait. You don't know about the broadcast? You *were* inside," I said.

"What broadcast?"

"The radio drama where they said Martians were invading Ecuador?"

She let out a slight smile, a crease of confusion in her forehead. "You're joking, right?"

I leaned forward. "No, I think you are. You really don't remember anything?"

She hesitated. "I wasn't . . . I wasn't at the station. I was talking to your dad in his office."

Of course, not everyone had been listening to the radio. So many people inside the building must have not known what was going on, especially the newspaper employees who only shared the building with La Voz. The puzzled look of the linotypist came to mind.

"Do you know what happened to him?" I asked.

"I was about to ask you. He was fine when I left the office."

What had been so important that my mom had to speak to my dad there and not at home? "Why did you go there, Mamá?" I said, cautiously.

She averted my gaze. "It's grownup stuff, Mati."

There was nothing that infuriated me more than when she treated me like a child. For God's sake, I'd just carried her out of a burning building! There was a soft knock on the door. The person didn't even wait for an answer before opening it.

"*Hola, prima.*"

The man walking in wasn't really my mother's cousin, though they affectionately called each other by that term of endearment. Julio Montero was, in fact, my father's cousin, son of his late younger uncle.

"How are you feeling?" he said, doing a terrible job at hiding a despondent expression.

"Hi," she said, her voice a whisper.

He patted my back. "Mati."

My mom and I both stared at him in silence, bracing ourselves for what was about to come out of his mouth.

"I'm afraid I have some sad news."

I didn't want to listen to him. I wanted to run out of the room and never come to this rotten hospital again. But Julio couldn't hear my thoughts.

"Unfortunately, my cousin passed away last night in the fire. They just found his body."

"Are you sure?" I asked.

He gave me a mystified look. "I wouldn't be telling you if I weren't sure, Matías."

"But how can they know?" I said. "I mean, wasn't he burned?"

Julio, usually a jolly man who loved a good party, with tasty *hornado* and imported whiskey, had never looked so ashen and disconcerted to me. It was almost as if he'd lost ten pounds overnight, not that he was thin from any point of view.

"I haven't seen his body yet, but as far as I know, a few employees have identified him."

"I want to see him," I said, feeling a rubber ball stuck in my throat.

"No!" Both of them yelled in unison.

"You don't need to see that, *hijo*," Julio said.

I'm not your son. I pulled away from him.

"Don't call him *that*," I said. "He's not a thing. He's my father."

"Mati," my mom said, sitting up, not a single tear in her eyes. "Julio didn't mean it that way. It's best that you don't see him."

I needed to get out of this place—now. I had an almost uncontrollable desire to break every object in the room. I turned around and ran as far away from that hospital as I could.

CHAPTER 14

Valeria

1957

Graciela and I pestered Tío Bolívar all through dinner to take us with him to the welcome party the producers of Ernesto Albán's movie were hosting for his co-stars, Alejandro Toledo and Juliana Isabel. Only a few important members of the press had been invited—my uncle being one of them. In the end, exhaustion trampled conviction. Tío Bolívar finally gave up and nodded, taking a satisfying drag of smoke after the hefty meal my aunt had prepared. Since she wasn't going—Tía Marga hated social gatherings—he agreed to take me and my cousin in her place.

Before he could change his mind, Graciela and I rushed upstairs to find something mildly appropriate to wear. Graciela ended up wearing one of her older sister's gowns—an emerald one—and I wore a black velvet pencil skirt dress with lace on top. It had belonged to my late mother. I figured this classic-cut dress wouldn't look too outdated. In fact, I felt sophisticated in it. This was my first time wearing my mother's clothes, but my aunt had been saving them for years in a large trunk she presented to me a few days after my arrival. My mother must have been smaller than me, as the top was a little tight on me, but it would do for tonight.

I had not told Graciela yet, but once we reached the party, I was going to demand my camera back from Alejandro Toledo's body-guard. Since my uncle didn't let us go to the press conference after the airport fiasco, I never got a chance to get it back.

The party was being held in the home of one of the producers, just a few blocks from my uncle's house. I remembered seeing this spectacular construction as a child and thinking it was a magical palace, but I never knew whom it belonged to, and never, ever, had I imagined going to a party inside.

A surge of excitement made my legs tingle as I maneuvered my mom's heels through the narrow cobblestone street.

"I want you near me at all times, Valeria," my uncle said. He still hadn't forgiven me for wandering about in the airport.

"*Sí, tío,*" I said, conciliatory.

For years, I'd been dreaming of going to parties in fancy places like these. I wasn't going to ruin it now. The sound of trumpets and drums could be heard from a block away. The music only added to my excitement. Graciela and I exchanged smiles, hers behind a gloved hand. We followed Tío Bolívar inside through the open gates and into a large patio where several tables had been set and an orchestra performed on a raised stage. The courtyard was surrounded by large columns and, above them, balustrades with long planters and red geraniums in bloom. The walls were a combination of peach, white, and vermillion. I tried to spot the Mexican celebrities among the crowd, without any luck. My uncle, however, approached the charismatic Ernesto Albán, who was wearing his customary bowler hat with its matching black tie and jacket.

Don Ernesto, otherwise known as his popular character Eva-risto, was a short, pudgy man in his mid-forties. Always kind, always smiling, he had an enviable diction that served him well in his performances in plays around the country. His career was taking off now as he was going to start making films with interna-tional stars.

When my uncle introduced me, Don Ernesto's smile grew even wider. "Don't tell me you're Leopoldo's daughter?"

I nodded.

"My God, I met you when you were this big." He lowered his hand all the way to his thighs. "Look how much you've grown." He held my hand with both of his appreciatively. They were warm and made me feel more comfortable in this gathering of strangers. "Your parents were wonderful people," he said. "I was very sorry to hear what happened to them."

About that—what exactly happened? I wanted to ask. Had it not been for the fact that my uncle was attentive to my every word and that I was in the middle of a party, I would have bombarded Don Ernesto with questions. I'd always wanted to know the details of my parents' demise or what brought them to that strange situation in the first place. I'd always had the feeling that there was more to the story than what Tío Bolívar had told me. Don Ernesto seemed open and nice enough to help me. So far, he'd been the only person I'd encountered who had spoken about my mother with affection.

"Were you there . . . that night?" I ventured.

"Nearby," he said. "During that time, Teatro Sucre was being remodeled, so I rented Teatro Espejo for my company to work in. That night, I—"

"There's Juliana Isabel!" Tío Bolívar interrupted, pointing at the beloved actress in her long spaghetti-strap silver dress, which highlighted all her curves. Her lovely honey-colored mane was lifted in a loose ponytail cascading on one of her shoulders. Her cherry lips looked full and moist.

The music stopped and you could almost hear a collective gasp—particularly from the men in the patio—as she smiled and greeted those next to her. Don Ernesto Albán excused himself and approached her. I would have to catch up with him later to get more information. In the meantime, I would find that wicked bodyguard who took my camera.

I searched behind Juliana Isabel for Alejandro Toledo and his security team, but I didn't see any of them in the vicinity, no matter how hard I looked. Among the crowd, however, I noticed someone staring directly at me.

Matías.

I'd suspected he might be here. I held his gaze for an instant, then looked away. If he wanted to ignore me, so could I. I was *done* playing the part of the stupid girl with a crush. I couldn't believe I'd been thinking about him for eight years straight! It was ridiculous. I didn't even know who he was anymore, and my assessment as a ten-year-old child may not have been accurate. He had appeared to be a nice boy back then, but clearly, he wasn't now. Arrogant and full of himself, that was what he was.

I turned to Graciela, who was talking to a man. Well, mostly nodding as he spoke and when she had to answer, she would bring a hand to her mouth first.

Someone ought to take that girl to a dentist.

"Valeria, look who's here!" My uncle said.

I turned to look at none other than Félix Recalde. He seemed taller and thinner than the last time I'd seen him. I didn't remember his hair being so bright and so red. I pinched my cousin's arm.

"*¡Ayayay!*" she said.

"Sorry," I said. The habit was too hard to break.

"Isn't it wonderful to find him here?" Tío Bolívar said, with a smile I rarely saw.

"H-how are you?" Félix asked me, stuttering a bit.

"Fine, thank you."

Someone came to greet my uncle and while he was talking to the other man, there was an awkward silence between me and Félix. I sneezed.

"*Salud,*" he said.

"Thank you." My nose had gotten so itchy.

"You have a beautiful voice," I said, recalling the serenade from the other night.

"Thanks."

We had thanked each other enough. What else was there to say? Félix and I smiled at each other like a pair of idiots.

"M-my p-p-parents would like to say h-h-hello to you," he said after yet another unbearable silence.

"Where are they?" Tío Bolívar asked, after disengaging from his other conversation and grabbing a champagne for the toast on the fly.

Félix guided us to his parents' table. Once again, I was subjected to the scrutiny and stares of Doña Caridad Recalde while her husband and Tío Bolívar spoke. I wanted to scream that I wasn't merchandise for sale!

One of the producers clicked his wineglass with a fork to garner everyone's attention. I could tell by his accent that he was Mexican. He thanked us all for coming and proceeded to make a toast for Juliana Isabel, Alejandro Toledo, and Ernesto Albán, and for the projected success of the movie they were about to film. I still hadn't seen Alejandro Toledo or his bodyguards anywhere. When I asked Félix, he told me that the Mexican singer hated crowds and gatherings, and didn't like to give interviews, so he'd opted not to come to the celebration. I collapsed onto my chair, sighing. Toledo had been my primary motivation to come to the party.

As the band started playing a *guaracha*, Tío Bolívar prompted me and Félix to dance. I wished he hadn't. Whereas Félix was a gifted singer, dancing was not on his list of talents. We stepped on each other's feet several times. In one of our stiff, forced turns, I spotted Matías laughing.

At me? I wanted to slap him.

My cheeks burning, I turned toward Félix and tightened my grasp of his hand. My left hand landed softly on his shoulder. I'd been dancing for years with my classmates, so I knew the steps. I just needed to get a hold of my nerves and my chagrin at having Matías watching me. My friend Rosaura had taught me a trick so that my hips would move more. I had to dance on my tiptoes. So, I did just that.

Matías wouldn't laugh at me when he saw what I could do! I

took a deep breath, listened to the rhythm of the song, and told Félix to slow down.

"Follow me," I said. "Listen to the beat."

He nodded and followed me obediently. Soon enough, we were doing a lot better. Our next turn went smoothly. I even started to have fun. I quickly glanced back at Matías. He was now dancing—very well, to my annoyance—with a cute girl in a red polka-dot dress. A different girl than the one from the airport. But he was flirting with her just as much. I shouldn't care about what he did. We'd never been anything but friends.

Instead of wasting my energy on that twit, I should focus on talking to Ernesto Albán about my parents. I got a feeling he was about to share something important earlier. But as the whiskey and *aguardiente* bottles were getting empty, and people got more and more affectionate, Don Ernesto became harder to reach. He'd shed his jacket a long time ago, displaying a pair of suspenders over his white shirt, and people often came to talk to him or offer him a drink. He was undoubtedly the most popular man at the party, whereas Juliana Isabel was the most popular girl. Even Tío Bolívar had asked her to dance. Don Ernesto danced, too, with his wife, who Graciela had told me was also a theater actress.

Félix and I were already on our fifth song. He was getting significantly better, so I didn't have the heart to tell him I was getting tired and thirsty, and wanted a break. What I had noticed was that the closer he got to me, the more frequently I sneezed.

I felt a tap on my shoulder.

"Now it's my turn to dance with Valeria," Matías told Félix.

I was shocked. Up until that moment he'd acted as though he didn't even know my name. But something about the way he'd approached us: with that smug smile, the faint scent of alcohol, and how he had taken "ownership" of me bothered me. Not to mention the fact that he'd apparently been laughing at me earlier.

"No," I said. "I'm not dancing with you."

I held Félix's hand and led him toward the table where Graciela was sitting. She'd run into an old school friend and was talking to her animatedly.

After a sip of water, Félix and I returned to the dance floor for a cha-cha. It was a favorite, and everyone stood up to dance. Matías had recovered quickly from my rejection and was dancing with yet another girl. Ugh, he'd turned into such a womanizer.

Félix was more comfortable with me now and was not stuttering as much. He was also learning the steps faster. The dance floor got crowded, and I lost sight of Matías. In the last few years, *cha-cha-chá* had become a popular dance in all of Latin America and I liked it because it was simple and fun to dance. But the first notes of "Los marcianos" by Tito Rodríguez made me stiffen.

I stopped dancing.

"What's wrong?" Félix said.

I needed to be alone. I couldn't stand that stupid Martian song for one more second. I made my way across the dance floor, pushing a couple of drunks who tried to grab me by the waist. Somewhere along the way, I lost Félix, which was a relief as I didn't want to have to give him any explanations. I found a hall that was quiet and dark, and stood there, leaning against the wall with my arms crossed. The hall led to another small patio, but I spotted a couple sitting on a bench under a dim light, so I stayed where I was.

"You don't like this song, either."

His voice startled me. Matías had been standing behind a column in the center of the patio.

"I hate it," I said.

"Me, too."

"You can't get away from it."

The blasted song was in every radio station and party, it seemed. It had come out a couple of years ago in light of the ongoing Martian craze around the world. Not only because of the drama that ensued here eight years ago, but also in other countries. The so-called alien invasion became the subject of graphic novels and movies, even songs such as this one, which tells the story of Martians arriving on a flying saucer and dancing the cha-cha-chá. If it weren't because the subject was so personal to me, I probably would've liked it as much as the next person, since the melody and lyrics were extremely catchy.

"It should be banned," he said, approaching me.

Of course he would hate it, too. His father had died in the same incident. The whole Martian fiasco, which seemed so outrageous and amusing for some, wasn't funny to us *at all*. Now that I had him close, I could tell he wasn't drunk, like I'd originally thought. He seemed completely sober. His eyes had that special shine they always got when they looked at me. At least, I had wanted to be-lieve it.

"Why didn't you want to dance with me?" he said, curtly.

"You've changed."

"Everyone changes."

I sighed.

"You have changed, too," he said. He was about to add something else but didn't.

"Your mother is not here today?" I asked, self-consciously.

"No. She hates parties. Ever since my dad"—he loosened his tie a notch—"ever since his passing, she doesn't go out anymore."

And yet, she'd married another man. I found that odd, especially because her new spouse was her husband's first cousin.

"Why were you laughing at me?" I asked him.

"I wasn't laughing at you. When?"

"Earlier. When I was dancing."

"Someone told me a joke."

"But you looked at me."

He inserted his hands in the pockets of his trousers. "That had nothing to do with it."

"With what?"

"The joke was not the reason I was looking at you."

"Then what was it?"

He shrugged. "You look like your mom now."

"And that's a bad thing?"

"I never said that."

"Well, is it?"

He cleared his throat. "No."

"Valeria!" My uncle's voice thundered behind me. He'd never raised his voice at me, and it was disconcerting. "What are you doing here? Félix got tired of waiting for you and left!"

He looked at Matías as though he were a monster emerging from a cave. Neither one greeted the other. I knew for a fact they'd met before. Matías and his parents often attended gatherings at my parents' house during holidays and birthdays, and Tío Bolívar and his family were always there. At some point, Graciela, Matías, Germán, and I had all played together.

Tío Bolívar grabbed my arm. "Come on."

I turned to Matías. Now that I'd finally gotten him to talk to me, I had to leave. I was going to tell him something about continuing with our conversation at another time, but he spoke first.

"Don't let me keep you."

I was so hurt I turned around and left without saying goodbye. On our way out, we heard Don Ernesto Albán singing a popular tango.

CHAPTER 15

Matías

1949

I stared languidly at *The Angel of Silence*, an Italian statue crowning the first mausoleum built in Cementerio San Diego, one of Quito's oldest graveyards. With a finger against his lips, the monumental angel gestured for all of us to remain silent. All around us were marble statues and eclectic mausoleums belonging to aristocratic families, former presidents, fallen soldiers, as well as religious figures and artists. The styles of these structures were as diverse as the people resting here: neo-Gothic, neoclassic, Baroque—all filling up this city of concrete among rows of trees and sporadic benches. My history teacher said most of these sculptures were brought from Italy to the gulf of Guayaquil, then transported to Quito on the backs of mules, to be assembled here. It was a pity that such elaborate constructions held nothing but lifeless bodies who couldn't appreciate the artistic greatness erected above them.

Our family's mausoleum sat next to the angel that had captivated me so. My father had been assigned to a premature niche inside the neo-Gothic structure, the final resting place of my grandfather and his father before him. It was probably going to be the place where I would be buried, too. Just like my family said

I'd been born with "the smell of ink" and an indisputable future in print—whether I wanted it or not—my final resting place was also part of my family legacy.

I wondered if Valeria's parents were going to be buried in this cemetery as well. So far, I hadn't seen anyone from her family—neither here, nor at my father's wake. When I'd mentioned them to my mother, she'd shut me down immediately and told me she wouldn't be attending their services and neither would I. I'd tried to ask why. Hadn't Valeria's mom been her best friend in the entire world, not to mention my baptismal godmother?

My mother said one day she would explain everything, but now was not the right time. She hadn't removed her sunglasses since she left the hospital and hadn't said much, either. As stiff as one of the statues around us, she held her black patent leather purse in her hand, the tip of her nose pink, her mouth void of any lipstick. She hadn't bothered fixing her hair in her customary pompadour, either. Her loose bun was more of an afterthought, while a black lace veil covered her head.

As the priest finished the Rite of Committal, the pallbearers—me included—lifted my dad's casket and inserted it into his crypt. My throat felt thick and achy, but I'd been told from a young age that men didn't cry, so I would wait until I was alone to do it—if I did at all.

"Your father will be missed," Raúl Cortés told me after, patting my back. I still didn't know how he'd survived the fire but my father hadn't.

Both acquaintances and strangers offered me their condolences, and my grandfather on my mom's side—the only grandparent I'd ever known—held my arm as we walked away from my dad among tombstones and patches of grass. Despite his age, my grandfather was still a big man, admired by women and men alike for his business successes and engaging personality. But in the last year, I'd noticed how his customary assertive pace had slowed down and his large shoulders slumped.

My grandpa and I shared a love for history and politics, and we often engaged in long conversations about the aftermath of the war in Europe and the Pacific, as well as the Peruvian invasion of 1941. But that was the extent of our conversations. I doubted he knew more about my mother's odd reaction to her friend's death, but even if he knew, he wouldn't tell me. My mother and he had their differences throughout the years, but my grandfather was loyal to her to a fault.

The rest of the afternoon was spent at home in the utmost silence. I couldn't stand seeing my mom's lethargic face as she sipped the *consomé* Delia had prepared for us, or locking myself in my bedroom any longer. Shortly after dinner, after my mom had gone to bed, I went outside to get some fresh air.

I hadn't planned to go to Valeria's house, but somehow, I ended up there. All the lights were off and when I rang the doorbell, nobody opened. I went to Benjamin's house, which was only a couple of blocks away, and mentioned Valeria and her parents.

"Didn't you hear?" he said. "Her uncle sent her to a boarding school in Riobamba. She left this morning."

CHAPTER 16

Valeria

1957

I followed Tío Bolívar and Graciela at a distance. I knew that if I stayed too close to them, I wouldn't be able to hide my ire. So, I walked behind them, tearing a branch I'd pulled from a plant on our way out of the party at the producer's house.

How dare my uncle talk to me that way in front of Matías? Who *the hell* did he think he was?

Not my father!

My father had been a kind man—maybe distant and busy—but he had never imposed his ideas on me or ordered me what to do. Not that I had him long. I was ten years old when he passed, so my memories of him were scarce. He was a genius—that much I knew.

Not only did he have the ability to run a radio station, dealing with all the administrative aspects of the company, but he was also a respected and talented writer and poet. Since *radionovela* scripts came from Cuba and used their own slang, my father—with the assistance of his producer—would end up rewriting sections of dialogue so that the Ecuadorian audience could understand every nuance. He also wrote plays of his own, as far as I knew.

And he had adored my mother. There was nothing he wouldn't do for her. My mother would get into strange moods sometimes when it was hard for her to get out of bed. Sometimes it lasted days—at which point my father would get so desperate he had to recruit the services of a less-talented actress, Beatriz Lara, to take her place in the nightly *radionovela*.

Then, as if nothing had happened, my mother would get up in the middle of the afternoon, wear her nicest suit, and head to the radio station to perform during the evening show. The next morning my father would be so contented he would bring her coffee to bed.

I had a few memories of my mother, like how she peeled off the skin of *every single* kernel on her corn on the cob until her plate had a pile as tall as the Cotopaxi. Or how she never threw away her old lipstick but kept them in the bottom drawer of her bureau. Once a week, she trimmed and filed my nails. I tried to escape the ordeal, but she would say that the care of a mother showed in her daughter's nails and hair.

Illuminated by the streetlight, I glanced at my nails. The misty rose polish was starting to chip. How I wished my mother were here today to take care of them.

Tío Bolívar opened the door for us, frowning.

"Good night, Graciela," he said, hanging his fedora on the hat tree by the door. Then he turned to me. "You, stay. I want to talk to you."

The house was dark and quiet. The grandfather clock in the living room signaled that it was nearly 11:00 p.m. I'd never been out this late.

"Sit down," he said.

I obeyed, immediately crossing my arms. He could be angry at me all he wanted—I was mad at him, too.

"I don't ever want to see you talking to Matías Montero again."

"Why?"

He undid his tie, the top button of his shirt undone.

"We're no longer friends with them."

"Why not?"

He sat on the sofa's armrest. "Because."

"Because why?"

He sighed. "I don't want to get into this so late at night. Just know that Matías Montero is off limits."

If he only knew that Matías had no interest in me. But this was my chance to understand what had happened between our two families. "You can't expect me to obey you blindly if you don't give me a reason."

"They're jerks!" he said, dropping his cigarette butt on the hardwood floor and not caring enough to pick it up. "They've spent the last eight years making disparaging comments about your mother and blaming your father for what happened the night they died! Is that enough of a reason?"

Looming over me, he looked big and menacing. Gone was the easygoing man I'd always known and liked. He was clearly not used to being questioned. Graciela couldn't be any more obedient, and I had seen the way his older children were always trying to please him—not to mention the two youngest.

I nodded, my anger melting.

He picked up the cigarette butt. "I'm sorry, Valeria, I didn't mean to yell at you. I just . . . I just can't stand those people. After everything my brother did for them. You know he bought the radio station from them? They were the original owners, but they didn't know what they were doing or how to run it. Polo bought it, restructured it, came up with the concept of having live music and radio dramas at night, not just news or religious ceremonies like the Monteros had done before. Radio La Voz surged with Polito. It became one of the top radio stations in the city—in the entire country—in just a few years. Moreover, he helped them at a time when they were struggling financially."

I was glad to hear that in spite of my dad's dreadful mistake, my uncle still respected him. I hadn't heard my dad's nickname Polito in so many years.

"But why did he broadcast that blasted script after what happened when Orson Welles did it in the United States?" I said, my throat closing in.

He shrugged, lifting his hands.

"I've been wondering the same thing for the last eight years."

Later that night, while Graciela was getting ready for bed in the lavatory, I finally peeked into the folder she'd hidden from me the night Tío Bolívar told me about the Recaldes and their intentions toward me.

It was the original script of *The War of the Worlds* with my father's pencil notes all along the margins. Some pages had burned down, but several were legible. Had Graciela wanted to spare me the pain of seeing this sad reminder of my parents' last night on this earth? In parentheses, my dad had indicated what sounds would go where and what utensils they would use to produce such effects. Nothing looked out of the ordinary except for one thing: my mother's name had been crossed out in several pages and above it—in big bold letters—he'd scrawled the name of Beatriz Lara, my mom's understudy.

I'd always thought my mother had performed at the station that night. Could there have been a mistake? Had she been somewhere else? And more importantly, had she survived the fire?

The next day, I attempted to get an answer from my uncle about my mother's whereabouts during the night of the broadcast. "Did you hear her voice during the radio drama? Are you certain she was one of the actresses there that evening?" I even mentioned I'd seen the script with her name crossed out.

Tío Bolívar gave my cousin a scolding look. "I told you not to save it," he told Graciela.

"I'm sorry, Papá," she said. "I couldn't bring myself to throw it away. It's a piece of history. Besides, the fact that it survived the fire must mean something."

"Like what?" my uncle said, skeptical.

"I don't know. A sign?"

"It wasn't the only object I found after the fire. Does that mean *everything* has a meaning?"

Graciela rolled her eyes—it was the first defiant gesture I'd ever seen from her.

"You're certain you heard my mother that night?" I insisted, bringing my uncle back on track. I still hadn't touched my lunch, even though it was *aguado de gallina*, my favorite soup.

"I already told you, I can't remember. It was so long ago. I didn't even hear the entire thing before I went to the station to see what on earth was going on."

"But everyone says her voice was so distinctive."

I looked around the dining room and my gaze settled on my aunt, the only other adult who might have memories of that evening. My little cousin was oblivious to our conversation, busily peeling the skin off his chicken's drumstick, while Germán looked at me mildly interested—chin resting on the palm of his hand, right elbow on the table, even though Tía Marga had forbidden it.

"I didn't listen at all," Tía Marga said. "I go to bed at eight."

"Why are you so interested in this now?" Tío Bolívar said, sipping his broth. "It happened so long ago. Of course, your mother was there, Valerita, otherwise she'd be here, right?"

"But did anyone see her body?"

Tío Bolívar shrugged. "I didn't, but her father—your grandfather—did."

My grandfather had passed away shortly after my mom died. He'd been sick for some time before that, and I barely remembered him. It was one of the reasons why I'd been sent to a boarding school instead of moving in with another relative. My mother had no more family left in Ecuador, as far as I knew.

"I have wonderful news," Tío Bolívar said, serving himself a glass of mineral water with a satisfied smirk. "Juliana Isabel has agreed to perform on *Canciones del Alma* next week."

And just like that, one of the most important conversations of my life was over.

After lunch, I received an unexpected visit.

Félix was standing in the middle of the living room, wearing a black leather jacket that looked like it had swallowed him whole. In his hands was a small package. We awkwardly said hello, not knowing whether to shake hands or hug.

"Nice picture," he said, sitting in front of me.

He pointed at a painting above the gramophone that had intrigued me since I'd arrived. Geometric shapes in orange and green tones gave shape to a minimalist woman sitting in a dark chair while holding a vase in her lap. A woman waiting. I identified with her, as my life seemed to be in a standstill while I waited for something I'd yet to figure out. I'd asked my uncle about this piece, and he said it was an oil from a female Ecuadorian artist he'd once met.

"The artist is Araceli Gilbert," I told Félix. "She's fairly young. In her mid-forties, I think. She studied art in Santiago de Chile, New York, and Paris."

When my uncle had told me about her, I couldn't believe it and had listened in awe. A woman artist. A woman who'd studied abroad and exhibited in Europe. I aspired to be like her, but of course, she was the daughter of a doctor and former vice president of Ecuador, so she'd had many opportunities that most of us didn't.

I could tell Félix was trying to say something else, but he probably didn't know what. His cheeks had turned even more flushed. I felt sorry for him. Some people couldn't stand silence, but I didn't mind it.

"I have something for you," he blurted out.

My gaze went to the package he'd brought with him. It was wrapped in brown paper and a string held it together. He stood up, formally, and handed me the box.

Oh, how I loved presents! Perhaps because I'd had so few in my life. It was probably perfume, but it was a little heavy. A music box? Excitedly, I unwrapped the package and revealed a cardboard box.

I opened it as quickly as I could.

I gasped.

"Your uncle said they stole yours."

"*Virgen del cielo*. A camera?"

I couldn't believe my eyes. I pulled it out of the box. A 35mm Leica with a fancy lens! A *professional* camera! Félix had bought me a much better camera than the one that idiot had stolen from me. I watched him in astonishment. "Thank you, but I don't know if I should accept this gift. It's too expensive."

"P-p-please do. I know you like photography, and you were heartbroken when you lost your camera."

"But a Leica?"

"You deserve it."

"Thank you, Félix. You're too generous."

I looked through the lens, zooming in and out. Félix had a big smile on his face, and I was happy to keep the camera, but something in the back of my head told me I was going to pay a high price for accepting this gift.

The pressure was overwhelming. Even Tía Marga and my older cousins had been talking to me about the wonders of Félix Recalde and his family. Given the fact that Tío Bolívar's family had sent me away for eight years just as soon as my parents died, I had a strong feeling they didn't want me around much longer and were trying to get rid of me. What better way than shipping me off with a rich husband?

I tried in every possible way not to be a burden to the family. I was agreeable at all times: I helped my aunt in the kitchen, served my uncle a glass of *jerez* every night after dinner and lent ears to his grievances about President Camilo Ponce's government. I occasionally took care of my cousins' children, listened to endless gossip from my cousins' wives, played cards with Joselito, accompanied Germán to buy his new guitar, and even listened to Graciela's poetry until the wee hours of the night while trying to conceal my yawns.

But it was not enough. They still wanted me to marry Félix.

A battle brewed inside of me: the need to be liked and accepted by my family as a means of survival, since I didn't have a home of my own or a job to support myself, versus the urge to be my own self and rebel against a forced marriage. It was against my nature to be so congenial. At school, I'd always gotten in trouble with the nuns for what they called "my nonconformist nature." I was always the first to lead the other girls into a rebellion over a variety of things: the food (meals not balanced enough for our growing bodies), wanting to start a theater club in the afternoons, not having to confess every Saturday out of obligation, asking questions about the doctrine that our religion teacher would shut down every time, having to go to bed at eight o'clock when girls who were only a year older got to stay up until nine.

There had always been something to complain about. But it all boiled down to me not caring about the consequences of my behavior. I didn't fear an expulsion. In fact, I would have loved nothing more. I didn't want to live in a boarding school in Riobamba during my entire adolescence. I wanted to be here in Quito, with my family, interacting with boys, being able to go to the movies and parties, and to try new things.

I was eager to live life. Getting married just when I was finally free seemed like another kind of prison. But what else could I do if they didn't want me here? My uncle was so worried about the station. They'd been losing money every year, he said, not getting enough advertisers, and they hadn't been producing *radionovelas* in years. In fact, he wanted to hire Beatriz Lara, who was now a well-respected actress. He believed she might boost their ratings.

Meanwhile the Recalde's stations, Radio Los Andes and Radio Luna, were excelling. It would be so much better to associate with them, he would say. Part of the problem, as I understood it, was that my uncle had never intended to run a radio station. He'd been in another line of work.

"Numbers are his thing," Tía Marga explained, while we rinsed and sorted out lentils to make *menestra* for lunch. "He doesn't have a single artistic bone in his body, and communications bore him. He's an introvert, *mijita*—he hates talking to people."

So, it was up to me to save the family. Indirectly, all of them had told me that my parents had brought disgrace to the Anzures name. In other words, it was my fault-by-association that my uncle was so miserable.

"Graciela is already engaged, or we would consider her as a potential wife for Félix," Tía Marga continued, as if they owned her. "Think about it, *mijita*. Where else are you going to find such a good match? After what happened with your parents, our family is tainted."

In a way, she was right. At a *melcocha* party Graciela and I had attended the other afternoon, a group of guys had mockingly asked me about the "Martian invasion." Others stayed away from us the entire time, and I hadn't seen Matías since the producers' party. Not that he had shown any interest in me.

His "don't let me keep you" still stung.

Félix, on the other hand, was so kind and sweet. He wasn't ugly, either. In fact, the more I looked at him, the more appealing he seemed. Not to mention that he'd given me an expensive, brand-new camera, and brought me a serenade. Plus, he was turning into a decent dancer.

I let out a sigh and rested my elbows on the kitchen counter. "All right. I'll do it."

"Really?" Tía Marga got up and hugged me.

I'd never seen her smile so widely before.

"Oh, I'm so excited. We're going to have a wedding! I'm going to call your uncle!"

As she darted out of the kitchen, I exchanged a glance with Clemencia, their maid, who looked at me in solemn disappointment.

A pang of regret hit me.

What had I just done?

CHAPTER 17

Valeria

1957

I was now officially engaged. I'd regretted it almost immediately. When my uncle told the Recaldes, Félix sent me a bouquet of violets, and that afternoon, he paid me another visit filled with uncomfortable silences and shared smiles. Before he left, he clumsily came to me and stamped a kiss on my cheek. My nose started to itch again, and the only relief came in the form of a sneeze. I was convinced I was allergic to Félix.

The only solution to my dilemma was to become self-sufficient. It turned out that I couldn't live off my inheritance since there wasn't any money left. My dad's house had gotten sold years ago, and my mom's father hadn't left me anything of value. In fact, he'd had so much debt that my uncle had covered it all with the sale of his furniture and other possessions. My uncle had simply tried to spare me the distress of knowing the full truth when I'd first arrived by hiding those unfortunate details.

But Tía Marga had told me the truth.

And now, I had a plan.

My uncle had all the insight on the Mexican celebrities visiting our town. Whereas Juliana Isabel had agreed to sing during the radio's evening show next week, the reclusive Alejandro Toledo (and my old camera) remained unreachable. Apparently, he was only seen on the movie set, and photos were not allowed. He would then return to his suite at Hotel Humboldt, where he would spend the rest of the evening. My uncle had heard from a friend of his at the set that a girl visited the singer every night and they ordered dinner from the hotel restaurant.

I had been thinking all night about my options and my only conclusion was that in order to break off my engagement, I needed a job. The only thing I could—and wanted—to do was take pictures. If *Crónicas* wouldn't hire me as a photographer, another publication might. And what was the *one* thing all the newspapers were currently after?

Alejandro Toledo.

If I managed to get a shot of him with his mysterious girlfriend, I could offer it to all the editors in town and see who paid me more, or better yet, who offered me a full-time position.

It was brilliantly simple.

But I couldn't do it without help. I needed Graciela to cover for me, because my plan could only take place at night, and I had to be in bed by nine. I also needed a key to Alejandro's suite. That might be trickier, but not impossible. Graciela tried to dissuade me. Félix was a perfectly acceptable match. He was romantic and generous, she said, what else could I want?

"A man who doesn't give me allergies?" I said.

"That is the stupidest thing I've heard. You're not *allergic* to him. It's all in your head."

"All right, then how about someone I love?"

Graciela led out a deep sigh. "That I can understand." So, she agreed to help me. But the plan required preparation.

It took three days and two visits to the Art Deco hotel, the tallest in all of downtown, to become acquainted with the building layout and come up with a strategy. Our plan required a secret meeting with one of the hotel housekeepers, whom we ambushed after her shift was over and she was waiting for the bus on a bench.

I hated to part with some of my savings, but I saw the transaction as an investment in my future, so I flat-out offered to buy her uniform.

"But *señorita*, it's dirty. I wore it all day. I was taking it home to wash it."

"Oh, don't you worry about that." I removed a couple of bills, and she took them without speaking another word.

From our observations and from pointed questions to Tío Bolívar, we got a good description of the girlfriend in question and learned that Alejandro Toledo was staying on the eighth floor, which happened to have a nice terrace with some lounge chairs to enjoy the city view.

My plan was bold, but if I wanted an exclusive, I was going to have to take risks and do something different from all the other photographers. The only problem was how to avoid the two mammoths who accompanied Toledo at all times. I would have to figure it out when the time came. Meanwhile, Graciela would cover for me at home, saying I had a terrible migraine and wouldn't be coming downstairs for dinner. She agreed hesitantly, as she didn't like lying to her parents.

I left home at 6:00 p.m. because the housekeepers finished their shift around that time. In a leather handbag I had borrowed from Graciela, I carried the uniform and most important, my camera. I discreetly walked past the bank adjacent to the hotel tower, then stood, gathering my courage, in front of the hotel's bronze double doors. I scanned the door's square panels, running my fingers over the embossed reliefs featuring scenes of everyday life. These panels were surrounded by geometric lines that gave the hotel entrance an ultramodern appearance, which highly contrasted with the colonial style of the buildings in the same block. Of course, Toledo would've stayed there. It was one of the newest and biggest hotels in the area.

I finally pulled the doors open and, taking advantage of the fact that the receptionists were busy tending to a group of tourists, I crossed the ample vestibule, my gaze on the cement tile floors. I headed directly to the lavatory, which Graciela and I had already surveyed on our reconnaissance mission.

I quickly donned the black shirtdress, which was a little short on me, and tied the white apron around my waist. Then, I went to the basement. For another ten sucres, the maid had told me where to find the keys to the rooms and Toledo's in particular.

"You're not going to rob him, right?"

"Not at all," I said, "I just want to see him up close. I'm his greatest fan."

Finding the keys and grabbing a cart full of cleaning supplies, I headed for the service elevator. The hallway to Toledo's room was empty, so I continued to his suite with confidence. My uncle had said that filming usually concluded after sunset, but Toledo never joined the crew or other actors for dinner. He came directly to the hotel.

I knocked on the door, just to make sure no one was inside. As there was no answer, I removed the keys from my apron's pocket. With trembling fingers, I opened the door to the suite and pushed it in. It smelled of fresh pine and wood. It was so spacious and nice! I wouldn't have minded staying there.

The suite had a fine living area, with a rosewood couch and matching lamps on either end table. A guitar was resting casually on top of the sofa. I pictured Alejandro singing romantic tunes to his lover in this very parlor. The coffee table was made of thick oak, with flower arrangements scattered throughout the suite and tasteful artwork hanging on the walls. In the bedroom was an oversized bed draped with a lime quilt, a small desk, and a sitting area in front of a long vertical window with a glass door next to it.

There was the balcony with lounge chairs my uncle had mentioned! The view of the city was breathtaking: a mosaic of pitched roofs, church towers, and domes tucked in a valley surrounded by evergreens and mountains. What made it most impressive were the kaleidoscopic colors in the sky, ranging from blues to crimson and purples, as the sun was being swallowed by the night.

Any moment now, Toledo and his bodyguards would be back.

I had to find a good hiding spot. The closet in the bedroom was where all of Alejandro's clothes were. He would probably take a shower or change clothes as soon as he got back. I contemplated hiding under the bed, but it was too low, and I didn't fit. Besides, if something were to happen between the two lovers, I didn't want it to take place on top of *me*!

In the hall between the room and the parlor was a closet with a gabardine overcoat hanging by its lonesome self. The weather in Quito was mild most of the year, and this had been a warm month, so there would be no need for him to reach out for this jacket. Thus, he probably wouldn't look inside the closet—at least I hoped so.

Hanging the camera around my neck, I went into the dark space and alternated between sitting and kneeling, trying to find comfort and relief for my aching legs. What if Toledo decided, this once, to go out to dinner? Then, I would be stuck in this closet for the rest of my life! I grabbed a broom leaning against the wall as a defense weapon against one of the bodyguards or anyone who might find me here.

The next thirty minutes felt like four hours, but I finally heard someone at the door. There were several male voices, but I couldn't make out what they were saying. The steps grew closer, and I thought I heard the words *"carne asada"* and "potatoes." This came as no surprise to me, as I'd noticed that the men in my family were always in the mood for meat, preferably beef, and a meal didn't seem to be complete without some form of animal protein. But why was he ordering dinner so soon? Shouldn't he wait for the object of his affection—or lust—to arrive first? What if she wasn't coming tonight? Then all of this would've been for nothing. Not only would I have wasted money on this uncomfortable uniform, gotten cramps in my legs and possible permanent back damage, but I was also about to miss one of my aunt's delicious meals. All this food talk was making me realize I was hungry as I hadn't eaten since lunchtime. Even worse was the possibility that they might send me to jail for trespassing or maybe even lose my brand-new camera! I cradled my Leica in my hands. All this sacrifice and risk could amount to—what? Some photos of Alejandro Toledo sleeping or having a drink by himself on the balcony?

After a moment of endless anguish, there was a loud knock on the door, followed by more steps and then a woman's voice! God had answered my prayers!

It turned out her name was Lupita, and she had a melodious, sweet voice. I was desperate to open the closet door and take a peek. She must be some kind of goddess to have won the affection of the elusive singer.

Who knows how long I was stuck in the closet? It had gotten pitch black after the sun had set. From what I could gather, they had eaten their meal already. I contemplated the possibility of sneaking out and taking pictures, but I didn't know about being so obvious and upfront. I didn't want them to see me, so I had set my hopes on the balcony. From the bedroom, I could safely take their photos.

But in the dark? Would the bedroom light illuminate them enough? I had a flash lamp, purchased with most of my savings, sitting inside my bag. I'd practiced a few times, and hoped it would work. I'd better take it out and be ready for that prized photo I was about to take.

The heels of women's shoes startled me as they came near the closet door. Was she about to hang her coat? Please, no. Instinctively, I crouched and lifted the camera against my face, ready to take the shot—even if it was that of a surprised woman. Hopefully, Alejandro would be nearby, and I could catch both of them in the same frame.

With my free hand, I slowly removed the flash lamp from Graciela's bag. Another set of footsteps followed and also stopped by the closet. That had to be *him*!

I held my breath, my legs trembling. I didn't think I could hold still for much longer, but this might be it. My one and only shot! They were probably kissing or hugging or *something*. Why else would they have stopped? I slowly straightened my legs from my crouching position. My knees ached, and my back was covered in sweat. What if it was the bodyguard? Would he shoot me if he found me here? I hadn't seen a gun, though that didn't mean he didn't carry one.

She was giggling now, but I couldn't hear Alejandro. I could open the door, take their photo, and run away. Except that one of the bodyguards might block my exit, and then what?

I shivered.

The woman laughed again, and this time her voice was more distant. If I was going to do something, I had to do it now. With my bag over my shoulder and a good grasp of my camera, I slowly opened the door.

No one in the hall.

The bedroom door looked ajar, and there didn't seem to be anybody in the parlor. Hopefully, the bodyguards had gone out for dinner to give the couple privacy. I stepped out of the closet. Fortunately, the flats I was wearing were soft and didn't make any noise when I walked.

Slowly, I pushed the bedroom door in. Just as I had predicted, Alejandro and Lupita—who struck me as an average girl in a lilac dress and not the goddess I had envisioned—were standing by the balustrade, enjoying the city view with a glass of wine in their hands. She giggled as he softly rubbed her back.

There was just enough light coming from the bedside lamp to make out Alejandro's characteristic Elvis-like pompadour and slicked sides. I would probably only get one shot, and this had to be it. I lifted my camera and the flash lamp and pressed the shutter.

They immediately turned around—*that damn flash!*

"Hey!" Toledo said.

I took another photo as they were both facing me now and I could get a clear view of their faces. As he came toward me, I dashed to the front door. Thank Heavens neither one of the bodyguards was in the parlor. I scrambled with the doorknob as Toledo came toward me, but I managed to open it and get out of the suite.

"Hey, what are you doing!" one of the bodyguards, coming down the hall with his partner, said.

"Get her!" Toledo yelled.

The two bodyguards didn't have to be told twice, and they sprinted behind me. Holy Mother, I'd never attempted to run this fast before. There was no way he was taking this camera from me, not my 35 mm Leica with a prime lens! He would have to kill me first. With the camera swinging side to side and the expensive flash lamp still in my hand, I scurried down the hall like a mad-woman. After a while, I couldn't figure out where I was or how to get out of this maze of shadowy halls and rooms with doors that looked exactly the same.

If only I could find the staircase—I didn't have time to wait for the elevator. Someone grabbed my arm and pulled me into a room.

Oh, no, they got me!

The room was only illuminated by a dim light bulb hanging from the ceiling, but already I could see that it was the janitor's closet. There was barely any space to move with an oversized trash can, cleaning supplies, brooms, buckets, and a vacuum cleaner. The hand, it turned out, belonged to none other than Matías Montero.

"Mati!" I said, reverting to his childhood nickname. "What are you doing here?"

He brought his finger to his lips so I would stay quiet. Then he pressed his cheek against the door. Fast footsteps approached and we held our breaths until the steps became more distant.

I repeated the question. "Why are you here?"

"The same reason you are," he said.

He was trying to get a shot of Alejandro Toledo?

"How do you know what I was doing?"

"I just saw you getting out of his room!"

"You take pictures?" I asked. "But you're the owner of the newspaper."

"Not yet. My mother wants me to start from the ground up and learn every aspect of working at a newspaper, so I've been spending time at every single department. Now, I'm doing journalism and photography, and after that—" He paused. "What's so funny?"

I didn't realize I was smiling.

"I just find it amusing, that's all."

"What?"

"You and me here! It's so ridiculous." I didn't want to say it aloud, but the sight of the heir of a publishing fortune stuck in a closet filled with cleaning supplies and brooms was comical.

He smiled and, for a moment, he reminded me of the young Mati. This was a different kind of smile than the ones I'd been seeing since I'd gotten back—that sardonic smirk I despised.

"How did you end up here?" I asked.

"Well, rumor has it that Toledo has been seeing Lupita Peña."

"Yes, I saw her. Who is she?"

"She's the daughter of the Mexican ambassador in Ecuador. Last week, the ambassador had a private dinner for Toledo, Juliana Isabel, and Ernesto Albán. Ever since, it's been rumored that she's been visiting him, taking advantage of the fact that her parents are out of town, of course."

My photos just rose in value. An ambassador's daughter!

"I followed her here, and she came directly to Toledo's room," Matías said. "I was hoping to see them stepping out or something."

"You silly man, don't you know that Toledo never leaves his suite? He dines inside every night."

"I guess I didn't know." Examining me from head to toe, he said. "What's with the look?"

I felt suddenly self-conscious. Here I was, finally in close proximity to the man I had hero-worshiped since childhood, and he was seeing me in this ill-fitting outfit and covered in sweat? And God only knew what my hair was doing.

"I had to borrow this in order to enter his room."

"Very clever. Did you get any good shots?"

"Of course. Do you want to buy them?"

"No, but my mother might."

"But she *hates* me."

He didn't have an answer to that, which only confirmed my fears. "I think it's safe to go out again," he said, turning the knob. "Shit, it's broken." The doorknob kept turning without releasing the latch bolt.

"Let me try," I said with the same results. The door was, in fact, jammed.

He smacked it.

"Shhh," I said.

We attempted to open it for several minutes. He turned toward the bottles of cleaning supplies. "We need some kind of tool, something sharp, like a knife or a screwdriver."

I helped him look, but there was nothing usable.

"Move out of the way," he said, lifting his leg.

"Wait! What are you going to do?"

"Kick the door open. What else?"

"But if you break it, someone might hear us and call the police. Or maybe Toledo's bodyguards will catch us and take my camera. I don't want to lose this one, too."

He lowered his leg. "What do you mean?"

"They took my other camera that day at the airport."

"Are you serious?" he said, indignant on my behalf. "They can't do that. That's robbery. You should press charges, so they return it."

I hadn't even thought of the possibility. "That's not a bad idea. I was very fond of that camera."

He was still studying the door, hands on his hips. "The hinges are on the outside so we can't remove them." He tried the door-knob again uselessly.

"Or we could just wait it out until everyone falls asleep and then you kick the door open? By the time they get out of their rooms, we'll be in the elevator or the stairs. Nobody will ever know what happened."

I was in no hurry to leave Mati's side, though I was nervous that Tío Bolívar or Tía Marga might have discovered that I wasn't in my bed. I also felt a little guilty that my cousin might be worried about me. Just not guilty enough to leave Matías. Who knew when we would have another opportunity to be alone again. Seeing as things had progressed between us, probably never.

He looked at his wristwatch. "It's almost nine. At what time do you think people will go to bed?"

"I don't know . . . midnight?"

"What about your family, won't they worry about you?"

I chewed on my bottom lip.

"What?" he said.

"They think I'm asleep. Graciela is covering for me."

There it was again, that faint smile of his. So adorable. He removed his suit jacket and placed it on the floor. "Here, have a seat," he said, pointing at his jacket as though it were some luxurious couch. Fortunately, the trash bin was empty, so the smell wasn't too bad.

I sat down and leaned my back against the wall. He sat in front of me with his legs crossed.

"Can I ask you something?" I said.

"I don't know. Can you?"

"Why *does* your mom hate me?"

He avoided my eyes and sighed. "You really don't know?"

"Know what?"

"She blames your father for what happened—for my father's death."

"But that doesn't explain the hatred for my mom. As far as I knew, they were great friends."

"I don't know exactly what happened between them," he said. "I've asked her many times, but she won't tell me."

"You remember that night?"

"How could I forget?" he stared at a crack on the wall.

"My uncle took me to see the building the day after the fire," I said. "I'll never forget the floor on the first story. It looked like a steel mirror. My uncle explained it was molten lead from the printing press. And the typewriters on the floor . . . they were all warped."

He looked at me as if wanting to say something.

"The stench of smoke was so strong, even then," I said, swallowing my tears into a painful lump. It happened every time I thought about my parents' last minutes inside that building. "Will you tell me about that night? I want to know everything." Only if I figured out what had been going on with our parents would I be able to move on with my life. Until then, I lived in a perpetual limbo, where most people despised my mom and dad—and me, by extension—but I didn't know why.

He ran his fingers through his hair. "There's very little I know about that night, other than the chaos in the streets of Quito. I've been wanting to know for a long time myself, but my mother is inscrutable."

"In that case," I said, more resolute than ever, "there's only one thing to do."

He lifted an eyebrow.

"We must investigate what really happened."

PART 2

Comadres

1929–1935

CHAPTER 18

Alicia

1929

My mother had been at the hospital for over a week and neither my father nor my grandmother would tell me why. When I asked if I could go visit her, they flat-out said children were not allowed in hospitals. Fortunately, my best friend in the whole wide world, Marisa, had come to my rescue.

From a white sock that rose all the way to her knee, Marisa removed a folded piece of paper. We were sitting in the patio, inside Colegio La Providencia, where we attended sixth grade.

"What is it?" I asked.

"The hospital's address," she said.

"How did you get it?"

"I have my methods."

She never said what they were, but that was how Marisa was. A mystery—even to me, her closest friend. She'd come to my school unannounced, in the middle of the school year, three months ago. We'd taken an immediate liking to each other. I had been in need of a best friend since the other girls in my class would often ignore me. They would only occasionally include me in their games, but I often spent recess by myself. Marisa, on the other hand, had been interested in me from the beginning, in spite of the other girls' attempts to befriend her first.

Later I found out she'd moved to Quito from the Coast, which explained why she was bolder than the rest of us, and so agile. At first, I thought she had formal acrobatic training, as she'd been able to hang upside down from a metal bar for several minutes. Her legs had hooked onto the bar as if it were the most natural thing in the world, and if that wasn't enough, she'd end the exercise with a jump, twisting quickly in the air and landing on her feet—all while wearing our uncomfortable uniform skirt.

That had made her the most popular new girl in the history of my school. After a month of friendship, she'd made a confession. There was no professional acrobatic training. Back in Guayaquil, she lived right next to a park, and there had been a bar on the playground where she practiced. She'd befriended a group of boys who taught her and her brother these and other tricks.

I thought she was the most interesting person in the world. Not only had she introduced me to the fun of physical play (I, myself, was now hanging from the same metal bar and performing a routine with her), but she was also a big reader and had introduced me to books filled with adventure and mystery.

"We'll go after school," she said, as I reread the hospital's address, trying to remember where the street was. "I already know how to get there. It's only a few blocks from here, by El Arco de la Reina." On the other side of the address was a map she drew herself. I gave her an excited hug. It was all set. I would see Mamá this afternoon.

Marisa and I waited until a couple entered the hospital and followed them inside. We shadowed them at a close distance so that people would think we were their children and wouldn't ask what we were doing there. Somehow Marisa had even figured out in what room my mother was.

As with many buildings in downtown Quito, Hospital San Juan de Dios had a large central patio with a fountain and a gigantic tree in the middle. We continued on our own after the couple entered a room. Marisa pulled me into a wide hall flanked by concrete archways. I fixed my eyes on the floor so that nobody would notice me, but before we reached our destination, a high-pitched voice hollered behind us.

"Hey, *niñitas*, you can't be here!" The stern nurse was quickly approaching us.

Marisa grabbed my hand and darted toward a set of concrete stairs. I ran as fast as my feet and my tight moccasins allowed. We darted through the upstairs hall, lost in a maze of white walls and mahogany doors. But somehow, with sweaty armpits and braids in disarray, we found my mother's room.

"How do you know this is the room?" I asked her.

"I just do."

Again, my friend's talents were a mystery.

"Hey, you!" Somehow the persistent nurse materialized.

Marisa opened my mother's door and pushed me inside. She stayed in the hall, where I could hear the nurse screaming at her.

When I entered the room, I identified a scent akin to rubbing alcohol, masked by a mild whiff of pine, and my mom lying on the bed. There was also an unpleasant odor I couldn't quite pinpoint. I rushed toward my mom before the nurse kicked me out.

Her eyes were shut.

"Mamita," I said.

She opened her eyes and produced a smile through chapped lips. "Alicia, what are you doing here? How did you get in?"

What had happened to her voice? She sounded like she was speaking through a cone.

I didn't know which question to answer first and besides, I didn't have time for explanations. "I miss you," I said, holding her bony hand.

She usually was well-groomed: the latest cloche hat, a smart two-piece suit, carmine lipstick, and her nails neatly manicured. But today things looked very different. Her mane rested wildly on her shoulders, the tip of her nose was red, and she wasn't wearing a lick of cosmetic. The final blow were her nails, stripped of any polish. As if things couldn't get any worse, her arm was connected to a tube that led to a glass container with a transparent liquid slowly dripping inside her veins. I felt an urge to cry just seeing her unkempt appearance.

"When are you coming home?" I asked her.

She started coughing uncontrollably, bringing a handkerchief to her mouth. I spotted yellowish mucus coming out. When she was done coughing, she finally answered. "I don't know." She was about to say something else but seemed to think better of it. "How did you get here?"

"Marisa found you."

My mom smiled. "She's such a good friend to you. I'm so glad you have her."

She had another coughing spell. I handed her a glass of water from a metal tray with long legs and tiny wheels. After she was done, I took the glass back.

"I want you to have this," she said, removing her necklace.

It was her favorite, the one she wore at all times, even with her nightgown. It had a gold pendant of a sun, which I loved. She put it around my neck. "Something to remember me by."

"But you are coming home, right?"

She wouldn't say anything, but her eyes filled with big fat tears.

The door opened abruptly. "Alicia? What are you doing here?"

I turned to face my dad.

"How did you get here?" He stopped speaking when he saw that my mom was crying—well, both of us were.

"We have to take her home," I said. I didn't care what the doctors said. I needed her home.

"We'll talk later, *hija*," he said.

My mom was coughing again, and this time a nun walked in. My dad pulled me back so she could do her work.

"I need you to step outside," the nun said.

We did as we were told and sat on a couple of chairs in the hall. There was no sign of Marisa.

Almost immediately, the nun came out of the room and scurried down the hall. Not five minutes had passed before she came back, followed by a doctor. I tried to go into the room, but my dad held me back with those strong hands of his. Two other nurses went into the room.

"What's happening?" I asked my dad.

He had paled, and he looked like he'd shrunk since we arrived. He didn't utter a word.

Fortunately, my grandmother arrived. Surely, she would know what to do. She was a confident woman who always had an answer and knew how to solve any problem in sight.

"*Hola, Mamá*," my dad said, sounding somewhat relieved at her presence. At least he still had a voice.

In spite of the fact that my grandmother and my mom had a sometimes antagonistic relationship, she'd come. And I loved her for that. I hugged her. She was not what you would expect from a grandmother. Most of my friends' grandmas were plump matrons who inspired nothing but hugs and cozy meals. Papá's mother had a sophisticated name, Azucena, and a slim, elongated body with hardly any hips or breasts to go with it. No matter the weather, she donned tubular, low-waisted dresses that she sewed herself; the kind of woman who would never be caught outside her house without face powder and lipstick or her stylized chignon. Most grandmothers I'd met bore mourning dresses and a few extra pounds after years of indulgent eating, but Doña Azucena Ortega broke all preconceptions. With a perfectly straight back, the poise of a ballet dancer, she assessed the doctor approaching us behind a pair of round, golden framed glasses.

"Can I speak to you for a moment?" the doctor asked my dad.

The two of them stepped aside while my grandmother held my hand with her cold one.

That mountain of a man who was my father looked stricken by the time he was done talking to the doctor. He came toward us while the doctor stood there, looking solemn. My dad squatted in front of me, his eyes watery, and hugged me tightly.

"I'm sorry, *nena*, we lost her."

His choice of words confused me. Surely, he didn't mean my mother was *dead*, did he? I was about to ask for an explanation when I heard my grandmother speak.

"That can't be, Manolo. She was only thirty-six years old. Are they certain?"

Was?

I let go of my dad and darted into my mother's room. Someone had covered her entire body—from head to toe—with a sheet, and there was a man writing something on a clipboard. I removed the sheet, but something had happened to her in the last twenty minutes. Her face was ashen, waxy, and her eyes partially open.

"Mamita!" I said, shaking her.

Someone held me by the shoulders—my dad again. "She's gone to heaven," he said. But it sounded mechanical to me. "She'll always look over you."

How? She's still here. I wanted to say. But I couldn't form the words.

My grandmother stood by the door, dabbing her eyes with the corner of a handkerchief. I stood there, staring at my mom. I wanted to hug her, but she looked so different now it was scaring me.

"You can touch her," my grandma said.

Hesitantly, I touched her arm.

"She's still your mother," she said.

I climbed on the bed and hugged her. My tears wetting Mamá's neck, they let me cry there for a long time. So long I completely lost track of time.

When the nun came back into the room, my dad held my arm. "Come with me, *chiquita*," he said, helping me step out of the bed.

Slowly, the three of us left the room. I was so small, I drowned in my father's arms. For as long as I could remember, people had been intimidated by him. He was taller than most men in Quito and had large, wide shoulders. But it was his raspy voice that made him so scary to all except for me.

Mamá claimed tobacco had ruined his vocal cords. "Don't you ever smoke, Alicia," she would say. "It's a vile habit."

I never got around to asking her what *vile* meant, but when I learned the word, months after I'd lost her, I inexplicably broke down and cried.

Once arrangements for my mother were made, the three of us finally left the hospital. It was dark already, and the moon looked blue. How many hours had I been inside? I grasped my dad's hand as I followed him down the street. When I turned to look back at the hospital, where my mother's body rested, I spotted a figure at the end of the street.

She was sitting on the curb, her back leaning against the hospital wall, her arms hugging her knees. When she looked up, I immediately recognized her.

It was Marisa.

CHAPTER 19

Alicia

1932

Marisa was always scheming something exciting and unexpected for our amusement. So here we were, in the midst of a declamation contest at a brand-new radio station, Radio Cantuña. Marisa was the youngest, surrounded by adult women and men in their best garments, practicing their speeches to themselves.

Having just turned fifteen, Marisa looked significantly older. Most people thought she was nineteen or twenty. I also looked older and took advantage of it: free bus rides, invitations to the ice cream parlor from older guys, cigarettes galore. Men, especially, treated young women more kindly than they did children, and I loved this newfound power.

Something had recently clicked inside me, stirred by all the attention men were giving me and my grandmother's careful guidance on how to look my best. I'd grown more confident than I'd ever been. Today, I'd gotten hold of my grandmother's powder and lipstick—which Marisa and I were both wearing—as we sat stiffly on our chairs, waiting for Marisa's turn to speak. We would have to make sure to remove any trace of cosmetic before Marisa's dad saw her and slapped the lipstick off her mouth.

My father was the exact opposite. I'd grown up spoiled by him and cuddled by my grandmother, who'd moved in with us shortly after Mamá passed away. When I wore rouge, my dad pretended not to notice, or even better, he complimented me, saying something like, "you look especially pretty this morning." If he'd been working long hours at his soda factory, he would give me money to buy myself something nice. I supposed that was the only advantage of having lost a mother at such a young age: Nobody denied me anything.

A man in a gray suit opened the door to the hallway where we were sitting, clipboard in hand. "Marisa Vallejo?" he said, reading the name from a list.

Marisa stood up immediately, smoothing the back of her black wool skirt. She was wearing her mom's white shantung blouse—unbeknownst to her mom—and the effect was professional yet stylish.

"Good luck," I said, winking at her.

"Do you want to watch?" the man said, assessing me from head to toe.

I didn't have to be asked twice. I darted behind my friend, both of us giggling, into a dark auditorium. I joined the people in the audience while Marisa ambled toward the stage, climbed three steps, and settled behind a tall microphone. Another one hung from the ceiling and connected to some device in the back of the auditorium.

Sitting on a cushioned maroon chair in front of her, I interlocked my fingers together over my lap until they stopped shaking. I was more nervous than if I had been the one onstage.

Marisa straightened her back, cleared her throat, and started reciting. I had heard my friend speak in public before, but never behind a microphone. The effect was mesmerizing. Her voice was soothing, yet powerful. It made me think of caramel, honey, and warm chamomile. She knew exactly when to pause, when to prolong a word, when to raise her voice for emphasis and when to talk in a whisper—all according to the content of her sentences. Sometimes, when girls at school recited, I sunk in my chair—cring-ing—and my cheeks warmed as if their shame was my own. With Marisa, I felt no shame. I sat up excitedly, holding back applause.

Marisa recited a poem of love and loss, one that was decidedly too adult for a girl her age, who should be talking about first kisses and holding hands, or flowers and blushing cheeks, not despair and heartbreak. Still, she delivered. I could see that the audience was just as enthralled as I was. I could feel the emotion in my own throat, a mix of pride and sorrow. I pitied the scorned woman in Marisa's poem. Marisa stopped being Marisa, and she became a grown woman who'd just found out about her husband's betrayal, someone who'd lost the man of her dreams to another woman and was left with nothing. The final thrust to the heart was Marisa's voice breaking in the last sentence, and the last word delivered with a barely audible whisper.

When she was done, there was silence.

I was afraid to look around, lest the audience would *boo* her. Perhaps I was getting emotional because Marisa was my friend, and I assessed her with loving eyes. I turned to see the teary woman behind me with a handkerchief pressed against her nose.

In unison, the audience applauded, cheered her, some men even stood up, cigarettes dangling from their lips, hats being waved around. Marisa smiled, and her face lit up. Her nose wrin-kled a tiny bit, and dimples appeared in both of her cheeks and by her eyes. Only when the dimples appeared, I knew she was truly happy.

She won second place.

The first-place winner was a twenty-three-year-old man named Reinaldo, with a tenor voice that was at the same time raspy and deep. Not knowing how young we were, he invited us to a celebra-tion at a brand-new dance hall. They had a wonderful orchestra, he said, and it was bound to become the most popular place in Quito. But there were limits to the things Marisa and I could get away with. Missing dinner wasn't one of them.

Generally, Marisa and I would spend afternoons together. Our families always assumed we were at each other's homes, but we were expected to be back by six or seven—at the latest—and would never be allowed to leave the house after dusk.

We thanked him, without ever bringing up our real age, and left the station, jumping up and down the cobblestone street in excitement with Marisa's medal and the unexpected invitation from an older, good-looking guy.

Not a week had passed before the radio station director himself called Marisa to invite her to participate in a commercial.

"We are enthralled by your voice," he said.

Now Marisa had to figure out a way to go without telling her dad. For the next three months, I was her cover. She told him I was teaching her how to type and she had to come to my house every afternoon to practice with my typewriter. It wasn't hard to believe that Marisa was behind in her typing. She'd never been the best student, and I frequently had to help her with homework and tests. Even so, she never missed school. I suspected it had to do with the fact that she hated being at home, though she always refused to tell me why.

One April morning, she didn't come to school. At first, I didn't think anything of it. Many girls at school were getting colds, but she'd been perfectly fine the previous day—no symptoms whatsoever. I decided to go to her house and find out what was going on. She was the one to open the door. Her cheek had a red mark, sanguine and vivid. She attempted to close the door, but I blocked it with my foot. Or so I thought. In reality, my toe got squashed.

"*¡Ayayay!*"

"Sorry," she said, reopening the door. "Are you all right?"

I lifted my hurt foot. "I suppose."

"Come in," she said hesitantly.

With her assistance, I hopped inside.

We entered a small parlor that shared its space with the dining table. Pretty curtains with embroidered lace hung in front of the windows, but the highlight of the room was the upright piano—her father's pride and joy. I'd only been to her house a couple of times. Usually, she came to mine.

I found a rocking chair, where I'd seen Marisa's dad read the newspaper, and sat down. I removed my oxford shoe. "So, what happened to you?" I said, removing my sock to check the damage.

She crossed her arms over her bosom. "My dad found out I was doing radio spots in the afternoons."

"*How?*"

"One of his musicians also works at the station and saw me."

Marisa's dad was the director of the symphonic orchestra in Quito, which was why they'd moved from Guayaquil five years ago.

"He doesn't want me to go anymore."

"Does he know how good you are? All the voices you can make?"

She shrugged.

"What if my dad talks to him?" I said.

"What difference would that make?"

"Then, let's have the station's director talk to him."

She unfolded her arms, sighing. She was such a pretty girl. It was a pity that she didn't make more of an effort with her appearance. I'd tried to pass on my grandmother's teachings about hair and cosmetics, but Marisa was hopeless. The world around us absorbed her too much—to the point where she had little time for introspection or her own looks. It didn't help that her mom was so neglectful of her own presentation, often wearing her husband's old collared shirts, with hair flying carelessly from her loose bun. She was more immersed in her gigantic paintings and sculptures than making sure her children's clothes were clean and fitted properly.

Marisa had grown up like a wild child, chasing her older brother and his friends across town in fun adventures, while her youngest sister—two years younger than us—spent every waking hour engrossed in a book. Having a father who was a musical genius but little to no social skills didn't help my friend. I'd often wondered if her dad's firm hand was an attempt to overcompensate for his wife's lack of attention and discipline toward her daughters.

My dad and grandmother weren't pleased with our friendship, as they determined that Marisa's family was chaotic, at best, but I often reminded them that my mother had liked her, and she was the only friend who truly mattered to me.

After thinking about my proposition to ask the radio's director for help, Marisa finally answered. "I guess it's worth trying."

It took some back and forth, but eventually the director at Radio Cantuña made a salary offer generous enough to convince Marisa's dad to give her his blessings. However, her becoming a working woman didn't deter him from getting periodic reports on all of Marisa's comings and goings. His stern control also affected me, but the two of us didn't lack the ingenuity to continue with our occasional outings.

Of course, things got worse after what her mother did.

Chapter 20

Marisa

1935

My first day at Radio La Voz, and I was running late. My insomnia was taking a toll on me. I couldn't sleep at night, and I paid for it the next day. Just an hour before sunrise, I would finally doze off, but then it was nearly impossible to wake up. I didn't even hear my alarm clock. If it hadn't been for my sister Tatiana, I wouldn't have made it to the station at all.

I was familiar with the five-story building on Chile Street, but I'd never been inside. All I knew was that the radio station was on the third floor, while the newspaper took the basement and the first and second stories.

The producer of Radio La Voz, Piero Zambrano, had heard me at Radio Cantuña and had come to see me, which was an unexpected honor for a girl my age. He'd asked if I had any theatrical training and I said yes, I'd been taking lessons for years at La Casa del Arte, where my father worked as an orchestra director.

"Wonderful!" he said and repeated the same praise throughout our conversation.

Wonderful this, *wonderful* that.

He said now that they were going to start airing *radionovelas*, they needed a female voice and had been looking for an actress. What better than one person who could do several voices? He'd heard me perform as a child, as an adult, as an old woman. "Is there anything you can't do?" he said, winking.

I said that in the last two years of doing commercials, I'd learned how to modulate my voice and do all kinds of *wonderful* things with it. He'd slipped a business card into my hand and instructed me to come punctually at 8:00 a.m. the next day. But I was already five minutes late, according to my wristwatch.

From one of the first-story windows, I spotted an upright metallic contraption with a keyboard and what looked like large metal above it. I rushed toward the front door and pulled it open. Inside the building was a small vestibule, painted white, where a man rested on his elbows behind a counter, reading the newspaper.

"*Buenos días*," I said in haste. "I have an appointment with Mr. Zambrano."

He barely looked up. "Third floor."

The staircase curled behind him. I rushed upstairs as fast as my heels allowed me, but as I was about to reach the second story, a man coming down with my same sense of urgency slammed against me. The papers in his hand flew all over the stairs.

"I'm sorry," he said, holding me by the shoulders to prevent me from falling.

I'd never seen a more imposing specimen, even with the thin moustache above his lip. His spotless gray suit, the hat covering the edge of his eyebrows slightly tilted, and the handkerchief poking out of his front pocket completed the perfect package.

"Are you all right?" he said, picking up my hat from the floor. "I apologize. I was distracted."

"I'm fine," I said, bending over to pick up his papers.

"You don't have to do that. You're in a hurry."

"Oh, I'm already late."

"Are you going to the station upstairs?" He squatted to collect papers.

"Yes, I'm meeting Don Piero Zambrano."

"Ah, you must be an artist then." He smirked.

Me? "No, that's my mom. I'm just a performer. I read scripts, that's all."

"Well, I'd love to hear you one day."

I smiled. "And you work here, at the paper?"

"Yes, unfortunately. But I won't bore you with that. You should go. Zambrano is a stickler for punctuality."

I was torn. I really wanted the job, but I also wanted to keep talking to this gorgeous man.

He finished picking up his papers. "Nice meeting you, and good luck!" he said, resuming his descent.

I stuttered. I wanted to know more about him—his name for starters, but I barely managed a "thank you" before heading to the third floor.

Zambrano pointed out that I was fifteen minutes late, and he let me know that if I was going to work here, I'd better be on time. People expected the show to start as soon as they turned their radios on—not one, five, or fifteen minutes later. I barely listened. My mind kept going back to the man on the staircase and the feel of his hands on my shoulders.

I'd never been in love, and I was curious about men. Unlike Alicia, who was always surrounded by admirers, I'd never had a boyfriend or anything close to one. Not only because I kept so busy with my acting lessons and the job at Radio Cantuña, but also because my dad kept an eagle eye on me. He'd always been strict and short-tempered, but ever since my mom left him for some vagabond artist, as my dad called him, he'd fortified his guard on me. He often said I was "just like my mother," so he expected a transgression any second.

If only he would pay as much attention to my other siblings, but Gabo was a man, so he had a free pass to do as he pleased, and Tatiana was the mellowest child. So studious and religious. She didn't have my rebellious streak, as my dad called it.

"It won't happen again," I told Zambrano, offering no excuse or explanation for my tardiness.

The truth was I was excited about the prospect of working on *radionovelas* at La Voz. They were going to be pioneers in the industry, as none of the other radio stations in Ecuador were doing radio drama yet.

He took me on a tour of the station, and I felt a little thrill as I saw the studio behind glass windows, the large microphones, the encyclopedia-size manuscripts resting on the desk. The scripts were sent directly from Cuba, he said, where most *radionovelas* were written.

Zambrano was a short, stocky man who must be using some special soles on the bottom of his heels to look taller. The wood scratched the floor with every step. A permanent layer of sweat made his cheeks and forehead shiny, and some kind of greasy product kept his hair stiffly in place. Around his neck was a gray scarf that he kept touching as he spoke. He frequently cleared his throat, and every so often, he would remove a mint from his trousers and insert it in his mouth. On one occasion, he offered me one. He said it did wonders for the voice.

I took it.

This station was much larger than Radio Cantuña. It even had a small library and an auditorium with a grand piano. I was told that there was also a cafeteria on the fourth floor.

I couldn't wait to start.

"What about the salary?" I asked shyly, knowing that only if they paid fairly, my dad would allow me to work here.

"How old are you?" he said as an answer, the green candy exploring every cavity of his mouth.

"Almost eighteen," I said. "But I've been working since I was fifteen."

He assessed me from head to toe. "We'll match whatever Cantuña pays you and add another ten percent."

"Fair enough."

"When can you start?"

"Now."

"Excellent. The rest of the actors should be here any moment.

Come, I'll show you the script of *La Intrusa*." He led me into the booth. "One more thing," he said, turning abruptly toward me. The mint showed up again, significantly smaller. He tapped his chin with his index finger. "I don't think 'Marisa Vallejo' will do. We will go with Marisa del Valle. It sounds more artistic, more lyrical."

I was astounded that someone I'd known for less than an hour had already decided to change my name, but I didn't dare argue with the producer. That was only the beginning of people making decisions for me.

CHAPTER 21

Alicia

1935

Taking advantage of my father's distraction, I poured a splash of vodka into my blackberry soda. A friend of his had brought him three bottles from one of his trips around the world, and I'd discovered that this liquor was magical. It could take on any other flavor while giving you a kick. And I needed something to relax me as I'd been dreading this party for weeks.

Not that I didn't like celebrations. On the contrary, I loved to dance and meet people—especially guys—just not under my father's watchful eye. For weeks, he'd been planning the launch of a brand-new soda flavor, blackberry, to add to his successful brand, Naranjada, which consisted exclusively of an orange soda. But he'd been talking about adding a new line of flavors for years, and the first success was here, in the form of this purplish drink that perfectly hid the vodka I'd poured inside.

For this momentous occasion, he'd invited members of the written press and the many radio stations he was affiliated with for advertising purposes. So many of them, I could barely keep track. Not that I wanted to anyway. Most of them were older men and utterly boring, but at least I'd been allowed to invite Marisa to keep me company during this torturous evening.

I handed her a drink of her own with the same magical liquor mixed inside.

"What is this?" she said, after the first taste, bringing the glass to her eyes so she could examine it.

"My dad's new soda, Morada." I couldn't hide a smile.

"Hum." She gave it another taste, then studied her drink again. "This is not just *mora*. I know you, Alicia—you put something else in it."

My answer came in the form of laughter. "Well, we have to get through this evening somehow."

"Oh, here you are." My grandmother startled both of us. As usual, she was the most elegant woman at the party. With an ankle-length silk gown in deep burgundy, her silver mane styled in her characteristic chignon, and two strands of pearls around her neck, she looked stunning—even at her age.

"Girls, you should mingle, especially you, Marisa, as you're going to be the star of the radio theater in no time," my grandmother said, keeping her back very straight and holding a wineglass filled with Morada soda. It was so strange to see her drinking soda instead of champagne, ("too sweet for my taste," she would say), but at least she'd insisted on having the soda served in a wineglass.

I'd forgotten that my friend Marisa was rising in status. For the last three years, she'd been doing live commercials for Radio Cantuña, but someone from Radio La Voz had just hired her to do *radionovelas*. It was a fresh new concept emerging in the world of communications, and everyone was excited about it.

"Yes, you go," I told her, feeling a pang of sorrow.

Marisa had already dropped out of school, as her commitments with the radio station and the theater group she belonged to were taking too much of her time, but now I was going to lose her to stardom.

Things were rapidly changing for us. For one, Marisa's mother had left, and I strongly suspected it had to do with another man.

Marisa, however, had said her mom wanted to "see the world" and find inspiration for her art, whatever that meant. The other change was how interested adults were in my friend now. For years, I'd been the center of attention, especially at the parties we attended—but now that she'd been *discovered* as the owner of a prodigious voice, everyone wanted to talk to her. Her talent represented ratings and thus, money.

As Marisa approached a heavy-set man who had been popping mint candy into his mouth all night, I spotted what could only be described as a Michelangelo sculpture come to life—with clothes on, that was. And not just any clothes: a tuxedo.

He nodded at me from across the room, holding a glass of soda in his hand. It was almost comical to see so much sophistication while drinking soda.

My dad approached the podium. He was a natural behind the microphone. With a glass bottle of Morada in his hand, a black bow tie, and a few silver hairs flying above his ears—the only sign that he was aging—he thanked all the guests for coming and announced this was just one of the many flavors he would be adding to the fruity collection of his soda company.

A waiter dashed in front of me with a tray filled with purple glasses.

"Since I founded this company twenty years ago, I knew we would make strides in this country. This is just our next logical step. I urge you to give it a try, my friends, and tell me what you think," my dad said.

Those who weren't holding a glass of Morada grabbed one from nearby waiters and prepared themselves for the sugary toast.

"To the success of this new magnificent soda and all the things we will do together to promote it! ¡Salud!"

I had no doubt that my drink and Marisa's were the tastier ones.

A general ¡salud! blasted throughout the salon. Immediately following the toast, a duet of musicians resumed their melodious repertoire, one strumming a guitar and the other one playing a pan flute.

Trays filled with tiny *empanadas de morocho* and shrimp cock-tails paraded in front of my eyes, but I was about to finish my soda and was ready for more of my special drink. I discreetly approached the corner table filled with alcohol bottles that my father had brought along to share with his guests as the night progressed into *guarachas* and *cumbias* for dancing.

In passing, I grabbed another glass of soda from one of the waiters. Making sure no one was watching me, I took hold of the closest vodka bottle—a full one, as I didn't want to make it obvious that someone had been drinking before the allotted time. I quickly poured a splash in my fresh glass.

"That looks like an improvement," a male voice said behind me.

Startled, I turned to face the Michelangelo smiling at me with straight teeth. I composed myself before speaking.

"It is. Would you like to try?" I asked him.

"Absolutely."

I poured some vodka into his soda, and he greedily tossed the entire glass.

"I'd never tasted a better soda," he said. "My congratulations to your father on the new formula."

How did he know who I was?

"I will let him know." I sipped my drink. "And who might you be?"

"Agustín," he said, extending his hand.

I offered mine and he gave it a kiss, followed by a wink.

"I don't know much about sodas," he said, "but I'd be happy to offer my services as taster for any other flavors that may come out in the future."

"Excellent," I said. I was finding him more attractive with each sip. "And what might your current profession be, when you're not tasting soda?"

"Something not as exciting as this. I guarantee it."

Another young man approached us. This one was shorter and swarthy with an air of hedonism.

Agustín patted his back. "Raulito, let me introduce you to"—he turned to me—"Alicia Sotomayor, right?"

I nodded, as I didn't think I could form coherent sentences anymore. Voices and faces were becoming more distant with time. I had to admit that the last serving of vodka may have been more than just a splash.

By the time the *guarachas* started, Agustín and I had become more or less acquainted with one another and had even danced a couple of songs. Inconveniently, a few drops of soda spilled on the front of my white sequin gown. Holding my hand, Agustín took me to the nearest lavatory and the two of us, giggling, got into the tiny room.

Grabbing a towel with ornate vine embroidery along the hem, he wet it under the sink and helped me wipe the stain from my dress before my father, or worse yet, my grandmother, would see it. As he worked, I stared at the close proximity of his hand to one of my breasts, but at that point, I was incapable of cleaning the gown myself as I had no coordination left whatsoever.

"Has anyone told you how striking your eyes are?" he said.

"Sure." I laughed. They were unusually green, an anomaly in this part of the world. "But thank you."

Marisa was waiting outside the bathroom and seemed taken aback upon finding me with the handsome stranger. "I've been looking for you all over," she said.

"Marisa, my dear, let me introduce you to Agustín-no-last-name." I sounded perfect to my own ears, but Marisa grimaced, eyeing the drink in my hand.

"How many of those have you had?"

"I apologize," Agustín said. "I should've stopped her. Listen, I can take her home before her dad or her grandmother notice her state."

"And what do I tell them?" Marisa said.

"Just say she was feeling sick and a friend of hers took her home."

"And how do I know you're not going to attack or kidnap her?

She is the heiress of a soda empire, after all," she said, but I wasn't sure if she was joking or being serious.

"Then you must come with us," he said, humoring her. "Just go tell Doña Azucena we're leaving."

"All right," she said, obediently.

I was surprised that Marisa had agreed so easily as she was usually wary of strangers. Then again, Agustín had a certain quality very few people had of making everyone feel immediately comfortable in his presence.

I had little recollection of the rest of the evening. All I knew was that after kissing so many frogs, I had finally found my prince.

CHAPTER 22

Marisa

1935

"Funny running into you here," Agustín said, as we left Alicia's house.

I'd also been stunned by the coincidence of seeing him at Alicia's dad's event, especially seeing him dancing and flirting with my friend all night. At least I'd learned his name—Agustín—not that it did me any good. Alicia would probably claim him already—even though I'd met him first a few days before at the radio station. It didn't matter, though, men always preferred her. She was so beautiful.

"So, what do you do at the newspaper?" I asked.

Agustín led me to his black Chevrolet sedan and opened the passenger door for me. I'd been impressed to see that he owned a car—and such an elegant one! Not many people I knew did. Only Alicia's dad, really, and he had an older model.

"My family owns it," he said, without a hint of arrogance but more in a matter-of-fact way. "My dad founded it almost thirty years ago, and I'm now attempting to learn the business so I can fill his shoes one day."

I liked his honesty. I sat in the front seat, where minutes before

Alicia had been—although I doubted she would remember anything about this evening in the morning. He asked for my address and then started the car.

"Do you have any siblings?" I asked him.

"I have two older sisters, but I might as well be an only child."

"Do tell."

"Well, the oldest married years ago and lives in Argentina, and the second one has been practically excommunicated from the family."

"How so?"

Agustín sighed. "She married a man—how should I put it?" He tapped the steering wheel with his hand. "Below her station in life? My parents warned her not to do it, but she didn't care because she said she loved him."

"What does he do?"

"He's a cobbler, but he's illiterate, which I think bothers my parents more than his profession."

"But she loves him."

"Yes. She gave him two kids."

"Have your parents met them?"

"Once. Briefly."

"He could get educated," I said. This would have been a cause my mom would have jumped on.

"I suppose," he said. "Did you get the job at the station?"

"Yes!" My excitement extinguished the second my house came into view. If my dad saw me arriving in the car of a stranger, I would pay for it. "Stop here!"

"Here?" We were in the middle of the intersection.

"Yes." I opened the door. "Thank you."

"Wait!"

I rushed to the curb, making sure no one was around. The last thing I needed was for one of the neighbors to tell my dad.

Agustín unrolled his window. "I'll see you at the station on Monday!"

Despite my fear of being caught, I got a small thrill at the possibility of seeing Agustín again. I waved back and gave him my most promising smile.

As I tiptoed inside the foyer, the gramophone was blasting Mozart's Piano Concerto No. 21 in C major, one of my dad's all-time favorites. I had been praying that he'd had a late concert tonight or he would've already gone to bed so that I could sneak into the house in the dark without being noticed, but here he was, practicing his conductor moves to the tempo of the concerto. He still had his tuxedo on, but he'd removed his white bow tie. It was going to be challenging to cross the parlor toward the staircase without being seen.

I bet he had already opened a bottle of whiskey. The more he drank, the more irritable he became. He never used to drink before since he was "the responsible parent" and my mom was "the crazy artist," whom he had to protect us from. But the day she left "to find herself" (in her words) or "to be with her lover" (in his), he'd bought the first bottle. It never stopped after that.

"Oh, there you are!" he said, coming to me with an open hand. "Late again!"

"Don't touch her!" my brother Gabo yelled from the top of the staircase.

My father froze while Gabo came rushing down, two steps at a time. He shoved my dad away from me and stood between us. He was now taller and stronger than our father, who was short to begin with. But in spite of his unimpressive stature, my siblings and I had feared him when we were younger. Now that Gabo was twenty, he'd become defiant. Things had changed from one day to the next. One morning Gabo had woken up and he no longer feared my dad.

Looking confused, my father took a step back.

"Come on," Gabo told me and led me up the stairs.

Ever since our mother left, my brother Gabriel, or Gabo as we called him, had become my protector. He was only two years older than me, but even when we were little, he looked after me and my sister. Our parents had always been too busy with their own lives: my dad working most weekends in the evening and rehearsing long hours during the week, my mom spending hours in her studio in the back of the house, which now sat empty, collecting spiderwebs.

Occasionally, if I wanted to feel close to her, I would go in there and look through her stuff. The gray linoleum floors were stained with multicolor paint drippings. The center table was still covered with a year-old newspaper that she had taped there to protect the wood. She'd left many canvases and brushes, and clay that had dried out months ago—all now unusable, but I'd never had the courage to dump it in the trash. What if she came back and found her things gone?

I was the only one who ever went in there. I doubted my father had set foot in the damp studio since she left. He deemed it too dirty, and he complained that it stank of oil paint and turpentine. My sister acted like everything was fine and we'd never had a mother, so being confronted with her forgotten things might prove too difficult, whereas my brother said the studio made him gloomy, so he would rather not go.

"I met someone," I told him as soon as we walked into his room. We were so used to my dad's outbursts, we no longer saw a point in discussing them, though my brother's hands trembled some.

"At the soda party?" he said, heading toward his desk.

Soda party was not exactly what I would've called the cocktail reception where Alicia had gotten drunk.

Gabo sat down and picked up a thin brush. He took a deep breath before dipping the brush in a small jar of black ink. He had inherited my mom's artistic talent, and he spent most of his free time drawing cartoons of politicians and historical figures, or simply people we knew.

"Sort of. I met him first at La Voz, but he was at the cocktail party tonight."

Leaning over his shoulder, I recognized the portrait of our former president, José María Velasco Ibarra, on the paper. With those bony cheeks, perfectly bald head, dark glasses, and abundant mustache, I didn't need to ask who it was. The man was the perfect subject for a caricature as he was so tall and skinny, and his facial features so dramatic. If Don Quijote were a real person, I imagined he would look like Velasco Ibarra.

"And?" Gabo said, tracing his pencil lines with the Chinese ink.

I climbed onto his bed. His desk faced the window, but there were only a few scarce lights outside as not everyone had electricity in our neighborhood.

"There is a problem. Alicia met him, too."

"So?"

"Boys always like her."

"Tell her you like this one. She has so many boyfriends anyway."

He was right. Alicia disposed of men as if they were chicken bones. "All right, I'll talk to her tomorrow."

I didn't like going to Alicia's house. Perhaps it was the fact that, in spite of having lost her mom at a young age, she was always surrounded by the love and attention of her father and grandmother, who'd more or less taken the role of Alicia's mom since she died. Our fathers were so different that the comparison always pained me, and now that I didn't have my mother, either, the disparity of our circumstances was even more obvious.

Alicia's dad looked as if he were made out of brick instead of flesh, whereas my dad was compact and plump. In addition to the physical differences, their attitudes and demeanors also diverged. Alicia's dad was engaging, and his laughter echoed in every corner of their opulent home, while my dad was prone to periods of moroseness, and minor inconveniences incensed him. We couldn't touch his things—that much we knew since we were small—thus his gramophone was forbidden. However, Gabo and I had figured out ways to use it when he was at work by leaving everything in pristine order after we were done—the same with his radio and his piano. If I was sufficiently motivated, I would even convince Tatiana, who had a penchant for sweets, to help me get a piece of the Spanish *turrón* he kept in his night-table drawer.

Alicia met me downstairs. Not a trace of her sorry state from the previous night. She was one of the few girls I knew who wore pants. She'd found a seamstress to sew her a white pair of sailor trousers—wide on the hips and bottoms—and paired it with a fitted powder blue short-sleeve shirt. Her wavy bob—held on the side with a single barrette—came to the edge of her chin, and she had just applied a smidge of peachy lip balm. She had so much style!

She snapped her fingers at me. "Marisa?"

"Oh, hi, sorry I was admiring your outfit."

She winked at me. "This old thing?"

"How are you feeling this morning?"

"Splendid!" she said, holding my hands and bringing me to the living room, where a soft tawny couch awaited. She folded one of her legs and sat on top of it. "I think I'm in love."

For a second, I worried she was going to mention Agustín, but there were many men at the cocktail party so she may be talking about someone else. At least, I hoped so.

"With whom?" I said, hesitantly.

"Who do you think, *tontita*? The newspaper man!"

One of her pencil-thin eyebrows arched upward—it always did when she was flirting or when she talked about boys.

Something twisted inside of me. She couldn't have him! I met him first—days ago! Didn't that count for something? I just hadn't told her about him. This was exactly what I was afraid of, although I'd been hoping her inebriation last night would've made her forget all about Agustín.

"He's so handsome and nice, and a great dancer, too! Do you think he liked me? Did he say anything about me after he dropped me off?"

"No."

I should just tell her. It was the only way to have a fair battle.

I was going to—just as soon as she stopped babbling about last night's events in excruciating detail, starting with how they'd met, how he'd held her while they were dancing, the way he'd sung softly into her ear during a *bolero*—with *that voice*—or how he'd laughed when she poured vodka into his soda.

"What about Mario Sánchez? I thought you were taken by him," I said, reminding her of a boy she'd met a few weeks ago at another party.

"Mario is *nothing* compared to Agustín. I'm surprised you would even think there is a comparison!" She slapped my leg, good-naturedly. "Did you take a *good look* at Agustín?"

Unfortunately, I had.

"You know what?" she added. "There's someone for you, too. Agustín introduced me to a friend of his at the party—what was his name?" She snapped her fingers, trying to recall the information. "I think it was Saúl or Paul, one of those two names."

I was mildly offended that she thought I needed her help getting a boyfriend. Then again, I'd never had one. I'd been so busy with my theater classes and the job at Radio Cantuña that I didn't have time to do things other girls my age did. Plus, I had an ogre for a father. Once in a while, though, I would go to *melcocha* parties with Alicia, but only if my dad had a concert that evening.

"It would be perfect!" Alicia said, applauding. "The two of us going out with two friends! We'll have so much fun."

This was why I never liked talking about boys with her—she was always trying to find me a partner. I bet that Saúl or Paul was horrible. She stood up. I could see by the shine in her eyes and her conspiratorial smile that an idea was forming in her mind—an idea I wasn't sure I was going to like.

"I know! We'll go see Agustín. We'll take him—I don't know, *pristiños* or something—to the newspaper, to thank him for taking care of me last night and for bringing us home. What do you think?"

"Today is Sunday, Alicia. We're supposed to go to church."

Even I knew that was a lame excuse. Ever since we turned fifteen, the two of us had stopped going to mass on Sundays. We had told our fathers we would rather go together to the later mass, and they had hesitantly agreed. My mother frankly didn't care. She'd never been concerned with religious doctrine, though she called herself "spiritual." She hadn't been going to church for years, as she said she felt closer to God when she was creating. After all, *He* was the one who had given her such a vocation, she would say.

Thus, Alicia and I would stop by Iglesia de San Juan, the church closest to my house, and we would pick up the *hoja dominical*—a piece of paper with the litany of the day's gospel, but instead of going inside, we would go grab the paper and ran to the bazaar at Mercado Santa Clara. There, rows and rows of vendors would extend long cloths on the ground and set their imported Colombian goods, such as brassieres and fabrics. Other days we would visit the seamstress. When we got home, we would leave our papers on the console table so the adults in our lives—who cared enough—thought we'd gone to mass.

That was not the only way Alicia had made me break the rules. When we were younger, she would mimic our parents' handwriting to perfection and she'd bring notes to the teachers saying we had a doctor appointment the next day. Odd as it might be that the two of us would have appointments the same day, our teachers never questioned us because Alicia had a true talent for forging signatures and other people's calligraphy. She used to say it was her superpower. And so, the day would be spent at the park and galivanting all over town.

At the mention of Sunday church, Alicia winked at me. "Great idea."

"It's Sunday," I repeated, "he's *not* going to be at the newspaper."

"*Crónicas* is a daily paper, Marisa. I'm sure he'll be there. He seems like the responsible kind."

"Well . . ." I was trying to come up with the perfect excuse. Something made me think that if I agreed to her plan, I would lose my chances with Agustín forever. "*Pristiños* are supposed to be served warm or they harden. How are you going to manage that if we have to walk all the way to *Crónicas*?"

Pristiños were fried pastries in the shape of a crown, drizzled with syrup. Just thinking about them made my mouth water.

She tapped her chin. "That's a good point." She paced the parlor, going back and forth from the console radio to the grand-father's clock.

"In that case, we'll just stop at the bakery on the way and get him *suspiros* and *aplanchados*. We could leave right away, without having to bake." The urgency in her voice made me realize how enthusiastic she was at the prospect of seeing Agustín again. I couldn't remember a time when she'd been this excited about a boy.

A cause for concern.

Then again, it was Alicia, a girl who changed her mind about people and things every day. This was no different. We'd gone through so many schemes with boys before, and it always came to Alicia getting bored with them after a week. I had nothing to worry about. But maybe I should tell her that I'd met him before, that I was meaning to talk to her about him but hadn't had an opportunity.

"You know *Crónicas* is in the same building as Radio La Voz?" I pointed out.

"Is it now?" she said, but I could tell she wasn't too interested as she headed for the stairs. "Tell me about it later, *amiga*, I'm going upstairs to change. I'll be back in a minute!"

She was already halfway up the staircase, leaving me standing by the radio, wringing the gloves in my hands. Something told me this was not going to be as simple as I'd originally thought.

CHAPTER 23

Marisa

1935

I hesitantly followed Alicia up the stairs of the *Crónicas* building. The guard downstairs had told us we could find Agustín in the newsroom on the second floor. I couldn't stop thinking about the moment he and I had met here on the stairs, just a few days ago: how our hands had briefly touched when I helped him pick up his papers, how our eyes had met, the smile, the conversation. Now Alicia was desecrating my memories of him with her loud steps and incessant chatting.

He couldn't have forgotten me so easily. If he was, in fact, here today, I hoped he would pay attention to me and not her. Why wouldn't he? He'd been so kind yesterday when he'd dropped me off. Alicia had made a fool of herself with how much she drank. Despite my misgivings, I was somewhat excited to see him again. Perhaps I wouldn't have to tell Alicia that I liked him, after all. Perhaps he would show his preference for me.

I straightened my back and entered the second floor. The newsroom took most of the floor, which had a small reception area that was empty. Over a dozen desks were scattered around the room with no rhyme or reason, a typewriter on almost every desk. I could only imagine the chaos of this room during weekdays.

Today, there were only a couple of reporters, and in the back, Agustín, wearing a pair of glasses, working on a Sunday morning, speaking to a guy of around his own age. We approached them, and Alicia was the first one to greet Agustín, claiming "we were in the neighborhood" and wanted to drop him these pastries as a sign of gratitude for taking care of us last night.

He gave us that debonair smile of his. Those glasses made him look even more attractive. "You remember my friend Raúl Cortés?" he said to no one in particular.

We both greeted him, and Agustín explained his friend was one of the editors of the newspaper. I didn't quite catch what Agustín did—upset as I was to see Alicia using her best tactics of flirtation. I had seen her use these strategies hundreds of times. First, something happened to her voice. Her tone got lower, more sensual. Then, she got giddy and laughed at anything the boy in question said. Throughout this conquest process, she fiddled with her hair. Her last weapon was sitting on one of the desks and crossing her legs, which gave Agustín the opportunity to see her perfectly shaped calves.

Alicia knew exactly what she was doing when she changed her trousers into a pencil skirt and striped buttoned blouse, which was tight enough to enhance her full bosom. I glanced down at my minimal chest. I stood no chance.

She mentioned something about her dad's soda factory, and both men expressed an interest in visiting the facility. Exuding enthusiasm, Alicia offered to take us on a tour herself. It was settled then that we would all go next weekend—given that my father had a concert, which I was almost certain he did. But this cozy arrangement didn't sit well with me. I didn't find "Raulito" attractive at all. He was nice, but that was about it.

He was too short—nearly my same height—and the dark circles under his eyes reminded me of a raccoon. His only grace was that he had straight, pearly white teeth. Agustín went along with Alicia's plans and seemed to perk up at the idea of visiting the factory. I didn't know if it was because he liked her or because Naranjada was a potential advertiser for his newspaper.

"It's going to be so much fun," she said, applauding childishly.

Normally the plan would've interested me—I'd always been curious about the process and the factory, as I had grown up drinking the famous orange soda—but not when I was so unenthusiastic about my date. I also found it telling and odd that all the years that I'd known Alicia, she'd never invited me to the soda plant, but she had been prompt to invite Agustín after knowing him for about five minutes.

A couple of times, Agustín's eyes met mine and he smiled. But he was so hard to read! Who did he like? Was he interested in Alicia *because* of her father's business? Had I read too much into things when I perceived some sort of chemistry between us the two times we'd been alone?

"Well, ladies, thank you so much for these delicious treats," he said, abruptly, and smiled at Alicia. "I look forward to seeing you on Saturday."

"Same here," Alicia said.

I nodded, without wanting to. Inside my jacket's pockets, my hands were closed in tight fists, but I tried not to give his smile any importance. I told myself that Alicia had been the one who extended the invitation to the soda factory and who had done all the talking while the three of us just watched her with uncertain smiles. Agustín was just being gracious.

My biggest concern was that he hadn't mentioned seeing me tomorrow, like he did the night before. Had he forgotten I now worked in this same building? Did he not want Alicia to know? I was supposed to be in this building at 9:00 a.m. to meet the other actors and rehearse the script. It would've been common courtesy to acknowledge my presence since we'd met before, but he didn't.

When we left, Alicia was jubilant, analyzing microscopically every gesture, every smile, and every word Agustín had spoken.

I couldn't get a single word in. Not that I wanted to. I was too confused, too frustrated. Agustín didn't seem invested in me at all. He had sort of gone along with Alicia's flirtation and shown politeness and good manners, but not much else.

I reminded myself he had been at work, and even though there were only a couple of reporters nearby, he was the owner's son—flirting with Alicia or me would've been most unprofessional.

"I can't wait until Saturday," Alicia said, skipping.

I did my best to hide my annoyance. I'd always been grateful to Alicia because when I first moved to Quito and gone to Colegio La Providencia, she had immediately befriended me—no matter how odd my family had been. My mother had never quite belonged to the conservative Quito society. Those ladies in minks and feathered hats, who devoted themselves to charity work, and went to church every Sunday, never gave my mom the time of day. I knew for a fact Alicia's grandmother didn't like her, even though my friend never said a word about it.

Not only was my mom different, because she'd grown up on the coast of Ecuador, which meant that she frequently wore short-sleeve dresses and lighter colors—something that was frowned upon in Sierra society—but also, my mother was an artist, and she saw the world in a unique way. Societal norms didn't matter to her as much as creating art. She had no time for long gossip sessions or gatherings to pray the rosary when she could be painting a portrait or crafting a bust and thus, immortalizing someone's likeness. The way she saw it, time was too precious to waste.

Initially, my parents had bonded because of their mutual love for the arts. My dad introduced my mom to classical music, and she enjoyed attending concerts with him and getting herself lost in renditions of Mozart or Chopin. My father admired her talent for drawing and painting, and the passion she brought to all her projects. He often said—when happy or sad—that he'd never met a woman like her before.

But they were too different in their essence. My dad was neat and meticulous in his appearance and neurotically orderly. Every object had its place and needed to be cared for and kept clean. Above all, he valued punctuality. My mother, like many artists, was more concerned with her creations than mundane details, like the upkeep of my father's precious things, or being on time for a concert. Those were simply not her priorities. Not when she was "hit by inspiration," as she called it, and in the middle of creating a potential masterpiece. As my dad became stricter with his rules, my mom became more relaxed, and the house turned into a battlefield—which ended the day my mom packed her favorite brushes and blank canvases, and left for good.

Alicia had been there for me then. I'd initially been embarrassed to tell her what my mother had done, but she'd figured it out on her own and guarded my secret. Unfortunately, such a big secret couldn't last. Soon, the neighbors started commenting that they hadn't seen my mother at the marketplace or outside our house in a long time. Rumors that she might be sick spread until my brother put an end to it all and told his friends in the neighborhood the truth.

Gabo had never been one to care what people thought and said, and that gave him a certain measure of freedom most people never had. Certainly not Tatiana, who was tormented with how others perceived us. Her refuge became the Church. Every week without fail, she confessed not only her sins but, I suspected, my mother's as well. She stopped visiting her friends and locked herself away to pray. Then, the fasting began. Last week, she said she wanted to join the convent next year, no matter how much I tried to dissuade her.

I normally enjoyed spending time with Alicia on Sunday afternoons, but I didn't want to listen to her talk about Agustín for hours on end, so I told her I was going home.

"Are you all right?" she said. "You've been acting strange all day."

"I'm just tired after last night's celebration and want to take a nap." I didn't have the energy to tell her how I felt about Agustín, so I just headed home in defeat. Something told me I had lost the battle before it even started.

CHAPTER 24

Marisa

1935

Microphones had a peculiar smell. Something about them always reminded me of that particular blend of alcohol and yeast that emanated from my father's beer bottles—an aroma he found irresistible. Microphones could be intimidating when you used them for the first time, as they commanded the attention of an entire room. Adults listened. People couldn't ignore you, even if they tried. So, you'd better have something important to say, as everyone had their eyes and ears on you.

I still remember the first time I used one during a declamation festival. The sight of the tall metallic stand in the middle of the stage and the microphone angled in my direction had made my palms sweat. So did the sight of over thirty people looking at me and waiting for me to speak. When I did, though, I was elated, beside myself. I not only got through my speech, which had been my goal, but also earned the audience's applause. This minor success gave me the confidence to do it a second and third time, but the nerves were always there.

Something changed when I started working at Radio Cantuña. The sight of the microphone, which had once tied my stomach in knots and made me want to pee every five minutes, now gave me a thrill. Soon, the nerves turned into excitement, and later, eagerness. I longed to stand behind the microphone every day. It was my vice. Microphones helped me find my voice. And my voice became my power.

When I was doing commercials or making announcements, nothing else mattered. Not my father's anger, nor my mom's disappearance. Certainly not my sister's strange behavior. But I couldn't deny I was thinking about Agustín when I met my fellow actors that Monday morning and stood behind the microphone with the script of *La Intrusa* in my hands. We were about to rehearse before my debut that evening.

Zambrano introduced me to four actors and the technical director, who was in charge of the sound effects. I was the only actress—for now—according to the producer. I didn't mind being the only woman in the room. I'd always felt comfortable around men, perhaps because my first and closest playmate had been my older brother. The truth was I'd never been close or fully comfortable around women. My relationship with my mother had always been distant, and I couldn't understand my sister's mind at all. My only female friend was Alicia, so I clung to our friendship in spite of the annoyances and frustrations, like yesterday's incident with Agustín.

When I delivered my first line, my voice came out a little bit broken. I was still shaken after my pilgrimage up the staircase. I'd been hoping to run into Agustín again and had paid special attention to my grooming and clothes that morning.

My choice for my debut as an actress was a cotton voile floral dress with short, flowy sleeves. To complement the gardenia print, I wore white gloves, which contrasted nicely with the navy base of the fabric. I'd even styled my hair. I curled the tips of my bob and wore a detachable braid across the top of my head. Alicia had given me the braid months ago, but this was the first time I'd worn it. Alicia said it was "chic" and American movie stars like

Bette Davis wore braids and curls all the time—I'd yet to find out who that actress was.

All that effort for nothing.

In the last couple of years, Radio La Voz had become one of the most popular radio stations in the country. Doing a *radionovela* was a dream come true, as it combined two of my greatest passions: radio and acting.

"Excuse my tardiness," a man, who must have been thirty or close to it, said. He removed his beige gabardine and handed his briefcase to a secretary who had been staring at our performance, wide-mouthed, for a couple of minutes. I hadn't caught her name, but she'd shown up with a tray full of espressos. I had one myself even though I'd never had coffee without milk before.

"You must be Marisa del Valle," the man in the trench coat said.

"Yes?" I said, uncertain about who I was talking to.

"Well, I'm glad you agreed to join us. I'm Leopoldo Anzures, the artistic director."

He gave me a few instructions regarding my character and how he envisioned my performance. I nodded at everything he said, eager to impress him and my co-workers, since I was the newest and youngest actress in the group. Halfway through the rehearsal, Anzures removed his jacket and rolled up his sleeves. Holding the folded script in his hands, he leaned on a desk facing us while the five of us stood around the microphone reading our lines.

He didn't miss a beat. If anyone made the slightest mistake, he caught it immediately. He interrupted us to make recommendations regarding our tone and delivery and with his free hand, he directed the sounds effect technician behind us. He reminded me of my father conducting a symphony and directing his musicians with his baton.

Anzures was just as serious as my father, but a couple of times, he smiled to himself when I read a humorous line or when I put enough feeling into one of my lines. His approval felt good and encouraged me to push myself. His direction had the strange quality of both infecting me with his commitment to the play and making me focus on the story as if I were there myself. He made me *feel* Gabriela, the main character, and even though he was demanding—a perfectionist—his presence relaxed me. He transmitted the confidence we'd been lacking before he arrived. He knew exactly what he was doing and what he wanted from us. I kept glancing at him, waiting for his nods to reassure me.

Later, when he dismissed us, the secretary, who introduced herself as Sandra, told me that Mr. Anzures was not only the artistic director, but also the owner of the radio station.

"But he's so young," I said.

"Yes," she said with a sigh. "His brother works here, too, as an accountant. Leopoldo—I mean, Mr. Anzures—is the older of the two. You'll probably meet the brother soon."

Sandra seemed to be the one running the station: she answered the telephone, greeted visitors, talked to advertisers, scheduled musicians and entertainers for the evening show, knew everyone's names *and* the names of their spouses ("Say hi to Flor for me!"), and, as if she weren't busy enough, she made coffee for everyone throughout the entire day.

As I sat next to her with my second *tinto*, getting the scoop of everyone's comings and goings, a voice—like thunder—made me nearly choke on my coffee.

> *"Caminante, no hay camino,*
> *se hace camino al andar."*

I immediately recognized the poem—it spoke about making one's own path as you walked, instead of taking the existing one. I'd memorized it for one of my first declamation contests when I was still in elementary school. The voice behind the poem was Agustín's, who'd just walked in and was looking at me with a nonchalant smile.

"Antonio Machado," I said, citing the poet.

"Very good."

"It's a wise one," I said.

I'd always liked this poem—maybe because it went against all the nonsense my mom always spewed about a determined and unmovable fate, which was what she was obediently following right now.

"Doesn't it contradict the concept of destiny, though?" I said, testing his views.

"That's why it's so great. It means you can start a new path every day, if you wish to do so. There are no limits or fixed paths."

He'd removed his glasses today and his brown eyes were shining. I sat up straight as his gaze traveled over my dress—he'd noticed.

"Good afternoon, Sandra," he told the secretary, as an afterthought.

She twisted one of her curls. *"Buenas tardes, Señor Montero."*

Montero. I liked it.

Marisa de Montero. It fit nicely.

"How was rehearsal?" he asked me.

"It went well, I think."

"Good. I look forward to hearing you tonight." He then turned to Sandra. "Is Polo available?"

"Yes, sir, I'll let him know you're here."

Agustín's comment was both exhilarating and terrifying. He was going to *listen* to me, which meant I had to give a perfect performance—no pressure there. But the thought that he was going to make the effort to find the dial, tune in, and listen to *my* play filled me with joy.

When Sandra went down the hall to get Polo, whom I assumed to be Leopoldo Anzures, Agustín turned to me. "You look very pretty today."

I didn't even know what to say. I'd never been good with flirtation; that was Alicia's gift. Usually, I was just a pal to men and a chaperone to Alicia on her outings.

"Thanks. So do you."

Had I just said that *out loud*?

He smiled. "Are you staying here all afternoon?"

"No. They said we could go home and just come back at seven for the show."

"Do you have a ride?"

Of course I didn't have a ride. I lived only a few blocks away.

"No."

"Can you wait until I talk to Polo? It'll only be a few minutes and then I can take you."

"Sure."

Sandra reappeared. "Go ahead, Señor Montero."

He winked at me before heading for the hall.

"Isn't he handsome?" Sandra said, just as soon as he disappeared. "He's the best-looking man in this entire building."

I nodded. How was it that "the best-looking man in the building" was taking *me* home?

CHAPTER 25

Alicia

1935

What in the world was wrong with Marisa? Since she'd gotten the job at Radio La Voz she'd been acting as if she was too good to be my friend anymore. Normally, she had a lot to say. She would tell me every detail about the people at work, and we celebrated and dissected every piece of gossip from her co-workers. In fact, I'd been looking forward to the inside story of La Voz since she started the new job. But so far, she hadn't told me anything, other than it was "fun."

I'd heard her the night of her debut, and she'd been fabulous. Her voice had trembled a bit at first, but by the end of the episode, she'd made me believe she was Gabriela, the protagonist of *La Intrusa*. From what I could tell, the *radionovela* was becoming popular in our circle. Everybody at school talked about it this week and some of the girls in my class, who'd met Marisa in elementary school, were excited that she was part of the production. They couldn't believe they knew a "celebrity"—even though they'd ignored her during our childhood.

Was that it? Was Marisa becoming conceited because of her newfound fame?

She'd never been vain before. Then again, she'd only been doing commercials. She hadn't been the star of an evening *radionovela* such as this one.

Since we arrived at my dad's factory, Marisa had said very little. I had been the one doing all the talking while we waited for the guys to arrive. I'd been bombarding her with questions, but her answers had been cryptic and incomplete. Maybe she was tired. She wasn't used to working nights. I wondered, too, if her father had been giving her a hard time about her new schedule.

When Agustín and Raúl Cortes arrived, she tensed up. Did she not like them? I would have to ask her later. Agustín looked adorable with his glasses on and a striped suit. I hardly noticed his friend, Raúl—as Agustín was always the center of attention—but both seemed excited for the tour. The only one with a somber face was Marisa.

We started outside the factory, where a truck had just arrived and a couple of employees were unloading wooden boxes filled with fruit. I'd chosen to start with the *mora* soda since it was my favorite and our newest flavor, so I picked a handful of blackberries from the open boxes and handed them to my guests. I put the last one directly into Agustín's mouth, surprising him.

Inside the plant, they poured blackberries into round metal tanks to be sorted out and given a chance to rest in water for about an hour. Once that was done, they covered the containers, and the fruit went through a special contraption that removed the pulp.

I explained each step of the process to the best of my recollection. I hadn't visited this place in a while, but when I was a child—before I met Marisa—I came frequently. I was fascinated by the fact that my dad owned a soda factory, as I always had free bottles at my disposal and occasionally the girls at school wanted to come over to drink endless amounts of soda. Now I would also be the first one to test the new flavors, according to my dad.

As we toured the factory floor, Agustín and Raúl asked lots of questions, but Marisa remained sour. She was starting to irritate me.

"After the pulp is removed, the juice is left to rest in these tanks for two days." I pointed at a couple of gigantic, sealed tanks. "And then, it goes through a pasteurization process in this machine."

Marisa yawned.

How dare she?

I explained to the men how the juice then had to rest for two more days in nearby tanks before it proceeded to the next room where it got mixed with water and other ingredients to create a syrup.

A couple of workers in white smocks greeted me as we walked by. As we turned around the corner, I removed Agustín's glasses and ran away with them. He followed me all through the bottling section, which was loud. I hid behind one of the machines, covering my mouth not to laugh.

"Alicia! I know you're in here!"

As he passed by, I grabbed his arm and brought him to me. I was wearing his glasses, and he chuckled when he saw me. I took a step forward. "If you want your glasses, it's going to cost you."

His smile vanished. "How much?"

I grabbed him by the collar and lowered him so I could kiss him properly. The few seconds our mouths touched felt like heaven, but he interrupted the kiss quickly as fast steps approached us.

Marisa and Raúl were coming; Marisa in the front. She was frowning. Maybe Raúl had said something unpleasant. The little I knew of him indicated that he was one of those people who were always trying to call attention to themselves by being funny, but in reality, he was just annoying.

"What are you doing?" she asked me.

I took off Agustín's glasses and put them on him. "Nothing. Let's go." I held his hand and resumed the tour as if nothing had happened. I pointed at a machine spraying bottles one by one. "Here's where the bottles get washed."

Marisa took a moment to catch up with us. When she finally did, she folded her arms across her chest. In front of us, an inspector made sure the bottles were spotless before he sent them through a conveyer belt to a circular contraption to get filled with the soda mix and then capped and branded.

The four of us then proceeded to the next room, where bottles were hand placed inside crates that were then arranged on pallets for transportation. I uncapped some bottles and handed one to each one of my guests so they could try it, but my attention was on Agustín's every move.

Everyone took a sip, except for Marisa.

"You're not going to try it?" I asked her.

"I'm not thirsty."

I shrugged, reaching under Agustín's arm and pulling him toward me. "And what did you think?"

"Tasty," he said.

"Well, I have to go," Marisa said. "I didn't tell my dad I was coming here."

"Are you serious? I thought we were going to Teatro Bolívar after this," I said.

"I can't."

"Well, maybe Raúl can take you home?" I winked at her, but she averted my gaze.

"It would be my pleasure," Raúl said, donning his hat.

"No," she said. "I'll just take the bus."

"You're not going on a bus." Agustín removed his car keys from his pocket and handed them to Raúl. "Just take my car. Alicia and I will take a cab."

She barely said bye to us, and Raúl promptly followed her.

"I don't know what is wrong with her today," I told Agustín. "She's usually very agreeable."

Agustín looked after her. "Is she really?"

"Do you still want to go to the matinee? My afternoon is completely open."

He assessed me from head to toe. I'd been very careful with my appearance today. I was wearing a cobalt-and-white polka dot dress with a red stash belt and a matching beret.

"I'd love to," he said.

CHAPTER 26

Marisa

1935

I'd never been so vexed with Alicia before. Did she not have any self-awareness? She was being *so* forward with Agustín, who most of the time looked uncomfortable with her advances. She thought that because she was rich and beautiful, every man would fall at her feet, helplessly in love with her. But what else was there? What could she possibly have in common with a man like Agustín?

Their mutual love for blackberry soda?

Please!

She was still in secondary school, for God's sake. She didn't know anything about the real world, whereas I had been working—a productive citizen—for three years already. Agustín and I had a lot more in common. We both worked for the media. We'd had so much to talk about the day he'd dropped me off at home. He was currently the advertising director at his father's newspaper, and I'd been doing commercials for years. We *understood* the business.

"What's wrong?" Raúl said, driving Agustín's sedan, his gaze alternating between the road and my legs. Ugh.

"Nothing."

"Be honest. You're not . . . interested in Agustín, are you?"

I turned to him, shocked. Had I been that obvious? Then, how was it that Alicia didn't notice—or did she not care? More than anything, I was stunned at Raúl's frankness.

"Why do you ask?"

"For one, you watch him all the time."

My cheeks burned.

"Listen, you seem like a nice girl. I wouldn't want you to get hurt. I've known Agustín since elementary school, and he's always had this—how should I put it—*gift* with women?" He accelerated and shifted gears. "He's not a bad person. He just doesn't take women seriously. He's focused on his work. When his dad passes, he's going to have to run the newspaper on his own, so that's where all his attention is."

"He doesn't want a wife?"

"Eventually. But he's only twenty-two. He's not ready for a commitment."

"Men his age marry all the time."

"He says he's not going to bring a wife to his parents' home. He wants to have something of his own before he gets married."

His words stung, but I wouldn't show it.

"Who says I want to get married?" I said defensively. I was, of course, bluffing. I wouldn't mind getting married to someone like Agustín. He was handsome, smart. We even worked in the same building!

"You don't?"

I shrugged, looking out the window at the pastel houses stacked next to one another, balconies, geraniums, trees. The only marriage I had observed up close was my parents', and it was definitely not the best example. And yet, I couldn't conceive a life without marriage. What would it be like to be single forever? How would I even support myself? The money I made at the radio station wasn't enough, and I didn't want to depend on my father for the rest of my days. He had an impossible temper.

"I, for one, am ready to get married," Raúl said. "I just bought a small apartment and I'm looking to settle down."

I studied his profile, with his fine chin and tiny ears. Had he just said those things about Agustín so that I would pay attention to *him*?

"Well, thanks for letting me know," I said. "I'll keep it in mind."

The next time I saw Agustín, he was standing behind a bouquet of gardenias.

"Happy birthday!" He extended the exquisite flower arrangement toward me.

"How did you know it was my birthday?" I could barely hide the excitement in my voice. He'd just rung my doorbell, and I'd been stunned to see him through the window.

"Have you forgotten I work at a newspaper?" he said. "I have my sources."

I took the bouquet and inhaled their sweet aroma.

"I figured you liked gardenias since they were splattered all over your dress the other day," he said, looking behind me, and then added as an afterthought, "I haven't been able to think about anything other than that dress in days," he said in a grave, low voice, followed by a sideways smile.

The comment was so unexpected I didn't even know what to say or do, other than to make a mental note that I should wear that dress every day.

"Do you want to come in?" I asked him.

Fortunately, my dad wasn't home. On Saturday mornings, he had coffee with his musician friends at Heladería San Agustín, which gave us a couple of hours.

"Sure," he said.

He walked in, examining every corner of the parlor and dining room. I was self-conscious that my home may not be up to par. Our furniture was old, and we had to mix and match chairs from a couple of different sets. On top of it all, our walls were bare because my father had been so upset after Mamá left that he took down all her paintings, which at one point had adorned every corner of our house.

If Agustín's family owned *Crónicas* and he paraded in such an expensive car, he probably lived in a mansion. But if he noticed something odd about our décor, he didn't say. He only commented on my dad's upright piano.

"Do you play?"

"Not in years. My dad tried to teach me and my siblings, but the only one who's any good is my youngest sister, Tatiana."

He ran his palm on the polished wood. If my dad would've seen him, he would've lost his mind. Agustín's innocent touch was going to leave fingerprints all over the instrument's surface, for sure. Nobody touched my father's piano, unless you were practicing arpeggios, and you had washed your hands thoroughly first. I made another mental note: *wipe piano with flannel after Agustín leaves.* Our furniture might have been humble and run-down, but we kept our things spotless. My dad wouldn't have it any other way.

Agustín sat on my dad's rocking chair and stared at me. "So how old are you now?"

I sat in front of him. "Eighteen."

It gave me a small satisfaction to finally be the same age as Alicia. She often made me feel as if I were her younger sister, especially when it came down to matters of the heart.

"No longer a child, huh?"

I resented the comment. "For your information, I've been working for the last three years."

"Have you, now?"

I lifted my chin. I resented the condescending tone.

He stopped rocking. "Did I offend you in some way?"

"Well, Agustín, I'm not a child. I've been running this house for the last year and also working. And before you hear it from someone else, my mom left us a year ago."

"Sorry, I didn't know. It wasn't my intention to make you feel bad." He got out of the chair and squatted in front of me, holding my hands. His touch gave me a chill. "I was just trying to tease you, but of course I had noticed that you're a grown woman, and you have the most melodious and soothing voice I've ever heard."

Before I could answer—to thank him for the compliment, probably—he cupped my face with both hands and gave me a soft kiss on the lips. As he slowly pulled back, I grabbed his face and brought him back to me for more.

After a couple of minutes of glorious kisses, which had the effect of weakening my limbs, the creak of the front door interrupted us. Agustín stood up abruptly and turned toward the entrance.

My brother walked in with a paper bag under his arm. Fortunately, it wasn't my dad, but I was still disappointed by the interruption. Every morning, Gabo brought us a loaf of French bread and if he had extra cash, he would buy *moncaibas*, my favorite cookies.

He stopped his humming as soon as he saw us.

"Gabo," I said, somehow recovering from my first kiss ever. "Come meet my friend Agustín."

The two of them shook hands and exchanged pleasantries. I didn't even hear what they were saying as I was so flustered. I'd been curious about what it would be like to kiss a boy for years and now I knew: It was wonderful, and I wanted more! I kept glancing at Agustín, but he seemed unperturbed, as if this was something he did often.

I gathered that he was asking my brother what he did for a living.

"I'm studying architecture," Gabo said.

"And he's a wonderful cartoonist!" I added, knowing my brother was too humble to mention it. "You should see his work."

We ended up taking Agustín upstairs so he could look at Gabo's drawings. He was particularly fascinated by the caricatures of politicians, so much so that he said he'd mention him to Raúl, who turned out to be the managing editor of *Crónicas*. The position was impressive for someone so young since, according to Agustín, Raúl worked directly under the editor-in-chief. No wonder he was "ready to get married," as he had told me.

Upstairs, Agustín also met my sister, who had become nearly a recluse. Agustín agreed to have breakfast with us, but he had to leave immediately after. I was not sure what our kiss meant. Were we officially boyfriend and girlfriend now? The thought delighted me. This was the best birthday of my life. There was only one thing disturbing my bliss: Alicia. I couldn't postpone my conversation with her anymore. I had to face her as soon as possible and tell her Agustín and I were in love.

CHAPTER 27

Alicia

1935

I only went to mass once a year—on the anniversary of my mother's death. They said those annual masses helped souls ascend to heaven. I often wondered how many years and how many more masses it would take. She had passed away six years ago. Shouldn't she be there already? Of course, I never expressed my doubts out loud, especially not in front of my dad, who never forgot to offer a mass for her, in spite of how many women he had been seeing that year. I pretended not to know about his indiscretions, and he knew better than to bring anyone home.

I dreaded these anniversaries. It made me relive all the sadness and confusion of having lost my mom. It was like time hadn't passed and here we were, in mourning all over again. I'd told Agustín about the mass, thinking he wouldn't make it, but here he was. Somehow, seeing him in church this Saturday morning made it more bearable.

I glanced at him over my shoulder, and he offered a sympathetic smile. I squeezed Marisa's hand, who was sitting beside me—like every year—and pointed at Agustín.

She didn't react, except for a soft nod.

A tangle of emotions conflicted inside of me: I was excited to see him, but also heartbroken that my mom had only been in my life for a short period, and she was missing so much. As usual when the priest said her name, I teared up. After it was all over, I stepped out of the church with Marisa on one side and my grandmother on the other—all of us connected by a chain of arms— when Agustín came to greet me.

His hat was slightly tilted and his dark suit contrasted nicely with his light skin and thick eyebrows. The scent of his cologne was irresistible.

I introduced him to my grandmother and my father and both of them were gleeful to meet him, as they had known his grandfather.

"My father and your grandfather used to play cards together!" my dad then turned to me. "Can you believe it? Such a small world."

"Well, this is a small town," my grandmother said.

"How about dinner tonight, Agustín?" my dad said. "I know this lady who prepares the best crab legs. I'll bring some tonight."

"Thanks, but—"

"Oh, come on, your grandpa loved them," he insisted. "He came a couple of times for dinner. Right, Mamá?"

She nodded.

My dad had never been this friendly with any of my other admirers. Today, he was at his most charming.

Agustín finally agreed.

"I have to go," Marisa told me in low voice. She was such a sensitive, empathetic person. My mom's mass had clearly affected her.

"I can drive you home, if you'd like," Agustín offered.

"No." She let go of my arm. "Thank you." She walked away before anyone could say another word.

CHAPTER 28

Marisa

1935

I was finally going to have a talk with Alicia. I had waited long enough, and things were getting out of hand. If it wasn't Alicia pressuring Agustín to spend time with her, then it was her father or grandmother. Agustín had been too polite to decline their dinner invitation, but even a blind person would've realized how uncomfortable he was with their attention. I myself didn't have the heart to accept his offer to drive me home after seeing how upset Alicia had been during her late mother's mass.

But now I needed to save him from their claws. He had made his preference known when he kissed me on my birthday. Besides, he'd been leaving me notes with poems at work with the question, "Who wrote this?" on top. I would then write the name of the poet, or finish the verse, and send him the note back in a sealed envelope to be delivered by the messenger boy. I had been planning to tell Alicia about our kiss the same afternoon when she'd come over to bring me a gift for my birthday, but there hadn't been an opportunity as we were never alone.

Since meeting when we were twelve years old, Alicia and I had celebrated every one of our birthdays together. What started with handmade cards and drawings evolved into more elaborate gifts. Her grandmother taught her to knit, so Alicia would make cozy blankets and hats—I had several of her creations. Personally, I had no ability with crafts, as much as the nuns at school—and later Alicia—had tried to teach me.

Today we were supposed to go to mass together, but as usual we were at the bazaar because Alicia wanted to get more wool for a sweater she was knitting for her dad. I sometimes envied how close the two of them were and wished my father would be a little like hers. As we walked between vendor stands, she gushed over some colorful fabrics. I was hearing her without listening. Instead, I was trying to come up with the perfect words to tell her about my feelings for Agustín.

With the tips of my fingers, I felt a corner of the tawny organza she was showing me. "So how was dinner last night with Agustín?" I asked.

"Oh, absolutely wonderful. He's so charming. My dad and my grandma loved him. *Amiga*, I'm in love. It's finally happened!" She reached out for a translucid white fabric and placed it over her head, as though it were a veil. "What do you think? Does it suit me?"

I was speechless. Somehow, I found my voice. "Nice." I forced a smile. "And how does he feel about you? Has he—has he said anything?"

"Oh, he adores me. I'm sure about that. He's always staring and, you know when a man is flirting. It's obvious."

"Have you . . . kissed yet?"

She let out a giddy laugh but kept walking without answering my question. I followed her at a distance as she made her way through fabrics and undergarments. Wait, what did that mean? Had they or had they not kissed? Her laughter and the shine in her eyes told me they had.

As many boyfriends as Alicia had before, I'd never seen her this enthusiastic about anybody. She would usually lose interest in whatever boy she was seeing within a few days. But with Agustín it was different. I had underestimated the situation. I had waited too long. I stood there watching her in her cloud of bliss, bargaining with vendors, trying on scarves, and I had the gloomy realization that it might be too late for me.

As much as I delayed my climb up the stairs of the *Crónicas* building, waiting to run into Agustín again, I hadn't seen him in days. The main problem was that we worked different schedules: My workday started late in the afternoon and went well into the evening, whereas he had regular working hours. Even so, I continued to answer his daily notes with poems that got more obscure and intricate with time. I had to ask co-workers if they knew who wrote them. Once, I even asked Leopoldo Anzures if he knew the poet in question—whom, of course, he identified immediately. I'd also been taking careful attention to my appearance—wearing my newer outfits and even the gardenia dress he liked. Who knew if he would work late one of these days or if he would come to the radio station again? What I didn't do was go into the second floor. I didn't dare. I didn't want him to think I was looking for him—that would've been unseemly.

At work, I was thriving. If I got a smile or two from Leopoldo Anzures during a performance, it meant I'd done a good job. A nod was enough to get me through a scene. I lived for those minimal signs of approval. I had seen him lose his temper with an actor who arrived late or if someone skipped a line or missed their spot when reading. But so far, he had never directed his anger toward me. He called me Señorita del Valle and was always respectful when he made suggestions. He was hard to read, but a genius—I had no doubt in my mind. He directed the *radionovela* with scientific precision, knowing when someone should pause, when a sound should come forward, how exactly to bring out the best from his actors. His creativity never ceased to amaze me, especially when it came down to sound effects. He and the sound technician, Tobías, would go over the required effects an hour before the show started. Leopoldo would make suggestions on how to re-create a sound. For example, they would use empty coconut shells against a table to mimic horses' hooves or speak behind drinking glasses to pretend they were talking on the telephone.

There was a lot to keep track of and coordinate. In so many ways, radio theater reminded me of my father's orchestra: there was a tempo to it, a group of performers working together in harmony, and someone on the other side synchronizing the whole production. My dad, however, did not see it my way. In fact, he had made disparaging comments when I'd drawn parallels between my work and his.

"How could you compare that lowbrow melodrama to a symphonic orchestra? That's entertainment for the masses," he would say, scoffing. "The storylines are so banal and overdramatic."

This was the first time he'd admitted to hearing my work. It filled me with shame to know that instead of feeling pride at having a successful daughter, he had been secretly mocking me.

"I know," I would say, trying to be agreeable, but in all truth, his comment had hurt me. I took pride in what I did. It was hard work to stand there every night, not only reading my lines but *performing*—making sure I transmitted the feelings and tone the writer had envisioned for my character while trying to impress the director and please the audience. How was that different from a musician playing an instrument? What made one type of artwork more sophisticated or relevant than another?

Ever since we started with *La Intrusa*, the ratings at the radio station had doubled. Everyone was talking about Gabriela's fate and the many tribulations she had to go through—Alicia told me as much. We'd gotten another actress, Beatriz Lara, who helped me with the female characters, but when she was too nervous, her voice would tremble—she still had a lot to learn.

The biggest surprise, however, had been to run into Reinaldo Cuevas—the young man who had beat me at the declamation contest a few years ago.

"Your voice is impossible to forget," he had said, as soon as he saw me.

He was one of the announcers at Radio La Voz, not only for our *radionovela* but also for *Canciones del Alma*, the evening musical show scheduled three times a week. Reinaldo and Sandra, the secretary, were the only people I talked to at work, since everybody else was so much older than me and Beatriz kept to herself at all times. I sensed she was competitive and resented me for being "the star of the show," as Reinaldo put it.

One evening, when I least expected it, Agustín showed up at my house.

"What are you doing here?" I said, forgetting my good manners. My dad would be home any minute.

"I wanted to see you," he said. "I went looking for you at the station today."

I glanced at my wristwatch. It was 7:00 p.m. Normally, I would be working at this time. "We don't broadcast on Sundays." I was hesitant to let him in, in case my dad showed up.

"I have good news," he said. "I talked to Raúl about your brother. He wants him to come in and show him his caricatures."

I was so excited I gave him a hug, not thinking about what I was doing. When I tried to push back, he held me tight. I left my arms on top of his shoulders, taking in the woody scent of his cologne on his neck. This hug felt right.

"Can I come in?" he said in a soft voice.

It might be better to let him in than to be seen by one of the neighbors hugging a man. There were too many gossipers on this street, and I didn't want my dad to hear stories about me. As soon as I let Agustín into the foyer, he tried to kiss me.

"No, Agustín, you can't do this."

"Do what?"

"You can't kiss me and then ignore me the next day when we're in front of Alicia."

He sighed.

I marched into the living room and sat on a sofa with the most hideous flower print repeated all over it—I'd been begging my dad to get rid of this old couch, but he had some kind of sentimental attachment to it. I crossed my arms and stared at Agustín. I was mortified when tears filled my eyes. I wiped them with my hand, angrily.

He approached and squatted in front of me, just like he had on my birthday. "I'm sorry. I didn't mean to hurt you. I thought—I don't know—I thought we were just having fun." He wiped one of my tears with his fingers. "We're still friends, aren't we?"

"Friends don't kiss each other."

He smiled. "I just can't resist your beauty."

I rolled my eyes.

"It's true." He grabbed my hands in his and kissed them. "Look, Alicia is gorgeous and full of life. It's never boring when she's around, but if you want me to break up with her, I will."

"So, you *admit* that you're going out with her."

"It's nothing serious."

"Just like us, right?" I removed my hands from his. "You're just *having fun?*"

He sat next to me.

"Alicia and I have been best friends for almost six years, Agustín. Do you know that?"

"I feel like a jerk now. I'm sorry. I didn't think any feelings would get involved."

I slapped the cushion. "Then you're an idiot!"

"Yes, I am, but it all happened so fast." He held my hand. "It's different with you, though. Alicia is enjoyable to be around, but you . . . You and me, we have a special connection. You must feel it, too."

Of course I felt it.

"Look, if you want me to stop seeing her, I will," he said, looking me straight in the eye. "Just say the word and I'll leave her."

There were defining moments in life; moments when one decision, one answer, one action, could change it all. This was one of them—I could sense it even at my young age. I could say yes, but that would mean my friendship with Alicia would be over for good. I knew in my heart she would never forgive me if I took

Agustín from her—because that was the way she would see it. After all, she had *claimed* him first, and she insisted that she was in love.

As cute and charismatic as Agustín might be, I didn't know if it would be worth losing my best friend over him. Raúl had told me he was a womanizer. He said Agustín didn't want to get serious with anyone, and marriage was the least of his concerns. His actions with me and Alicia proved Raúl had been speaking the truth. Agustín had no intention of getting serious with either one of us—and who knew if there were other women in his life?

He clutched my hand, still waiting for my answer. How could I say no to him, though, when he was looking at me like that? All I wanted, really, was for him to kiss me again. But then I remembered all those times Alicia and I had spent together: looking for four-leaf clovers in her garden, reading stories to one another, watching clouds and trying to make out their shapes, braiding each other's hair, making *humitas*, talking for hours about what the perfect man would be like. All of that would be gone for good. All for someone who may leave me for someone else in a few days.

Alicia came across as a strong confident girl, but the truth was that she was a sensitive, sometimes insecure person. I'd lost count of how many times she'd cried with me over her mom's passing. I had still to shed a single tear for my mom's abandonment. I despised crying. Today had been a sorry display of weakness in front of Agustín.

"No," I said, removing my hand from his. "Don't leave her." I stood up. "I think it would be best if you left now."

CHAPTER 29

Marisa

1935

Alicia was the last person I expected to see at Radio La Voz, particularly at this time of the night. It was almost 9:00 p.m., and we were nearly done with tonight's episode of *La Intrusa*. She stood outside the booth, hands inside her coat's pocket, hat and gloves still on. She searched for me with inquisitive eyes until she found me among my workmates, script in hand, reading our lines. Upon exchanging glances with me, Alicia's brow furrowed just a bit, and I immediately knew something bad had happened. Her grandmother? Her father? *Agustín?*

The two of them had officially been dating for about three months now. I'd ran into him occasionally in the building but barely exchanged greetings and pleasantries. A couple of times, he attempted to have a conversation with me, but I had found excuses to leave immediately. He had also stopped sending me poems, which I had been looking forward to every workday before, and now I missed them terribly. You would think that now, with my brother was working at *Crónicas* as an illustrator, I could come and go as I pleased in the newsroom, which was right next to the advertising department. But I didn't. The second floor was forbidden to me, and if Gabo wanted to talk to me, he knew he had to come upstairs.

Apparently, Gabo, Raúl, and Agustín had become good friends, and through my brother, I found out bits and pieces about Agustín's life. For example, I learned that everyone admired him at the paper, and several secretaries were in love with him. Gabo had also met Agustín's parents: The mom was apparently a sophisticated socialite and the father a bald, chunky man who carried around a pipe and was always throwing orders around.

I nodded at Alicia, signaling it wouldn't be long, that I would be there for her, as usual.

Leopoldo Anzures turned toward her to see what was demanding my attention. The transformation on his face upon seeing my friend was undeniable. His frown released and his mouth gaped a little. This was the effect Alicia often had on the opposite sex. When we walked down the street, men were always turning their heads, assessing her from head to toe, some would whistle, throw compliments at her, or attempt some feeble pickup line. It was exhausting. But somehow, I didn't expect this animalistic reaction from Anzures, who was intellectually superior to the majority of men and whose pursuits were definitely more refined. With me, Beatriz, and Sandra, he had been nothing but professional, even though I had noticed Beatriz's attempts to flirt. Thus, this display of male admiration over my friend's good looks bothered me—in spite of his attempt to compose himself and return his attention back to us as we concluded tonight's episode.

After we finished and he gave us the last instructions for tomorrow's episode, I stepped outside, where Alicia didn't seem aware at all that she had disturbed every man I worked with. As they walked outside the booth, they all nodded or tipped their hats at her. Anzures stayed inside the booth for a moment, arranging the pages of the script, grabbing his jacket from the coat hanger. It didn't escape my notice, though, how he kept gazing at us—at Alicia in particular.

She held my hands in her gloved ones.

"What happened?" I inquired.

"Something terrible."

Dared I dream that Agustín and her had broken up?

"What? You're making me nervous."

"My dad is getting married. He told me tonight over dinner."

"Well, that's not so unexpected. He's been a widower for years."

"Marisa, she's only five years older than me. She's a witch."

At that moment, Anzures stepped out of the booth.

"Good evening." He lingered by our side, pretending to check the locks of his briefcase. "Good job tonight, Señorita del Valle."

I supposed he was idling around so I would introduce him to Alicia.

"Thanks," I said. "This is my friend Alicia Sotomayor."

He extended his hand to shake hers, who responded somewhat mechanically.

"Nice to meet you," he said. "Sotomayor. Any relation with Don Manolo Sotomayor, the owner of Naranjada?"

She sighed. "He's my father."

"Oh, that's wonderful. Agustín Montero recently talked to me about the possibility of Naranjada becoming one of our advertisers."

She gave him a polite nod, but I could tell she was eager to continue her conversation with me.

"Are you also an actress?" he said. This was the first time I'd heard him talk about anything other than our play.

"No. I'm about to graduate from upper school in accounting."

"Excellent. We're always in need of people who can keep track of our money."

One thing Alicia's dad had done was insist that she finish her high school education. He had high hopes that she would either run his company one day or marry someone who would. The way he saw it, the more educated she was, the better the chances of being able to work or find a good husband.

"Well, it's a pleasure to meet you," he said, shaking her hand again.

Then Reinaldo came up in haste. "Mr. Anzures, can I speak to you for a moment?" His show was about to start in the auditorium.

I looked after Anzures as he rushed behind Reinaldo. A fleeting thought came to me. If he was so interested in Alicia, who was to say she couldn't be interested in him? It was well-established that she changed her mind about men frequently, and she hadn't said anything about Agustín in the last couple of weeks.

Perhaps Leopoldo Anzures was the solution to my problem.

I perked up.

"Don't worry, *amiga*, we'll figure something out. But first, you need to calm down. Why don't we go watch the evening show for a little bit? I think they're having a trio of *boleros* tonight, and you haven't seen the auditorium. You can relax there, and then we'll come up with a plan."

She hesitated. "But what about your dad? Won't he be upset that you didn't come home immediately after work?"

Of course he would be angry—it was his habitual emotion. But I was willing to earn a slap or two if it meant Alicia would show interest in a man other than Agustín.

"I think he had a concert tonight. He'll probably be home late."

She produced a tentative smile. "You're right, *corazón*, there's no use in me being so upset over this." She clung on to my arm. "Show me your famous radio station and let's go watch the show."

Something woke me up in the middle of the night. Did someone say my name?

"Marisa!" Tatiana said, knocking at my door.

I got up and opened it. She was in her salmon nightgown, her wavy head in disarray, a large crucifix—which had belonged to my mother—hanging from her neck.

"What is it?" I said.

"I think Agustín is outside, calling your name."

I darted to my window. "What time is it?"

"One in the morning."

So late? I slightly moved the lacy curtain. Tatiana was right—it was Agustín. Under my long gown, my legs trembled in anticipation.

"Is Papá home?"

"Not yet."

I led out a sigh of relief.

Agustín was looking up, trying to find me, perhaps.

"Marisa!" he yelled.

"I'd better go talk to him before he wakes up all the neighbors." I turned on my lamp and looked inside the armoire for something decent to wear. As his yelling continued, I grabbed the first dress I could find. My hair must be a mess. I ran into the lavatory to brush my teeth and wrap a chiffon scarf around my head.

By the time I reached the street, I was out of breath.

"What are you doing here?" I said.

"Oh, hi," he said, smiling. "I wanted to talk to you."

His speech came out slurred. Living with a dad who drank often, I'd learned to identify all the signs of excessive drinking.

"What is it?"

He gently lifted my chin. "You know I listen to you every night?"

Something fluttered inside me. "And you came all the way here to say that?"

"I've missed our notes." He took a step closer. "I haven't been able to stop thinking about you."

I didn't like the effect his touch, his proximity, had on my body—it made me lose perspective.

"Are you drunk?" I said, trying to refocus.

"I may have had a few drinks, but I know exactly what I'm doing. You and I belong together."

The intensity of his gaze was disarming me. "What about Alicia?"

"She's not the one I want." He slowly leaned over me and caressed my chin. "You're so beautiful."

Nobody had ever called me *beautiful* before.

He gave me a soft kiss, and I was unable or unwilling to push him away. I rested my hands on his neck, getting more comfortable with the deepening kiss when a voice—like thunder—shattered the stillness of the night.

"Marisa!" My father was marching toward us, cussing indistinctly. "What kind of spectacle is this? ¡*Casquivana!*"

I pushed Agustín away from me and scurried toward my dad, standing between the two men, chest heaving.

"You're just like your mother!" he said, raising his arm to slap me. I shut my eyes, almost feeling his harsh palm against my cheek. But the blow didn't come and when I opened my eyes, Agustín was holding his arm.

"Don't you dare touch her!"

"Who *the hell* are you?"

They struggled; my dad attempting to punch Agustín, who kept dodging. Since he was significantly taller, my dad stood no chance. Agustín got hold of my dad's arm again.

"Calm down," he hissed, twisting my dad's arm and shoving him against the wall.

"What's going on here?" Gabo had just arrived and immediately held my dad down as he was about to lunge toward Agustín again.

"Your dad, *hermano*," Agustín said, fixing his jacket. "He tried to hit your sister."

"That son of a bitch was *disrespecting* your sister!" my dad said, arms flailing.

"You should leave," Gabo told Agustín, while forcing my dad into the house.

Agustín looked at me, inquisitive. Several lights in the street were now on and the neighbors—some more discreetly than others—were staring at us.

"Thanks," I said, "but my brother is right. You should go."

His expression changed from a somewhat hopeful expression to pain, masked by irritation. With quick movements, he picked up his hat from the ground and adjusted it on his head. I watched him leave, fighting the urge to follow him and continue where we'd left off. But my feet were frozen. I didn't know if there was any way of coming back from this.

PART 3

The Shadow

CHAPTER 30

Valeria

1957

At midnight, Matías kicked the closet door open. Just as we feared, the price for our freedom was a ruckus that would most likely give away our hiding spot. I shivered just thinking about Toledo's bodyguards catching us and having us arrested for trespassing. I didn't even want to think about what Tío Bolívar would say about having a convicted niece, not to mention the trouble poor Graciela would get into for helping me.

Matías and I ran as fast as our legs allowed through the empty halls toward the elevator. At one point, he had to come back for me and hold my hand so I would move faster. Men's voices and fast steps followed us somewhere on the fifth floor.

They had heard us! I pressed the elevator button repeatedly while Matías explored the foyer. He pushed a door open. "Here! Come on!"

The stairs!

I darted behind him at the same time I saw the bodyguard who had stolen my camera.

"Hey!" he shouted.

Matías and I ran down the stairs, nearly tripping. I followed him, holding on to the banister for balance. Fortunately, he was carrying my new camera, because we both established early on that he had a better chance at escaping security, and we *needed* those pictures. I shrieked when I heard the bodyguard at the top of the stairs, following close behind.

"Stop!" he said.

"Come on, Vale, you can do this!" Matías said nearly a floor ahead of me.

He had reverted to the nickname he had used for me when we were kids, and I was about to lose a game. Earlier, I had told him not to wait for me. The photographs and the camera were too precious. At first, he'd been adamant. He wouldn't let me take the fall. But I had eventually convinced him. What would be the point of *both of us* getting arrested? Someone had to save the photos. We had to make this little adventure worth it.

Somehow I didn't feel so confident anymore. In fact, I was terrified at what these men would do to me. I didn't want to get arrested and spend the night in jail! Mati and I had agreed that if we got separated, he would meet me outside Teatro Bolívar, which was half a block away.

It was looking more and more like we were going to get separated. As the men were getting closer to me, I took a desperate measure: I reentered one of the floors, which according to the sign, was the third. I darted toward the elevator and pressed the button, glancing over my shoulder every other second.

I was aware of the extreme risk I was taking, but I figured that they were going to catch me, anyway. This way, I still had a chance to divert them as they were probably still hearing Matías's steps. The elevator opened, and thanks to the Virgin and all the saints, it was empty. I got inside and pressed the button to the basement, where I had hidden earlier.

When the elevator doors opened, the floor was completely dark. Of course, all the employees had gone home to bed already. I hesitantly stepped out. If I remembered correctly, there was an employee exit at the end of the hall, but to which side of the elevator was it? Maybe I should go to the first floor—there was a casino there, and maybe I could mingle with the crowd. But what if the men were waiting for the elevator there? What if the casino had closed already? Too risky. At least here, the darkness would help me hide.

But I hated darkness.

As a kid, I begged my mom to let me keep my lamp on all night, or, at the very least, a candle. But she had said I wouldn't be able to sleep with such a bright light, and a lit candle could start a fire. How ironic, considering the manner in which she had died. In the end, she'd let me bring her teal Telefunken radio to my nightstand and the light behind the dial panel and the music would ease my nightly fears. At the boarding school, I had been forced to sleep in the dark from the first night, but at least there had been other girls in the room with me, and knowing I wasn't alone had calmed my nerves.

Well, there was no time for fears today. I had to make a decision.

I chose the darkness.

I stepped outside, and within a few seconds the elevator doors closed, leaving my surroundings pitch black. With my arms extended, I felt the wall to my side and chose one direction, hoping it was the right one. I shuffled forward, one hand on the wall, the other one ahead for protection. After a while, my eyes seemed to adjust to the penumbra and things didn't seem as scary.

Minutes seemed like hours. I kept calling Matías in my mind to come save me, but if he hadn't been caught, he'd be at Teatro Bolívar by now. What if he got tired of waiting for me and went home? I shivered at the thought of walking home by myself in the middle of the night. How would I get into the house? Graciela and I hadn't planned for that, since the thought that I would return after midnight didn't even cross our minds.

When the tips of my fingers felt a vertical, metal surface, I stopped. Slowly, I touched it with both hands. A door! *Please let it be unlocked!*

I found the knob and turned it.

Thank goodness.

The darkness outside was tinted with a bluish hue, much lighter than the basement. I'd never been happier to see the full moon in the sky. As I crossed the street toward the theater, the silhouette of a man standing by a light post came into view. I slowed my pace, bracing myself.

He turned toward me, and I made out his facial features, letting out a deep sigh of relief. It wasn't one of Toledo's men. Matías was leaning against the rose-colored ticket booth at the entrance of Teatro Bolívar. Behind him was the ample vestibule with mosaic tile flooring.

"There you are!" He dumped a cigarette butt on the ground and stepped on it.

Mati smoked?

It shouldn't have come as a surprise, since most men did.

"What took you so long?" he said. "I was getting worried. I've been waiting for ten minutes."

My camera was hanging from his neck. In my excitement at seeing both him and the camera intact, I hugged him. He stiffened from my touch.

"Sorry," I said, as he didn't reciprocate the hug. I took a step back. Hopefully, the dimness of the night would hide my embarrassment.

"I'll walk you home," he said. And so, we did—each briefly catching up with our side of the story and how we had escaped security.

"I still think you should report them to the police to get your old camera back."

I nodded. "I'll show you the photos as soon as I have them."

Something had changed in Matías. Locked in the closet for three hours, he'd been less guarded, and he'd been happy to share all the details from the infamous night when Martians supposedly invaded our city.

The streets were wet from the evening rain and the lights from the buildings cast elongated shadows on the puddles we were avoiding.

"What's wrong?" I said, as he'd grown silent.

"I don't like walking around here at night. It brings back memories," he said.

We were approaching Plaza Grande, which was not far from the old *Crónicas* building, now housing the restored Radio La Voz and some private offices on the first two floors. I reached out for his hand, and he grasped mine. If anybody understood what he felt, it was me.

We walked in fragile silence the rest of the way and stopped in front of my uncle's house. All the lights were off, which gave me some relief. I tried the doorknob, but it was locked.

"Graciela must have fallen asleep," I said, glancing at her window in the second story. I picked up a small stone by my feet and threw it against the window, with such bad aim it hit the wall instead of the glass.

"Allow me," Matías said, grabbing a stone of his own.

"Just don't break the window," I said.

The glass made a cracking noise.

"Oh, shit," he said.

Lights went on almost immediately.

"Go before my uncle sees you."

Adjusting his hat as he looked up, he said, "I think it's too late for that."

I followed his gaze to the window next to Graciela's—correction, the window Matías's stone had hit, which happened to be the *wrong* one. My uncle was glaring at us through the window, his room brightly illuminated. In less than five minutes, he was downstairs at the other side of the door, his expression graver than I'd ever seen it.

"What the hell is going on here?" he shouted, then turning to me, "Do you know what time it is?"

"It's all my fault, sir," Matías said. "I wanted to have a word with your niece, and she came down to talk to me. Unfortunately, the door got locked and we were trying to wake Graciela."

"Why are you dressed like that?"

Oh, yes, the maid uniform. Small detail.

"Would you believe me if I said I got a job at a hotel?"

Matías pressed his lips together, trying to stifle a laugh.

My uncle crossed his arms in front of his chest. "Get inside!" he said. "And you, Mr. Montero, I don't want to see you here ever again."

CHAPTER 31

Matías

1957

I couldn't stop thinking about Valeria since last night. She was still the same rambunctious girl I knew as a child. She'd always had the exceptional quality of making me laugh, even at the most critical moments—like when her uncle caught us outside his house after midnight.

"Good morning," my mom said, entering the dining room in a gray two piece-suit, silk stockings, heels in place, and her mane already fixed in the tight chignon she wore daily. As usual, she was ready for work before anyone else.

"*Hola, Madre,*" I said.

At forty, she was still a good-looking woman, but that shouldn't have come as a surprise given the way she cared for herself. She meticulously watched everything she ate—nothing greasy or sweet, not too much salt, and cigarettes only on occasion. She never exceeded one glass of red wine per night, and she only drank because the doctor had said it was good for reducing cholesterol. Ever since she'd turned forty, she'd become fanatical about her health and Julio's.

There had been a time when she'd been lenient about the simple pleasures in life: preparing succulent new meals for friends, staying up until the last bottle of *aguardiente* or vodka was empty, filling an ashtray with cigarette butts until the last of the gossip was shared, dancing until her heels broke. But that had been years ago, before my father died. In spite of not engaging in social events ever since she'd become a widow, the vices had continued in private.

Everything had changed after her fortieth birthday. No matter how many times Julio and I told her how young she looked, or how often people in the street assumed she was my sister instead of my mother, she didn't believe us.

"You say that because you love me" or "They are just being polite" became her standard answers every time someone voiced a compliment. But the truth was she *did* look younger and she could pass as my sister. After all, she'd had me when she was barely nineteen years old.

I'd often wondered if her preoccupation with her health had to do with the fact that her mother had died young, a fact she mentioned often.

"You came home late last night," she said, taking her seat at the head of the table. "Where were you?"

"*Señora*, don't ask what you don't want to know."

"Fair enough." She clicked her glass with a knife, making a bell-like sound.

Delia, in her maid uniform—which wasn't too different from the one Valeria had been wearing last night—entered the dining room.

"*Buenos días, señora*. Would you like your usual?"

"Yes, please."

"*Sí, señito*."

"What's with that smile?" she told me as Delia went back into the kitchen.

I hadn't even realized I was smiling.

"A smile like that has to do with a woman."

I took a sip of my coffee. "Not necessarily."

"I know you better than anyone else, *corazón*. When you smile like that, it means there's a new girl in your heart. That also would explain how late you came home last night—even if you don't want to tell me why."

My mom *did* know me well, but if she even suspected that the woman occupying my thoughts was Valeria Anzures, she would throw a fit. The name of anyone in that family had been forbidden in this house for years. Just the other week, after Valeria showed up at the newspaper, Mamá had been in a terrible mood for days.

I waited to speak until Delia brought my mom's *café con leche* and diced papaya—I knew better than to bring up a sore subject when my mom was hungry.

"Mamá?"

"Yes?"

"You've never told me what you were doing at the radio station the night of the fire."

She nearly choked on her coffee. "This is too hot! Delia!" She hissed at me. "Where is this coming from? You know I don't like to talk about that night."

"And why is that?"

She looked over her shoulder. I wasn't sure if she didn't want Delia or Julio to hear her. "Because it's painful. Why should we talk about hurtful things?"

"Because, Madre, I want to know. You've been drilling in me the importance of good reporting and sharing information. You've wanted me to learn first-hand every aspect of working at a newspaper, with a special emphasis on journalism over everything else. It is ironic that you would be so cryptic about this. I'm an adult now. You can tell me."

She tossed the napkin on her plate—still halfway full—and got up.

"Well, I don't have time for memories and reminiscing right now. I have to go to work. Julio! Julio! Are you ready?" she shouted toward the staircase.

"You know I'm going to keep asking until you tell me," I said.

"We don't talk about that night, Matías." She turned to me, eyes glinting. "The past is gone. Let it be."

My stepfather, Julio, entered the room, fixing his comb-over hair with chubby hands, briefcase falling off, tie crooked. What a contrast the two of them created. My mother was the epitome of class and beauty. My stepfather was a walking disaster, short and chunky. But how he loved her. He would do anything to please her. Even working at the newspaper when he was, in fact, a law-yer. He'd come to her aid immediately after my father passed away. My mother, of course, was strategic and knew she couldn't possibly run one of the biggest newspapers in the country by her-self without any prior experience in the field. She knew, however, that the paper was going to stay in the family. Julio Montero was my father's first cousin, the only one who could take charge until I came of age, as my aunts were nowhere in sight and had no inter-est in the business, particularly after the scandal that ensued after the fire.

Julio, on the other hand, had been a bachelor, with nothing go-ing for him. He'd always been especially attentive to my mother. I wouldn't be surprised to know he'd always loved her. Many men did.

Julio Montero had also taken the role of my father. At first, our relationship had been forced and awkward, as I had been resentful that my mother had remarried so quickly after my father's pass-ing, but Julio had been kind to me, and from the first day, he'd recruited my help to complete his daily crossword puzzle, which I suspected he was perfectly capable of finishing on his own.

He'd also invited me with him to Café Chapineros, where he would meet on weekends with his friends for coffee and politi-cal conversations. I'd been extremely bored at first—being only fourteen years old—but with time, I'd gotten to know and love his idiosyncratic friends: the Italian immigrant who always told sto-ries about the war, the consummate Communist who constantly fought with the car salesman with a boisterous laugh, the dentist who couldn't be a minute late for lunch or his wife would cut him off sex for days, the postal worker who would only come for thirty minutes during his lunch break, and many, many others who were instrumental in my formative years.

And yet, in all my conversations with Julio, I'd never asked him if he knew what really happened the infamous night of the fire. Maybe my mother had shared more with him.

"Ready?" my mother told Julio, running her hands over her hips, and picking up her purse from the cupboard.

"Ready!" he said, like a conscript responding to his sergeant.

"Don't take too long, Mati," my mom instructed me as the two of them walked to the front door.

There had been no question that I would run the paper one day. Ideally, I would've had a choice between *Crónicas* or my grandfather's soda factory—which sometimes seemed more appealing to me—but my mother had deemed the newspaper a more worthy cause. I suspected her choice also had to do with the fact that she had been estranged from her father for a few years after he remarried a woman close in age to her. They hadn't made their peace until after he finally divorced said woman. Now my grandfather had sold his company and retired.

From the window, I watched my stepfather open the passenger door for my mother as she reprimanded him for whatever it was he did wrong. Clearly, I was going nowhere with my mother, but Valeria had managed to make me curious about a night I had tried to forget a long time ago—a night that had been pivotal in my life. I didn't know if there would ever be the perfect words to persuade my mother to tell me what happened, but that didn't mean I would give up. I might just have to find a different course of action.

CHAPTER 32

Valeria

1957

Eight years had passed since I'd seen this house. And yet, it was still etched clearly in my memory, particularly the terrace on the rooftop, where Matías and I would look at the stars and the astounding city view while our parents danced downstairs—no end to the celebration in sight. Oblivious to the sacred history of this house, the new owners had painted the outside wall in a tasteless ochre. I still remembered it in vanilla.

It was fortuitous that I would come back here with Mati. That was, if he remembered to show up. I had called him on the telephone last night and told him to meet me at my old house at noon. He agreed, but he sounded half asleep, or maybe he was just tense, since I was almost positive that his mother had answered the phone. However, he'd seemed fully awake when he told me to bring the film from the photos I took. I still hadn't decided if I should trust him with my most prized possession—my entire future depended on those photos—but I tossed the 35 mm film in the bottom of my purse anyway.

At times, the cool Quito air did its best to remind you that

you had bones in your body—bones that ached as the relent-
less chill seeped under your skirt, ignoring that you had gone to
great lengths to put on a pair of your finest nylon stockings or you
had carefully chosen your best-fitting pencil skirt, just for looks,
weather be damned.

But who cared about the cool temperature when the love of
your life stood in front of you?

As soon as I spotted Matías crossing the street with his confident stride and sandy hair billowing with the wind, something lit
inside my core, and I forgot all about my earlier discomfort.

"*Hola*," he said, approaching with a faint smile.

"Hi. Thanks for coming."

"You want to tell me what we're doing here?" He stared at the
house where I'd spent most of my childhood years.

"I need you to help me retrieve something."

Mati dug his hands inside his pockets.

"I know it's a long shot," I said, before he could tell me how far-
fetched my plan was, "but the day my mom died, I saw her hiding
a tin box in a small compartment under the staircase. I meant to
see what it was the next morning, but with the fire and all, I completely forgot. Shortly after, I moved away."

He was quiet for a perturbing moment. "Well,"—he rubbed his
forehead—"at this point, that's all we have. My mom flat-out re-
fuses to say anything about that night."

I exhaled in relief.

"But how do you plan to go inside?" he said.

"That's where you come in. Do you have your press badge?"

"Yes."

"Excellent. I'll do the talking. All you have to do is distract
whoever opens the door."

"How am I supposed to do that?"

Before he could change his mind, I held his hand and crossed
the street. "You'll think of something."

Standing in front of the familiar ornate door, I removed the camera from my bag and hung it over my neck. Then, I rang the doorbell. An old lady opened the door. Her hair was mostly white and oddly reminiscent of a bird's nest.

"Hello, *doñita*," I said. "My name is Valeria Anzures, and this is my . . . colleague, Matías Montero. We work for *Crónicas* newspaper and we're doing a report on historic homes in colonial Quito."

"A reward?" she said.

"A *report*. As in an article? I was wondering if we could come inside to take some pictures of your house and ask you some questions."

Matías flashed his press badge in case she needed extra convincing.

She looked at me, then at Mati's nonplussed expression.

"May we come in?" I asked.

"What did you say your name was?"

"Valeria." I refrained from repeating my last name as she might recognize it as that of the previous homeowners.

"What newspaper?"

"*Crónicas*," Mati said with a smile.

"Oh, yes, that's only a few blocks away."

Undoubtedly, she was thinking of the old, burnt building.

I cleared my throat. "I can bring you a copy of the paper when the article comes out." I hated lying like this, but it wasn't like I was going to steal from her. Technically, that tin box belonged to *me*, as it had been my late mother's.

"I'd like that," she said, finally opening the door for us. "You know that a count lived here?"

A count? Certainly not my dad.

"Really?" Matías said, following the thin woman who surprisingly had generous hips in spite of her bony structure. "Tell me about it."

The smell in the foyer was different than I remembered. More pine and more lemon. I couldn't recall the previous scent, but I knew it wasn't this. The parlor was smaller, too, and the interior courtyard, where my dad's bar used to be, was now covered with planters and bird cages—several parrots talked in unison, upset with our unannounced presence.

The staircase where my mother had hidden her tin box was inside her room. It led to a small loft where I loved to sneak away to and draw for hours on end.

"If you don't mind, I'm going to start taking photos while Matías interviews you," I said, but the woman was no longer concerned with me. She was leading Mati into a floral loveseat where the two of them fit cozily together. Matías looked up imploringly as the woman placed her hand on his knee and talked nonstop about the mysterious "count."

Before she could change her mind or someone else showed up, I rushed toward the stairs, as my parents' bedroom had been on the second floor. The beige wallpaper in leaf motif was still there, but it had faded considerably in the last eight years. It brought me comfort to see it intact—not every memory of my family had been wiped out by time and tragedy.

I took a picture of the hanging chandelier and the old wallpaper, as a souvenir. When I reached the second story, a balloon seemed to expand inside my chest. In the back of the family room, where my parents had read the newspaper daily or listened to the radio, was a built-in concrete planter I hadn't thought about in years. As soon as I saw it, a memory sprang through my mind.

I'd barely turned eight when my dad had called me from this very same room and asked me to help him plant three small ivies, "one for each one of us," he'd said. My father had always loved gardening. He'd been the one to fill the upstairs terrace with pots and flowers. I wondered now if, like this planter, they were still here.

"Plants often outlive us," he'd said. "These ivies in particular are very resilient. They require little care. Let's see which one outlives the other."

The three plants had been tiny then. Now the three of them were entangled and overflowed the planter where they dwelled. My eyes filled with tears. I still remember the smell of moist soil as I dug my fingers inside the dirt to make a hole for the plants' roots.

"Just like that," he'd said, even though he had to dig with his own shovel after me to make an appropriately sized hole.

I could almost hear his perfect enunciation and low baritone in that *lojano* accent of his. He had been a patient man who rarely raised his voice. I'd never seen him lose his temper with anyone, but my uncle Gabo had once said those were the kind of people you should fear the most.

"When they finally lose their temper, brace yourself," my uncle had said.

I rushed past the humble furniture toward the planter and touched the ivy's dripping leaves. They were so long now they touched the parquet floor. They had recently been watered as a few drops wet the wood.

For years, I refused to think about my parents. Of course, I had a natural curiosity to know what exactly happened to them—a question that my uncle and Doña Amparito had dismissed every time—but alone in my bed, during those endless nights at the boarding school when memories of my family would populate my mind and my thoughts would grow dark, I'd choose to ignore them. I would immediately switch my thoughts to my grand plans once I graduated, or what I would tell Mati when I saw him again (in my plans, I didn't become a mute like I did in real life). I would be eloquent and cultured—a cosmopolitan, modern woman who engages in the most fascinating subjects: art, history, politics. If the insomnia was too bad, I'd resort to the cherished recollections of our times together: how we would sit on the terrace, legs dangling from the banister, and laugh at the drunkards who stumbled out of the cantina at the end of the street. Sometimes they would sing at the top of their lungs; at other times they would quarrel with whoever happened to look at them funny. When the night was quiet, Mati would point to the constellations and planets—a series of bright dots swimming in the black sky—

and tell me their names. But this often happened at the end of the evening, when we were done playing card games, dominoes, and hide-and-go-seek. Since my house consisted of many levels and had several additions, it was easy to find new hiding spots every time.

It had been easy to get lost in those memories and ignore any unpleasant thoughts about my parents. But now, confronted with the place where they'd spent a big part of their lives, it was impossible not to think about them.

How *had* they died?

Had their bodies calcinated to ashes while still alive?

But if so, why did Mati's mom—my very own *godmother*—resent them so much? Shouldn't she feel compassion for them instead? What had caused the drift between two friends who'd loved each other like sisters since childhood—the two *comadres*, as they often referred to one another. And why in the name of everything holy had my father decided to broadcast that sinister show?

The old woman downstairs was still talking, though I could barely make out what she was saying, and yet, her voice was getting louder. Had she decided to give Matías a tour of the house herself? I had no more time to waste—I needed to find my mom's box immediately. I rushed to my parents' bedroom, which now housed a different canopy bed, a disjointed choice as it didn't match the pearl dresser or the cherry night tables.

However, I had no time for design observations. I turned to the staircase by the door, which led to the loft of my youth—where I'd loved to hide from Mati during our games. There, underneath one of the stairs, in the precise corner where the steps turned, was a compartment that would hold all kinds of treasures. I inserted my hand underneath the wood and felt the space for the tin box, my heart beating like a drum.

Where on earth was it? I looked inside the dim area, collecting spider webs. It was completely empty. Had this woman found my mom's precious box and disposed of it?

How dare she?

The palm of my hand filled with dust as I felt for the box again and again.

"And right around the corner is my bedroom," the woman said. "The same quarters where the count had slept in."

Right when I was about to give up, I felt something with the tip of my finger, something that happened to move further back.

Matías coughed as the woman's voice approached. "Wow, these ceilings are so high," he said with a voice louder than usual. "Look at those *vigas*!"

I had seconds before they came into the room, but I couldn't give up so easily. I extended my arm as far as it would go and again, felt something solid with the tips of my fingers. I searched for a tool around the room. The only thing that could remotely help was a comb with a long handle.

"Oh, yes, it's oak," she said.

With the comb in my hands, I stretched out my arm underneath the step, hoping I wouldn't push the box further. Then I softly tapped it toward me until the box came into view at the same time as the woman entered her bedroom.

I straightened up and hid the comb behind my back.

"Oh, here you are," the woman said.

Upon seeing me, Matías pointed at a painting above the bed. "That's an enchanting landscape," he said, "who's the artist?"

The woman faced the other side of the room. "My cousin Federico," she said, beaming with pride.

I carefully set the comb back on the dresser. Then, I pointed at said painting with my camera—though there was nothing special about that plain landscape—and took a picture. Discreetly, I took another one of Matías's profile staring at the hideous painting as I didn't have a single photo of him.

"There's an attic upstairs," the old woman said, "Do you want to see it?"

I shook my head at Matías.

"Maybe later?" he said. "I'm eager to see the terrace you mentioned with the spectacular views."

"Oh, yes, the terrace."

As they left the room, I got hold of the tin box and inserted it inside my purse, my fingers barely able to shut the clasp. Then, I casually followed them for the rest of the tour, shooting as many photos as I could in an attempt to take every single corner of the house with me.

The terrace—*our* terrace—hadn't changed at all.

"You were right," Matías told the lady, but looked at me as he spoke, "it's a breathtaking view."

My father's flowerpots graced the front of the balustrade facing the street. His roses had also grown substantially under the unforgiving Quito sun. I teared up again while the woman spoke endlessly about the neighbors across the street, people who, according to her, had noble lineage.

My attention, however, was on this moment, on this place, on Matías. I wanted to go back in time, I wanted to have my parents dancing downstairs and having drinks with their *compadres*. Matías nodded at me from above the woman's head, as if he felt the same way. This was not just any place. This had been the framework of our childhood.

Later, when we'd thanked the talkative lady and left the house, Matías held my hand and led me to a nearby park. "Did you get it?" he said, his voice raspy.

I nodded, because if I spoke, I might cry.

We sat on a bench, side by side, and I removed the tin box. Inside were several pieces of papers—notes. I pulled one out. At the very top it said: *Who wrote this?*, followed by a poem. On the bottom of the page—in my mom's handwriting—was the name of the author. Some were fragments of poems, completed with different penmanship.

"My mom wrote this," I said, pointing at the bottom half of a poem.

Mati pursed his lips. Then brought one of the notes close to his eyes. "This could be my dad's writing."

We exchanged a silent look. My expression must have been as puzzled as his. He searched through the rest of the contents in the box. There were dozens of notes, folded in halves, with poems in them. Like they had written them together? Or maybe one was quizzing the other?

"Do you think that"—he cleared his throat—"Do you think my dad and your mom were . . . involved?"

"This could be anything," I said. "A game of some sort. It doesn't mean they had a—what?—an *affair?*"

He gave me a pensive look. Even I knew how naïve I sounded. Why would they write poems to each other when they were both married to *other people?*

"If it didn't mean anything," he said, "then why did she keep the notes *and* hide them?"

I took a deep breath. This was too much to process. I tried to recall anything unusual about our parents' get-togethers. I didn't remember anything strange about my mom and Don Agustín's behaviors. Had they sat together during dinner? Or stared at each other? Or whispered to each other in one of the hallways?

Nothing came to mind.

Other than my mom's bursts of melancholy, where she would stay in bed all day, there had been no indication that she'd lived an unhappy life with my dad. I'd always thought it had to do with the fact that she couldn't have any more babies after I was born.

"Did you ever notice anything unusual about them?" I asked Matías.

He shook his head, but he didn't look me in the eye.

Does he know something else?

"Let me give this some thought," he said.

"I hope it's not true," I said.

He turned to me, a crease between his eyebrows. His eyes softened and he held my hand, giving me goosebumps. "I'm sorry."

"Mati, it's not your fault. Whatever they did—"

"No. I'm sorry about not contacting you after what happened to them. You must have gone through a lot."

My eyes started to burn.

"I think I was in a state of shock after everything," he said, wiping my tear with his fingertips. "But if it's any consolation, I thought about you. A lot."

"I get it. You were a kid, too."

"I always felt guilty about not writing you. I just didn't know what to say. I was inside the building that night, you know?"

The other night, he'd only told me about the hysteria across town—not that he'd gone inside. "Did you see my parents?"

"No, I barely made it inside the building. I found my mom unconscious and I had to take her outside before the flames got to her." He absently rubbed my hand with his thumb. "Everything was so chaotic. Nothing made sense. I've blamed myself for years for not going back in there and saving my dad."

"How could you? You were only thirteen."

He nodded, but his expression told me my argument wasn't convincing enough.

"What was your mom doing there?" I said.

"She doesn't want to tell me." He looked at me, giving me a soft smile. "Don't worry, we'll figure it out."

"Did you go to your dad's funeral?" I asked.

"Yes."

"They didn't let me go to my parents'. They said funerals weren't for children."

He shook his head. "They were *your* parents." He grabbed my hand and gave it a soft kiss. "I'm sorry, Vale."

When he let go of my hand, I was parched. He held my gaze for a moment. My face was on fire. I wanted him to kiss me so badly.

"Do you have the roll of film?" he said.

His question took me off guard. The last thing on my mind right now was Alejandro Toledo.

I hesitated. "Well, I . . ."

He extended his hand, and the way he looked at me disarmed me. I didn't want to disappoint him now that he was finally paying attention to me. My fingers fumbled with my purse's zipper, still uncertain if I should trust him with my precious film. Against my instinct, I removed the roll and placed it in his palm.

CHAPTER 33

Matías

1957

My mother was sitting behind her desk when I entered the executive editor's office. Technically, my stepdad was the publisher and chairman of the newspaper, but for all intents and purposes, my mother was running the operation. When my dad had died, she had little work experience. She'd done some bookkeeping for her dad's business, but didn't know much about journalism. So, when she became a widow, she relied heavily on Raúl Cortés, my dad's editor-in-chief. She also received business guidance from her own father, and for all legal matters, there had been Julio Montero, her brand-new husband and unconditional ally. She'd been smart enough to know that nobody would've put up with a woman publisher—even if she was Agustín Montero's widow—so Julio and her had worked as a team ever since.

I greeted her as she was going over some papers, a cup of *valeriana* for her nerves by her side. As usual, it had probably gotten cold already.

"How is your story coming along?" she asked, referring to my piece about the inauguration of some boring governmental building.

"Fine," I said.

As she finished signing papers, she sat back in her chair and looked at me, cup in hand. "What is it, son? You never come here without a reason."

Her tone was soft, like any concerned mother would use, but she was no ordinary woman. However, this might be my one chance to get some vital information from her, though only yesterday she had shut me down. How could I bring up the subject without being greeted with a cup of tea on my forehead?

"Mamá," I said, "I know this is a sensitive subject, but I *really* need to know." I cleared my throat. "Was my father having an affair with Valeria Anzures's mom?"

The cup flew over my head, thank God.

"Have you any neurons left in your brain or have they all been scorched?" she said. "I thought I made it perfectly clear yesterday that I don't want to talk about the past!"

I left the office before she was done insulting my mental faculties.

Tato Paredes was what some might call a "yes man." He was the only photographer in the organization I trusted, as he didn't have the arrogance and impertinence I'd seen in the others. He rarely partook in chitchat with his co-workers, and his introverted nature fit well with his profession, as he spent most of his time with his face behind the camera or in that cave he called "his" darkroom. He was easily startled, which made me wonder if he was some sort of spy or, more likely, if he worked on his own photographs during work hours.

"Tato!" I said, secretly hoping to scare him, as it always gave me a small pleasure.

"*¡Madrecita Santa!*" he said, invoking the Virgin after he hit his head against the amplifier in the darkroom.

"Are you all right?"

He nodded, rubbing his forehead.

"I need an urgent favor," I said. "Top secret."

The red light in the room could be deceitful, but I could still make out his raised eyebrows. "What?" he said with the eagerness of a child.

"You have to develop this film and then print me a contact sheet. It's urgent. Also, don't let anyone else see it."

Salivating like a greedy canine, he grabbed the film from my hand.

"Be careful when you develop it. It's *very* important."

"I'm a professional, Matías. I've developed hundreds of rolls."

Tato, like many of the employees, had been here since I was an adolescent, and they hadn't graduated to call me *señor* yet.

"Fine," I said. "Come see me in the newsroom when you're done."

The newsroom, it turned out, was in a state of chaos. A radio news bulletin had just reported that the famous Spanish *matador*, Tomás Escobar, aka Tomasín, was clinging to life by a thread after being gored by a bull. Last we heard they were transporting him to the hospital. Raúl Cortés sent me there to get an exclusive, as one of his secret sources had told him which hospital it was. This was big news and must be reported in our next edition with no delay. The opportunity I'd been waiting for to get an important story was finally here—maybe even my own exclusive. I was tired of reporting car accidents or chasing government officials all over town.

With barely any time to tie my shoelaces, I donned my hat and ran down the stairs, making my way through a mass of people toward the first empty cab I could find.

CHAPTER 34

Valeria

1957

Someone was following us.

Graciela and I had just left Tío Bolívar's house to go to the movie theater. The sun had already set and above the mountains, the twilight sky displayed a cocktail of yellow, ruby, and indigo.

Steps echoed close behind us, and for a second, I hoped it might be Matías. When I turned around, I could only make out a black wool fedora tilted so low it covered the man's face almost entirely. On the fly, I spotted a thick mustache. His body was engulfed in a beige gabardine trench coat, his hands buried in his pockets, making it impossible to assess the man's age or shape.

I didn't say anything to Graciela as I didn't want to scare her, especially minutes before planting ourselves in a dark room full of strangers for the next two hours. And besides, when I turned around again, he was gone.

I forgot all about him during the movie. *Abajo el telón* was a popular comedy featuring one of México's biggest talents, Cantin-flas, and I managed to get immersed in the story. After the movie, as Graciela and I animatedly pointed out to each other the actor's dance performance and his delivery of certain lines, and as the street became less crowded, I thought I saw the strange man again with my peripheral vision.

That was it. I was going to confront him. I stopped and abruptly turned around. Behind me was a woman with a basket. She was so distracted by her own conversation with another woman that she bumped into me.

"Sorry!" I said.

The woman screeched, dropping her basket and its contents—potatoes and *yucas*—all over the cobblestone. I continued to apologize as I picked up tubers and searched behind the incoming bodies for the man in the hat, but with such an abundance of legs and coats passing me by, it was a useless effort, especially not knowing who exactly I was looking for.

"What's come over you?" Graciela said, as we collected the last of the potatoes and renewed our walk home. "You're so jumpy."

"A man has been following us," I said.

"What?" She turned around and searched behind us. "Are you sure?"

"No, I'm just making it up to be interesting." I fixed the strap of my purse. "*Of course* I'm sure."

As we resumed our walk home, Graciela murmured something about my wild imagination. I'd been considering telling her what Mati and I discovered about our parents in the morning—mostly to know if she'd heard something about it from her parents, but I didn't want her to blame it on my so-called *imagination*. I wasn't crazy or delusional. A man *had* followed us from the house to the theater. And I was almost sure I'd just caught a glimpse of him.

I hastened my pace, offended and annoyed at her distrust, and thought about the poems in my mother's box. I still hadn't come to terms with the possibility that my mom might have had a relationship with Matías's dad. It would've been wrong on so many levels!

There had to be another explanation. Maybe Matías and I had

confused the handwriting and assumed it was my mom's and his dad's. But what if it belonged to someone else? Then again, if there was nothing illicit going on, why had my mom hidden the notes? I had a couple of notebooks my dad had left behind with story ideas for *radionovelas*, and the penmanship in the poems was certainly different.

No, it wasn't unreasonable to believe there had been an affair between my mom and Don Agustín. After all, there *had* to be a reason why Matías's mom despised my family so much and, by extension, me. Especially after being so close to my mom for most of their lives.

When I got home, I waited until Graciela went to the lavatory to hide my mom's box in the bottom of my valise, which I then slid back under the bed.

I couldn't sleep that night. My stomach ached the way it did every time I was nervous. I kept heading to the window and looking down—just to make sure there was no one in the street. Surely, I was imagining things. It was perfectly normal that a man had been walking behind us. The street was a public place! He might have been going to the movie theater himself, and really, how many men with fedoras and gabardines walk the streets of Quito?

Probably hundreds.

I dropped the curtain and was about to go back to bed when I spotted a dim light by the post across the street. I drew closer to the glass. Someone was lighting a cigarette, and the flame in the man's hands partially illuminated his silhouette. He was medium-sized, wearing a long coat and on top of his head was, in fact, a dark fedora.

An irritating sound woke me up from a very pleasant dream where I was in some kind of paradisiacal beach taking photos of Matías. It was my cousin's voice calling my name relentlessly. Maybe if I didn't open my eyes, she would go away, and I could go back to my dream.

"Valeria, Valeria, Valeria, your *suegra* is downstairs waiting for you!"

Suegra? But I wasn't even married, let alone have a mother-in-law.

I squeezed my eyes shut. I wanted to go back to the dream where no one was chasing me down a deserted street and I didn't have to marry a man I didn't love.

Graciela pulled the pillow from my head. "Did you forget she was coming to take you to the seamstress?"

Oh, yes, the seamstress. Tía Marga had mentioned her during dinner last night, when I couldn't think of anything else but Matías's warm lips on my hand. Doña Caridad Recalde had told my aunt she wanted to make sure I went to her seamstress—the only one she trusted—for my wedding dress. With the movie and the mysterious man standing across the street, I'd forgotten all about Félix's mother. I hadn't fallen asleep until dawn, when my mind had finally given me a rest from all my worries.

"You can't make her wait," Graciela said. "She's paying for your dress, you know?"

In spite of the old tradition that the bride's family had to pay for all wedding expenses, Félix's parents had graciously offered to take over the burden. They'd known better than to assume that my uncle would pay for anything.

"I'm going to tell her you're almost ready—but hurry up!"

Graciela vanished just as suddenly as she'd appeared by my bedside. I was going to have to put an end to this engagement. But how? Perhaps I could fake an illness? I ran my hand by my forehead, but it was cool to the touch. When I was small and didn't want to go to school, I would pretend I had a fever by hopping up and down to get warm and sweaty before my mom walked into my room to wake me up. It worked once, but after the initial thrill of my successful deceit, I'd been so bored at home I never tried it again.

Today, I didn't have the energy. I could barely keep my eyes open. But if I went to the seamstress and she got started on my dress, it would be much harder to back down from this ridiculous commitment later. I hadn't been myself when I'd agreed.

Maybe if I talked to Félix's mom in private? She looked like a nice, reasonable woman. It was in her best interest that her son married a woman who loved him, not someone who just didn't know how to say no and whose uncle was willing to marry her off for money.

Hesitantly, I slipped out of my nightgown and donned a magenta gingham shirtdress that had belonged to my mother. Lately, I'd been using her old clothes more and more. An idea came to mind. If I managed to make it so the Recaldes rejected me as a potential wife and not the other way around, then my aunt and uncle would have to resign themselves to the dissolution of my engagement. More important, they wouldn't be cross at me, and I wouldn't have this awful feeling of being a stray cat that somehow owed my only relatives loyalty and obedience.

But I had to be smart about it. If I behaved like a dunce, Mrs. Recalde would tell my family. I had to be more subtle than that. I took a final glance at myself in the mirror. Every hair was neatly tucked inside my ponytail and a light coat of strawberry lip gloss added the finishing touch. She didn't even answer my greeting, much less smile, and her arms didn't budge one millimeter from their tight cross over her generous chest.

How could I have thought that she might be reasonable?

"Finally," she said. "I've been waiting for fifteen minutes."

My aunt was with her, smiling and apologizing for me. "You know how girls are nowadays."

But Mrs. Recalde didn't seem to know or care. She kept staring at me, flying hairs escaping her bun, and a thin layer of sweat varnishing her face. The oil in her skin had apparently smeared a mole close to her mouth. Ever since Marilyn Monroe had showed us that moles could be sexy, lots of women were mimicking hers with eyeliner.

"Well, I'm here now," I said.

Tía Marga stood up. "Isn't this exciting? I'll go grab my purse."
She was coming, too? But what about her hundreds of obliga-
tions?

Mrs. Recalde continued to assess me from head to toe with a
loud sigh, and I wondered if this woman was the reason why her
son hadn't found a wife yet.

The older women did most of the talking while I sat on the
back seat of Mrs. Recalde's black automobile. Since she had a
chauffeur, Félix's mom sat on the passenger seat while Tía Marga
and I were in the back. As far as I knew, not even the Monteros
had a driver. No wonder my uncle was so impressed with this
couple.

Mrs. Recalde didn't talk to me, but she examined me whenever
she turned to chat with my aunt. I kept my gaze out the window,
recognizing long-forgotten buildings and signs. Ever since I went
to my old house, I'd been thinking a lot about my parents. Old
memories had resurfaced, like the nights when my mom would
lock herself in her room and my dad would take me out for long
walks. I still remember the feel of his big hand holding mine inside the pocket of his jacket because it was so cold outside. Sometimes we would stop by a vendor, and he would buy me a bag of
tostado.

He didn't like candy or anything sweet, because he said it
would ruin my taste buds forever. I didn't even know what taste
buds were, but I knew I didn't want to lose mine. For years, I was
cautious around sweets until I noticed that the girls at my school
gorged on *espumilla* and *dulce de guayaba* without restraint, and
their taste buds worked just as well as mine. The day I figured my
dad had been lying, I had *dulce de leche* for breakfast, *naranjilla* ice
cream for lunch, and strawberries with cream for dinner as a sign
of rebellion—and didn't regret it one bit.

The seamstress we were visiting today was as old as time.
There were wrinkles inside her wrinkles and a slight curvature

in her spine, but she wore a tailored lime suit with matching emeralds in her earrings and necklace. Her shop was tiny and barely fit all four of us, but I could tell by the gowns on display that she had exquisite taste.

Nobody ever consulted me on the model of dress I wanted. Mrs. Recalde gave her directions, and the woman took my measurements. That was it! I had to end this immediately. I couldn't live for the rest of my life under the Recalde regime. I had a brain and my own tastes. She couldn't ignore me just because I was younger and poorer than her!

When my aunt excused herself to go to the lavatory and the seamstress went to the back of the shop to bring sample fabrics, I spoke. "Mrs. Recalde? There's something—"

"I met your mom, you know? She had a lovely voice."

Her comment was so unexpected, I forgot how exactly I was going to break off my engagement. Instead, I let her words sink in. This woman had known my mom. And her tone had been cordial and conspiratorial. Maybe the breakup would have to wait a little longer.

Before I could ask what she knew about my mom, the seamstress returned with cuts of satin and organza to show us.

"Yes, I like this," Félix's mom said, feeling the fabric between her fingers.

I touched the soft material, too, out of obligation. The truth was I couldn't care less about my wedding dress, but this woman had suddenly become a person of interest to me. Her demeanor earlier made me think there was something she wasn't saying and wanted to tell me, but didn't have the time. And now that Tía Marga was back, I would have to wait for the right moment to mention my mom again.

"I know this may seem like a humble shop," Mrs. Recalde said, as we stepped out of the minuscule parlor, "but she's the best seamstress in town."

"What about the invitations?" I said, as if I cared about the wedding details.

"Well, we would have to set a date for the wedding first. The dress won't take more than a few weeks. Doña Berenice is really fast, but I'm afraid we would have to speak to the men about the date so that everyone is in agreement."

I rushed behind her. "And what about flower arrangements? Couldn't we look at some today?" At this point I would've said anything to prolong my time with Mrs. Recalde. "If you have things to do at home, Tía, we could probably drop you there, right, Doña Caridad?"

Félix's mother lifted a thin eyebrow before speaking. "I'm sorry, Valeria. We will have to leave that for another day. I have a hair appointment in thirty minutes."

As soon as we got home, I waited for Tía Marga to go into the kitchen before I snuck into Tío Bolívar's study to borrow his telephone. I shut the door behind me and hurried to the desk, shaking. Pressing the black receiver against my ear, I talked to the operator.

"Could you transfer me to *Crónicas* newspaper, please? I need to speak to Mr. Matías Montero."

As I waited for the connection to go through, I impatiently tapped my fingers on the cherry wood surface of my uncle's desk. Honestly, my news about Mrs. Recalde wasn't too impressive, but any excuse to talk to Matías worked for me, and this might lead to an interesting discovery. Perhaps he had some input as to how to approach the subject of my mother with this lady.

"I'm sorry," the operator said. "He's not in the office at the moment."

I hung up the phone, disappointed. But that was nothing compared to the heartbreak of seeing the ultimate betrayal sitting right in front of my eyes. Right there, on top of my uncle's desk, was the entertainment section of *Crónicas*. On the front cover was the photo I had taken of Alejandro Toledo and Lupita Peña in the hotel balcony.

* * *

Graciela's voice reached me as if through a haze, faint and distorted. I couldn't make sense of what she was saying. All I could do was stare at Alejandro Toledo staring directly at *my* camera in a surprised expression that betrayed his shock to see me. Yes, *me.* The one who'd hidden for hours in that closet space to take said photograph, not the person receiving all the credit—this Tato Paredes, whom I'd never heard of in my entire life.

"Didn't you hear me?" Graciela said. "We have to get ready for Juliana Isabel's show tonight at the radio station! Don't tell me you forgot about that, too?"

How could Matías betray me like this? He knew how important it was for me to get the photographer job. He'd taken the one and only opportunity I had, and he'd given it to this . . . to this Paredes person, who had gladly taken credit for a photograph that wasn't his!

"What's wrong?" my cousin said.

The newspaper trembled in my hands, tears of rage burning my eyes.

She took the paper. "Oh, no, someone beat you to the exclusive." Her eyes flew up and down the article. "How weird. That same night." She lowered the paper. "Don't worry, Vale, there will be another opportunity. You can take photos of Juliana Isabel tonight."

"You don't understand. This is *my* picture."

She brought the paper close to her face. "But it says here . . ."

"I know what it says! That doesn't mean it's true! *I* took this photo and was so dumb as to give Matías the roll of film to develop so he could *steal* it from me and give it to this . . . this *con artist.*"

She looked at the photo again. "Are you sure it's this one?"

"Yes! I was there! I caught them on the balcony after I was stuck in that stupid closet for hours!"

She sighed. "There has to be an explanation, *prima.* Matías is not a dishonest guy. Why would he do this to you?"

"Because his family hates ours!"

He must hate me, too. The thought was too painful to say out loud. Damn, I couldn't believe I'd been hoping he would kiss me. He must have been laughing at how gullible I was. Maybe he'd been nice just so I would give him the film. How could I have handed him my most valuable asset—my only ticket to the career I'd always wanted?

"Calm down, *prima*, take a breath. You're so pale you look like you're going to faint any second. Let's keep this in perspective. Perhaps he lost the film, and this man found it, or something like that. Let him explain. Come on, let's go to the kitchen to get you some water before my dad finds us here. He doesn't like anyone in his study."

She grabbed my arm and took me to the kitchen, where I did as was told. Little did I care if I was drinking water or poison at this point. I couldn't believe Matías had done this to me. After he'd been so sweet to me yesterday. No wonder he'd kissed my hand and been so perky after I gave him the film—he already had a plan of his own! His mother had probably turned him against me. That *witch*!

"Valeria!"

My aunt looked at me with a puzzled expression. I hadn't even noticed her in the kitchen.

"You'd better go change. Your uncle is coming to pick you and your cousins up in twenty minutes. Don't you want to go to the radio station?"

Sure, I'd go, but what I really wanted was to go to *Crónicas*, throw my camera at Matías Montero's face, and tell him all the bad words in my lexicon!

It was no surprise to anyone that Félix Recalde was standing in line to enter Radio La Voz. I glared at my uncle, who didn't seem to notice (or care) how much he'd annoyed me for having invited him without telling me. But my oblivious uncle rushed to greet my future husband.

"What are you doing standing in line, *hombre*? You're my guest of honor!" Tío Bolívar patted Félix's back as he eagerly searched for me among my cousins' heads. Once our eyes met, he waved and smiled.

My nose started to itch.

Like a long chorizo, the line to enter the former *Crónicas* building took the entire block and turned around the corner. Tío Bolívar led us all to the front of the line—much to the protests of those who'd been waiting for hours under the drizzle. The guard immediately opened the door for us.

This was the first time I'd been to this building since the fire. As I understood, it had taken two years to repair the damage. Thus, the radio station had been closed during that entire time. But the newspaper had sustained the majority of the loss. The printing press had been severely affected and they'd had to use another newspaper's press to print the daily news for nine months. Even though they'd been competitors, the owner of *El Día* had been generous in solidarity with the Monteros. If he only knew the kinds of people he'd been dealing with!

My legs stiffened as I entered the lobby. I'd come here a few times as a young girl and had been fascinated by this world. The smell of ink, the sound of the press printing thousands of copies of someone's thoughts and words for others to read, images recorded forever, the making of history, and then, upstairs, the magic continued: My mother's voice echoing throughout the entire country, my dad's stories—those *radionovelas* that had introduced me to the adult world, with its passions and betrayals, bliss and sadness. A place that held such precious memories had, in one day, turned into my parents' mausoleum.

Their last hours were spent here.

"Hurry!" Germán was telling me, without an inkling of empathy for my memories, as he followed Tío Bolívar to the auditorium on the third floor. My younger cousin must have been excited for tonight's event as he usually didn't say a word to me.

In the hall, there were framed photos of actors reading from the scripts in the middle of a performance, of my father writing on his desk, and one closeup of my mother behind the microphone. I stopped in front of it and ran my fingers over her pompadour. I still remembered the smell of her rose perfume, her soft waves falling lightly over her shoulders, and how much I liked the blouse she was wearing in the picture, with its blue bow. I couldn't believe these photos had survived the fire. Or had my uncle brought them after?

"Valeria!" Joselito said, eagerly.

He was so young, he probably had no idea that the woman in the photo was my mother—or what had happened to her, since the subject of the fire was something my uncle's family never spoke openly about.

The last photo in the hall showed my dad's theater group posing for the camera. There were two rows of actors; ten men and two women—my mother and Beatriz Lara. My mother, no doubt, was the prettier of the two, as proven by the fact that three of the men in the picture had their heads turned and were staring at my mom as she smiled openly at the camera. Beatriz was somewhat attractive, too, but in a meeker way. She wore a light short-sleeve sweater with a handkerchief around her neck.

"Valeria!" my uncle and Germán called. "Come on!"

My uncle and cousin were holding the small auditorium's double doors open for me. I finally peeled my eyes off the photos and went inside the room. The seats were almost as I remembered—red velvet, but maybe a shade darker than in my mind's eye—and long, thick curtains flanked the stage where the musicians had already set up. One microphone stood in the center of the stage, and another one hung from the ceiling, connected by a long cable to a radio transmitter in the back of the room. An announcer sat behind the equipment, wearing a pair of earphones, ready to broadcast the performance throughout the airwaves.

We were the first ones in the auditorium. Tío Bolívar led us to the front row—the perks of being related to the owner.

Félix sat by my side but was much too shy to hold my hand.

Germán was more animated than I'd ever seen him (according to Graciela, he had a *big* crush on Juliana Isabel), so he talked non-stop about the young actress and her movies.

"Did you know her father practically owns an island?"

I had little interest in the details of the woman's life, but I was glad to have my cousin talking to us, as I didn't think I could endure any more conversations about the weather with Félix. Germán went on and on about Juliana Isabel, and once in a while, Félix would ask a question. He confessed he knew nothing about Mexican entertainment. He was so kind to everyone, it was hard not to like him.

I kept staring at the microphone in the center of the stage. How many times had my parents stood behind it? My father used to say there was an invisible power in the microphone and the "magic box" they called radio. It could reach millions of people at once and they would believe anything that came from it without question.

The show started an hour later, and we had to sit through several pieces from the band before the main attraction. When she finally came on stage, the whistles and applause behind me were deafening. As usual, she looked stunning in a baby blue sheer halter top gown that reached her ankles, her maple hair in an updo. Her look was effortless and chic.

As we listened to her syrupy voice, Graciela encouraged me to take photos of the Mexican star, but just the sight of my camera in its bag made my blood boil all over again. What could I possibly achieve by taking photos of someone singing at a radio station? Where was the interest in that?

"We ought to go backstage and meet her," Graciela said, star-struck. "If you get something good, you could sell it to the competition."

"*What* competition?"

El Día had shut down in 1953, and all the other publications in town were minor in comparison to *Crónicas*. I didn't take a single shot of Juliana Isabel. In fact, I couldn't wait for the evening to be over and go home. Normally I would've enjoyed myself, but tonight I was in no mood for celebrations.

"You kids go on without me," Tío Bolívar said when the show was over. "I still have things to do here."

It wasn't a long walk to my uncle's house, but Félix offered to drive us there.

"It's still early. You should go for ice cream," my magnanimous uncle said.

"Oh yes, can we?" Joselito said, applauding.

"I think that's a g-g-great idea," Félix said.

With the enthusiasm of a clam being boiled for ceviche, I followed the group half a block before I realized that I'd left my shawl in the auditorium.

"Wait! I have to go back. I forgot something." Before Félix would volunteer to come with me, I rushed back to the building.

My silk shawl was exactly where I'd left it. I rushed back downstairs, taking a short break and deep breaths in the middle of the staircase. As I stepped out of the foyer, something made me stop. My uncle was helping Juliana Isabel—wrapped in a fox mink—into the passenger seat of his car. He was holding her hand, smiling, and I'd never seen him looking so gallant. Instinctually, I felt for my camera, but no, I couldn't do that to my uncle. I had to draw the line somewhere.

I was probably reading too much into it, anyway. Of course he would drive her back to the hotel. She didn't have a car. But she did have a security team, a makeup artist, a hairdresser. They had all been at the airport surrounding her like a precious jewel. I'd never known of my uncle—the station owner—driving any performer anywhere. My father didn't do it, either, as far as I knew.

Before the starlet got into the car, he swiftly kissed her hand and rushed around the hood, lightly tapping it, like a youngster on his first outing with a girl.

"Oh, here you are," Félix said, startling me. "I could've brought the shawl for you."

"It's fine," I said.

As I descended the four concrete steps outside the entrance, I caught a glimpse of Matías Montero standing across the street. He smiled at me, and it looked like he was about to cross.

I turned to Félix, grabbed him by the lapels, and planted a kiss on his mouth.

CHAPTER 35

Matías

1957

Attending the symphony with my mother was dreadful, and not because I didn't enjoy the music. It had everything to do with her behavior and how furious she'd made me. I almost didn't come tonight. But why should I sacrifice? I'd been looking forward to this concert for weeks. The orchestra had flown all the way from Berlin.

The classics were my favorite, especially Tchaikovksy's Piano Concerto no. 1, which was on the program for tonight's performance. The Russian composer sure knew how to transmit his passion for life and intense emotions in one complex piece of music. At least he had this magnificent concerto to unleash his demons— whatever they might have been—whereas I had no creative outlet for mine.

But I could certainly identify with strong emotions, particularly the pure and unadulterated rage I'd been experiencing for the last five days.

I *needed* this outing.

We were in the ample foyer of Teatro Sucre, waiting for the concert to begin. I stood by my mother and stepfather as they greeted friends and acquaintances. When nobody was watching, she straightened her husband's bow tie and attempted to fix my pompadour, but I pulled away. I wanted nothing to do with her.

Even though my mother didn't go out much anymore, she'd been quite popular as a young woman, so people appeared excited to see her. She and my father had been a power couple in the Quito society, and she'd become sort of a mythic creature—the beautiful young widow who ran the largest newspaper in the capital.

"Your coverage of Tomasín Escobar was fabulous," a heavy-set woman with carrot hair—whom I had no recollection of but apparently had met as a child—said. "What a pity. So young."

Part of my frustration tonight had to do precisely with the *matador*, who hadn't made it. He hadn't reached twenty years old yet and had been considered a child prodigy in the world of tauromachy. I'd been rooting for him to survive and stayed at the hospital overnight to be the first to know the results of his surgery. After the doctor had notified the media of his passing—at dawn the next day—I'd rushed back to the paper to write the article on no sleep.

Upon arrival, I'd been confronted with the appalling news that my mother had been looking for me in the newsroom the previous day and had run into Tato Paredes, holding the contact sheet of Valeria's photos against his chest. As much as Tato had attempted to hide the sheet, my mother had gotten a hold of it. I can only imagine how mysterious and nervous Tato must have behaved. My mother could be so perceptive. You couldn't hide anything from her.

Seeing the gold mine in front of her, she'd forced Tato to print Alejandro Toledo's photo and had one of the other reporters type a few words about it as the entertainment cover story of the day. I was sure the photo would get reprinted in most Latin American major newspapers, as he was famous internationally.

Of course I'd given my mother a piece of my mind. "For your information, Valeria Anzures took that photo, not Tato!" I'd told her. "You need to pay her, at the very least, since you gave credit to someone else."

At first, she'd shrugged. "Tato never said he didn't take the photos." Her shamelessness knew no bounds. "But what were you doing with that girl's film anyway? I told you I didn't want you anywhere near her."

"You *must* print a correction and give credit to Valeria for the photo," I'd said, and my mother knew better than to contradict me, but I had yet to see the correction printed. Immediately after the encounter with my mother, I'd tried to call Valeria at her uncle's house to explain what happened, but she was out. I continued calling, even after I saw her kissing that idiot in the middle of the street the other night, but they kept saying she wasn't home.

Hence, my current, *enhanced* state of irritation. I hadn't spoken to my mother since, but I was making an exception tonight, in front of her friends anyway.

"Did you hear the latest?" the woman with the carrot hair continued. "The Recalde's boy, Félix, is getting married to Leopoldo Anzures's daughter! You know, the girl they sent away for years? Well, apparently, she's back—and such a *lagarta*, she's already snagged the richest bachelor she could find."

My mom threw a quick glance at me. Inside the pockets of my trousers my hands balled into tight fists. Valeria engaged? No wonder she'd kissed that fool the other night. I'd been trying not to think about that and pretend it didn't bother me.

"Not only that, the Recaldes are throwing an engagement party tonight—out of the blue—and they had the gall not to invite us, right, Pepe?" she elbowed her husband, a thin old man with an eagle nose, who answered with a "*what?*" and then a "*who?*"

"Alfonso and Caridad Recalde! I told you about their party this afternoon. If you'd only listen to me once in a while!"

The man, chewing on a toothpick, winked at me.

"The nerve of those people!" she said. "We invited them to the weddings of both of our girls, and these are the thanks we get?"

My mother shook her head in solidarity.

An elongated woman, with an embroidered blouse that came all the way to her chin and spectacles at the tip of her nose, rang a small bell by my ear, signaling that the show was getting ready to start and we should take our seats—praise the Lord.

I sat through the first half of the concert. It was mesmerizing, electrifying, more than I would have anticipated. And yet, I couldn't stay there one more second. I got up, still in the dark, and made my way to the end of the aisle—not a word to my mother, but I could hear her hissing my name. I strode out of the auditorium, rushed through the foyer, and out to the misty street. It had been raining earlier, and the cobblestone was still wet.

I didn't need directions. I knew exactly where to go. Lifting my lapels and digging my hands inside the pockets of my jacket, I hurtled down the street without looking up. I couldn't believe Valeria had gotten *engaged*. She was much too young. And why had she not told me? It couldn't be true. I had to see it *with my own eyes*.

A car honked at me as I crossed the street without looking. What had come over me, anyway? Why did I care about what this girl did? She'd been away for years, and I had barely thought of her during that time. If I did, it would always be with pity. Poor Valeria this, poor Valeria that. But seeing her as an adult, a grown woman, had shaken me to the core.

I reached the parking lot where we kept my dad's sedan—even after all these years—and I unlocked the driver's door. I always carried the key with me, since I often had to drive around town to find my stories, unless I was too far from the lot, in which case I would take a cab.

Of course, everyone in the media knew who the Recaldes were and where they lived, me included, but unlike the carrot-haired woman, I wasn't surprised that they hadn't invited us. Valeria's uncle couldn't stand us, and she probably despised me now as well, so that may have had something to do with the slight.

I drove fast, checking my watch from time to time. The party would be in full swing by now. From a distance, I could make out the shape of the Recaldes' neocolonial villa. They had a mansion, unequivocally: an old castle that had belonged to a marquis or a count of some sort during the last century. Not a lot of people knew there were actual castles in Quito. In the last twenty years, they had been building many of them in the district known as La Mariscal, where the city's aristocracy had been moving to get away from the ever more crowded downtown area. Some were impressive displays of architecture, while others stuck out like sore thumbs next to the colonial and modern buildings emerging near them. I had heard there were several, and I'd intended to write a series of articles about them. The visit to Valeria's old home had rekindled this desire. There had been some talk about moving into this area in my family, also.

The construction in front of me was an eclectic blend of Renaissance finials, symmetrical lines, and colonial details in the form of wooden window frames and balconies. Adding to this ensemble was a large palm tree flanked by a handful of smaller ones inside the property. Bright lights pointed at the balcony archways spread throughout the second story, and two towers crowned with jade pitched roofs gave it the look of a European castle. I imagined Valeria locked inside one of those towers if she married into this family, her photojournalism dreams tossed into the nearest trash can.

I parked half a block away and, fiddling with my keys, followed the voices and laughter to the front metal gate, which was wide open. I let myself into the property, walking past an immaculate garden and a large stone fountain. There was a small cluster of people in the garden, enjoying drinks and so distracted that none of them seemed to notice me. Conveniently, I was wearing a tuxedo, so I blended in well with the elegant guests.

As I stepped into the crowded foyer with its saffron walls and spiral staircase in the back, I kept my eyes open for Valeria; so far, I hadn't seen her. I'd better find her before her uncle kicked me out, so I couldn't be too brazen about my presence here. On the fly, I grabbed a glass of champagne from a stiff waiter carrying a tray full of drinks, and I slowly migrated from the spacious foyer into a grand salon surrounded by tall windows and a candelabra chandelier hanging from a carefully carved ceiling resembling a geometric maze.

In the corner of the room, a quartet of strings played Vivaldi. The room was packed as people mingled and laughed—and there, guarded by her many cousins, stood a very serious Valeria.

In black?

Her dress tightly hugged all her curves. It had puffy sleeves and some kind of lace covered the entire fabric. She was even wearing heels, which enhanced a pair of shapely calves I hadn't noticed before. I'd been mistaken to think of her as too young to marry. There was nothing childlike about this woman. Not her red lipstick, nor her wavy hair in a sophisticated updo, the glass of champagne in her hand, and certainly not the notorious pearl on her ring.

A mixture of anguish and regret took over me. I needed to talk to her. *Immediately.*

"Excuse me," I said to a group standing between us as I squeezed past them toward her.

Her eyes widened upon seeing me and then, that irresistible frown. She held my gaze for a moment until the clicking of glass drew everyone's attention (except mine) to the back of the room.

A man's voice over a microphone echoed throughout the salon, welcoming the guests who'd actually been invited to the event, offering a toast to the bride and the groom. The voice belonged to Alfonso Recalde, an older version of his son Félix, except that he carried the confidence that age and success gave men—something his son was sorely lacking. If anyone was a child here, it was Félix Recalde, who approached Valeria and stood like a broom by her side. He was significantly taller than her, but he still had the body of a teenager: long, bony arms and legs, a perky nose, and a face full of freckles.

He didn't deserve a woman like her.

Valeria's uncle, Bolívar Anzures, spoke next. I could tell by his slightly slurred speech that he'd been drinking for a while, perhaps to gather enough courage to talk in public. A general *"salud"* followed Anzures's hasty speech, and all drank their champagne. I had already finished mine but could certainly use another to help my ire subside, if nothing else.

As the guests slowly made their way to the dining room, where I was sure succulent dishes probably awaited—based on the exquisite smell—Valeria drifted away from the group and gravitated toward what I assumed to be the lavatory.

I followed her, and before she could enter the room, I held her arm. "I need to talk to you."

She dropped mine as if I were a burning pot.

"What are you doing here?" she hissed.

"Why didn't you tell me you were engaged?"

Looking around, she led the way to another room, which turned out to be a library covered in wooden panels and bookshelves. At its center was a stone chimney with flanking carved statues of pre-Incan tribesmen, who appeared to be glaring at me.

"I didn't think you would care," she said. "Not after what you did to me!"

"I've been trying to call you for almost a week to explain!"

She crossed her arms.

"I've been feeling terrible about what happened, and I know it looks awful, but I promise I didn't do it on purpose. It was all a big mistake." I explained to her the situation with the *matador*, and how I'd been gone that entire afternoon and night. "We're going to pay you for the photos," I said, "even if I have to do it myself with my own salary."

She didn't say anything for a while, but I could see that her rapid breathing was slowing down a bit.

"Am I supposed to be touched by your act of kindness?" she finally said. "I haven't forgotten that your family *owns* the newspaper. I didn't just want the money. I wanted the job!"

I took a step closer to her, but she didn't budge. "I know. It looks bad. It may be hard to believe, but my mother and my stepfather are the ones in charge. I have no say in any editorial or administrative decisions. My mom wants me to learn every aspect of the business before I can move up. Once I understand the basics and get good at it, I'll move up in the organization. She says she doesn't believe in nepotism, and she won't make me director until I have a keen understanding of what it is to work at a newspaper."

She let out a sigh. My eyes couldn't look away from her full lips. When did she become so stunning?

"That's all very commendable, I suppose," she said, "but where does that leave me? I still have no job. At least if I had the photo, I could've sold it to another publication and perhaps they would've hired me."

"I know, Vale, I'm sorry. But I'll make it up to you. I promise." I gently brushed her bare arm. She seemed to be trembling. "Are you cold?"

"No."

I picked up her hand, unable to avoid glancing at her hideous ring.

"I still don't understand why you're here," she said in a low voice.

"Because I heard you were getting engaged."

"Yes. And?"

"I can't let that happen. I won't let you marry that *tarado*."

"Why? What business is it of yours?"

I couldn't fight it any longer. I held her face with both of my hands and kissed her.

CHAPTER 36

Valeria

1957

I was still submerged in a cloud of bliss, courtesy of Matías's kisses, when my uncle's thunderous voice brought me back to reality.

"What the *hell* is going on here?!"

My uncle had never been intimidating to me, but he was now. I pushed Matías away, electricity still coursing through undiscovered areas of my body. Tío Bolívar marched toward us and, before anybody could react, he punched Matías square in the jaw with a resounding crack. Matías fell back, against a bookshelf, his head being crowned by a particularly heavy volume of *Enciclopedia Espasa-Calpe*, carelessly placed on the edge of the shelf.

I was mortified, but before I could assist him, my uncle lunged toward him. Fortunately, my older cousins rushed into the study and got a hold of his arms.

"Calm down, Papá!" Jorge, the oldest and the living portrait of my uncle, said.

"What's come over you?" said Arturo, his second-born and the tallest of all.

Tío Bolívar shrugged his sons off of him, while Matías rubbed his jaw and attempted to stand up straight.

"This *desgraciado* was disrespecting your cousin!"

The two of them turned to Matías, glaring.

Holy Mother, could this get any worse?

"Really?" Jorge said, assessing him from head to toe. "No surprise there, I guess. What else could be expected of a Montero?"

Arturo grabbed Mati's arm. "You have no business here!"

"Get your damn hands off of me!" Matías said, shoving Arturo against one of the sofas. "I know the way."

Fixing his lapels, he turned toward me and gave me a sideways smile. "Good night, Valeria."

"Don't you speak to her!" my uncle said.

As Matías walked away, my uncle shouted, "I don't ever want to see you near my niece again, you hear?"

Whether he heard or not, he was out the door before Félix and his mother made it into the library. I wanted to throw the damn encyclopedia at my uncle's head. He'd just ruined my chances with Matías!

"What was that ruckus?" my future mother-in-law said.

"Oh, nothing to worry about, Doña Caridad," Jorge said. "Just some party crasher that insisted on speaking to my cousin, but we already took care of him."

"Yes, he won't be coming back here anymore," Arturo said, fixing his jacket as it got disheveled with Matías's push. "Come on, *prima*. Let's go eat."

I sighed heavily. Before walking away, I shot a glance at my uncle, who watched me pensively. He knew exactly what had been going on, and it had nothing to do with disrespect.

That night, I couldn't sleep from the excitement.

Matías loved me.

And he hadn't betrayed me, like I'd thought. It had all been his mother's fault.

I finally knew what a kiss from Matías felt like. Who could sleep at a moment like this? Now the only problem was what to do about Félix. We were getting more and more entangled. He'd even given me a pearl ring that he said had belonged to his grandmother.

A noise coming from the street startled me.

Matías!

Another serenade from Félix?

No, God, please.

Graciela was fast asleep by my side, so I tiptoed to the window. At first glance, I couldn't see anything but the lonely street and the dim light post in front of the bakery. I identified some movement—the shape of a man. He appeared away from the light, but I was almost certain there was a person there. He wore that fedora I had seen before, and I knew it wasn't Matías because of the grayish mustache. What could this man possibly want from me? Or was he after Graciela?

I was tempted to go downstairs and demand to know why he was following us, but I didn't want to look like a fool if it just happened to be some random person in need of fresh air or waiting for a friend. Besides, it could be dangerous. What if it was, in fact, some delinquent or someone who wanted to harm me? And what would my uncle say if he saw me nonchalantly dashing into the street in the middle of the night after the spectacle with Matías he'd witnessed at my engagement party?

He hadn't said anything else about it, but he'd stopped drinking altogether and during dinner, I caught him staring at me. It was only a matter of time before he confronted me. I didn't know what I would tell him. Things with Matías were inconclusive and it was obvious that the animosity between the two families had not diminished with time but was growing like the roots of an oak tree. I wondered if Matías's mom knew I had taken Alejandro Toledo's photo and printed it just to spite me. I ought to go to *Crónicas* myself and demand an explanation, a correction, and *payment* from them after their act of thievery.

It would also be an excellent opportunity to see Matías again.

* * *

The guard greeted me as I walked into the *Crónicas* building the next morning and called the elevator for me. I was glad he remembered me as I didn't feel like lying about having an appointment with my *madrina* again.

As the elevator ascended, my courage descended. I had been rehearsing all I was going to tell Matías's mom, but I didn't know if I could bring myself to do it. Every step from the elevator to her office felt like I was heading for my execution. Then I reminded myself of what this woman had done—how she'd given credit to someone else for my work, after all my sweat and blood, after risking my physical well-being and, potentially, my freedom (if Toledo had called the police).

I walked past the receptionist and marched toward my godmother's office. I opened the door without knocking. She lifted her head from a piece of paper where she was writing, startled. All I noticed were the glasses and the chignon.

"What are you doing?" she said, standing. "How dare you come in like that?"

"I came to collect my money and *my* film."

She faltered for an instant, but then straightened her back and raised her chin. "You could've made an appointment, or at the very least, knocked."

"That would be more kindness and respect than you've given me."

She assessed me. "You're just like your mother."

I crossed my arms. "Really? How is that? When I was little, you didn't seem to mind how she was."

"I'm not going to discuss your mother with you."

We held each other's gaze. I wasn't going to be the one to look away first. She opened the top drawer of her desk and removed a checkbook. She wrote an amount I couldn't see and signed the check. Then, she opened another drawer and removed an envelope.

"We'll print a correction in tomorrow's edition." She handed both things to me. "This concludes our business."

Our business? The amount on the check was more generous than I had imagined, but hardly enough money for me to live on. Inside the envelope was my film, cut in four long rows.

She sat down, her hands rubbing the cognac leather arm's rest. "I'd appreciate it if you closed the door behind you. And Valeria?"

I looked up from my purse, where I was inserting the check and the film.

"Stay away from my son."

Oh, how I wanted to throw one of my shoes at her arrogant face, but instead, I took a deep breath. Acting like a petulant brat would be beneath me. The door burst open and Matías barged into the office, out of breath. He looked around the office with a worried expression, as if trying to assess the damage to furniture or humans.

"Nobody knows how to knock anymore?" his mother said.

"Sorry." He turned to me. "Are you all right?"

"She's fine, Matías. She was just leaving."

I walked to the door. As he started following me, his mother spoke again.

"Matías, please stay. I need to talk to you. It's urgent."

I nodded at him and left the office. Underneath my skirt, my legs were shaking.

I was filled with regret during my entire walk down the hall, during the elevator ride downstairs, and as I headed into the bright street. *I should've said this. I should've said that.* This had been my opportunity to find out what exactly had happened the night of February twelfth, but I'd been too proud, too upset to think strategically. By the way she spoke of my mother, it had been more than apparent to me that she despised her, and the only logical conclusion was that, in fact, my mom and Matías's dad were having an affair. Women only hated in such a fierce way when it had to do with a man and a betrayal. My years of reading literature and theater had taught me as much.

I turned to see if, by a miracle, Matías had followed me outside.

No such luck.

Given how much our families hated each other, a relationship between the two of us was impossible. I felt like a modern-day Juliet immersed in one of my mom's *radionovelas*. It was a ridiculous situation. And yet, I'd never felt more drawn to Mati than I did now. When I'd seen him at the newspaper, it had taken all my might not to throw myself at him and cover him with kisses.

My head was a jumble of contradicting ideas and feelings. How was I going to deal with the Redhead Dilemma, aka my engagement? I felt awful about kissing Matías during my engagement party, but also exhilarated because I'd been dreaming about that moment since I was ten years old. I liked Félix—he was sweet, and he'd given me my Leica, the best gift anyone could've given me. And also a ring.

I glanced at it for a moment. If I broke off my engagement, I would have to return it to Félix. But Matías hadn't promised me anything. He'd only given me a kiss. That didn't mean he wanted to marry me, or even have a relationship with me. And this check—I tightened my purse against my side—this money wasn't enough to give me the independence I wanted.

It would be a good start, though.

There was a bank adjacent to Hotel Humboldt, the place where Toledo was staying. Maybe I could open a savings account? Doña Amparito had one. I'd gone with her several times to deposit money from the restaurant. If I took more photos, I could sell them to other publications—it was obvious that *Crónicas* wouldn't be conducting any further business with me. But I didn't think I wanted to specialize in stalking celebrities for gossip.

As I double-checked for any cars before crossing the street, I noticed *him* again. *My shadow.* The man who had been following me for days. For an instant, I'd thought—and hoped—it might be Matías, but the familiar beige gabardine told me it wasn't him.

Enough of this!

I kept trudging along the curb until I walked past a narrow alleyway. I took a sharp turn and grabbed a rock in each hand.

Sure enough, the man turned after me. I threw one of the rocks at his face. He let out a groan and brought a hand to his forehead.

"Who the hell are you?" I asked him. "Why have you been following me?"

Rubbing his forehead, he slowly removed his hat. "It's me, Valeria . . ."

The voice was familiar. I immediately recognized his eyes. But what happened to his hair? It was almost all white, and his mustache had thickened.

I dropped the other rock.

". . . your dad."

CHAPTER 37

Valeria

1957

My *father* standing in front of me? I couldn't believe my eyes.

He took a step forward. I wasn't dreaming. It *really* was my father. Sure, he'd aged considerably, but the way he squinted when he looked at me, his angular nose, the mole above his eyebrow—all those traits left no doubt that it was him. He tried to hug me, but I pushed him back. Any desire I might have had to hug him back clashed with my shock at his long deceit.

"*Hija . . .*"

"Why?" I yelled.

"I'm sorry, I . . . It's a long story."

I crossed my arms. "You've waited long enough to tell it."

He looked around. "Here? Couldn't we go somewhere more private?"

"Well, you're the one who took this approach."

"You're right." He fidgeted with his hat. "I apologize. I didn't mean to scare you. I knew you had graduated, and I wanted to see you, even from afar."

"That's why I don't understand. Why the need to be so secretive? Why lie? Why abandon me and lead me to believe you were *dead*?"

He peeked all around us. "Listen. I'm going to explain everything, but can we go somewhere else? I'll buy you a juice or a soda, or whatever you like."

My own father didn't know what I liked to drink.

"There's a café nearby," I said.

He nodded nervously. I led the way.

My dad and I sat in the back of Café El Madrilón. As the name suggested, the owner's wife was a blonde. Admittedly, not natural, but I'd heard her say it was "her color," because she'd paid good money for it at the salon. After which, she would let out a guffaw. Today, she was nowhere in sight, but I scarcely noticed. I couldn't believe I was here *with my own father*—the man I thought was dead.

We chose the dimmest and most private table in the café, and we kept our order simple.

Two coffees.

Papá raised his eyebrows.

I was an anomaly since the women in my family always prepared their coffees with a cup of warm milk and a tablespoon of instant coffee or *esencia de café*, which was its liquid form. Sugar was optional and to taste, but Graciela put in at least three teaspoons. I, myself, drank *tinto*—the blackest of all coffees, concentrated, bitter, small.

Today it matched my mood.

Sure, my father being alive was *good news*—I'd missed him so much. But my emotions were in a heated battle because I was so hurt—so furious—that he had deceived me, that he had *abandoned* me.

"You don't want a flan or a pastry?" my dad said, facing me, his back to the front entrance.

Who was this man offering me a dessert? Had he forgotten all his objections against sweets?

"No," I said. I wasn't going to make things any easier for him.

"You've turned into a lovely woman," he said, then added hesitantly. "You look so much like your mother."

I wanted to ask about her (was she alive, too?) I had so many questions, but before I could say anything, the hefty waiter—his bow tie so tight it looked like it might be choking him—brought the two porcelain cups full to the rim.

I let mine sit there and stared at my father. The last eight years had not been kind to him—pronounced purple circles under his eyes, deep lines flanking his mouth, his forehead a confluence of rivers. On the side of his temple was a red mark where my rock had hit him. At least it hadn't broken the skin, but it might bruise. He'd lost weight, too, and the gray had conquered most of his former chestnut hair.

"Well, don't look at me like that."

"Like what?"

"Like I'm a disappointment." He took a sip of coffee. "Let me explain what happened first and why I left . . ."

I wanted to add "like such a coward" to his sentence.

He dodged my gaze, as if reading my thoughts, ". . . the way I did."

"Where have you been all this time?"

He coughed. "Perú."

Perú? That was a lot closer to Riobamba than Quito.

"The night of the . . . the broadcast . . ." He coughed some more. "I never thought something like that could happen. I never thought our own people would turn against us. We were one of the most well regarded radio stations. They loved us—they loved your mother. They recognized her in the streets from time to time, you know? Her photo was frequently in the paper whenever a new *radionovela* was starting. And apparently, as I grimly found out that night, people knew me, too."

Of course, he'd been president of the Association of Radio Broadcasting around that time and an active member of Quito's cultural circle—a poet, in fact—not to mention the owner of the ever-popular Radio La Voz. I, too, had seen his photo in the paper more than once.

"I still can't believe our citizens would turn so violent. That night," he dodged my eyes, "after the crowd started burning the building, I looked for your mother all over without any luck. Zambrano dragged me upstairs to the terrace. I figured she managed to get out, so we jumped onto the roof of an adjacent convent and then nearby other rooftops, as several buildings on the block were connected."

The thought of my father—so prim and proper—climbing on terraces and jumping from one perilous pitched roof to another was somewhat comical, but I was in no mood to laugh.

"They'd handed me a linotypist's smock," he said, "but I didn't have time to change. When I finally descended through a wall that was still in construction, a group of men recognized me and beat me senseless. If it hadn't been for Zambrano, who got me into a taxi, they would've killed me. I have no doubt about that."

He was now the one staring at his coffee without drinking it. "That night I fled to Loja, where Camilo Rey, my best friend from elementary school, lived. His family had a farm. You met him a couple of times, remember?"

"No."

"He took me to a clinic where they took care of me for a few days. After I recovered, I wanted to come see you and your mother, but a lawyer friend told me that if I went back to Quito, they would charge me for the deaths of the people in the building. I had been the instigator and the direct cause of their doom. That's when I found out that your mother didn't make it."

His moist eyes set on the black liquid. "I wanted to come get you immediately, but my friends talked me out of it. What future awaited you with a fugitive for a father? Running away from the law all your life and not having a stable home? I decided to lay low until things calmed down and then come back for you—but things didn't calm down. Not for a while. The police ran an exhaustive search all over the country. A friend of mine, who was a former *Crónicas* editor, had moved to Lima a few months prior and offered me a job at the paper there. I figured it would be better for you—for the entire family—to believe I had died that night, to save you the shame and pain of having a father in prison for the negligent death of so many people."

"So, you thought it would be better for me to be an orphan?"

"No, I was planning to come back, but at the time I thought you'd be better off with your uncle and your cousins. You loved spending time with them. You wanted a sibling so badly."

"Well, I didn't love it. Tío Bolívar sent me to a boarding school in Riobamba."

He looked positively shocked.

"I just moved back a few weeks ago," I added.

"I didn't know. I assumed— I thought you'd been living with your uncle this entire time." He brought a hand to his forehead and rubbed it. "I'm sorry, *hija.*"

"Why didn't you ever send for me or write?"

"I thought about it, but if anybody suspected I was still alive, they would've come after me. People wanted justice—they felt mocked. I was sure they would've killed me, like they tried that night. I had to let everyone believe I had died so that the police would stop looking for me. Even the people who helped me out of the building that night didn't know what happened to me afterward."

"What about my uncle?"

"He didn't know, either. If he knew, I would've endangered him—he would've been my accomplice, and he would've demanded that I come back to the radio station. He can be very persistent."

Didn't I know that.

"But that was the last thing I wanted. I could never go back to the station after what happened to your mother there. I couldn't handle the guilt. The only two people who knew I was alive were my two friends from Loja: Camilo and Ramón Súarez, the lawyer who got me a fake passport and helped me cross the border."

And none of them had the compassion to let me know my father was still alive.

My dad reached out for my hand, but I guarded it under the table. "Please forgive me, Valerita."

"I don't go by *Valerita* anymore," I said acidly.

He finished his coffee. I hadn't even started mine.

"Why are you back?" I said. "Why now?"

"I figured you might have graduated from high school and as an adult, you could understand certain things. Plus, enough time had passed. Even if they were still looking for me, I wouldn't be a priority anymore."

Then why was he still hiding under a hat with that ridiculous mustache, standing in dark street corners at nighttime?

"That night—that broadcast—was the biggest mistake of my life," he said before I could throw my own accusations. "If I could go back in time, I would have done things differently."

"You thought you'd be the next Orson Welles, didn't you?"

Unlike my father, who'd fallen into disgrace, the American adaptation of the same novel gave its creator instant fame—the good kind. He went on to direct and act in famous movies after his Mercury Theatre performed and broadcast *The War of the Worlds*.

I'd recently wondered if Welles's example had motivated my father to do the same.

"No," he said, taken aback. "I didn't. I just thought it would be a breakthrough from the boring melodramas we'd been performing until then."

I was still livid, which was part of the reason why I'd mocked his decision to broadcast that show after the chaos it created in New Jersey and New York, but I wanted to know more before he vanished again. "What about my mother? Are you sure she died?"

"Not a hundred percent, but that was the rumor back then. I couldn't find her anywhere on the third floor, and when I tried to go downstairs, the smoke had taken over. I just saw a couple of people fleeing the newsroom in the staircase. It was so chaotic. All of us had been locked in the studio, recording, and when the mob started throwing rocks and burning newspapers, everyone panicked."

"Was she there"—I interrupted—"during the recording?"

He shook his head. "Well, at first, yes, but she left after a while. She"—he cleared his throat—"she didn't have an important role."

"How come?"

He shrugged. "Just the way the script went. There weren't strong female lead roles, and she was used to being the star, so she wasn't too happy to be an extra."

"But Beatriz Lara was."

He looked stunned. "Yes . . ."

I examined his every expression. I hadn't seen him in eight years, but I was almost certain he was hiding something else.

Once my father and I parted ways with a robotic wave, I let out the tears I'd been holding back for the past hour. What was wrong with me? Now I was feeling bad for not hugging him, for being so unforgiving. He'd asked me not to tell Tío Bolívar or anyone else that he was still alive. But how could he expect me to keep something so important to myself? Honestly, I didn't think I could hide it for long, especially from Graciela. He'd said that even though things had died down in the last few years, there were still some who were seeking justice for the events of February twelfth.

I was openly sobbing now. What if he never came back? He'd left me once before, and I didn't even know how to find him. He was staying at a hostel, but he wouldn't tell me which one or how long he was planning to remain in Quito. Furthermore, he wouldn't tell me the pseudonym he'd been using since he left. It was understandable that he would change his name, as his real one had lost all credibility from the public, even internationally, but it hurt that he wouldn't share this detail with me. Did he really believe I would send the police over? What kind of daughter did he think I was?

"It's not that I don't trust you," he'd said. "But it would be best for you not to know too much."

I didn't think he was only talking about the hostel where he was staying. There was more, and what I really wanted to do was call Matías and tell him everything. He would know what to do. But with our families' mutual hatred, things were getting awkward between us. My cousins had manhandled him, and I'd been rude to his mom—with good reason—but who knew if she'd poisoned him against me after I walked out?

Maybe I should've asked my dad more about that night or mentioned my suspicions regarding my mom and Agustín Montero, but I'd been so angry when I found out he'd lied and left me here alone that I couldn't think straight.

My stomach started hurting again. I'd let my pride take over. I'd missed my chance to fix my situation. If anyone could help me, that was my father. He could talk to Tío Bolívar about my engagement. If things went bad, I could always move to Lima with him and work at the newspaper he mentioned—not that I had forgiven his abandonment—but Lima was a big city with several newspapers that hadn't branded me as a pariah.

Yes, I would tell him about my conundrum.

Wiping my tears, I turned around, but my dad was gone—the street behind me eerily empty.

A thump outside the window woke me up. I sat up as another pebble hit the windowsill. There was no denying the person's intent. I rushed to the window.

Matías!

He was standing by the light post, looking up.

I waved back at him.

Madre mía, what was I going to wear? I was most definitely not going downstairs in my nightgown. But I had to hurry up before my uncle saw him or Mati got tired of waiting and left.

In the dark, I pulled out the first shirtdress and sweater from the armoire, and rushed to the lavatory to wash myself and spray some of my aunt's violet perfume. It wasn't until I was downstairs that I realized I was wearing a lavender dress with an orange sweater. Not the best combination, but commendable given that it had taken me only five minutes to look relatively decent and well-groomed.

As I stepped outside, I rearranged the buttons of my sweater, which were mismatched.

Leaning over his sedan with his arms crossed, Matías looked at me with an amused smile.

"What are you doing here?" I said, making sure no one was watching.

The street was relatively empty, except for a drunkard singing out of tune at the end of the block.

"I need to show you something."

"I appreciate the urgency to share, but couldn't this wait until the morning?"

"Yes, but I didn't want anybody to see me here. Your uncle and your cousins have you well guarded in your tower. I figured I had a better chance to reach you while everyone was sleeping." He caressed my cheek, smiling. "Come on."

He opened the passenger door.

"What? I can't go anywhere at this hour. My uncle will kill me."

"Come on, Juliet. I know you're not afraid of anything."

Juliet? My heart was thumping against my rib cage. He was implying that we were— *what?* More than friends? I closed the front door and against my better judgment, I got inside the car.

"Wait, how am I going to get back in?" I said, realizing in my haze that the door had locked behind me and I didn't have a key.

"We'll figure it out," he said with a wink, and drove away. He parked in a dark, empty street and looked at me.

"What are we doing here?" I asked.

He leaned over me and gave me the kiss I'd been waiting for since I saw him. It was better than the first time, maybe because we weren't interrupted by some brutes who wanted to kill him. Tonight, he had time to linger in this kiss he seemed to be wanting as much as I did. He undid the top button of my shirtdress and kissed my neck. What was this strange sensation? I felt it all the way to my knees. I couldn't believe I'd been missing out for so many years. With his lips trailing down my neck, he spoke.

"What are you going to do about," another soft kiss on my collarbone, "about your engagement?"

Why did he have to bring up that subject at a moment like this? I pulled back. "I don't know. Do we have to talk about this now?"

"Vale, your wedding is in, what? A couple of weeks?"

I sat back. "What do you propose I do, then?"

He didn't say anything. Of course he wouldn't ask me to marry him. It was too soon, and besides our families would kill both of us.

I buttoned up my shirt and folded my arms.

"What did you want to show me?" I said.

Sighing, he removed a small wooden chest from the glove compartment and handed it to me.

"What is it?"

"I found it buried at the bottom of my mom's armoire. Open it."

There were over a dozen photographs of two girls in various stages of their lives, from puberty all the way to their late teens.

"It's my mom," I said, recognizing the dimples in her cheeks, her sweet smile that I had seen so seldomly toward the end of her life. The last photo showed Mati's mom in her wedding gown, hugging my mom.

"At one point, they loved each other," he said.

Underneath all the photos was a folded powder blue scarf with meticulously illustrated doves.

"And this?"

"I have no idea. My guess is it was a gift."

"If your mom is still holding on to all this stuff, she must not hate my mother as much as she says."

I felt an inkling of hope. Perhaps there could be a future for us.

"Well, she does a good job at hiding it. I wanted you to see it before my mom notices it's missing. I know there are no big revelations here, but I thought you would like to see those photos nonetheless."

"Thank you, Mati." I folded the scarf back into the chest. "I do have a big revelation of my own." I stopped fumbling with my mom's photos. "It turns out my dad is still alive."

His mouth gaped open. "What?"

I went on to explain—as best as I could—my encounter with my father that afternoon, but before we could make sense of my dad's presence in our lives and what that could mean for all of us, a knock on the window startled both of us.

A policeman.

"You can't be here," he said, gesturing for Matías to roll down the window and spewing something about *indecent acts* and *nothing good happening after midnight*. As much as Matías tried to explain that we weren't doing anything wrong, the man wouldn't hear him.

"Do me a favor and scram!"

Well, at least he kicked us out politely.

And so, we left. Now the only problem was how to get back into my uncle's house?

As soon as we arrived at my uncle's house, Mati and I used the "pebble on the window" trick to try to wake up Graciela, but there was no response. I should've known better—she was a deep sleeper: She never heard her alarm clock in the morning.

At some point I accidentally hit my uncle's window, which was next to ours. I covered my mouth with both hands to keep from laughing.

"Let me try," Mati said. He squinted one eye as he aimed at the perfect angle of Graciela's window. He threw the pebble and hit the middle of the window, causing a minor thump that died next to the engine of a car roaring behind us.

Ever so slowly, I turned around only to see Tío Bolívar's Ford Fairlane parking in front of Matías's car.

"My uncle," I said, dropping my stone on the ground.

Invoking all the saints in the heavens that might be available,

I waited for my uncle to get out of his car. My face had never burned more. I pictured my head rolling into a wicker basket, like Marie Antoinette's.

"What's going on here?" he said aloud. "Didn't you have enough the other night?" He was coming toward Mati, gesticulating with both arms. But this time I was prepared. I lunged toward my uncle, standing between the two men.

"Stop it, Tío!" I turned to Matías. "Please leave, Mati."

"Are you sure?"

"Yes!"

"You are engaged, Valeria. And these are not visiting hours!" my uncle was saying.

I kept blocking him until Matías got inside his car.

"If these aren't visiting hours, then *who* were you with tonight, Tío?" I asked.

My uncle frowned. "What? I wasn't visiting anybody."

"No. You were you just dropping someone at her hotel, right?"

He took a step back. "I don't know what you're talking about."

"Tío, I saw you the other night with Juliana Isabel."

He stuttered. "Well, I was just . . . just—she needed a r-r-ride."

"And my aunt knows about this grand favor?"

The color drained from his face.

"Don't worry," I said. "I won't tell her anything, and I suggest you don't say anything about Matías, either. Look, it's late. We're both tired. What do you say we just go to bed and forget about all this?"

He nodded, removing his keys from the pocket of his trousers. Neither of us said another word as we entered the foyer, our quiet steps weighing heavily on the creaky wooden floors—the only discernable sounds in the stillness of the house.

PART 4

A Night of Martians

$\mathcal{C}$HAPTER 38

Alicia

February 12, 1949

I had done *everything* to make this marriage work. From being the most indulgent wife—always looking my very best, cooking Agustín's favorite meals, waiting for him with a glass of whiskey after a long workday, listening to his tedious political talk—all the way to casting spells and rituals carefully crafted by a renowned witch to help me keep his love. Not to mention the small detail that I had given him his one and only son, Matías, the heir and hope for his family's publishing business.

Unfortunately, it hadn't been enough.

Something had been amiss for months.

The mysterious phone calls that invariably resulted in silence at the other end of the line; the unaccounted-for jewelry receipt; Agustín's unexplained absences accompanied by what I was certain were lies; and, of course, that expensive fountain pen that had appeared out of nowhere and he couldn't explain.

Folded inside his old Chevrolet sedan, I searched in the glove compartment and under the front and back seats for any evidence to confirm my suspicions—suspicions that had been tormenting me at all hours of the day and night, making it impossible for me

to sleep or live my daily life in peace. My nerves were in shambles, and I was drinking more vodka than anyone ought to, but
it was the only way to suppress the tremor in my hands and legs.

As usual, Agustín had walked to work since the newspaper was
only a few blocks away from home. In addition, our house didn't
have a garage, so he paid a monthly fee to leave his sedan at this
parking structure. Most people who lived in downtown Quito and
owned an automobile did. This old colonial area where houses
were stacked like domino pieces didn't have room for garages or
carports.

Thus, it had been relatively easy for me to rummage inside his
car while he was at work. And then, my careful planning and effort
had paid off as soon as I spotted the wing of a dove in a powder
blue scarf carelessly lying under his back seat.

The most unexpected sensation took over me: *relief.*

The satisfaction of a job well done.

I wasn't crazy. I wasn't just seeing things, like Agustín had said.
I was *right.*

But this feeling was short-lived and quickly replaced by a deep
ache in my chest. He had *another woman.* I wasn't enough. I had
never been. Even more heartbreaking was to make the ultimate
connection, the realization of who this furtive mistress was.

This scarf had come into my life on one of those Sundays when
Marisa and I had skipped mass together and gone to the marketplace instead. I spotted it immediately among a dozen others.
But this had to be it. I'd seen one just like it around the neck of
a ravishing movie star in a film the previous night and I'd fallen
in love with the look. I wrapped it around my neck and wore it as
my only adornment for the next few days. On occasion, I'd used it
as a headscarf. It made me feel worldly, glamorous. And everyone
complimented me on it.

After Marisa had her baby—Valeria—she was never the same
again. Something dark clicked inside of her. Instead of the bliss
I'd experienced with Matías's birth, Marisa lost the energy and

drive she'd always had. It was as if she'd given up on life and would
spend her days in bed. Leopoldo had to hire a nanny—Ada—to
take care of Valeria.

In an effort to cheer Marisa up, I gave her the powder blue scarf
with its stylized doves. She'd always liked it, and when I bought it,
she searched all day for one like it at the bazaar without any luck.
She kept looking in the following weeks, but never found another.
It was one of a kind.

I handed it to her in a box wrapped with a red bow on top. She
smiled behind teary, swollen eyes, and had even made an effort to
remove it from the box.

"Let me do it," I said, and wrapped it around her neck in a stylish knot. "Beautiful. Now all you need is a little lipstick and rouge
and you'll be ready to go out."

"Thanks," she said, undoing the knot, "but I don't want to go
out."

"Marisa, you haven't left your house in weeks! Valeria is two
months already."

She shook her head and pulled the covers over her again. No
matter what I said, or in what tone, it didn't change the fact that
Marisa was not the same girl I knew. Now I finally knew why.
Marisa, my childhood friend, nearly my sister, was having an affair with my husband. This item only confirmed what I had been
fearing for weeks.

Had she been in love with Agustín all along? She'd cried at my
wedding—I remembered as much. But I'd thought it was the emotion of losing her best friend so soon. I'd barely turned nineteen,
but was already expecting Matías, so I had no choice in the matter. We both knew things would never be the same now that I was
going to be a married woman and a mother. Had there been more
to her sorrow?

After my wedding—or during the party—she'd finally accepted
Leopoldo, who'd been smitten with her for the past two years, but
she didn't marry him for another two years. Those early years of

marriage had been ideal. Our husbands were good friends, and so were we. Plus the three of them worked in the same building.

It had come natural for us to raise our kids together. Despite the three years' difference in age, Matías and Valeria had practically grown up together. Matías had always been so protective of her. It would break their hearts to know about Marisa and Agustín's betrayal. But I didn't have the fortitude to think about them now or about any of the implications of my discovery. What I really wanted was to slash all his tires, break every window of his precious car, yell at them, hit them, and make them suffer as much as I did.

Holding the scarf in my hands, I knew exactly what I had to do.

When I arrived at the *Crónicas* building, my legs were shaking so much I had to hold on to the rail to climb up the stairs. I tensed up as I walked past the second story. I didn't want to see Agustín. Not yet. I would have a word with him later.

Could *she* be there with him—shamelessly conducting their affair in his office? I ought to just go in there and make a scene. I paused halfway up the staircase, staring at the door leading to the second floor. No, it would be better to talk to Leopoldo first. He would know what to do.

The radio station was busy, as usual. People excused themselves as they walked past me. I knew many of them, as I used to visit Marisa here while she performed, but I barely answered their greetings. Marisa might be here already, and not with Agustín, as I had imagined. What would I tell her then? Throwing the scarf at her face was the only course of action I could think of.

I caught Leopoldo in his office speaking in a rather agitated tone with Fermín Alcazar, a Chilean actor who'd been working at La Voz for a few months now.

"That would be irresponsible, Fermín! I said no already."

"But Polito, it would draw more of an audience than this silly love story." He waved a thick manuscript in his hand. "We've made dozens of them! People are ready for something new, some-

thing groundbreaking. The competition between *radioteatros* is
pretty steep nowadays. Look, I even made copies of the script."

"Don't you remember what happened in the United States
with Orson Welles?"

He waved a hand. "We did it in Chile and there were no mis-
haps whatsoever."

"I heard someone had a heart attack."

"A coincidence. The truth of the matter, Polito, is that it was
a very successful show with great ratings. We'll just make sure to
tell people at the beginning that it's a novel and we'll mention our
sponsor frequently. I doubt anybody would be so dumb or gullible
to believe it's true."

"No. We're doing *Gloria*, and that's my final word."

Leopoldo saw me then, and his nose scrunched a little. Years
ago, he'd had a thing for me, but it was short-lived. Marisa, with
her unassuming charm and her angelic voice had a way of winning
people over. Unfortunately, it had worked on my husband, too.

"Alicia, what a surprise," he said. "Marisa isn't here yet. You
know how she is."

I knew all about her habitual tardiness. "Actually, I need to
speak to you."

He got up from his desk as Fermín walked past me with a nod.
Always the gentleman, Leopoldo pulled out a chair in front of his
desk for me, but I was too shaken to sit down. I didn't even know
what I was going to tell him yet.

I gripped the back of the chair.

"Is something the matter?"

"Yes."

He assumed his most solemn stance, the way he did when he
was directing actors during a performance—so different from the
relaxed tight-lipped smile he displayed during our get-togethers,
once he had a few drinks inside him. He'd grown a mustache in
the last few years, which made his demeanor even more grave.

He closed the door while I took quick breaths, gathering the
courage to speak and shatter his world, just like mine had been.

There was no way to say this in a subtle way, especially not at this time. Any minute, Marisa would show up and they would have to start the *radionovela*.

"I have reason to believe Marisa and Agustín are having an affair."

At first, he looked like he might smile—as if he didn't understand or believe what I was saying. He tilted his head just so, and his eyes narrowed as he scrutinized my face.

"What are your reasons to believe this?"

I removed the scarf from my purse and placed it on the desk.

"Recognize this?"

"It looks familiar."

"I gave it to Marisa years ago. I found it today in Agustín's car. But there's more: he's been acting strange lately, he's rarely home, and he shows no interest in me. Also . . ."

"What?"

"At Gabo's funeral, didn't you see the way they hugged, how they *looked* at each other?"

He paled, the vein in his temple beating. "It's understandable," he said, stumbling over his words. "Gabo and Agustín were very close."

"You can believe me or not, but I'm a hundred percent sure of what I'm telling you. I could go through a long list of irregularities, but we don't have the time right now. The question is: What are we going to do about it?"

CHAPTER 39

Marisa

February 12, 1949

As I hurtled toward the third floor of the *Crónicas* building, I nearly bumped into Alicia. She was coming downstairs in as much haste as I was going up. She must have been looking for me at the station.

"Oh, hi," I said, "what are you doing here?"

She didn't bother answering, but simply continued her way down the stairs. Had I not been so late for the show, I would've followed her and demanded an explanation for her rudeness. Since when did she not greet me—her so-called best friend *in the entire world*? Maybe something bad had happened. I would have to visit her later.

At La Voz, it was chaos as usual. I went directly to Polo's office to grab my script. Today we were starting *Gloria*, a *radionovela* from a local writer where I was the protagonist. The manuscript was not in his office. Neither was my husband.

I found him in the conference room, where he was heading some kind of meeting I knew nothing about. At first, I thought it might be a sales meeting, but all the actors were there and also Piero Zambrano, the producer. Why had Polo not told me about this? It was not the time for impromptu meetings, either. In less than twenty minutes transmission would start. He didn't even look at me when I entered the room, but everyone else did. They each had a booklet in their hands.

Without a second's pause, Polo continued giving instructions to Reinaldo and Fermín. "Reinaldo, do you think you can play the minister of government?"

He read from the script in front of him. "Unfortunately, compatriots"—his voice became more nasal—"I suspect our weapons do not have the mechanical capacities to counter those of the colossal enemy."

Everyone laughed.

"Excellent," Polo said.

I looked at the title of one of the scripts. *The War of the Worlds?*

What on earth? I knew Fermín had been trying to push this Spanish adaptation of the famous novel on us for weeks, but Polo had always said no. In fact, he'd told me last night he was fed up with Fermín bringing it up all the time.

For a split second, Polo glanced at me, but quickly turned toward one of my colleagues. "And Gonzalo, you will be the mayor of Quito."

Immediately Gonzalo read his line. "People of Quito, allow us to defend our city. Our women and children should go to the high surrounding areas in order to leave the men free for action and combat."

Everyone applauded. It was a masterful impersonation of our mayor. I hadn't seen this much energy coming from our group in years. My understudy, Beatriz Lara, was there, too. I turned to my husband, indignant, but he was oblivious to my presence—or so it seemed. I knew better than to interrupt him when he was giving directions. I prided myself on keeping things professional at work.

It had always been that way for us. In fact, it had taken two years of working together and an exorbitant amount of *aguardiente* for him to tell me how he felt. Alicia and Agustín's wedding had been the last push I needed to let go of my unrequited love. If not emotionally, at least physically. Seeing Alicia in Agustín's arms all night in that gorgeous pearl headband and her long, fluted moiré silk wedding gown had been too much. It had been natural to accept that first dance with Polo. Up until then, he had never even hinted that he had a romantic interest in me, but sometimes I would catch him staring at me for too long during our performances or when I spoke to someone else. When I turned in his direction, he would immediately return to his script as if nothing had happened.

That first *bolero* had led to many others and a declaration of love by the end of the night. Polo Anzures was not a bad-looking man, but he was closer to thirty than twenty, and I had just turned eighteen. With Agustín, I'd always been more at ease; not only because he was younger, but also because he was approachable and fond of telling jokes. Polo, for the most part, was a quiet man—except when he was directing. He had a lot to say then. The other, little problem in this burgeoning relationship was that he was my boss.

It had been a slow courtship with awkward hand holding, prolonged silences, shy smiles, and secretive outings. "Nobody at the radio station can find out," he would say, though I didn't fully understand why. We were both single and he'd hired me long before our relationship started.

I would shrug and follow along. What I really wanted was to forget Agustín once and for all—not an easy task since we worked at the same building, and he was married to my best friend. Not to mention the minor detail that he was going to be a father to my future godson in a few months. Alicia and I had made a pact years ago that we would be *comadres* one day, each godmothers to our future children.

When Alicia had told me that she was expecting—barely a month prior to the wedding—I would've rather had the roof collapse on top of my head. I'd considered that Agustín and Alicia might have been intimate, but it had been nothing but a suspicion. Her current reality *confirmed* it.

Deep down, I'd been hoping he would come back to me, choose me instead of her.

He hadn't. As soon as Agustín found out about the baby, he proposed. From that bleak day on, they were in a race against time—lest anybody would see her growing stomach. There had been tricks she'd had to pull, like wearing a corset and keeping a large orchid arrangement close to her midsection during the entire ceremony, but as she waltzed with the man of our dreams, I could see the small bump with Agustín's child underneath the layers of fabric.

I found my consolation prize in Polo. He was so attentive, so talented. He went above and beyond to please me. Two kids later (theirs and ours), I learned to live with my buried feelings for Agustín, like a dull molar pain that doesn't go away. But ignoring the pain didn't mean the problem was gone. With my brother's untimely death, Agustín and I had grown close again. It had been inevitable—he'd been the one to deliver the devastating news that my brother had been hit by a bus while riding his bicycle to work.

Gabo, the most talented cartoonist at *Crónicas* and the only person who knew about my true feelings for Agustín, had died on impact—leaving me alone and more vulnerable than ever. I couldn't even count on my sister Tatiana as she'd joined the convent years ago. Agustín had consoled me that afternoon, offering me a much needed hug.

"Any other questions?" Polo said to the group, interrupting my thoughts with a resonant voice that contrasted with his ordinary even tone.

What had come over him?

Of course I had questions, but I wasn't dumb enough to ask them aloud. He looked at me defiantly before marching out of the conference room.

The plan, as I understood it, was to start with the variety show instead of the *radioteatro* and soon after, they were going to interrupt the music and mention the alien invasion in the form of a news bulletin. This format had been first conceived and adopted by Orson Welles, the now-famous American actor and director.

Fermín Alcázar had claimed this setup was more dynamic and gripping than just reading and performing the novel.

Polo had already gathered a group of performers, who were settling in the auditorium, and the highlight of the evening would be a famous duet, Benitez y Valencia, the most beloved *pasillo* singers in the country. I'd known they were coming today, but I doubted they knew what my husband was up to. It was going to be a sacrilege to interrupt them.

I darted behind my husband as he rushed to the auditorium, papers in hand. I knew better than to bother him when he had an agenda in mind, but I couldn't help it. He was slighting me in front of the cast, in front of the entire radio station.

"Polo!"

He kept walking. I scurried behind him as quickly as my heels allowed.

"Leopoldo!" This time, I screamed, and several people turned to look at me.

He finally stopped. "What?"

I caught up with him. "What's going on? You're doing *The War of the Worlds*?"

"How perceptive of you." He'd never spoken to me with such disdain before.

"Why?" I said. "You said it would be dumb and irresponsible."

"I changed my mind."

"How come?"

"I really don't have time for explanations. The show starts in two minutes. Perhaps if you would've been on time, you'd understand the change of plans."

"But what about *Gloria*?"

"I'm tired of those stupid love stories."

"Stupid? They're the bread and butter of this station."

He crossed his arms. "Well, no more. A change is much needed."

"So, am I even going to be in the show? Beatriz Lara is here."

He shrugged. "You can be one of the people screaming in the

background. But frankly, you're not needed. You may leave if you want."

What?

He was about to resume his walk, but I grabbed his arm. "Polo, what's happening?"

For an instant, I recognized the love in his eyes—the affection he'd always had for me—but just as quickly, his expression turned icy, and there was a harshness in his brown eyes I'd never seen before. He remained silent.

"Does this have anything to do with Alicia?" I said, groping for clues. "I just ran into her outside the station, but she didn't say a word to me."

"I don't have time for explanations," he repeated his mantra. "We'll talk later."

He was maniacal, unrecognizable. I'd never seen him this agitated. It wasn't only in his speech or his abrupt change of heart; the booklet in his hands shook a little bit, and there were tiny drops of sweat on his forehead. He'd also removed his jacket and was walking around the office in his white shirt, sleeves rolled up. It was out of character, as he'd always been so formal, especially at work. Even his tie was loosened.

He let go of my arm and strode into the auditorium, where the voices of Benitez y Valencia boomed while they rehearsed before they went on the air. I gripped my mother's aquamarine pendant, which hung from my silver necklace. She'd left it behind years ago. She used to say that this stone had the power to release fear and give you courage. But no matter how tightly I held it or how much I tried to rub away the pressure in my chest, I still couldn't shake off the ominous feeling that something wretched was about to happen.

CHAPTER 40

Alicia

February 12, 1949

Agustín raised his head as soon as I opened his office door unannounced. He'd been writing something with that fountain pain *she'd* given him. My rage grew. A constellation of creases formed on his forehead upon seeing me. At least he wasn't in the arms of another woman. Even though I was fairly certain that Marisa was his mistress, there was the slight possibility that I might be wrong.

"What are you doing here?" he said, and not in his kindest tone.

Things hadn't been exactly smooth between us lately. My jealousy, my constant suspicion and distrust had put him on edge—I admitted it. But the way I saw it, I was completely justified. Especially *now*. The one thing I could never tolerate was betrayal.

Many women put up with cheating husbands—I knew that—but they didn't have the means to support themselves or an education to pursue a career, so they had no other option but to turn a blind eye on their men's indiscretions. I didn't have that problem; I had my own money. My father still owned the soda factory, and I occasionally helped with payroll and other administrative tasks. I worked part-time, as my priorities were my marriage and Matías.

However, being financially solvent didn't mean I was ready for the stigma of divorce—even less to share my husband with my so-called best friend.

"I should ask the same thing," I said. "It's Saturday night."

"And as you can see, I'm behaving responsibly *at work*."

He looked so handsome in that new striped gray suit, I had a fleeting urge to forget all about the dove scarf.

"What was so important that Raúl couldn't handle, especially on a weekend?" I asked. I hadn't yet decided whether to throw the evidence in his face or ease into the subject of what I'd casually found in *his* car.

"What's so important that you had to come to my office in person? Is Matías all right?"

"He's fine."

"So?"

I hated that harsh tone that emerged more frequently the longer we were married. What had happened to the carefree, charming man I had met? But if he was going to be hostile, I had no reason to be kind or subtle. *I* was the offended party. I removed the scarf and placed it on his desk.

His ears turned bright red. He recognized it—I knew it.

"What's this?" he said.

And still, he had the gall to lie to me.

"You tell me. I found it in the back seat of your car."

"I don't know what you're talking about. Alicia, we're on a deadline here. You know we go to print at ten p.m. I still have to approve this article and send it to the linotypist."

I couldn't care less about deadlines. "Answer me." I picked up the scarf from the desk and waved it. "What was this doing in your car?"

He brought both hands to his head. "I. Don't. Know."

"Stop lying!"

"Alicia, couldn't this wait until later? There's been rumors that Velasco Ibarra may come back, and you know the kind of political unrest that would cause."

"Who cares about that!" I slapped the desk.

"It's our duty to report what's happening."

"Velasco Ibarra is not coming back, and you know it. He's happily living his exile in Buenos Aires. Why would he want to come back here?"

"You don't know that."

"Whether he returns or not is the least of my concerns now. Stop trying to distract me." With shaking hands, I shoved the scarf back in my purse. "I know you're having an affair with Marisa."

He stood up, as if propelled by a spring.

"You don't know what you're saying, Alicia. You're blinded by jealousy."

"I know exactly what I'm saying. I gave her this damn scarf years ago. And this is how she repays years of friendship?"

He shook his head, looking at me as if I were a disgusting insect.

"Dare to deny that you love her!" I despised how my voice cracked at that moment. "I always suspected there was something between the two of you. *Since we met.* She changed after I started dating you, and she was never the same. I've seen the way you look at her, Agustín. How you didn't say a word the day of her wedding to Polo. How you drank yourself into oblivion every night after she got married. For *weeks.* And then, you didn't want to meet her baby until she was, like, four months old already!"

He circled me, like a watchful lion.

"Not to mention the *hug* you gave her at Gabo's funeral last week!" I said. "You guys nearly *melted* into one another!"

"He was one of my best friends. He worked for me for years. His death was tragic!"

"Yes, and she clearly took advantage of the tragedy—using your shoulder to cry on!"

"You're seeing things, Alicia. There's nothing between Marisa and me."

For a heartbeat, I wavered. Had I fabricated the whole thing in my mind? My throat ached, not only from my screaming accusations, but also from the pain of what I had just realized.

He hadn't denied that he loved her.

My eyes burned.

"You complain of all the secrecy," he finally said. "But have you ever considered your part in my behavior?"

"Now you're going to say it's my fault?"

He rubbed his eyes with the palm of his hands. "You're not an easy woman to live with."

I'd had enough of this. He would *never* confess, he was just going to throw accusations at me and blame me for the failure of our marriage.

I grabbed my purse and stormed out of the office.

But something stopped me.

Right there, in the empty reception area, was my former best friend.

The rage was stronger than me. I took two steps toward Marisa and slapped her so hard it hurt my hand. Her shock was obvious. Wide-mouthed, she brought a hand to her face.

"What are you doing?"

"What am *I* doing? Why are *you* in my husband's office?"

Behind me, Agustín grabbed my arm as I attempted another swing at her. "Alicia! You've lost your mind. Calm down!"

"No! I'm not going to calm down!" I told him, then turned to Marisa. "After all that we've gone through, all those years of friendship, this is how you treat me? Sleeping with *my* husband?"

She looked like a wounded animal. "I don't know why you're saying that."

Fingers trembling, I fumbled inside my purse for the scarf-in-question, and that was when I felt the cold metal barrel of my dad's revolver, the one he'd given me years ago for protection.

I still didn't know why I'd put it in there. To threaten them? To give it to Leopoldo so he would take matters into his own hands? I'd never used it before, but this felt like the right time.

I took it out and pointed the gun at Marisa.

"Alicia, put the gun down!" Agustín said. "You're mistaken. Marisa and I have never disrespected you."

I'd never felt more hatred toward anybody as I did at this very moment against Marisa.

"How could you do this to me?" I said, still pointing at her chest. "I considered you my sister. You were supposed to be my one true friend out of all those meaningless associations."

"I haven't done anything to you."

"You're going to deny your feelings for *my* husband?"

She peeked at him, and her expression revealed everything.

"No, and I should've told you years ago. But that doesn't mean I ever acted on it."

"I don't believe you!" The gun trembled in my hand.

How dared she confess her love for my husband as if it was *nothing,* as if she wasn't married to another man, as if Agustín weren't mine? She'd always been frank. I gave her that. She wasn't a good liar, either, which was why her deception was so out of character. And yet, she couldn't deny the mountains of evidence against her. There were too many things to ignore, and I was absolutely certain that my husband was being unfaithful, but at the moment I didn't feel like going through the list—I just knew I wanted her to suffer as much as I did. I wanted to wipe that grim expression from her face that told me I was an idiot for not realizing how she felt for him all along.

I pulled the revolver's hammer back but before I could fire, the weight of Agustín's body crashed into mine, knocking me to the ground. In a flash, Agustín was on top of me, trying to take the gun from me. I tightened my grip on the pistol, even though I knew it would be futile—he was much stronger than me.

A shot escaped the barrel, loud and definitive. Marisa screamed. I stiffened my body, afraid to look around. Had I hit *her?* No, God, please.

"Are you crazy?" Agustín yelled.

His body was still on mine, so I couldn't see Marisa. My legs turned to gelatin. Something sharp hit one of the windows and shattered the glass. Whatever it was—a small torch covered in flames—fell on one of the desks and lit a pile of papers.

A shout came from the threshold, but it wasn't Marisa's voice. "They're attacking the building!" the woman's voice said. "We have to evacuate!"

Agustín was still holding my wrists down with both of his, so I couldn't get away, but behind his head, I spotted Beatriz Lara, some actress wannabe who always found ways to insert herself into our lives. She was frantic, saying things that didn't make sense about some angry people outside. But where was Marisa?

That awful woman kept talking. "They're throwing rocks and torches at the building! We have to get out!"

"Why?" Agustín asked.

"The broadcast. People are furious."

"What broadcast?" He looked annoyed more than worried.

"*La guerra de los mundos*," Beatriz said.

He pulled me up. "You have to leave. Right now." He shoved me and my purse toward the staircase door. "Wait for me at the house!"

My last glance was of Marisa's body crumpled in the corner of the foyer.

$\mathcal{C}$HAPTER 41

Valeria

1957

One week before my wedding, I finally had a chance to be alone with my future mother-in-law. So far, Tía Marga had made it impossible for me to talk to Mrs. Recalde about my mother, since she had been there every step of the way: from picking flowers and choosing invitations to talks with the parish priest, visits from my fiancé, and the dreadful task of making a guest list. I only had a few guests of my own: Doña Amparito and my friends from school, but I had resisted sending out their invitations as I still believed and hoped—deep down in my heart—that something would stop this farce. And yet, the days were passing by with unrelenting speed and all my commitments with Mrs. Recalde and Tía Marga had made it impossible for me to come up with a plan for an escape.

At night, I would come up with alternatives and solutions that I hadn't yet dared to try: I could run away when I went with Graciela to the market, or ask for a job at a photography studio I'd spotted on one of our walks, or find my father and beg him to take me to Lima with him.

At least today, I would finally have a chance to speak freely with Mrs. Recalde about my mother and, hopefully, uncover the truth about her. For the first time since the wedding preparations had begun, Tía Marga didn't deem it necessary to attend my dress fitting, so I had Mrs. Recalde all to myself.

I couldn't deny that the gown was coming out beautifully. The bodice was made out of fitted lace all the way to the long sleeves. A thick satin band, wrapped around my waist, gave way to a full organza skirt. As a final touch, Doña Berenice placed a tulle veil on my head. If only I could wear this dress to marry Matías, but he might never propose. I hadn't even seen him since our little escapade—not under my uncle's watchful eye.

"What do you think?" the seamstress told my future *suegra*.

"Perfect, Doña Berenice. You've outdone yourself!"

They both turned to look at my reflection in the mirror—at the fraud I had become. Getting married to someone I didn't love. And for what? Financial security? Appearances?

"Come to my house for tea," Mrs. Recalde said. "That way you can see Félix."

I agreed immediately. This was my chance to ask what, if anything, she knew about my mother's last days.

I decided to approach the subject in the car. Even though her driver was listening, it would be better than Félix or Mr. Recalde being present.

"Doña Caridad," I said.

She sat by my side in the back seat of her fancy car.

"The other day you mentioned you had met my mother."

"Yes. She did a few commercials for us."

From what I remember of my childhood, voice actors and actresses got jobs at different radio stations to do spots or shows since it was difficult to make a living exclusively from their profession. My mom had moved from one station to another until she married my father and fully committed to the *radioteatro* at Radio La Voz.

"She was so talented," Félix's mom said.

"Were you friends with her?"

"I wouldn't call her a friend, but she knew who I was. She was always pleasant and kind to me."

"What about Alicia de Montero? Do you know her?"

"Of course. We all know each other."

"But you're not close."

"No. Alicia was always more difficult. It was hard to believe she was such good friends with your mother, who was so approachable. Of course, the rumors didn't help their relationship."

"What rumors?"

"Oh," she waved a hand, "let's not talk about that. It's all in the past. I shouldn't have even brought it up."

"Please tell me more. I lost her when I was so young. I'm eager to know about her."

She looked out the window as we were leaving downtown.

"Please?" I said.

"Oh, people are horrible. They love to gossip, and there was a time when they liked to say that Agustín Montero and Marisa were too close for their own good."

"And you believe that?"

She shrugged. "I don't know anything about them, but Agustín was a complicated man."

"What do you mean?"

"You know, he was so young when he took over the administration of *Crónicas*. His father was in a fatal traffic accident and passed away shortly after, so Agustín had to take charge with hardly any preparation. That's a lot of responsibility for someone so young that also happened to have a new wife and a small son."

What did youth have to do with fidelity?

"What are you saying?" I told her.

"That I wouldn't put it past him to have an affair. Men are different than us, especially in our country. But I don't think your mother was like that. She struck me as a decent woman. I don't think she would've done that to your father or her closest friend."

The Recaldes' mansion came into view, which meant our conversation was about to come to an end. She turned toward me, rather abruptly.

"Have you met Beatriz Lara?"

The question was so unexpected, I didn't even understand who she was talking about.

"She was my neighbor during those years," she said.

What did Beatriz have to do with my mother, or this conversation?

"I know she was an actress," I said, cautiously. "She was my mother's understudy."

"Yes. Agustín used to visit her, you know."

"Really?" I asked. "And whereabouts did you live then?"

"Oh, across from Hospital San Juan de Dios. Her house was cobalt blue. Unmistakable."

We parked in the driveway and the driver opened the door for her.

"Do you know if she was there that night?" I asked her.

"What night?"

"The night the radio, you know, the night they died."

She looked at me with an unreadable expression. "I don't know, *mijita*, but I wouldn't be surprised if she was."

I barely participated in the conversation during tea, and I only had one *alfajor*. Fortunately, Félix and his mother filled all the silences as she updated her son with our progress for the wedding preparations. I nodded occasionally, while Félix kept his eyes on me. But my mind was elsewhere. I was still thinking about what Doña Caridad had been saying about Beatriz Lara and making connections as though I was putting together a jigsaw puzzle.

When Félix offered to take me home, I promptly agreed and thanked his mother for all her kindness. Despite my reservations, I was starting to like her. She was certainly opinionated and somewhat crass, but so far, she had treated me with affability, which was more than I could say for Matías's mom.

"Do you know we're getting married on a full moon?" Félix said, after several attempts at small talk that I had dodged. "It's supposed to bring abundance and f-f-f-fertility." He avoided my gaze as he said this last part. I was surprised he knew—or cared—about moon cycles and myths.

"Yes. I've heard the full moon is ideal for starting new endeavors," I said, barely present. "That's why they say you should cut your hair on a full moon for it to grow faster and healthier."

An idea occurred to me.

"You know what, Félix?" I said. "I almost forgot I have a hair appointment in fifteen minutes. Could you drop me off at the salon instead of my uncle's house?"

"Sure . . ." he said, dumbfounded. "But I don't think there's a full moon tonight."

"That's all right, I'll take my chances," I said, perking up as my plan took shape in my mind.

"How will you g-g-get home? Should I wait for you or pick you up later?"

"No, no, don't worry about me. It's only a couple of blocks from the house. I can walk."

"Are you sure?"

"Absolutely." This plan had given me an energy I'd been lacking all week.

Hesitantly, Félix parked next to Peluquería Florencia. He tried to give me a kiss before I stepped out of the car, but I pretended not to notice and opened the car door.

"Thank you, Félix. Have a wonderful evening!" I shut the door and waved at him before walking into the beauty salon, where a row of women sat with their heads under hair dryers, looking like extraterrestrial creatures.

"How can I help you?" A slim woman with an arrogant smirk said.

"Can I borrow your telephone?"

"Are you going to purchase any of our services?"

I looked around. "What's the quickest thing?"

"We could wax your eyebrows."

I brought a hand to my eyebrows. They had always been on the thicker side, and I'd never even considered reshaping them, but I so desperately needed the phone. I couldn't waste this opportunity.

"All right," I said. "But let me make my call first."

The woman pointed at a teal phone, and I asked the operator to call *Crónicas*.

"You look different," Matías said as I glided out of the salon, feeling like a new woman with my new polished eyebrows.

"In a good or bad way?"

"Let's say that if there weren't all these people around us, I would give you a kiss."

Well, that was reassuring. I was so excited to see him after so many days, I fought the urge to hug him. Before any of my family's acquaintances saw me there, I entered his sedan. Quito may have grown in the last few years but, at its core, it was still a small town where people in neighborhoods knew each other.

"Tell me again where we're going?" he said, getting into the driver's seat.

I hadn't been able to explain my entire plan to him over the phone, but my conversation with Caridad Recalde had given my investigation a new direction. I gave him the address to the blue house.

Along the way, I explained who Beatriz Lara was and what Mrs. Recalde had told me about her. It didn't escape my attention that he frowned when I mentioned Félix's last name.

"So, are you set on marrying him?" he said.

"Can we not talk about that now?"

If he wasn't going to contribute to the solution, then I definitely didn't want to discuss my ominous fate with him.

Like my almost *suegra* said, the house was unmistakable. It stood out like a flower in the middle of the dessert. From my parents' conversations, I remembered that Beatriz had been a young widow. Her husband, who'd also been an actor, had some kind of odd accident a few years prior to my dad purchasing the radio station. In fact, my parents had never met him when Beatriz came looking for a job.

We rang the doorbell. The woman from the photo at the radio station materialized in front of me, but this was a faded version of her—unlike Alicia de Montero, who had gotten more attractive with age.

The roots of Beatriz's hair were darker than the rest of the dried-out, strawlike dye in her bob. It gave me an urge to drive her to Peluquería Florencia immediately. Also, something had happened to her skin. There were blemishes scattered throughout her cheeks. In her defense, we hadn't warned her of our visit, and in the past, she'd used layers and layers of foundation. Now I could see why. For a second, I wondered what my mother would've looked like now, nearing forty.

"Can I help you?" she said, twisting her full lips.

"Señora Beatriz?" I asked. "I'm Valeria Anzures and this is Matías Montero. My mother was Marisa del Valle. You know, the director's wife?"

A significant pallor came to her face.

"We were wondering if we could have a word with you," I said before she shut the door.

She watched us both. Matías flashed her one of those smiles capable of disarming any woman.

"It'll be quick," I said.

"Yes. Valeria, of course," she said.

"We met when I was a little girl."

"Yes, yes." She seemed nervous.

Matías attempted to shake her hand. "My dad was Agustín Montero, the newspaper owner."

She hesitated, but took his hand, nonetheless.

"We just wanted to talk for a few minutes," Matías said.

"Five minutes, *no más*," I requested.

She forced a smile. "All right."

The floors had been recently waxed, as they felt slippery under my slip-ons, and a strong scent of wood polish invaded the entire living room.

"I came here once with my mom," I said, recognizing the heavy cherry furniture. "For a rehearsal."

"I'm sorry the house is such a mess," she said, turning off the console radio and picking up a set of playing cards from the coffee table. "Had I known you were coming, I would've worn something nice."

When she smiled, I finally recognized the pretty young woman she once had been. Her face had aged some, but her body hadn't. She was still the curvaceous woman I remembered who used to turn heads in the streets of Quito. She wore a fitted beige blouse with buttons barely closing over her ample bosom.

It didn't escape my notice that Matías gave her a once-over. Ugh.

"Would you like something to drink?" she said. "I have this Portuguese *oporto* I've been waiting to open for when I have company."

We thanked her. She turned toward her cupboard and removed the wineglasses. Matías helped her uncork the bottle and served the three of us the burgundy liquid. I sat on a stiff leather sofa. Around us were photos of people I'd never met and behind the dining room table hung a large wedding photo of a very young Beatriz with a man who I assumed to be her late husband, the actor.

She grabbed one of the wineglasses Matías had set on the coffee table and drank greedily. "So, to what do I owe this honor?"

I tried my *oporto*. It was surprisingly good, sweet with a slight taste of passion fruit. "Well, I just moved back to Quito from Riobamba and was curious to meet some of my mother's friends."

I wasn't sure if "friend" was the right term to describe her, but Beatriz had been present for many years of my mom's life. She sat on a chair in front of me and grabbed a cigarette box from the end table. She offered us one, but we declined.

"Your mother was kind," she said, as Matías lit her cigarette. "But she kept her distance, you know? I don't know if it was because she was the director's wife or because we were surrounded by men all the time. She couldn't be too friendly, or they might have taken it the wrong way."

"You weren't close then?" I said.

She served herself more Portuguese wine, the top of her teeth turning maroon. "Not really."

I glanced at Matías, pleading for his help with my eyes—uncertain of how to continue.

"So," he said, sitting next to me. "Valeria and I were talking about how little we know about what happened that night at the radio station. When our parents died, we didn't know many people who worked with them, so we didn't know whom to ask. But Valeria remembered coming here once, and we thought—well, maybe she knows something about that night, about why her father went along with the broadcast."

She blinked repeatedly. "I don't know why he did it. He changed his mind barely an hour before transmission."

"And my mom. Did she participate in the show?"

"For a little bit, but then she left." She drank some more. "When the fire and smoke reached the inside of the building, it was utter chaos. People were running in all directions. Some went to the roof, others jumped to adjacent buildings. Some even attempted to form human chains outside the windows to escape."

"They did," Matías said, pensively.

She took a long drag of her cigarette. "People like to speculate that *Crónicas* had political enemies who used the radio hoax as an excuse to burn the building."

This was the first I'd heard of such conspiracy.

"And you believe that?" Matías said, leaning forward.

She shrugged. "I honestly don't know what to think. It's been eight years, and I still cannot make sense of that night."

"How did you escape?" I asked.

She avoided our gaze. "By the stairs. I was fast enough to leave the building before the fire got too bad. Unfortunately," she finished her drink, "your parents didn't have the same luck."

Though her behavior was somewhat erratic, I couldn't blame her. The memories of that night were probably traumatic. A heaviness came over me. My mother's last minutes alive must have been horrific. For months after the incident, I had nightmares about my parents.

"So you stopped acting after that?" Matías said.

"I took a break after the fire. I didn't have the need to work since my late husband"—she made the sign of the cross—"left me this house and an adequate inheritance."

I looked around the large home. How strange that a radio theater actor in this country would've made enough money to afford such a nice house and sustenance for his wife for so many years.

"After your mother's passing, other radio stations contacted me," she said. "It's not a lot of money, but I like it, and I've done well for myself."

"What about your other colleagues who were there that night?" Matías said. "Are you in touch with them?"

"Not really, but your Tío Bolívar contacted me recently for a new *radionovela*, which we're starting in a couple of days."

"As the protagonist?" I said, unable to hide the bitterness in my voice. She was booking all the jobs my mom should've had.

"Yes." She smiled, proudly.

"What about the newspaper people? Are you still friends with anyone there?" I said.

"No."

I finished my drink so I could gather the courage to ask the next question, the reason for us being here. "But you were friends with Matías's dad, right?"

She scraped the label of the *oporto* bottle with her nail. "Not really. I mean, I knew him for years. But who didn't?" She studied one of her chipped nails. "He came a couple of times, because he was interested in purchasing some paintings my husband had left me. My Lorenzo had inherited them from his grandfather, and they were valuable pieces from the Escuela Quiteña in the nineteenth century."

Matías looked surprised. "Did he buy them?"

"No," she said, avoiding our gazes. "I ended up selling them to the city's museum."

Well, that explained Agustín's visits. Now what?

We left Beatriz's house disappointed. Our investigation had led us nowhere, and we didn't know what to think of our parents. Per my request, Matías parked a block away from my uncle's house. He held my hand for a moment and kissed it. He was about to say something else—I knew it—but he changed his mind and simply uttered a goodbye.

CHAPTER 42

Matías

1957

Valeria was getting married tomorrow, and I failed to do anything about it.

The truth was that I liked her. *A lot.* But that didn't mean I was ready to make any kind of commitment to her, especially with all the animosity between our families.

I needed to find her father. Only he could stop this nonsense. He had more power over her life than her uncle. All afternoon, I'd being going from hostel to hostel asking about him, but it was nearly impossible to find someone when you didn't know his alias. All I had was a newspaper clipping of what he looked like eight years ago—when other newspapers were reporting the burning of the building and the police search for Leopoldo Anzures.

The people at the reception desk thought I was crazy when I showed them the blurry photo of Valeria's dad and asked them if this man was staying here. Why had I waited so long to do this?

I supposed I didn't really believe Valeria would marry that *pelele*, Félix Recalde. She didn't seem happy with the engagement, at least not when she was kissing me. But she never wanted to talk about the subject.

Deep down, I'd been hoping she would call the whole thing off. So far, she hadn't. Now it was up to me to do something. I'd been to every hostel in the downtown area without any luck. The last option was Hotel Majestic, but I doubted Anzures would be staying at such an expensive place. Nonetheless, I went inside.

This was the first time in years I'd stepped into this lobby. I'd been avoiding this building since that dreadful night, when someone jumped off one of the balconies and that woman was about to deliver her baby. The reception area was more elegant than I remembered, with its shiny checkered floors, the cherry wood furniture, and an ostentatious red rose arrangement in the center. At the front desk, I gave my usual speech about trying to find a long-lost uncle and flashed the photo of Leopoldo Anzures. The curt man behind the counter said guest information was confidential, and he had customers behind me to tend to.

I migrated toward the bar area, where I could keep an eye on the people coming and going. I ordered a whiskey on the rocks with mineral water—this place was much too classy for a simple *puro*. Next to me was a young man sporting sunglasses—inside?—and drinking the same thing I was just being served. I lifted my glass to him and took a sip.

He did the same.

There was something familiar about the shape of his jaw, but his tilted hat covered his eyebrows and forehead.

"Who are you looking for?" he said. "I couldn't help but overhear you."

I showed him Anzures's photo. He grabbed the paper and looked through the article.

"Have you seen him around here?" I asked him.

He shook his head and read the paper I handed him in silence. "I had no idea about this. Were you here that night?"

He was not from Quito—his accent told me as much—but something about him inspired my trust, or maybe it was the whiskey since I wasn't used to hard liquor. I went on to tell him all about *The War of the Worlds* and Valeria and our parents.

He bought me another whiskey and casually removed his sunglasses.

And then I recognized him. "Aren't you?"

He nodded, rubbing the bridge of his nose.

In front of me was none other than Alejandro Toledo.

"What are you doing here?" I said. "I thought you were sort of a recluse."

"Sometimes I like to mingle with regular people to feel normal again."

I realized then that in one of the tables behind us were his two bodyguards.

"I thought you were staying at . . . a different hotel," I said.

"I change places frequently to throw off the fans and the press. Tonight, I felt like coming downstairs for a drink." He swallowed his whiskey, pensively. "You know, that story you told me about the radio broadcast, would make a great movie. But in the end, of course, you have to win the girl." He winked at me.

"Well, I think you could help me with that."

I still didn't know what I was going to tell Valeria, but I was hoping that she would be excited to see her beloved camera again. When I'd told Alejandro Toledo that his bodyguard took her camera at the airport when she tried to take his photo—since she was such a big fan (no need to share her true intentions), he'd ordered them to give it back to me immediately. So, one of them had begrudgingly gone to his room and brought it downstairs while Alejandro and I had one last drink together.

Valeria would be thrilled to hear the story of Alejandro Toledo at the hotel bar. After we had chased him relentlessly, he had showed up when I'd least expected it.

I rang the doorbell to her uncle's house. I didn't care what Bolívar Anzures had to say. I had a good reason for being here. I had something that belonged to Valeria, and I wouldn't leave until I saw her.

Her cousin Germán opened the door. I vaguely remembered

him as a small child from occasional get-togethers between the families. He glared at me from head to toe—apparently the hostility transcended generations.

"Is Valeria home?" I said before he threw the door at me. "I have to return something of hers."

"No," he said.

Was he lying? I checked my watch. It was 8:00 p.m.—strange that she'd be out so late—especially the night before her wedding.

"Do you know where she went?"

"No. She left with Graciela and my dad."

Even more odd.

"But you can leave whatever it is with me," he said.

"No." I tapped the pocket of my jacket where I kept her camera. "I'll give it to her in person."

I waited outside her house for about thirty minutes, but there was no sign of Valeria. The light of the room she shared with her cousin was off, so Germán hadn't been lying. After a while, I decided to head to the radio station. It was the only place where she could be that made any sense. Unless they were invited to her fiancé's house? But Germán had not mentioned his *parents*, only his dad. If there was a dinner or something of the sort, Valeria's aunt would've been invited, too.

There was a long line outside the station's building. I so hated to come here. But the crowd indicated there might be a special event. Valeria was probably here then, like the night she'd kissed that moron in front of me.

The man at the door was handing out numbers and I took one. I followed the line of men and women up the stairs and into the third floor. Maybe someone big was performing, like Julio Jaramillo or the duet Benitez y Valencia, who'd grown in fame in the last few years. Maybe even another foreign singer. If that was the case, though, I would've heard about the event at the newspaper, wouldn't I?

I entered the auditorium, where we were to sit in order of entrance. I looked around, trying to find Valeria or her family, but I didn't recognize a single face. There was no band onstage, just a microphone at the center with a long cable that went to the ceiling and all the way to the back of the seats, where some sort of radio equipment was, including a recording device.

We were given directions. This was not a presentation; this was a *live* contest to find the next big radio announcer—obviously an attempt by the radio station to raise their low ratings. I couldn't think of anything worse. Normally, I would've walked out, but the two and a half whiskeys I downed (I hadn't quite finished the third one) made me numb and uncaring.

They were handing out typed scripts with information about the songs and artists we were to present, but improvisation was encouraged. That was, if we knew a tidbit of information that would be of interest to the audience. The whole thing was amusing. There were some good voices in there, and I already had my favorites. It took me a moment to realize the announcer—Reinaldo-something—was looking at me and apparently waiting for me to come onstage.

"*Señor, pase por favor,*" he repeated.

He was telling *me* to go? Everyone was looking at me, but my reflexes had significantly slowed down, together with my balance. Everyone's voices sounded like they were coming from the end of a tunnel.

"Sometimes nerves get the best of people," Reinaldo was saying as I slowly made my way to the three steps that led to the stage (or were there four?). "I would know, I was discovered through a radio contest twenty-five years ago." He extended his arm to welcome me. "Well, he made it—our next contestant. Please state your name first."

With the paper loosely held in my hand, I gripped the microphone pole. "Wow, it's larger than I thought."

"Your name, please," Reinaldo hissed.

"Matías," I said. "Matías Montero."

"And the song you're going to announce?"

I skimmed through the cheat sheet in my hand and cleared my

throat. "I'm sure you all know our next ballad by a young singer who rose to fame last year. Originally written by the Puerto Rican composer Benito de Jesús and turned into a *bolero* by Rosalino Quintero, "Nuestro Juramento" has become an anthem to lovers of all ages, and its singer, Julio Jaramillo, one of the most important singers in our country, thanks to his golden voice." I stopped reading and looked around the packed room.

Reinaldo loosened his bow tie a bit. A man in the front row dried the sweat off his forehead with a handkerchief. I could see the horror in the faces across from me. Most people weren't comfortable with silence, or public embarrassment.

I finally spoke. "I, myself, would like to take a moment to express my own feelings and dedicate this song to Valeria, who's getting married tomorrow to a full-time idiot, but I hope with all my heart that she's listening and doesn't go through with it. Vale, I should have told you earlier how much—"

The strings of a guitar started as the first notes of "Nuestro Juramento" interrupted my impromptu speech, right before I could express my undying love. Reinaldo, sweaty and hot, pointed at the other end of the stage for me to get out.

As I stumbled down the steps, a woman grabbed me by the arm, breaking my fall.

"That was beautiful!" she said. "I hope Valeria was listening."

$\mathscr{C}$HAPTER 43

Alicia

1957

Sometimes I didn't recognize the person I'd become. And it wasn't just the obvious signs of aging I examined every morning in the mirror. The stranger living inside this familiar body had no joy left. She'd been stripped of the innocence she once had, the blind belief in others, the wonder and excitement of what every day could bring.

That Alicia—that stupid, lively girl—was gone forever.

In her place was a cynic, a woman riddled with guilt and uncertainty; someone who harbored hatred and bitterness in her heart, and whose only belief in herself lay in her power over everyone, in the empire she'd built, of the self-confident image she presented every day.

I'd learned to live with this stranger, even though I despised her. The pain no longer hurt, though—I'd become numb to it—but I carried it with me like a cloak. Sometimes I wished I could be the old Alicia again, but I didn't know how. This new woman had become a habit. To act or feel differently would be like fighting the current of a torrential river.

In the stillness of the night, I heard the door latch open downstairs followed by Matías's footsteps. He was finally home. God only knew where he'd been. I got out of bed, careful not to wake Julio by my side, and grabbed my robe. I never slept, so talking to my son would be a welcome distraction from my tormenting memories. I met him in the living room, where he tumbled onto the tan sofa.

"Are you all right?" I said.

After last time, I knew better than to ask where he'd been. He reeked of alcohol, but didn't seem drunk.

"No."

"What's the matter?"

He looked me squarely in the eye. "I'm in love with Valeria Anzures, but she's getting married tomorrow to Félix Recalde."

The news would've come as a surprise had I not seen the way he looked at her when she came to my office the other day, not to mention his mysterious absences.

I let out a sigh. "It's best that she's getting married."

"I don't understand you," he said. "Her mother was your best friend! How could it be that because of one mistake—one stupid radio broadcast—you changed your mind about her and her husband forever and decided that you hated them?"

"It wasn't the stupid broadcast!" I yelled.

He didn't look surprised. In fact, it seemed to me like he knew this already. As much as I'd wanted to save his dad's reputation in Matías's eyes, I couldn't be quiet any longer. "Your father was having an affair with Marisa." It was the first time I'd uttered those words aloud since that infamous night. "They betrayed me—two of the people I loved the most." I hated the crack in my voice.

"But how can you be sure about that? Did they confess?"

"No, but they didn't deny their feelings for each other."

"That didn't mean they *acted* on their feelings—not necessarily."

I'd given this some thought, but knowing they loved each other was just as bad.

"I had proof," I said, "lots of it."

"Like what?"

"I found a headscarf I had given her in the back seat of his car—but I don't want to go into all the details right now. Just trust me when I tell you it's true."

"Did you *see* them?"

"What do you mean?"

"Together."

I was taken aback. "Of course not."

"Then anything else is circumstantial. You can't condemn anyone on that basis. Have you considered the possibility that you could've been wrong all these years? You've been nurturing a hatred for Valeria's mom and her entire family without real proof."

"She admitted that she loved him," I said, almost to myself.

"So what?" Matías slapped the side of the couch. "Your ego cannot stand that she loved your husband? Hasn't she paid for that sin already? Hasn't *he*?"

I'd never seen my son like this. The worst part was that he was making sense, and I—I felt like a child next to him.

"That's not all of it," I finally said. He had to know the real reason why a relationship between him and Valeria was impossible. "I think . . . I'm afraid I may have shot her that night."

"What do you mean you *think* you shot her?"

Without realizing it, my face was covered in tears. "I had my dad's revolver. I pointed it at her. Your dad and I struggled for the gun and a shot fired but there was so much confusion after that. Someone broke a window and threw a lit torch inside. There was a lot of smoke after that. All I could see was Marisa's body on the ground, but I didn't know if she was dead or alive. I couldn't see her face."

My heart was racing as if I were there again, I could almost smell the smoke and see the sprouting flames. "Your dad dragged me out of the office before I could do anything, and there was so much smoke in the stairs. I couldn't see anything. I couldn't stop coughing and that's when I passed out, when you found me."

I looked at my son, begging that he would forgive me after this. "Don't you understand?" I said, sobbing openly. "I may have killed her, or at the very least wounded her. If it weren't for me, your father and Marisa could have escaped the fire."

CHAPTER 44

Valeria

1957

If someone had asked me what I planned to do the night before my wedding, sitting in the waiting room of a hospital would be the last thing on my mind.

But here I was, or I should say, here *we* were: Graciela, Tío Bolívar, and I.

Earlier that evening, my uncle had burst into our room saying he had an important, unbelievable announcement. "Your dad is alive, Valerita."

Well, at least I hadn't been hallucinating. I had truly seen him a few days ago.

"Really?" I said, because it was expected of me.

"You don't seem too surprised."

I avoided his gaze. "No, I am."

Graciela, in contrast, brought a hand to her throat, like the heroine of a *radionovela*. "*Dios Santo*, I can't believe it!"

"I'm afraid that's not it," my uncle said, his nervous tics fully on display. "He's in the hospital right now. The maid at the hostel where he was staying found him nearly unconscious this morning. Apparently, he had a hard time breathing."

We didn't even have dinner. We rushed to the hospital, where my dad had been admitted and was going through some testing. My uncle paced the waiting room, repeating to himself and to us that he couldn't believe his brother was alive. He alternated between excitement and indignation. How could Leopoldo have hidden his whereabouts from us—from *him*—for so long? But this was not the time for recriminations, Graciela told her father. I just sat there numbly, tuning out the voices around me, the radio in the background, the complaints of other patients, my own thoughts.

Just when my father was back, I was about to lose him again.

"I knew he was alive," I said at last.

My uncle stopped his pacing and stared at me incredulously.

"He followed me home the other day," I blurted out. "He said he's been living in Lima this whole time, but he was afraid to come back and face an arrest and a sentence for what he did. He made me promise I wouldn't tell anyone that I saw him."

Tío Bolívar was shaking his head. "You should've told me."

"Yes, I should have, but I had no idea this would happen." I looked over my shoulder, making sure no one could hear us. "There's something I don't understand, Tío. How did you bury my father if there wasn't a body?"

My uncle scratched his head. "Some of the bodies were unrecognizable, Valeria. We did what we could. I suppose we buried the wrong person under his name."

The thought was horrifying.

A plump doctor with eyes that appeared too close to one another stepped out of the room.

"Bolívar," he said as a salutation. My uncle had mentioned earlier that the doctor was a family friend.

"How is he?"

The doctor let out a deep sigh and when he spoke, his voice was more grave than earlier. "I'm afraid I don't have good news. Apparently, Polo was diagnosed with pulmonary emphysema a couple of months ago."

"What's that?" Graciela said.

"Basically, his lungs are damaged and don't work properly. This causes him to have shortness of breath and can lead to other lung diseases, like chronic bronchitis, which I'm afraid is the case here. Emphysema can be the result of heavy smoking or smoke inhalation." He gave us all a meaningful look. "We've managed to get his symptoms under control with some antibiotics, but the prognosis is not good. I can go over some treatment options later. He's awake now, so you may go see him, but he must rest as much as possible."

I had a hard time processing what he was saying. Everything around me seemed to be moving too quickly. It was now a cold, hard fact: I was going to lose my father once again. It seemed like a cruel twist of fate. And why hadn't he come to us—his family—and shared his diagnosis? We could've helped him. At least, I *wanted* to believe we could have.

The doctor opened the door for us, but Graciela stayed in the waiting room. Inside, the curtains were drawn. Papá lay on a high bed, his face ashen. An IV was connected to his arm. He turned toward us, cheeks sunken, thinner than the last time I saw him. He hadn't shaved in a couple of days, it seemed, but had recently gotten a haircut that revealed his crown was thinning out. Tío Bolívar greeted him in a low voice, stiffening as the two of them exchanged glances.

My dad shook his head. I couldn't tell if he was angry or embarrassed that we'd come to see him. I sat on a chair next to his bed while Tío Bolívar stood in the back, gripping the metal bar at the foot of the bed. He was about to say something, but I spoke first.

"Why didn't you tell me you were sick?" I said, reaching out for my dad's cold hand. Since I already had time to process that he hadn't died eight years ago, I didn't feel the urge to reproach him today.

"I'm sorry, Valeria. I meant to, but I couldn't find the right words." His voice was so hoarse. He looked at Bolívar, cautiously. "My treatment in Lima was going well. I thought I had more time to make amends."

"You should've come to the house," my uncle said, firmly.

My dad coughed for a long, uncomfortable moment.

"I apologize, *hermano*," he finally said. "All those years that you had to do my job. What I did wasn't fair to you. Trust me when I say that, if I could go back in time, I would've made different choices."

My dad's cough sounded like the sharp bark of a dog.

My uncle raised his voice. "Why did you disappear like that?"

My dad avoided his brother's gaze. "Cowardice, mainly. But also, I was uncertain about what to do. I acted recklessly, which I had never done before, and I didn't really know how to handle the consequences. That damn show got out of hand. And that's just the half of it."

"What's the other half?" I said, cautiously.

The doctor had warned us about his fragile state, but maybe my dad wanted to talk, maybe he *needed* to clarify things after all these years.

My uncle chose a chair in the back to sit down. Under normal circumstances, he might have corrected me for being nosy, or asking questions at the wrong time, but I think he wanted answers, too.

My dad was silent, which made my uncle's breathing faster.

"I don't understand what happened, Polo," Tío Bolívar said, impatiently. "You had just told me that morning you decided to go with *Gloria* and not *The War of the Worlds*."

My dad let out a deep sigh. "*Gloria* was a good story, but it lacked the novelty factor. We thought *The War of the Worlds* might appeal to our male population, too. Alcazar said it had been successful in Chile, with minimal casualties, so we thought that as long as we let the audience know it was a novel, we would be fine."

"But you guys didn't do that!" my uncle said, slapping his own leg.

"Tío . . ." I said, attempting to appease him.

"I think we did," my dad said, scratching his head. "It's all a little fuzzy now. We thought that it would be obvious since our regular sponsor—that orange soda—was constantly being announced."

"Well, it wasn't obvious to the people who panicked in the streets or to those who died that night. It was all about your ego, wasn't it? And then, you left me with this terrible mess. You left Valeria!"

"I know, I know." A coughing spell came over him. "I only thought about myself, but honestly, I believed Valeria would be better off with you. I've been tormented by guilt ever since she told me you sent her to a boarding school all these years."

"I didn't have any room for her!" my uncle said, avoiding my gaze. "Marga was about to have another baby, and I already had five children."

"I'm not blaming you," my dad said. "You did what you thought was best. The truth is, I didn't plan to leave for so long. At first, I thought I'd only be gone for a few months, just until things in Quito calmed down, but after I got settled in Lima and got a job there, it was hard to come back to a place where everyone hated me. I thought my presence might make things harder for all of you." He reached out for my hand. "I'm sorry, *hija*. For everything."

There was so much pressure inside my throat, I feared it might explode in an embarrassing outburst.

"It's about time you know the entire truth," my dad said, clearing his throat again. "The promise of better ratings wasn't the only reason why I decided to broadcast H. G. Wells's novel. An hour before the show, Alicia de Montero came to the station to tell me your mom and Agustín were lovers. She was certain of it. And I"—he turned to me, his eyes filled with sorrow—"I adored your mom more than words can say, so this was a terrible blow for me. I admit that I'd been suspicious myself. I knew your mom cared for me, but she'd never been in love with me, and I'd seen the way she looked at Agustín all those years. Of course, I'd chosen to ignore it. After all, Marisa loved Alicia like a sister, and I didn't think she would ever betray her."

His story was sporadically interrupted by coughs, but he continued, nonetheless. "Agustín was not to be trusted. I'd seen the way women threw themselves at him. He was a good-looking man, he was charming, and he had a lot of money. I was no competition for him. When Alicia told me about them, I knew she was right. I decided right there and then that I didn't care about anything anymore. Transmitting *The War of the Worlds* would be a blow to Marisa's ego, as she was the star of a *radionovela* we were about to launch. What better way to punish her than that? And that would only be the beginning of my revenge, consequences be damned." He sniffed. "Little did I know that I would pay dearly for that reckless decision."

The walls in the hospital room closed in on me. I took in deep breaths. One thing was to suspect that my mother had been in love with Agustín Montero, but another one was to get confirmation from someone who had witnessed it all. I still wanted to believe that my mother had been a good and honest woman. I wanted to believe that Alicia was wrong in hating her. I could feel Tío Bolívar stiffening next to me, but he didn't utter a word.

"I admit I got carried away during the broadcast," my dad said. "I became immersed in the moment. I figured that since I was doing it already, I might as well excel and give the performance of a lifetime. I don't know if I achieved this. Some people have called it 'pathetic,' but that was exactly what I was aiming for. A pathetic man who saw death in front of his eyes. For a moment, I wanted it to be true: I wanted Martians to wipe me from this earth as my entire world was collapsing in front of my eyes."

He was silent for a moment, dabbing a handkerchief on his lips.

"Where was my mother during all of this?" I said, finding my voice.

"She participated for a little bit and then left. I figured she was angry, so I didn't give it a second thought. A live show of that magnitude required a lot of concentration and coordination. Twenty minutes into the broadcast, someone called the radio station to tell us people were on the streets in a panic." More coughs. "It was a strange feeling. I was horrified, of course, but also satisfied that our acting and production had been so successful. We tried to appease the citizens, explaining that there was no alien invasion, and it was all radio drama, but that only angered the crowd even more. I don't have to tell you what happened in the city that night—only that when they started attacking us, I worried about your mother. We always went home together after the show, so I didn't think she'd left the building. I looked for her all over the floor, but someone told me they'd seen her go to Agustín's office, and that infuriated me." His eyes filled with tears—I'd never seen a grown man cry before. "I started going there, but when I saw people rushing down the stairs, I left her there."

I removed my hand from his arm, where it had been resting for some time.

"I regretted it almost immediately," he said, "but it was too late. Everything happened so fast."

The doctor entered the room, followed by a nurse with a clipboard. He went over some treatment options that would extend my dad's life, but the inevitable was coming sooner or later. I watched the brittle man listening to the doctor's instructions and pitied him, but at the same time, I was filled with indignation. If it hadn't been for his reckless act of jealousy and pride, my mother would still be here with me.

CHAPTER 45

Matías

1957

I was fifteen minutes late for Valeria's wedding.

The traffic around me had come to a sudden halt. Hitting the steering wheel and honking relentlessly didn't work, even though several of us had more or less resorted to the same frustrated measures. I got out of the car and stormed ahead. There was a brutal crash involving a bus and two vehicles. No sign of moving anytime soon. Normally, I would've stayed to help, but these were no regular circumstances.

I returned to my car and attempted to park by a curb. Conventional wisdom said the bride was always late, so I was counting on Valeria following the old tradition and not rushing to make the biggest mistake of her life. Unfortunately, everything seemed to be running on course when I'd stopped by her house in the morning and the maid told me the bride-to-be went to get her hair done.

I locked my car and strode toward the church, but no matter how much I hustled or how many people I dodged, I was still late. When I finally arrived at Iglesia de San Francisco, the church was empty except for exotic arrangements of lilies and orchids at the end of every pew. I double-checked my watch. It was 12:30 p.m. According to an invitation I'd snatched from a reporter who'd gone to school with Félix, the ceremony was scheduled at noon. I imagined the service would've started already, but not end so quickly.

My steps echoed inside the cavernous nave of the basilica as I looked for someone—anyone—to give me a hint as to where the bride and groom and all their entourage went. As I advanced through the nave, I expected to see a few guests remaining, or at the very least, the satisfied priest who'd just united two souls for eternity, but I was completely alone in the incense-saturated sanctuary. I didn't even encounter a church mouse.

This was one of the oldest and most grandiose structures in our city. Like many churches in downtown Quito, it had taken decades to be completed—this one over 150 years—so it had gone through several phases, resulting in a notorious combination of architectural styles: Mannerism and Renaissance in the facade, Baroque and Mudéjar in the interior details, particularly the lavishly carved columns and intricate ceiling. It was impossible, after just one visit, to note every detail—every cherubim engraved on the golden archways, every sculpture and painting of a saint, every depiction of Christ, every star gracing the dome above the altar. I'd meant to write a series of articles about the impressive constructions in downtown Quito, but I'd been too distracted to begin the project.

But who cared about architecture at a time like this? Apparently, the ceremony was over quickly. Perhaps, I'd mistaken the time. I felt my back pocket for the invitation, but I'd left it in the car. It was entirely possible that Valeria was a married woman now. I had the urge to curse out loud, but the various holy men surrounding me made it impossible. I left the church before my dark thoughts set in.

I was disconcerted. Perhaps I'd gotten the church wrong—not an impossibility, since there were dozens of religious buildings in historic downtown. Now I doubted that I'd read the right location. I didn't even remember where the reception was going to be held—I hadn't thought that far ahead, as I had planned to stop this nonsense during the ceremony. The only option was to go back to Valeria's house and get some answers from the maid. I certainly didn't want to sit at home and mope. I had to do *something*. Undoubtedly, it would be faster to walk to her house than attempt to unbury my car from the mountains of traffic and drive. I headed over there with long strides.

By the time I reached the Anzures home, I was sweating—not the best look to persuade anyone to give me information about the wedding, or worse yet, to convince Valeria to annul her recent marriage and choose me instead.

I rang the doorbell several times, but nobody answered. The maid must have gone to the reception or gotten the rest of the day off.

Of course, Valeria wouldn't be here. She was at her reception celebrating, and I, the biggest idiot on the planet, had been late while the woman I loved started a new life with someone else.

CHAPTER 46

Valeria

Four hours earlier

With the emotional roller coaster of my father's revelations and my impending wedding in the morning, I had tossed and turned all night, getting little to no rest. I didn't even have to wait for Graciela's alarm to go off.

From the early hours of the day, excitement buzzed around me. There was ironing of shirts and trousers, and long gowns, shoe shining, nail polishing, and rollers on everyone's heads—except for mine, as my future mother-in-law had made a special appointment for me at her favorite hair salon at nine o'clock. Graciela was especially enthusiastic because she said she hadn't attended a wedding in years.

I was in no mood for parties. How could I be after what I learned about my mother last night and my dad being so sick? After my dad's confession and the doctor's visit, Graciela had come into the room to greet my father and we'd gone home shortly after. I'd briefly mentioned my upcoming wedding to my dad, but he hadn't had much to say other than the Recalde family were "good people" and he was glad I'd finally have a home of my own. I'd been hoping he would offer a solution to my dilemma, but with my uncle in the room and in my dad's current state, he had no mind for anybody else's problems. It was understandable, I supposed.

In spite of Graciela's curiosity during the drive back home, neither my uncle nor I had said another word about the night my mother died—both of us emotionally drained from the hospital visit.

A knock on the door interrupted my thoughts.

"Valeria?" Tía Marga poked her head into Graciela's bedroom.

I was sitting on the bed, staring at the gorgeous wedding gown lying by my side, still in my cotton robe.

"You're not dressed yet? You have to be in the hair salon in twenty minutes!"

I couldn't disappoint my family. They'd done so much for me.

"*Sí, tía.*"

I went through the motions, without letting myself stop to think, as if one of those androids in the sci-fi novels Germán read had taken over my body. I washed up and put on the first shirt-dress I could find. Grabbing my gloves and my purse, I headed for the stairs. I just had to worry about taking one step after another until I made it to the hair salon, then the church, then the party, and finally Félix's house, where we were going to live until they finished building the apartment the Recaldes had bought for us as a wedding present. Perhaps this was what I needed, a new life away from my family and all the sad memories they brought.

A taxi was already waiting for me outside the house, and Tío Bolívar rushed me into the back seat. "See you soon," he said, offering a kind smile and shutting the door for me. He probably couldn't wait to get rid of me.

The radio in the taxi was blasting at full volume as we drove to the hair salon. It was a lovely, sunny day. Flowers in full bloom, thick trees with leaves gently swaying in the wind, quaint colonial balconies, not to mention the sublime churches on almost every block. But I couldn't appreciate the beauty around me. There was an unbearable weight on my shoulders. Life as I knew it—unfulfilled dreams and all—would be over in a matter of hours.

One of the most popular songs of the year, "Nuestro Juramento," started playing. I squeezed the gloves in my lap and spoke to the taxi driver for the first time.

"*Señor,* I need to make a stop before we go to the salon."

The closer the villa came into view, the more I shrank into my seat. Perhaps this was not the grand idea I thought it would be a few minutes ago. When the taxi stopped by the gate, I had the urge to tell him to go back to the salon, where it was safe.

The driver turned toward me. "*¿Aquí?*"

I swallowed. "Yes, here is fine, but can you wait for me for fifteen minutes? It shouldn't take longer than that."

"Sure, but I have to charge you for my time."

I nodded. I wanted the certainty that if things got ugly, I could flee immediately.

"Señorita Valeria?" the hefty maid, Rosario, said behind the door.

I had met Rosario the day of my engagement party when I hid in the kitchen for a few minutes as things got too overwhelming. She'd been kind to me and had made me try one of her succulent fried coconut shrimps.

"It's normal," she'd said, referring to my nerves. I didn't feel like explaining myself today. This wasn't just "nerves."

"*Buenos días,*" I said. "Is Félix here?"

"Yes, *niña,* but it's bad luck for the groom to see the bride before the wedding."

Given my current circumstances, I believed it.

"It's important," I said, "please tell him I need to speak to him."

Shaking her head, Rosario made a *tsk* sound with her tongue and opened the door for me. She pointed at one of the sofas in the foyer.

"Sit there." She was old enough that she didn't care what people thought about her or how she came across. I still liked her, though, and stared after her as she wobbled up the stairs. She was short, but her wide hips made up for it.

I only hoped Félix's parents—his *mother*—wouldn't show up before he did. I might lose my courage then. To think that I could live in this gorgeous home.

At least Félix hadn't changed yet. He was wearing his everyday clothes: a buttoned-up shirt and gray trousers. His frown revealed his concern to see me.

I stood to greet him, and he held both of my hands in his. I sneezed.

"Valeria, is there a problem?"

I didn't know whether to sit or stand. At this point, it didn't matter so I just sat down and sunk in my seat. What had I been thinking when I decided to talk to him? I should've thought this through. I couldn't break Félix's heart. And besides, what would become of me?

"No," I said, in a last preservation attempt. But then a memory came to mind. Last night, after my uncle and cousin had stepped out of the hospital room, my dad had held my hand and quickly said, "Sometimes the right thing to do is the hardest. Learn from my mistakes, *hija*."

I hadn't thought much about his words then.

"Valeria?" Félix said, eagerly.

"Yes, Félix, there is a problem."

He sat in front of me, eyebrows arched.

"I hate myself for doing this to you," I said, "today of all days. But after giving it some thought, it's probably for the best."

"What? You're scaring me."

"I can't marry you."

He looked confused, a greenish vein in his temple stood out.

"I'm sorry, Félix, I should've ended this a while back, but I didn't have the courage. The truth is I shouldn't have agreed, but my family pressured me."

"Is there someone else?"

I couldn't answer.

"That doesn't matter," I said. "Things have changed. My dad showed up last night after eight years. He's at the hospital and he's very sick and I . . . I just don't know what's going to happen with him now. I can't be making life-changing decisions right now. Besides . . ."

Would it be too cruel to tell him I didn't love him?

"Besides *what?*"

I glanced down. "I barely know you. I mean, I like you, but I don't think it's enough to get married."

He stood up, hands trembling. "And you couldn't mention this a little earlier?—like yesterday, or better yet, last week—*not* the day of the wedding."

I'd never seen Félix upset before, but he had every right to be.

"I'm sorry."

"Valeria?"

My almost mother-in-law came from one of the downstairs rooms.

"What are you doing here?"

"She just canceled the wedding," Félix said, redder than ever.

"*What?*"

I stood up. If they were going to attack me, I'd be better off closer to the door.

"Doña Caridad, I'm so sorry. I was just telling Félix that my father showed up last night. He's in the hospital. He has emphysema. I just don't think this is the right time for me to—"

"The right time? When *everything* has been purchased and all the guests are getting ready? Are you *insane?*"

The excuse that my father was back didn't seem to be working. Nobody seemed remotely interested in him or his fate.

"Well, I'm sorry," I said. "I'll pay you back."

She chuckled. "You'd better!"

"I should leave," I said.

"Just like that?"

"Would you rather me stand up Félix at the church? That

would've been a lot easier than coming here. You still have time to notify the guests."

"Does your uncle know about this?"

The hairs in my neck prickled. "No. But I'm an adult and can make my own decisions."

She laughed again. "*Niñita tonta,* you don't know anything about life. I'd like to see you support yourself or that foolish man you call your father."

That was it. I grabbed my purse and headed for the door, no longer feeling an inkling of guilt for what I had just done.

CHAPTER 47

Matías

Right when I was getting ready to walk away, the door to the Anzures household finally opened. To my surprise, instead of the maid I'd encountered in the morning, Valeria herself was the one to open the door. She was wearing a simple linen shirtdress, not the white gown I had expected to see.

Did I get the date wrong? I searched behind her head for any guests.

She smiled. "Hi."

"What are you doing here?" I asked, perplexed.

"I could ask you the same thing."

"Shouldn't you be at *your* wedding celebration?"

Sighing, she took a step outside and quietly closed the door behind her.

"There's been a change of plans."

"Meaning?"

"Meaning I changed my mind."

"But there was nobody at the church. Did *everyone* change their minds?"

She chuckled. "No. Just me. I was on my way to the hair salon this morning, but instead, I went to see the Recaldes and had a talk with Félix."

"Is that so?" I held her hand. "That took a lot of bravery."

"I suppose." She ambled down the curb. "Of course, nobody here is speaking to me, except for Joselito."

"Your little cousin?"

"Yes. Even Graciela is mortified, because she invited her friends from school, and Germán had asked the girl he likes to the wedding. Everyone was looking forward to the celebration."

I caressed her cheek. "Well, if it's any consolation, *I'm* glad you canceled it."

She smiled, biting her lower lip. "Why did you go to the church?"

"I don't know. I was going to stop the ceremony somehow."

"You were?" She grinned. "How?"

I shrugged. "I didn't have a concrete plan. Somewhere along the lines of screaming your name from the church's entrance, like a *radionovela* hero, or maybe—for a more dramatic effect—I could have punched Félix, carried you over my shoulder, and stolen you."

She laughed. "I think I would've preferred yelling from the main entrance. Félix doesn't deserve to be punched."

"How did he take the news?"

We reached the end of the block, and she leaned on a light post. "Relatively well. He didn't cuss at me or anything, but he seemed upset. In the long run, he'll probably be glad that I canceled instead of not showing up at the church at all. His mother, however, wasn't too happy with the idea of canceling the wedding the same day. She said we now owe them the money for the flowers, the dress, the food, and the invitations, which of course, infuriated my aunt and uncle. I feel so bad about it, but I couldn't go along with the farce."

A couple walked past us and stared. Valeria lowered her head.

"Disgruntled guests?" I asked in a low voice.

"Yes. Our neighbors. Can we go somewhere else?"

She held my hand, ready to go.

"Wait a second," I said. "I want to give you something."

I pulled out her Kodak Brownie from the pocket of my jacket.

She covered her mouth. "What? How did you get this?" She hugged me and gave me a smack on the cheek before I could give her an explanation.

On our way to the plaza, I told her all about my encounter with Alejandro Toledo and how he'd given me her camera back. She was ecstatic and wanted to know every detail. We stopped by an ice cream cart for *helados de paila*. The vendor was an old man whom we'd met as kids. I was hoping Valeria would remember that our mothers used to bring us here when we were small. Her radiant smile confirmed that she did.

We sat on a nearby bench, holding our cones.

"What made you change your mind about the wedding?" I asked.

She licked her lower lip, which was turning into a deep burgundy from the blackberry. "I heard you on the radio."

The heat rose to my face. I'd been drunk last night. I couldn't even recall everything I said during that ridiculous radio contest. Something corny about my feelings for her and that overly dramatic song that had become sort of a lovers' anthem. I shoved vanilla ice cream into my mouth.

"I was already thinking about breaking off the engagement," she said, "but hearing you on the radio only confirmed my decision. And then, the last push came this morning in the taxi when I heard 'Nuestro Juramento' on the radio."

She watched me with a wide smile.

I felt like an idiot, so I just finished my ice cream in silence.

"Don't be embarrassed. It was sweet." She rested her head on my arm, watching me with amusement. "You wouldn't believe where I was when I heard you."

"Where?"

"In the waiting room of a hospital."

"What were—?"

"My dad. He's very sick."

No wonder I couldn't find him in more than a dozen hostels and hotels. "What's wrong with him?"

She told me about his emphysema and how it might have started the night of the broadcast after inhaling all that smoke. The doctor had told them some people had it for years and didn't know it until the symptoms became more obvious.

"I'm sorry," I said. "Are you going to go to Lima with him?"

"I'm not sure. We didn't talk about that." She turned back to her cone. "But I found out a lot about what happened the night of the broadcast between our parents."

She proceeded to tell me a story that completed my mother's tale and gave me a clearer picture of what had happened that night.

"My mom mentioned the scarf in the box," I said.

"The one with the doves?"

"Yes. Apparently, she'd given it to your mom and found it in my dad's car. That was the last proof she needed to confirm her suspicions."

She was pensive for a moment, her ice cream mostly untouched. "I have an idea."

"What?" I said, fearing she may be recruiting me for another one of her adventures.

She tossed the last of her ice cream in a nearby trash can and stood up. "We have to go."

CHAPTER 48

Alicia

The phone call came right after sunset. We'd just sat for dinner, Julio and I, when Delia burst into the dining room to say some mysterious caller was on the line saying it was *very* important that he speak to me.

I hadn't heard his voice in eight years, but I immediately recognized his hoarse *lojano* accent. It couldn't be *him*. He'd died that night.

"Polo?" Had I heard right?

"Yes."

Trembling, I stared at the translucid sails of a ship painted in oils, hanging right in front of me. Agustín had loved this painting.

"We need to talk, Alicia," he said.

He gave me some odd explanation about being in Perú all along, but now he was at a hospital in Quito, and he had something important to share with me. Julio wanted to come with me to see him, but I declined his offer. This was something I had to do by myself.

When I entered the hospital room, I was shocked to see Polo in that condition—a prematurely old man.

"Thanks for coming," he said. "You look as radiant as ever."

Of course, being away for so long, he had no idea how much I'd cursed his entire family since he left. Or what I'd done to his wife.

"What's wrong with you?" I said, approaching the bed.

"Emphysema."

I paused midstep. I'd heard it was a terrible illness with no cure. "I'm sorry."

"It's ironic, isn't it?"

"What?"

"That the thing that is going to kill me is a consequence of my actions that night."

What was I doing here? I didn't need to add his guilt to mine.

"Have a seat," he said, pointing at a chair by the bed.

As I approached him, I noticed something in his lap—a framed photograph. It was a group of people, but I couldn't quite see their faces.

"We made a terrible mistake, Alicia. You and I."

"Why do you say that?"

He extended the picture toward me.

"What is this?" I said, standing.

"My daughter just brought it to me."

"Valeria?" I focused on the people in the photograph. It was a group shot of Polo's theater group, *Radio Voices on the Air*. My eyes settled on Marisa's pretty face. My God, she'd been so young then. My throat thickened. I couldn't believe I've been hating her for this long.

"I remember this photo," I said in an effort to speak without crying. "It used to hang by the radio booth."

Polo nodded. "What else do you notice about it?"

"I don't know. What am I supposed to notice?"

"Look at Beatriz."

She was sitting in the front with her legs crossed, the same sculptural calves that made men turn their heads when she'd walked up and down the *Crónicas* building. What else was there to see? Just the same vile woman who'd been blackmailing me for years.

She'd called me shortly after the fire to tell me she knew what I had done to Marisa. After Agustín had sent me downstairs, Beatriz and him had tried to tend to Marisa, but it had been too late. Marisa had died from a gunshot to the chest—the gunshot *I'd* delivered.

Or so Beatriz said.

Then, when Agustín had attempted to carry Marisa outside to see if a doctor could help, a beam had fallen on top of him. Beatriz said she'd tried to pull him out, but the beam was too heavy, and she didn't want to die, so she left the two of them there.

It was all my fault. And she was ready to tell everything to the police if I didn't pay for her silence. She claimed her husband's inheritance had barely lasted her a year after he died, and she didn't want to have to sell her house to support herself.

And so, I'd been paying for years. Every month, Beatriz received a hefty check for her silence.

"Look closely," Polo said.

I examined every detail in the photograph and that was when I realized what he wanted me to see. Beatriz was wearing a scarf around her neck and the wing of a dove stuck out from one of its folds, like the scarf I'd given Marisa.

"The scarf?" I said.

"Yes. When Valeria brought the photo today and pointed at the scarf, I remembered something. One time, we were rehearsing a *radionovela* and Beatriz was running a fever. She'd been coughing and sneezing all afternoon, so I told her to go home, but it was raining hard, and nobody could drive her home because the *radionovela* was about to start. Well, Marisa removed the scarf from her neck and tied it around Beatriz's head so she wouldn't get wet. I'd forgotten all about it until today."

I felt as if someone had just slapped me. "What are you saying?"

"They weren't lying, Alicia. They weren't having an affair. Beatriz never returned the scarf. *Beatriz* was Agustín's mistress, not our Marisa."

I fell back on the seat, shocked, confused. That couldn't be true. I couldn't have been so wrong about her.

"But she admitted she loved him," I said, weakly. *What* had I done? Not only had I—what?—killed my best friend, I'd been hating her for eight years *for no reason*. It had been so easy to blame her for the loss of my husband, of my home.

Unfairly.

"Marisa was too kind, too forgiving," he said. "I remember being surprised at how nice she'd been to Beatriz that day when just a week prior, Beatriz had yelled at her over the smallest thing and ended up throwing all kinds of accusations at her, saying she was tired of playing minor roles, of Marisa always getting everything she wanted. We had no idea she'd felt all this venom toward Marisa—so much envy. She'd even tried to come on to me once at a Christmas party." He shook his head. "I should've known better."

I broke down. The tears I didn't shed at their funerals were now pouring out, without control, without measure. Not for my husband, for my friend, for how unfair I'd been. My friend, my sister, how could I have been so hateful, so unreasonable, so cruel to her daughter—to anyone associated with Marisa?

I cried for what seemed like hours right there, in front of Leopoldo, who watched me with compassion, with solidarity. He'd also been despising Marisa unfairly for eight years. And our jealousy had caused a tragedy that could never be repaired.

When I was done sobbing, I stood up, said goodbye, and left.

I knew exactly where I needed to go.

CHAPTER 49

Valeria

Tío Bolívar was waiting for me in the living room, cigarette in hand. He'd barely reacted when I told the family that morning that I'd just canceled my wedding with Félix. The most outspoken and disheartened had been Tía Marga. She'd shaken me by the shoulders, tried to persuade me to call Félix immediately and take my words back. When she realized nothing was going to make me change my mind, she blamed it all on the pearl ring Félix had given me. ("I knew pearls were bad luck!") Graciela had followed suit with a disappointed air and questions pertaining to her complicated chignon and her brand-new dress. ("When will I be able to wear a dress this nice again?") Germán had uttered a *"chucha"* to which my aunt had responded with a slap on his face as he wasn't allowed to say such a foul word in front of her, whereas Joselito had happily removed his tie and continued playing with his soccer ball. All along, Tío Bolívar had stared at me in silence. What had followed was a series of phone calls to all the guests, split between Graciela and me, telling them the wedding had been canceled due to a family emergency—not entirely a lie.

But I couldn't avoid my uncle any longer.

Matías and I crossed the room, holding hands. We decided not to hide anymore. There was no point, no reason, as the two of us were already adults, and my own father had given us his blessing earlier today, when we'd all realized that my mother had been unfairly judged all these years. I remembered seeing the photograph of Beatriz with the scarf the night of Juliana Isabel's show, so after ice cream at the plaza, Matías and I had gone to the radio station to grab the photograph and show it to my dad at the hospital.

After visiting my father, Matías and I went to dinner together for the first time to a nice restaurant, but we couldn't delay my return home any longer.

My uncle didn't react to Matías's presence. He simply took a puff of his cigarette and pointed at the couch in front of him. We both sat down.

A long, uncomfortable silence followed.

"I have to apologize to you, Valeria," he said, appreciatively looking at his cigarette. "It was wrong of me to try to shape your life to my convenience. First by sending you to that boarding school in Riobamba, and now by pressuring you to marry the Recalde boy."

Before I could answer, my uncle spoke again. "And my apologies to you too, Matías, for being so obstinate. I should have realized, a long time ago, that the two of you were meant to be together. I used to watch you two when you were little. You were so close, always playing together. We even joked about it, your parents and I, how the two of you would end up marrying one day."

Mati slid his hand into mine.

"I appreciate it, Don Bolívar," he said.

The phone ring startled me. My uncle answered it, frowning and nodding at whatever it was they were telling him. His seriousness, his silence, was making me nervous. Had my father had a relapse?

"Are you sure?" he said to the caller. He nodded a couple more times before he hung up the phone.

"What's wrong?" I asked.

"Don't worry. It wasn't about your father." He remained pensive, and didn't offer any more.

"Then what was it about?" I said unable to control my eagerness.

He tapped his chin with his finger. "Oh, just about a woman who was going to work for me in a *radionovela*."

I glanced at Matías. "What woman?"

My uncle leaned forward. "Do you remember Beatriz Lara?"

I couldn't believe I was here again after so many years, after so much hatred—formally invited to tea with none other than Alicia de Montero. Unlike the owner, the house had aged significantly. The hardwood floors creaked as we stepped inside the foyer, where a crystal chandelier I remembered well hung low. Paintings from emerging local artists plastered the walls, and in the ample living room was my mother's former best friend.

Alicia was standing by a grandfather clock in a green taffeta skirt and a white satin blouse, her hair in a simple updo. She was so effortlessly elegant.

"Sorry we're late," Matías said. "We went with Valeria's uncle to the police station."

"That's all right, *corazón*," she said, hands inside her side pockets, and turned toward me. "*Hola, Valeria*." She smiled sheepishly. Had I not known any better, I would've thought she was nervous. But confident women like her didn't get nervous.

"Good afternoon, Señora Montero," I said.

"Call me *madrina*."

Godmother?

Matías squeezed my hand, initiating a smile.

"Please come in," she said, leading us into the dining room. "Everything's ready."

The food had already been set. A teapot sat in the middle of the table, surrounded by a tray of pastries and another one of cheese empanadas. The cups and saucers were made of fine porcelain, with moonflowers hand-painted on the side of each piece. The ornate embroidery in the tablecloth must have taken hours to complete—and the strain of some patient woman's eyesight.

"Please, have a seat," Alicia said.

I did just that, dumbfounded. I'd never been invited to tea before, so I didn't know what was expected of me. Before we walked in, Mati had confessed that he'd never partaken in this kind of invitation, either.

As soon as I sat down, Mati's mom filled my cup with tea and offered me some sugar.

"There's something I need to tell you," she said, clearing her throat, her eyes set on the water being poured into her cup. "I want to apologize for the way I've treated you. There's no excuse for my behavior, but I will make it up to you."

I nodded. It was all I could do.

"Matías says the two of you are in love."

I nearly choked on my tea.

"I think that's wonderful, *hija*. Have you given some thought to when you would like to get married?"

Matías cleared his throat. "*Madre*, that's a little soon, don't you think? We haven't even talked about that ourselves. Besides, Valeria just got out of one engagement."

"Of course, my love. I just wanted to make it clear that I'm fine with whatever the two of you decide."

My cheeks must have been bright red—I just knew it. But this kind of pressure didn't feel anything like my earlier engagement. In fact, the thought of marrying Matías—whenever that might be—was exhilarating.

She then served her son. "What were you two doing at the police station?"

"I meant to tell you this morning," he said, "but you were in such a hurry, I didn't have a chance. Last night, a news man from Radio La Voz called Valeria's uncle to tell him one of his sources at the police station had said they found Beatriz Lara dead at her house."

Alicia lifted an eyebrow. "Beatriz?"

"Yes, the actress who worked with my mom. You know her, right?" I said.

"Yes. We met several times, but we weren't friends."

Matías studied her. "But you know about her relationship with—"

"Yes, Valeria's father filled me in last night." She took a sip of her tea. "So why did you go to the police station?"

"They wanted my uncle to identify her body since he was one of her employers. Apparently, she doesn't have any family left, at least not in town. Matías came with us to cover the news as she was a minor celebrity, I suppose."

"I'll be done with the article tonight for tomorrow's edition," he said.

"Good." Alicia served herself a *moncaiba*. "And what happened to her?"

"They think it was a suicide," Matías said.

"She left a note," I added, "but the police wouldn't tell us what it says."

Alicia swirled her tea for a long time. Then, she set the spoon on the saucer and took a sip. "Well, that's unfortunate, but I'm glad justice has finally been served."

CHAPTER 50

Alicia

I'd always had a talent for mimicking other people's handwriting, but I never thought my skill would come in so handy.

Of course Beatriz had been surprised to see me. I never visited her. I just sent the money through the mail. In fact, I hadn't been in her house in years.

"That's odd," she said. "Your son came only a couple of weeks ago to see me, and now you. By the way, he's turned into a *very* attractive man, just like his father."

Her defiant smile made me want to slap her, but I resisted the urge and walked into her parlor. Overly decorated, of course, with *my* money.

"I should be grateful that the legendary Alicia de Montero is honoring my humble home with her presence. Would you like something to drink? I have the most expensive wines," she said, mockingly.

"No. I just want to talk to you."

"As you wish." She sat down and lit a cigarette.

"I wanted to come in person to tell you that your lucrative business is over."

Her hideous smile faded. "Are you sure? I can still go to the police and tell them what you did to Marisa. I have the murder weapon—*your* gun—carefully stored."

It took all my willpower not to attack her.

"Now that you mention that night. What really happened? I know now that Marisa wasn't Agustín's lover."

She frowned, confused. "Of course she was."

"No." I stood up and pointed my finger at her. "*You* were."

She tried to laugh it off, but her unease was evident. She loosened the scarf around her neck, which only reminded me of the dove scarf and how mistaken I'd been about Marisa.

"What else have you lied about?" I asked her. "At this point, I doubt Marisa was even dead when I left the office."

She avoided my gaze, her earlier confidence crumbling.

"Why don't you tell me what really happened, Beatriz? I deserve it after supporting you and your lifestyle all these years."

She stood up, exhaling a blue cloud of smoke. "You want to know? Fine! I'll tell you." She paced the living room. "I could never stand your arrogance, your airs, your smug superiority. Yes, Agustín was my lover. A woman like you can never satisfy a man like him." She scoffed. "And that stupid friend of yours was too meek to do anything with him, even though he would've left *everything* for her. She couldn't appreciate what she had: She practically owned a radio station, she was a respected actress, she had a husband who worshiped her, a lovely daughter. On top of all, she had Agustín's adoration, and yet, she was miserable. Well, I have no tolerance for people like her. Agustín broke things off with me that morning. He couldn't handle the guilt of cheating on you any longer, and after Marisa's brother died, he'd gotten close to her again. I knew how he felt. It was so obvious. I couldn't believe you didn't see it back then. Well, I wasn't going to just take it. I wasn't going to lose him *for her.*"

"*Dios mío, you* shot her. Didn't you?"

She didn't deny it. She slowly circled the room. "You idiot. You thought she was dead." She chuckled. "But she was just protecting herself from the shattering glass."

I couldn't believe her shamelessness. "And you thought you'd get away with this."

She lifted her chin. "You'll never be able to prove it."

"Probably not, but I'll do something better than that." I removed Agustín's old revolver from my purse and pointed it at the side of her head.

"Wait, Alicia, what are you going to do?"

"What a toxic, poisonous person like you deserves. All this time, you fueled my resentment, my anger toward Marisa and her family, not to mention the guilt of what I thought I'd done to her. But it was *you*. All along. You took my husband from me, not Marisa. You smeared her reputation and on top of all, you *murdered* her."

"You won't be able to live with yourself. You're not a murderer."

"You're wrong. I've already lived with myself. And it was much worse, because I thought I killed someone I loved."

She extended her arms. "Please, don't do it. Alicia, I'm sorry. I'll make it up to you. *Please!*"

But I was done talking to her.

I pulled back the revolver's hammer and shot.

EPILOGUE

Valeria

Two years later

It was unconceivable that all these people were here for us.

Granted, many of them were family members: Matías's parents and his maternal grandfather, my uncle and all his offspring, Graciela and her sailor, who'd finally come back and married her. But there were more than a dozen strangers, too.

The only one missing was my dad, but at least I'd had six months with him before he passed away, and he'd been a good guide and mentor for Matías and me as we embarked on this project. Between bookshelves and chairs, there was hardly any room to move in the tiny downtown bookstore, but we were ecstatic. As people formed a line to get copies of our book signed, I squeezed Matías's arm.

"Can you believe this?"

"No," he said, autographing the first page for one of our readers.

It had taken two years of hard work and investigation to get here. Matías had come up with the concept: a book about the monumental churches in Quito. He would write the text, and I would take the photographs. It had been *almost* perfect, as my coauthor and I had occasionally bumped heads, but in the end, we had this magnificent project in our hands.

I sat next to him to sign.

An old woman in a colorful dress approached us.

"I've been waiting so long to meet you, Valeria," she said.

There was something familiar about the shape of her eyes, about her smile. But the book had just come out this week. We couldn't possibly have admirers already. I smiled back, politely. She was an old woman; she was probably confusing me with someone else.

"To whom do I write this dedication?"

"Luisa de Vallejo," she said.

I lifted my head. Vallejo had been my mother's maiden name before they renamed her Del Valle and before she married my father and became an Anzures.

"Or you could just write *grandmother*."

Matías stopped writing and raised his head, equally shocked. My grandmother had been missing *for years*. As the story went, she'd left my grandfather when my mom was still in her teenage years. Nobody had seen or heard from her in decades. And she was here—today?

Now that I examined her facial expressions, the way she squinted at me, the shape of her chin, I could see my mom's features. "*Abuela*," I repeated, uncertain of what else to say. "Where have you been? We didn't think you were still alive."

"I've been all over, *querida*. Traveling the world. Making art. In more recent years, I settled in the Galápagos."

Matías and I exchanged a shocked look. Only adventurers and rogues lived there.

"I have a lovely little house in San Cristóbal. You're both welcome to come, of course. You'll find the most marvelous views and creatures there—perfect for photographs, just as stunning as the ones in this book." She tapped the cover of her copy. "You've inherited my talent, *mi reina*. I'm so proud of you and I know my Marisa would be proud of you, too."

The thought that my mother would've approved of me brought tears to my eyes. We didn't have time to talk any more, but she left me a piece of paper with her address.

My crazy grandmother.

When everybody left the bookstore and all our books had sold out, I interlaced my fingers with Matías's. "I think it's time for us to start a new project."

"By any chance, does this new project involve exotic animals and beaches?"

I offered my most convincing smile.

"Oh Lord, you're serious."

"You know you want to do it," I said, poking his side.

Through the glass door, he looked after my grandmother's bright dress as she stepped into a taxi. "When do you want to go?"

Author's Note

The idea behind *The Night We Became Strangers* was born from a disturbing event in Ecuador's history: the 1949 broadcast of the novel *The War of the Worlds*. This radio drama used a fresh format based on fictional news bulletins, which caused massive panic in the streets of Quito—the capital—and a disastrous aftermath.

To many, the decision to broadcast the novel was puzzling since eleven years earlier the same "experiment" had been carried out in the United States by Orson Welles and his Mercury Theatre, which also sparked hysteria among the populations of New Jersey and New York.

In my novel, I attempted to come up with a logical explanation for why my radio station's artistic director adapted Orson Welles's broadcast. Those of you familiar with my writing may already imagine that my fictional reasoning behind this event is far more convoluted than the real-life drama. In fact, the real radio station (Radio Quito) was owned by one of the largest newspapers in the country (*El Comercio*), and both were housed in the same building. However, for dramatic purposes, I decided to separate the ownership of these two entities, give them new names, and create animosity between the families as an aftermath of the infamous broadcast.

Aside from a few historical figures mentioned in the novel, all other characters are fictitious. The names of the radio station, the newspaper, and the soda brand have been altered to serve the narrative.

For the true history of the American and Ecuadorian broadcasts, please refer to the following nonfiction books used in my research: *Waging the War of the Worlds: A History of the 1938 Radio Broadcast and Resulting Panic* by John Gosling, *The Invasion from Mars: A Study in the Psychology of Panic* by Hadley Cantril, and for Spanish speakers, *El Comercio 100 años de historia y testimonios* by Jorge Ribadeneira, *Radiodifusión en la mitad del mundo* by Alvaro San Félix, and *El radioteatro en Quito de 1940 a 1965* by Mirian Félix and Patricia Robalino. Other valuable resources in my research, aside from countless online articles, were the podcast Radio Ambulante (Episode 17: Los Extraterrestres), as well as the novelization of events written by a first-hand witness—who also happened to be the artistic director and brains behind the broadcast in Quito—*Los que siembran el viento* by Leonardo Páez.

Acknowledgments

A million thanks to all who made this book possible:

To my mom, for helping me navigate the streets of downtown Quito and answering the endless flow of questions about life in the 1950s.

To Natalie, my first reader, for her careful editing and encouragement, and for being my faithful companion for all events and research expeditions.

To Robyn Arrington for her speedy and spot-on corrections.

To Deborah Condit, whose enthusiasm for books (and this particular novel) is contagious. I'll be forever grateful to you for reading this manuscript and for your undying support of the literary community of New Mexico.

To María Elena Venant and Shea Berkley for their acute understanding of storytelling. Both of you have helped me numerous times untangle the knots I've gotten myself into and land on my feet by the end of the novel. An extra thanks to María Elena for helping with my research and fact-checking.

To Andy, for making me rewrite a crucial scene in the novel, as much as I resisted it.

To Giancarlo Tescaroli for helping with my research about one of the organizations that inspired this story.

To my family and friends in both Ecuador and the US for continuing to support my writing, and to Danny, for all our years together and for telling everyone who will listen about my novels.

As always, my deepest gratitude to Rachel Brooks for being the perfect agent I always dreamt about.

To my editor, Leticia Gomez, for her fresh excitement about my work and for making a seamless transition for me, and to Norma Pérez-Hernández, for loving this idea and pushing me to write something new.

Last but not least, thanks to the entire Kensington team for all your help and support!

DISCUSSION QUESTIONS

1. Were you surprised with people's reactions when they thought their death was imminent? What was the strangest behavior you read in the novel? How do you think you would react if you thought you only had a few more hours (or minutes) to live?

2. Have you ever experienced a situation of massive panic? How did it play out? Did you witness any odd reactions?

3. Were you familiar with Orson Welles and his broadcast of *The War of the Worlds* in the United States? In your opinion, was he deliberately deceptive or do you believe he was experimenting with a new radio drama format (as news bulletins)? What about the radio broadcasters in Ecuador?

4. What do you think about the power the media has over the public? Do you think something like this could happen in current times? Can you think of any instances of media manipulation in recent history?

5. Do you believe there's extraterrestrial life? If so, do you think these beings have the ability to come to our planet?

6. Alicia is a complex woman whom some may consider admirable for her strength to continue with her husband's family legacy, but some may judge harshly for holding on to resentment and bitterness for so many years, thus affecting her son's life. What do you think about her?

7. Do you think Agustín truly loved Marisa or Alicia? Were you satisfied with their resolution?

8. Do you think Valeria made a mistake by accepting an arranged marriage with Félix? Have you ever met someone who married without love? Do you think arranged marriages work or have worked in the past?

9. Who did you think was a better match for Valeria: Matías or Félix? Please explain the reasons for your selection.

10. What do you think about Leopoldo Anzures and his reasons for going along with the broadcast? Do you think his deceit to his family was justified?

11. Tío Bolívar picked up the pieces after Leopoldo left. Do you think it was fair to him? Did he make the wrong choices with regards to Valeria?

12. Who was your favorite character in the novel? How did you identify with this person?

13. What were some of your favorite scenes from the book? Did anything surprise you about this novel?

Visit our website at
KensingtonBooks.com
to sign up for our newsletters, read
more from your favorite authors, see
books by series, view reading group
guides, and more!

Become a Part of Our
Between the Chapters Book Club
Community and Join the Conversation

Submit your book review for a chance to win exclusive
Between the Chapters swag you can't get anywhere else!
https://www.kensingtonbooks.com/pages/review/